Raptor's Quest

Raptor's, Volume 2

Lois Jaye

Published by Jaye Bird Books -- Casper, 2024.

Raptor's Quest

Copyright © Lois Jaye Evenson 2024

All rights reserved.

No part of this work may be reproduced, distributed, or transmitted in any form or by any means, including photocopying, recording, or other electronic or mechanical methods, without prior written permission from the copyright holder, except in the case of brief quotations embodied in critical reviews and certain other noncommercial uses permitted by copyright law.

This work may not be stored in, used by, or processed by any artificial intelligence system, machine learning model, or other automated technology without explicit, prior written agreement with the copyright holder.

This is a work of fiction. Names, characters, businesses, places, events, and incidents are either the product of the author's imagination or are used in a fictitious manner. Any resemblance to actual persons, living or dead, or actual events is purely coincidental.

First Edition

Dedication

This book is dedicated to Marri, David, and Eric,
and,
with sincere affection, to all who read

CHAPTER ONE

Jennifer Bradley's morning didn't get off to an auspicious start. Her frustration level could well have matched that of the poor paint store clerk by the time she pulled into the employee parking lot behind the Big Cup Café, twenty minutes late. Four years, she'd worked for Frank, and she knew the kind of nasty flak he would dump on her. Frank didn't like late – unless it was his lateness. And today of all days, when she had just decided to broach the subject of getting the weekend off so she and her son could paint his room.

The familiar odor of stale grease and onions settled into her nose. Debbie, another waitress and all-round good person, was just going into the storeroom with an empty silverware tray as Jen ducked into Frank's tiny and cluttered office to clock in.

"Keep your head down," Debbie whispered, "the old fart is on the warpath. What kept you?"

"Long story," Jen whispered back, "I'll tell you about it at break." Hurrying to tie her apron and slide her order pad into the pocket, she headed to the front. "Who's covering my station?"

"Me," Debbie called after her, "and thanks for the extra tips!" she grinned.

As Jen passed the kitchen door, Frank stepped through to block her, his eyebrows pulled into a single dark and hairy line above his squinty eyes. "I pay you to be here on time!" he growled, as he jabbed a finger hard just below a collarbone, and crowded her up against the wall.

"I'm sorry I'm late, Frank. I'll make it up at the end of my shift," Her eyes flared and her chin jutted, "but you don't pay me enough to put your hands on me. Don't do it again." She smacked his hand away and he backed up a step.

"Clock out at 8:00 as usual," he snapped. "I don't pay for a minute you don't work." He winked a fat and grotesque wink, "You might be able to make up the difference by opening the top buttons on your shirt," he snickered.

She almost expected him to slobber and drool. "If I need money that bad, I can earn twice what you pay me, at any tittie bar in Wyoming." He ducked and bobbed, as though he expected a slap. She spun away and almost ran over a man coming out of the men's restroom.

And not just any man. This was the man whose smoldering quick look could curl her eyelashes and melt her knees. She felt her mind clench and her face flame as she rocked off balance, inches from Detective Lieutenant Houston Whitehawk, of the Casper Police Department, and looked up into those deep black eyes.

How much had he heard through those paper-thin walls, she wondered? He was a cop. She doubted those eyes ever missed much and his ears even less. His face never showed much, and it was hard to read what went on behind that inky gaze. He looked away, beyond her to Frank, his jaw tight. Frank wilted against the door jamb, but pretended to merely lean.

If Frank had any sense, he would back away into the kitchen and start flipping burgers. If she had any sense, she would get out onto the floor, where she belonged. *She had no business drawing undue attention to herself.* It was one of the rules.

Frank attempted a snarl from the doorway, "I've got two people out sick, so don't count on any time off. Now get to work." A second later she heard the swinging door to the kitchen squeak shut.

"You must have heard that. I'm sorry," she apologized. Houston's eyes dropped back to her face, and she felt the color rise again up her neck.

"Do you have to put up with that often?" His eyes lost their hard glitter, but his jaw had relaxed only fractionally.

"Our boss is an equal opportunity bully," she shrugged, struggling to bring her color down, "and I was late." She moved to step around him. "I need to get to my tables." But he fell into step beside her, and followed her into the dining area where he veered off to settle himself into 'his' booth, one of her stations. He knew which tables she covered. As much as she would have liked to ignore his presence until she could get her emotions under control, but color still high, she pulled out her pad and walked up to the booth.

"Coffee?" she asked, although she already knew the answer.

"Always," he smiled, and she had to stiffen her knees, "and maybe a slice of that pecan pie."

"Will anyone be joining you?" It was often the case; he and his brothers as well as assorted friends regularly came in together. Sometimes his younger brother, Hawk they called him, brought his significant other with him; Savvy Mills, a woman who had barely survived a horrific encounter with a serial killer a few months ago. Jen liked her. Despite her ordeal, Savvy always seemed ... unflappable.

"Not today, Jen."

"Okay, I'll be right back," she nodded.

She tried not to notice that he lingered longer than usual over his pie and coffee, or that his eyes tracked her as she took care of her other customers, but it was impossible. She had no business thinking the thoughts his interest triggered, but for months she'd felt that interest in each look they exchanged, and God help her, she couldn't ignore the magnetic tug on the very feminine part of her heart that responded.

It was a dangerous game she played in her mind, but she clutched the feelings to her like a much-loved teddy bear. Nothing could come of it, but it was so nice to feel something other than soul-deep fear, at least for a few minutes, whenever this man came into the restaurant.

For a time, she'd thought her nightmare would come to an end, eventually, but she finally had to admit that this was her life, hers and Link's, forever and ever, until every member of the Lucano family was dead.

No matter how attracted she was to the handsome cop, the risk of becoming involved was simply too great. She had to empty her mind of an impossible dream and get it back into reality. *Keep her head down, avoid any undue exposure and don't make waves.* That rule – again.

After lingering over his coffee and pie for more than an hour, Houston dropped some folded bills on the table and left, just as a family of five came through the doors. Jen breathed a huge sigh of ... relief – yes, that's what it was; relief.

Houston's booth was a corner booth and the only table in the place large enough to accommodate five. She waved brightly at the Mom and hurried to bus the table to get them seated. The bills went into her apron pocket with his ticket as she dropped his dishes in the pass through and hurried back to welcome the family.

When she had a moment to take a breath, she pulled out Houston's ticket and cash from her pocket. He had included a generous tip. It was the custom of the Big Cup to pool tips and divvie them up among the staff at the end of each shift. Frank insisted that he was part of the 'staff' and demanded 'his' share. As she straightened the crumpled bills into the till, a folded square of paper fell to the floor. The word 'Jen' stared boldly up at her. Like a school kid getting a mash note in class, her heart kicked up even as her common sense chided her for it. She looked around to see if anyone else had seen it drop, then bent to snatch it up and stuff it into her pants pocket, where she could swear it warmed her thigh.

It was after three, the lull between the lunch crowd and the dinner rush, before she had a chance to take her first, and as it turned out, only break of the day. She snagged a bottle of water, the only thing Frank allowed his staff for free, and went out the back door for a breath of fresh air.

Debbie was sitting on the low wall separating the door from the loading platform. A cigarette dangled between her fingers. Jen hoisted herself up onto a hand railing on the other side of the steps, away from the cigarette smoke.

"Wow," Debbie said with a low laugh, "I just about split a gut when Houston stared Frank down and sent him back-pedaling into the kitchen."

"You heard all that?" Jen's face flamed anew.

"Of course. I was eavesdropping through the crack of the storeroom door. I saw it all. I really loved the way you knocked Frank's hand off! It shocked him that you stood up to him like that. I thought he'd fire you on the spot."

Jen was sure that wouldn't happen but there were a lot of ways Frank could retaliate that could make her sorry. Not sorry enough to tolerate future physical confrontations but she knew her little rebellion would not go unremarked. So much for asking the weekend off to use the paint she'd just bought, so she and her son could paint his room.

"I don't think he expected revolt in the ranks," Debbie puffed on her cigarette and slanted twinkling eyes at Jen, "but he's had it coming for a while." She chuckled, "It looked like he was going to press you, until Tall,

Dark and Dangerous stepped into the hall, then it looked like he was going to swallow his tongue." She laughed again.

Jen sighed, then told Debbie about her stop at the paint store where the clerk was trying to make a customer happy by remixing the paint she'd selected, then the woman decided it wasn't just the right shade of mauve puke, only to change her mind after the clerk had mixed the next batch, and decided to take the first gallons she'd ordered. "I was already frazzled when I walked through the door, ready to do a *Mea Culpa* for being late, but when he put his hand on me, my temper flared. I don't like to be touched, anyway, and I really don't like his constant sexual innuendos. I've told him that before. Either he still doesn't believe me, or he thinks the rules of polite society don't apply to him I know I haven't heard the last of this. Now, I'm trying to do my job with a smile on my face while waiting for the other shoe to drop."

"I don't know," Debbie gave it some thought, "after a cop heard him spout off, he might be less inclined to make an issue of it. Maybe he'll back off, for a while anyway." She checked the time. "I've got to get back on the floor. Talk to you later."

"Sure," Jen responded, knowing Debbie's prediction was a pipe dream.

With a few minutes left of her own break, she pulled the folded paper from her pocket and reread the word printed on top, bold and large, like the writer himself. Unfolding it, she sucked in a breath when a tightly rolled fifty-dollar bill dropped in her lap. "This is just for you," he'd written inside, "not to share with the others. Just in case you need some incentive to look for another job." A glow of happiness brought a wide smile to her lips. She couldn't keep the money, of course, but she basked in the regard it showed for a few moments before she stuffed the fifty back into the note and returned it to her pocket.

THREE BLOCKS AWAY AND around a corner, on the first floor of the Casper/Natrona County Hall of Justice, Houston finished his reports and leaned back in his chair in the squad room. He'd lingered longer at the Big

Cup than he should have, and to plow through the stack of reports he'd just finished was his penance. On the plus side, he was all caught up.

The little episode he'd overheard between Jen and her boss had played over and again in the back of his mind all afternoon. He'd gone to lunch early today with the ultimate goal of persuading Jen, whose beauty he thought beyond compare, to go out with him. He had annual leave starting tomorrow and had planned to press his suit, but that brief exchange in the hallway had set off his radar and killed any opportunity to follow up on his original plan.

He already knew Jen was gun-shy. He'd watched her walk a fine line with all the men who tried to make points with her, himself included, when he'd first noticed her. She somehow kept them at arms distance, yet not driving them away. He'd been wise enough to back off, bide his time, let her interest build as she began to take notice of him as well. It was amusing to watch her deal with them all, like a buddy or a really cute therapist, but she managed to deflect them with a quip and a smile and had them laughing when they left the Big Cup Café.

Was it just ego that made him think he had a better chance than all the others? He didn't think so. The electric pull he felt every time their eyes met wasn't all one-way. She felt it too, he thought, but in all the time he dawdled over his coffee, ever since he'd walked with her back onto the floor, she had refused to meet his eyes except to ask or answer a direct question.

Having become a regular customer of The Big Cup since Jen started work there, he'd heard rumors about Frank, but no formal complaints had ever been filed against the man. He'd never before seen any questionable interaction between the man and Jen but he was only there for meals. She was there for hours at a time. She had shrugged it off as just Frank being Frank but he had to wonder if she and the other women he hired – and they were almost all women – were subjected to that type of behavior on a regular basis. If she'd been putting up with that kind of harassment since she'd started work there, he had a feeling the situation was coming to a head. The incident in the hallway had raised a red flag. Maybe he should dig a little deeper into Frank.

He shut down his computer, filed his reports and headed to his car, still juggling the thoughts cruising around his brain. Of course, people who worked for pittance wages and tips, were usually reluctant to file charges against their bosses, for the simple reason that doing so usually guaranteed that they could never find employment in similar positions anywhere in town. Then again, there was something in the quiet waitress' air of calm competence that told him she was capable of working anywhere she chose to plop that cute little backside. Which thought made him wonder why she'd taken the job there in the first place. He also wondered if Frank had been peeved enough to fire one of his top employees.

It was nearly eight now, almost dark, about the time Frank had told her to clock out. Pure curiosity, that's all it was, made him turn his vehicle in the direction of the café, just to see if she was still there. He parked on the street at the end of the parking lot driveway where he had a clear view of the employee lot, lit by a single light over the doors of the loading dock. He got out and leaned against the hood of his car, arms folded.

"JUST A MINUTE, JEN. I need to talk to you." Frank's strident voice halted her halfway to her car. With a silent groan, she turned and squared her shoulders. She waited, to make Frank come to her. A bum leg made his progress down the steps slow and tricky, she felt a twinge of guilt, but quickly cast it out. She was so fed up with his bilge that the little revenge gave her a sense of satisfaction.

"Can't it wait 'til tomorrow, Frank? I have just enough time to get home to my son before he goes to bed."

"Let's just get this cleared up now." He had his finger aimed at her again and she glared at it pointedly. He curled the finger into his fist and dropped it to his side.

"I already apologized for being late. I won't do it again." He could take that any way he wanted.

"You know I can't fire you but if you use that fact to challenge my authority within hearing of any of the other employees again, the situation can change like that," he snapped his fingers and his little eyes glittered. "And don't count on Irene to protect you."

Her simmer rose to a low boil and her voice rose with her ire. "I'm heartily sick of the way you talk to your employees, especially the women, and if you put your hands, or finger, on me again, I will change our situation myself. So, if you decide to change our situation, just keep in mind I know enough of your secrets to make you regret it." She tightened the grip on her purse to keep her hands from fisting, too. "Am I clear on that?"

"Your cop boyfriend has made you damn cocky," he snarled. She didn't bother to correct him. As much as the thought warmed a place in her heart, Houston was not her boyfriend and never would be. "But," Frank spat, "he can't help you if someone should just accidentally leak your location."

Houston, at the other end of the parking lot, had only been able to pick up scraps of their conversation, only enough to understand that deep conflicts were at play, but even in the dim glow from the flood light over the back door of the restaurant, he saw the change in Jen's stance and heard the harsh breath she sucked in. With quick decision, he began walking toward the pair.

Frank saw him coming and the change in his demeanor was almost comical. He had raised his hand to ward off Jen's furious response, but the focus of his interest changed to a point over her shoulder.

She spun around, and felt a thrill, a tightness of fear that quickly changed to surprise then back to fear again as Houston Whitehawk strode toward them.

He waved a quick hand, "I was hoping to catch you before you left work," Houston kept his tone bland, leaving them to guess how much he might have overheard. "I accidentally dropped a larger bill when I paid for my food today and I thought maybe you might have found it."

Jen saw his ploy for what it was, a way to neutralize Frank's suspicion, and she jumped on it. "I did," she said, fumbling in her purse to free the fifty from the note, "and I started to call the station, but we were extremely busy, and by the time I had a few moments, I thought you must surely have left work. Figured I could catch you the next time you came in." She handed him the bill.

"Thanks," he palmed it. "Sorry to interrupt."

"No, that's fine. We were finished." She looked at Frank, daring him to challenge her. Whether he believed the exchange between her and

Houston, or not, was a moot point. He might be a world-class asshole, but he wasn't stupid.

"Yep," he responded after a brief hesitation, "all finished. Just work stuff." He limped over to the stairs and disappeared inside.

When she heard the door click shut behind him, Jen turned away toward her car, but Houston grabbed her hand and put the fifty back in her fingers, curling them around it. An electric shock raced up her arm, reached her brains and short-circuited her thought processes. She bit back a quick gasp, but it still took several seconds before her mind could form a coherent thought. His shining black eyes held hers for a moment.

"No, please," she shook her head to clear it as she forced the bill back into his hand once more. "It was a very generous gesture, Houston, but I can't accept it."

"You don't accept big tips? You were going to, until I interrupted." And she remembered that he was a cop, with a cop's ready suspicion.

"No! I wasn't. I fully intended to give it back to you."

"Why? It was a tip, not a bribe." His voice held a sharp edge, and it cut.

"No," she said, "it was just a kind reaction to what you saw in the hallway." She shook her head. "Very kind but not necessary." She turned her back on him and continued to her car, her mind working furiously. She knew he was not going to let this drop. She could see it in the set of his jaw and hear it in his footsteps as he followed behind her. If she couldn't come up with a plausible explanation for what he'd overheard, he would start digging. And he had the resources to dig much deeper than she could allow. She had to deflect him somehow.

Houston tapped her arm, "Who is Irene?"

"A relative," she shot back, without looking, "as is Frank. Do the Casper Police force themselves, uninvited, into family spats now?" She dug into her purse for her keys.

"Kissing cousins?" That drew a startled laugh from her. The storm that had been building within her died away, but still rumbled softly.

She stopped and turned toward Houston, to explain, "I'm not sure of the exact relationship since he's related somehow to Irene. But, as big a jerk as he is, he stepped in and gave me a job when I desperately needed it and I owe him for that." She pushed the key fob. The lights flashed on her car, six steps away.

"I've watched you since you started work here. You don't strike me as a person who would have trouble finding work anywhere you chose. Why were you desperate?"

In the brightness of her headlights, he saw a haunted look flicker in her eyes, but that was quickly replaced with irritation.

"I don't know how much of our conversation you overheard," she yanked her car door open, tossed her purse across the seat, "but, at the risk of repeating myself, I need to get home to spend a little time with my son before he goes to bed." She settled behind the wheel and started the engine. With her hand on the door, she finished, "So unless you're planning to continue this interrogation at the station, I'm going home."

"Wait," he caught the door when she tugged on it, crossed his arms on top of it. "I'm sorry if it sounded like an interrogation. Occupational hazard. I don't care for Frank."

Her lips twitched. "It's hard to argue with that."

"What I heard made me suspicious."

"All you heard was a difference of opinion between two bull-headed people." She pinned him with a glance as she reached again for the door handle. "I'm sorry you got caught in our little spat, but I don't need pity, and I'm not getting another job." She pulled on the door, and this time he didn't stop it. Executing a K turn, she left him. He remained, standing in the nearly empty lot, turning her words over in his investigator's mind. As plausible as she'd tried to sound, he wasn't buying it. His gut told him something was off, and he'd better back off his pursuit of the delectable Jen until he had more information. She was in some kind of trouble, and he needed to find out what kind, before he got in so deep he might risk his job.

CHAPTER TWO

Irene met Jen at the door. It wasn't even nine yet but the older woman was already in her nightgown and robe. It struck her that Irene, who had been her rock for nearly twenty years, was looking less like a rock and more like paper maché. Maybe it was time to try to lighten her load but that paper maché still covered an iron spirit which would be insulted if she tried.

"You're late. I was starting to worry you'd had an accident or something."

"Sorry," Jen dropped her keys in the wooden nut bowl on the table by the door and toed off her shoes. "Little problem at work. I got held up for a few minutes. Is Link still awake?"

"He's in bed but I doubt he's asleep," Irene smiled. "You know he fights it until you're here to tuck him in."

Jen grinned and patted Irene's arm. "Thanks. Why don't you go on to bed. I'll get him to sleep and then I'm headed for my bed, too."

She dropped her purse on the coffee table and asked, almost as if accidentally, "You haven't heard anything today, have you?" It had now been ten weeks since Jill's last call. Jill had always called, faithfully, every month. It wouldn't do any good to call the last number she'd called from, because that phone would already be destroyed. Jen was worried sick that something awful had happened to her sister. She had checked the major newspapers, online, from the cities she knew Jill had lived in; sifted through them for any tidbits about unexplained deaths or accidents. Especially if there were pictures of the victims. It was torture, but she couldn't help herself.

"No," Irene gathered Jen in a hug, her face as troubled as Jen's heart, "not a word yet."

Hugging her back, Jen said, "Good night, now." before heading down the hall to Link's room. She found him wide awake and engrossed in his latest comic book.

"So what's Spiderman up to today?" she ruffled his hair as she settled on the edge of his bed.

"He's trying to save the city from an alien monster, Mom," he grinned, "and the alien can make webs too, so Spidey has to keep from getting trapped in the alien's web."

Jen laughed. "Sounds like a metaphor for life," she tickled his tummy.

"What's a metapor, Mom?" His easy use of the word 'Mom' tore at her heart. Jill had given birth to him but Jen had been his 'Mom' since Jill had had to go on the run only six months into his life. What were the chances her sister would ever hear her son call her 'Mom', she wondered? And, if she ever did, how would Jen ever be able to give him up? She swallowed the pain and answered him.

"Metaphor," she emphasized the "f" sound, "It means something that is very similar to something else. Now, go to sleep," she shut off the bedside lamp. "Love you," she whispered and tucked Link in, kissed him on the forehead, and stood to go.

"Love you, too," he turned on his side and closed his eyes.

Back in the kitchen, she fixed herself a cup of tea, opened her laptop, and pulled up the Arizona Republic news site. It was a huge newspaper and a search took some time but she went through it carefully. She even checked the personal ads for the emergency notice she and Jill had agreed on, unsure what she would do if she even found it. Or where they would go. Jill had only said they would have to pack up and get out of wherever they were and wait for further instructions.

She closed the computer, swallowed the last of her tea, went into the bathroom, ran a tub of hot water, stripped, and sank into it with a tired sigh. Worried sick about her sister and what her non-contact could possibly mean, she couldn't stop the sudden tears but was able to stifle the sobs.

HOUSTON, BACK IN HIS pickup, made his way back to his apartment and considered his options concerning Jen Bradley. He could run her through the various databases he could access but he had no real cause beyond personal suspicions, to use department resources. And the thought of invading her privacy in such a manner didn't sit easy on his mind. Funny, he smiled grimly through the windshield, that the dispute triggering these thoughts didn't cause any qualm at all when he applied the same argument to Frank.

Put it out of your mind detective, he told himself. He knew he wouldn't, couldn't. His brain wasn't wired to let go of a puzzle until he had all the pieces firmly in place. No, he would find a way to dig out Jen's secrets, and hopefully, be able to remove that haunted look that passed over her face from time to time.

In the meantime though, he'd best turn his attention to getting hold of Darrell Candlemoss. The sketch artist occasionally worked with the police department but was, at this moment, scuba diving in the balmy waters off of Cozumel.

Hawk had asked him if he thought Darrell would be willing to work with Savvy on a sketch that played prominently in another nightmare she'd had, years ago, which involved a college professor she had reason to believe might have killed a young Navajo boy. All Savvy had to go on was a piece of pottery, a hand with a distinctive pinkie ring that she had recognized in her dream and the blood soaked face of the boy.

There was a time Houston would have scoffed at such a bizarre bit of "evidence", but not anymore. At least not if it came from Savanna Mills. The woman's nightmares had solved the years-old case of a serial killer who had been hiding in the hills just a few miles southwest of Casper.

She was the real deal. If she could help law enforcement with those dreams, Houston would help her any way he could.

He wheeled the pickup into his parking spot behind the apartment building. A quick glance around confirmed that Hawk wasn't here. Not surprising. His brother might just as well have moved into Savvy's apartment; he was there all the time anyway. He was certain that if Savvy hadn't shared the rent and the apartment with her sister, Hawk would have persuaded Savvy to share it with him, but Hawk's things still took up some space in Houston's place.

CHAPTER THREE

When Savvy walked out of her bedroom, makeup in place, she saw Hawk, sitting at the kitchen table, a cup of coffee in one hand and a sheet of paper in the other.

"The girls have gone grocery shopping," he looked up as she entered. "It says to call if we need something special for dinner tonight." Picking another cup from the tree on the island, Hawk reached for the carafe, poured coffee in the mug for Savvy and topped off his own.

"Do you want anything particular for dinner?" she asked.

"Maybe some raw oysters and an extra thick steak," he rubbed his stomach as he gave her a slow smile that had her own stomach tightening, "but, right now I'm just looking for some meat for breakfast." Hawk frowned as his stomach concurred loudly. "I'm feeling a little drained this morning. And the refrigerator is decidedly bare." "Hence, the grocery shopping," Savvy pointed out. "It's after twelve and we have to meet the real-estate guy at two to sign the lease for the office space. Why don't we just have some eggs and toast with this coffee." She set her cup on the counter beside the stove and added cream.

"Okay. I'll pop for an early supper at the Big Cup when we're done. We can talk about what we'll need for the office, over a burger basket, what say?" he grinned at her, as he rose and crossed to the fridge. "Seriously," he said, "we need to keep to the basics for the office," he handed her the carton of eggs. "Just a couple of desks, a couple of chairs and some filing cabinets."

"We can't leave Bryn and Lacey out of the decorating, you know." She eyed his frown of doubt as she turned on the burner under the skillet and added a tiny pat of butter.

"We can see what they have in mind," he hedged, as she opened the eggs, "but I will draw the line at sheer curtains over the windows." Savvy laughed, "Over easy or cheese omelet?" "Do we have anything else to go with the cheese?" "Nope."

"Then three over easy," Hawk reached for the bread and dropped some slices in the toaster. Returning to the refrigerator, he collected a jar of jam. "Apple, orange or grape juice?" "Orange, please." Savvy adjusted the heat under the skillet, added a drop or two of oil to keep the butter from browning too quickly and cracked four eggs into the pan.

The whole scene seemed so domestic. At least, as far as her memories of old TV shows had portrayed domesticity. Her young life had been a far cry from it. As a child, she'd had to scrounge in the cupboards and fridge for something to eat. Marva, her mother, could seldom be roused to cook anything before noon. But the experience had taught Savvy to cook. Something she loved to do, now, and she really loved working side by side with a man who pitched in to help without being asked.

It always amazed her at how seamlessly she and Hawk had adapted to each other, as though their minds had connected as readily as their bodies. Their thought processes meshing like finely woven fabric. She flipped the eggs gently and gave them a light sprinkle of salt and pepper.

"I've been doing some research on ol' Professor Bickstauffer." Hawk buttered the toast when it popped up, cut the slices into neat triangles, placed them on a saucer and transferred them deftly to the table. Taking plates from the cupboard and silverware from the drawer, he added them to the table and poured juice in their glasses before he took his seat.

At the mention of her old college professor, a primordial chill tiptoed up her spine. Savvy slid the eggs onto their plates, set the skillet off of the heat and pulled out her own chair. "And?" she added jam to a slice of toast and cut into her egg.

"It seems he will be going on another dig in Arizona during the spring semester next year." Hawk applied himself to his own breakfast.

"He used to go every year, but Lacey said he'd cut back to every other year before she finished school." They ate in silence for a bit before Savvy asked the question uppermost in her mind, "Are we going to follow him?"

"I'm going to follow him," Hawk chewed thoughtfully. "He knows you and you'd stand out like snow in the Caribbean. Whereas, I can blend in with the natives. It's the perfect cover for surveillance."

"I could get a wig," she suggested, finishing off her food, "or dye my hair. I might even be able to identify the location where the body was, if I saw it again. His group goes to the same area every year, I think."

"You would also have to dye your skin and wear colored contacts. No, it's just too risky." He ran a bite of toast around his plate, gathering up the last bit of egg, and stuck it in his mouth.

He was probably right, she agreed silently, but damn, she wanted to be there if they found enough evidence to arrest and charge Bickstauffer with a crime. She would give it some more thought. She was, after all, good at finding ways to make things work.

"Dad told Houston about a retired sheriff down in Tucson by the name of Benjamin Chee who has a big file, with pictures, of unsolved murdered and or missing people from the reservation." Hawk stood and began clearing dishes.

"Darrell Candlemoss does witness sketches for the Casper police. He's excellent. When he gets back from his vacation, Houston is going to see if he will sketch a picture of your nightmare. I can take that to Chee and see if it matches any of the pictures in his files." He looked at Savvy. "Will it bother you to relive the nightmare in hard detail?"

Every time, she thought. *Every time*. They all replayed often in the back of her mind, sometimes in the front, and the anguish never lessened; the nightmares were a part of her life. They never went away. She shook her head. "No."

IT WAS AFTER FIVE WHEN Jen looked up at the sound of the door chime to see Hawk and Savvy, accompanied by Bryn, enter The Big Cup Café. The eatery wasn't busy yet, just a smattering of people, singles and couples, mostly, but the booth they usually claimed was occupied by three uniformed cops, all of whom acknowledged them with a nod.

The police force were well acquainted with Detective Whitehawk's brother and Savvy Mills. Jen had heard the whispers about Savvy's psychic abilities. The majority of the whispered talk wavered between cautious acceptance or equally cautious skepticism, but so far, they had kept the rumors 'in house'. Jen suspected that no one was eager to broadcast to the world that the information that brought down a serial killer had come from a "psychic".

Savvy and Hawk seemed so much a unit. She knew they were looking for office space to open a private investigation service. She'd heard the couple, their hands clasped under the table, and their friend Lacey Billings, discussing paint and furnishings for the new office. Maybe that's what love did for you, gave you balance. Jen sighed. It was unlikely she would ever know.

The trio took a table near the booth and waited. Jen made her way over to them only pausing long enough beside another table to ask if they needed refills. At their nods, she promised to return as soon as she checked the new customers.

Pad in hand, Jen smiled at Hawk, then included Bryn and Savvy in her greeting. "Hi, guys. What can I get started for you?"

She jotted down their orders, two burger baskets and a Cobb Salad, with quick efficiency and a promise to return with their drinks; Pepsi, ice water and iced tea with lemon, as soon as she sent their food orders to the kitchen. Snagging a coffee pot, she hurried back to the other table with their promised refills and returned to the counter to fix the drinks for Hawk and the girls.

Since the group hadn't hesitated with their orders, she suspected that they weren't expecting anyone else, and her heart gave a little jolt of pain. She had to keep reminding herself that she had no right to feel anything, anything at all, for Houston Whitehawk, but there it was, just the same. Maybe after last night, in the parking lot, he'd decided to take her at her word and stop coming around.

"Are you sure you want that office space?" Jen heard the doubt in Bryn's voice when she set their drinks on the table. "I think you should keep looking. The view out your windows is depressing. A brick wall less than twenty feet away, then an alley full of dumpsters. It's not too late to back out. I mean, the ink isn't even dry yet."

"It's what I can cover right now," Hawk stripped the paper from his straw and set the wad aside. "Besides," he grinned at Savvy's sister, and stirred the Pepsi in his glass, "I'm counting on you females to make it look like a kick-ass Private Investigator's office. My hope is, you don't break the bank doing it."

"I'll have your food up in just a few." Jen told them, checking the tables in her section with a sharp eye. When no one seemed in need, at the moment, she lingered, remembering a time, a lifetime ago, when she had made her living as a decorator. "Where is your office located?"

Even the faint scar that traced down her jaw to her throat couldn't dim the wattage of the smile Savvy beamed as she reeled off Hawk's new address.

Jen hadn't spent much time getting acquainted with this town since they'd landed here four years ago. There hadn't seemed much point since she knew their stay could be temporary, but she had a general idea where Hawk's office was. If she was right, it was an older building in the old Yellowstone District – just off downtown. The district had been for years, they said, all rundown and nearly abandoned but it was picking up, with a spurt of renovation and re-vitalization, although that particular building had not yet been targeted. "Third floor of the building?" she recalled the suite number.

All three of them nodded.

"I would love to see it ..." She heard the door jangle and looked up as two of their regular customers, an older couple, walked through the doors, followed a few seconds later by a single male. She paused. "Excuse me," she stepped back and went to greet the newcomers as they found a table.

The man who had followed the couple went to the counter and took a stool at the far end where he scanned the other diners before turning to the menu Chloe set in front of him.

As business started picking up, Jen didn't have time to continue her conversation with Hawk, Savvy and Bryn, but she locked the information in the back of her mind as she and the two other waitresses remained busy until long after the three had paid their tab and left.

When she'd first started working here, Frank had rotated the waitresses into a pseudo-hostess position behind a small counter at the door. Later on though, he decided the extra touch of 'class' was putting too much load on the wait staff, but rather than hire another server, he did away with the 'class' and let the customers seat themselves. Still, Jen and Debbie tried to greet new customers at the door and suggest appropriate seating for them.

Most of the customers were regulars but occasionally a new face or two would walk in. Jen always made note of the first time customers, out of curiosity she liked to think, but had to admit it was really from the constant fear of exposure. You got pretty good at sizing up people who were strangers. Like the guy at the end of the counter. It wasn't the way he was dressed, dark jeans a ratty t-shirt and a black jacket hanging loosely from his shoulders, that was standard garb anymore, but there was something about the way he worked his way through his hamburger without making any real attempt to respond to Chloe, who was manning the counter tonight. Chloe was friendly, funny, and cute as a button, and it was unusual for her customers, especially the men, not to connect with her banter. This one sat silently and watched the room.

Jen was too far away to hear his occasional words over the general noise of the busy café but she kept him in her peripheral view until he finished his meal, dropped a bill beside his plate and left. She could almost hear Chloe's sigh of relief.

"Are you losing your touch, Chloe?" Jen kept her voice soft, as she clipped a new order on the wheel.

"Mr. Charm, you mean." Chloe kept her voice low as well since the counter was crowded. "He plopped his butt on that stool, looked at the menu, ordered a hamburger and a beer. When I said we didn't serve alcohol, he got this sour look on his face and decided on coffee instead. Never said another word, just grunted or shook his head if I asked if he wanted refills or dessert, until just before he left, then he asked what time this joint closed, like 'open 24 hours' isn't painted right under the name," she huffed. "I put his ticket on the counter, it was $9.85, he drops a ten by his plate and walks out," she chuckled. "I guess he figured a fifteen cent tip was sufficient for 'this joint'. Personally, I'm just glad he's gone."

There was no chance to respond as Chloe was hailed by another customer and Jen turned back to her stations. It took all kinds. Not that they didn't get an occasional oddball customer, but something about that man had set off her radar. The way he had watched everyone. She tried to shrug off the uneasy feeling, but the interaction was odd. She'd been living an odd life for the past six years, and yep, she really hated odd.

CHAPTER FOUR

Had the employee parking area been washed down, or even swept, in the last five years or so, Jen would have removed her shoes as soon as the back door of the restaurant closed behind her. But caution prevailed and she waited until she got in the car before she leaned down to loosen the laces so she could kick off the painful reminders of a tough day on her feet.

Just as she dropped her head, she heard firecrackers go off somewhere close and something hit the windshield like a baseball bat. Safety glass blasted her like stinging pellets from a sandstorm. She screamed.

From outside her car, she heard a louder report that left her ears ringing. Her car door was yanked open. Rough hands dragged her out of the seat and down to the gritty asphalt. She screamed again and fought against the hands that held her immobile.

"Be quiet and stay down," the oh-so-familiar voice of Houston Whitehawk broke through the ringing in her head.

The scream that was already building in her lungs, died with a sob. If her hands and knees hadn't been pressed into the bed of the parking lot, she would have flung herself into his arms, smart move or not. In the unearthly quiet that settled over the scene, Jen heard the back door of the restaurant grind open.

"What's going on out here?" Frank's strident and somehow whiny voice echoed into the silence.

"Get back inside and call 911," Houston ordered. "Tell them 'shots fired in the employee parking lot'. And keep everybody else inside. Nobody leaves!"

Houston released her arm as he pulled out his own phone. "Stay down."

It was an unnecessary order. She was frozen to the spot.

Her lungs struggling for air, as though she'd just finished a marathon, Jen's mind scrambled to make sense of what had just happened. Had the firecrackers actually been gun shots? Firecrackers didn't break windshields, did they? And the loud report right at her driver's window had definitely been a gun shot, from Houston's gun.

And how did Houston just happen to be right beside her car, anyway? Gun in hand? Had he been after a suspect that had just happened to run through the parking area behind the restaurant? Maybe she'd just been caught in some crossfire.

A sick feeling made her stomach roll. Or could this have anything to do with Jill? Or the Lucano mob? But what could they possibly have to gain by killing her? Unless, and the thought squeezed her heart painfully, Jill was already dead and they had somehow zeroed in on her and Link. What better way to eliminate any custody disputes than by eliminating her?

Her panic ramped up as she wondered if Antón, or his father, had already managed to find Link. She tried to crawl back into the car to get to her cell phone but Houston, with both hands occupied and his harsh baritone barking orders over her head, still managed to drag her back down behind her car door.

"I need my phone!" she struggled in his hold.

"Stay down, damn it!"

In the distance, she heard the wail of sirens. That was really fast, she thought, but cops were never far away from the Big Cup. The main cop shop in the Hall of Justice was maybe a half-mile away.

"I believe the shooter has already left the area. I heard footsteps running down the alley but I'm trying to keep the victim under cover until backup arrives ... Must have been an automatic ... at least three muzzle flashes ... centered above the steering wheel ... I pulled my gun and returned fire ... he took off."

She had been the target. As Houston's words finally began to register, she fought against the urge to vomit and repeated to herself, over and again, the words, 'I refuse to give in to that ultimate humiliation'. What she'd lived in terror of for the past six years, had finally happened.

"I need my phone! I have to call home!" Her words, loud enough to trigger a question from the other end of Houston's call, finally got a response from him. He muttered something into his phone and ended the call.

"Is it in your purse?" At her nod, he said, "You stay down." and reached across the driver's seat himself to retrieve her purse and drop it into her hands. With palsied fingers, she dug her phone out of its pocket and hit the speed dial for the house just as two patrol cars, sirens abruptly shut off but lights still flashing, pulled up behind them, and another entered the alley in back of the dumpsters. She swallowed hard, as she waited, prayed, for Irene to answer. She had to choose her words carefully.

When Irene picked up, Jen didn't waste time on an explanation. "There's been a problem here at work …" the husky rumble that left her lips didn't sound like her at all. She coughed to clear her throat. "… no, I'm fine, but I'll be late getting home … everything's okay … I don't know how long … I'll try not to be too late. I just didn't want you to worry. Yes, fine. Will you check Link's bag for his overnight camp trip tomorrow? Make sure he has everything he needs? … Okay, thanks. Be there as soon as I can." She hung up.

Irene would know what to do.

She closed her eyes tight and willed away the quaking that shook her body. And if she didn't get home tonight, she knew a clue would be waiting for her when she finally walked in the door. She would be able to find them.

Realizing Houston had probably broken rules to let her use the phone, she looked at him apologetically. "Thanks," she said. "Irene worries if I'm late, so does Link, and she doesn't need that kind of stress at her age."

Houston stood up as another patrol car rolled to a stop. With a motion of his hand, he directed the officers, who were unloading from the vehicle, to spread out and begin searching the area where he'd seen the muzzle flashes. He ordered one of them to secure the restaurant, and as another patrol car pulled in behind the others, directed the officers that got out of it to begin with the patrons and the staff of the restaurant to see if any of them had seen anything or heard anything suspicious around the time of the gunfire.

Realizing she was still on the ground where he'd left her, he pulled Jen up beside him, "Are you hurt?" He stared grimly at her as he wiped a trickle of blood from her cheek and brushed some glass fragments off her shoulders.

"No," she shook her head and lifted her purse strap over her shoulder, "ju ... just shaky." That was putting it mildly.

"Stay put," he said harshly, as he brushed more glass off her car seat and guided her back into it. "I need to check with the men. I'll be right back. And then," he added as he stepped back, "you're going to tell me who wants to shoot you, and why."

There was a hole in the windshield the size of a softball with a webbing of broken glass surrounding it, and there was a long gouge in the dashboard above the instrument panel. The glass pellets that had blasted over her head glittered like rhinestones on the seats and floor. She twisted around to look at the patrol cars that had effectively blocked any chance of exit and thought, since her legs were too unsteady to run, his admonishment to "stay put", was really unnecessary.

Unbelievably, a fire truck and an ambulance rolled up further blocking off the parking lot entrance. Overkill, the thought ran through her brain. Dropping her head to the steering wheel, she fought for a calm that stayed just out of her reach. Her fingers felt a harsh tear in the leather cover of the steering wheel, right where her head would have been if she hadn't reached down to loosen her shoelaces, and fresh terror assaulted her. Her teeth chattered like castanets and she clamped her jaw shut. It was going to be a long night.

IF HE'D EVER SEEN A rabbit ready to break and run, that was Jen, Houston thought to himself as he rechecked the area where he'd seen the muzzle flashes. He hoped he was prepared to hear the answers he was now determined to get.

Shit, another thought popped into his head. He wasn't just a witness, he'd fired his weapon. He, himself, was now part of the investigation. He couldn't question her about a damn thing. Frustration ground at him. But, he still intended to get answers, somehow.

The long and heavy Mag light, which he'd borrowed from one of the officers who had gone into the restaurant, now resting on his shoulder, he scanned the ground and found the spot, an area about six feet long, of trampled down weeds, where the gunman had waited, concealed behind the dumpsters and a section of old fence.

It had sounded like a heavy automatic, so he searched for spent shells but found nothing. Had the shooter had time to police the area before he ran off? Not a chance in hell, but the officers who had swept the area moments ago might have bagged them already. If not, they would search again at sun up. He spotted a fresh, shiny groove at the corner of the dumpster. His lips curved in a grim smile. His return shot must have been close enough to have the assailant wetting himself. A little closer than he'd planned, but who knows, if the round shattered, the assailant might have caught a fragment or two. He returned to the parking lot.

Jen didn't look much steadier when he got to the still-open car door, and she trembled as if the temperature was sub-zero. They both saw paramedics approaching.

"They'll want to take you to the ER." he told Jen and watched the panic flash in her eyes.

"No!" she shook her head violently. "I'm fine!" her voice rose as another shudder shook her like a chew toy.

The closest medic had heard her vehement refusal, but saw the blood on her cheek and asked anyway, "When the call came in, we were advised of "possible injuries". Are you sure, Ma'am? You should probably let the doctors check you over, just to be on the safe side."

"No! I don't need to go to the hospital. I'm fine!" she repeated, keeping a death grip on the steering wheel to stop the shaking in her hands.

"There weren't any injuries," Houston assured them, "but I'll keep an eye on her for a few minutes. If she changes her mind, I'll call you back in."

Dismissed, the paramedics hung around for a bit before returning to the ambulance.

The parking lot was a beehive of activity. Jen lost track of time. It could have been minutes, it could have been hours, as she leaned her forehead against the wheel and fought to bring her nerves under control.

"Come on," Houston said, "let's get you warmed up."

Would she ever be warm again, she wondered? She lifted her head from the steering wheel and nodded but she didn't speak as he helped her to rise, her purse bumping against her hip, and led her to his vehicle. He steadied her as she stumbled on a shoelace. The one that had saved her life. In some disconnected part of her brain, she noticed that the ambulance and fire truck were gone.

Pulling a jacket from behind the seat, he helped her put it on, and zipped it up. It swallowed her from neck to knees and she hugged the added warmth to her gratefully.

"Th ... thanks."

He opened the passenger door and got her settled in the seat then picked up her foot and tied her shoe. She didn't question his actions until he climbed behind the wheel and started the engine. "Where are you taking me?"

"Nowhere. Just turning on the heater."

She subsided into silence until it stretched to an unbearable length, then she asked, "Aren't you s ... supposed to t ... take my statement, or something?"

"Someone will, but not me. I'll have to give a statement too since I'm a witness as well."

Just then, Captain Bricker, in his official SUV, pulled up beside Houston's vehicle. Setting the brake, he left his car running and came around to where Jen huddled. He opened her door. She knew him, of course. Like many on the force, he stopped into the Big Cup often enough that they all knew her, too.

"It was your vehicle that was shot at?" he looked her over carefully, noting the bloody nick on her cheek with a frown. At her mute nod, he turned his attention to Houston. "And you returned fire?"

"Yes," Houston answered.

"Why is Jen..ah..Mrs. Bradley in your vehicle, Detective Whitehawk?" he growled.

"She was going into shock," Houston answered, "and I had a jacket in my car, and a heater, which she seemed to need."

The Captain frowned and muttered something about cowboys but Jen didn't catch it all. The comment, however, elicited a low growl and a frown from Houston although he refrained from responding. She wondered if, because of his Indian heritage, the term cowboy had a negative connotation.

"Mrs. Bradley," Bricker placed his hand on her elbow, "if you will come down to the station with me, I need you to tell me what happened tonight. We'll try to get you home as soon as possible."

"Of course," she said, though without much conviction. She climbed out, away from the heater and missed it immediately.

"Detective?"

"I'll follow you in," Houston nodded.

CHAPTER FIVE

It was after eleven by the time Jen took her first breath of fresh air, outside the cop shop. She had repeated her story over and over. Had choked down nearly a gallon of the worst coffee she'd tasted in years. Its only redeeming virtue was it was scalding hot, and yet she still couldn't get warm. And now, her gut was churning; from the coffee, and the fear that continued to pump through her body. Fear for Link and Irene, for Jill and for herself.

Her gut twisted into knots as she thought of Link and what must be going through his mind right now. Irene would only be able to keep him calm for a time, then he would start to pick up on the urgency of their flight, and the fear. And she wasn't there – which would only increase his anxiety.

It had been torture to try to stay calm during the questioning, with her mind rebelling against every second that ticked by. She wasn't completely sure she'd managed to keep the mask in place for the duration. The captain, and the female officer that sat in on the questioning and ran the recorder, had played tag team with the 'looks' they cast her way and the ones they volleyed between themselves. How many times had she repeated the lie that she had no idea who would want to hurt her.

"Thank you for your patience and your help," Captain Bricker finally said, pushing up from the desk and handing her a business card from a slot in the center drawer. "I think we've got all we need for now. We may have more questions for you later. If you remember anything else, call me. Officer Wells will take you home."

Dismissed, Jen followed the woman to the parking lot and to another police car where, this time, she was ushered into the back seat of the sedan for the ride home.

"Where to?" Officer Wells asked, as though she hadn't heard Jen repeat her address multiple times tonight.

A retort rose to her lips but she swallowed it. Getting snippy at this point wouldn't help her cause. Even if they couldn't prove it yet, she knew they thought she hadn't told them all the truth. Which, of course, she hadn't.

The ride out to the house off Cole Creek Road was over soon enough that, when the heater finally started producing, blessed little heat had managed to make it to the backseat. Chills played a vicious game of tag through her body.

God, why couldn't she get warm? She wondered, still burrowed deep in Houston's jacket. Loaning her his jacket had been a kind gesture. She would have to make sure he got it back, even if she never saw him again. Tears welled in her eyes at the thought. Maybe she could send it back to the station with Officer Wells.

"I still have on Detective Whitehawk's jacket," she said, as they rolled to a stop at her sidewalk and Officer Wells started to climb out. "If I leave it with you, will you see that he gets it back?" Reaching for the door handle proved fruitless, she realized belatedly. The back seat of cop cars are made to keep people in until an officer lets them out. Officer Wells circled the vehicle and opened Jen's door.

"You'll probably see him again before I will," she said. "We work different shifts. It's a great jacket. I wouldn't want to just leave it draped over his chair at the shop."

Really? Were there people at her office she wasn't sure she could trust?

Jill's words came back to Jen: 'Antón's father and grandfather own both state and federal officials and judges all over North and South America. We can't trust anybody.' And another quake shook her body.

"Thanks for the ride." Jen looked toward the pale kitchen light they always left on, where it filtered through the living room curtains.

"I'll see you in," Officer Wells fell into step with Jen as she moved along the uneven sidewalk.

"That's not necessary," Jen shook away the offer. "My son is a very light sleeper and I don't want to wake him if Irene managed to get him to sleep." Officer Wells stopped when she reached the top of the porch. "Okay, I'll just wait here until you're inside." Digging out her house key, Jen made her way up the three short steps to the porch and fitted it in the door lock. She turned to wave at Officer Wells as she pushed the door open and reached for the light switch. When the lamp in the living room and the porch light lit the area, her escort returned Jen's wave and descended the steps back to her car.

Leaning against the door, Jen closed her eyes as exhaustion washed over her. But she didn't have time to rest. She took off Houston's coat and draped it over the back of the couch where it would be easy to spot. On the table beside the couch, a tourist brochure lay open. She looked it over, spotted what she sought, then started for Irene's room.

It took some strength, but Jen managed to pull Irene's big dresser out far enough that she could get to the cubbyhole in the wall behind it. Opening it, she found the new passport and other papers she would need and the cash she and Irene had squirreled away. She emptied the contents into her purse.

Pushing everything back into place, she headed for her bedroom, stripping off her work clothes as she went. A dark canvas back pack sat by the door. She knew Irene had packed it but she went through it carefully anyway. Satisfied, she added her purse to the contents and went back to her dresser. There were black leggings and a black, long-sleeved shirt in the bottom drawer, which she threw on the bed, then dug out fresh underwear and socks. Her work shoes were black as well, and reasonably comfortable if she could stay off her feet for a while. She smiled bitterly. That wouldn't be hard to do for the next few hours. They would do. What she lacked was a black jacket. Gray was the best she could manage for now. Houston's jacket was black, the thought entered her head, but no, she would not add theft to her many transgressions.

Dressing quickly, she returned to the kitchen and grabbed an apple from the fridge. Hopefully, that would help settle the coffee acid and the fear that burned a hole in her stomach. A thin thread of hope was all she had at this point. That, and a healthy spark of self-preservation.

Unable to help herself, she removed Link's drawing from under the magnet on the refrigerator, and folding it carefully, tucked it into a side pocket of the back pack.

Taking a bite of the apple, she flung the back pack over her shoulder and opened the kitchen door, to head for the back yard gate and the abandoned house, a real fixer-upper, on a street about four blocks away.

The houses there were widely spaced, nearly two acres per lot, and backed up to what had once been considered 'green space'. There was nothing green about it any longer. The neighborhood was in the county, outside the Casper limits, and had been 'developed' during the last oil boom. That had come crashing down, as do all booms, in the 2008 debacle, and a good many of the houses and trailer homes were empty.

She'd heard rumors that this particular abandoned place had been a crack house where several people had died in an explosion, and the bank that held the mortgage apparently didn't feel it was worth trying to rehab or sell. So, it sat empty, waiting for the county to reclaim the property and demolish it. Several houses in the area had sale signs anchored in the front lawns. The isolation had been the deciding factor for Jen when she first came to town.

The only thing that had been added to the property was a new lock on the door of a dilapidated cinder block tool shed; the only thing left whole, at the far back of the acreage, following the explosion. She knew the lock was new because she'd added it herself, when she'd hidden the motorcycle in the shed shortly after moving here.

She rode the bike occasionally, late at night, just to keep the engine tuned. With a helmet on, she was just another rider.

The bike was not in her name and Irene made sure the license on it was current. The county didn't know about that. And as long as she didn't get a ticket, her secret was safe. Pausing for a couple of moments to say goodbye to the old house and the scruffy yard, she chewed her bite of apple and swallowed. They'd planned to re-sod the lawn but had never gotten around to it. But Link had played out here, and he'd loved that old tire swing in the cottonwood tree. Sadly though, he wasn't a baby anymore and she wouldn't be able this time to stick a pacifier in his mouth when he started asking questions.

Their charade was unraveling around them. She couldn't see any good end in sight, but still she must go on. She tightened the straps on the pack, stepped out onto the porch, and made to descend the steps when a blur of movement behind the bush at the bottom of the steps surprised a soft squeak from her. Reflexively, she dodged sideways, lost her footing, caught her heel on the top step, and tumbled down the short flight into a hard body. Her fall surprised a grunt out of her assailant, definitely male, as they both hit the ground, him bearing the brunt of the impact.

Strength she didn't know she possessed surged through her body, and she used the heaving chest under her to rebound up and away. She might have made it, too, if a strong hand hadn't clamped around her ankle, bringing her down hard.

With no body to cushion the fall this time, and the weight of the back pack adding impetus, her head hit the packed ground like a church bell clapper. All the stars above danced wildly to the ringing in her brain while her lungs sucked frantically for air, as the man she'd landed on scrambled to his feet. And that hand around her ankle was dragging her inexorably back toward her launch point.

She braced herself to fight. Find a vulnerable spot, she told herself. He was wheezing but so was she. When she tried to stand, he gave her leg a vicious, one-handed twist. Pain radiated up her leg but it paled against the terror that flooded her whole body. From deep inside, she pushed back the pain and fear to find the cool reason her self-defense instructor had told her was critical to survival. "Fight through the fear and pain. Find a vulnerable spot." he'd said.

She screamed at the top of her lungs. Suddenly he dropped her foot as his rough hands grappled to drag her upright and cover her mouth. For just a moment she was free and had both feet on the ground. Digging for all the strength she could muster, she struck out with one foot, and, her aim true, caught his kneecap. A howl of pain erupted from his mouth, right by her ear. Cursing and limping, he dragged her back toward the porch.

"Where are they?!!" the man growled. "Answer me!!" he said, louder, but then seemed to realize that he still had his hand over her mouth.

The pressure eased enough that she was able to comply but she had no intention of doing so. She knew what he wanted.

"Where's what?" she panted, still looking for a chance to deliver a blow that would free her.

"Don't play fucking cute! Where's the boy and ... Shit," he muttered as the back porch light came on.

He changed direction, trying to get them behind the tree but the shift loosened his grip on her right arm and she twisted in his hold. Knowing she only had a fraction of a second, she levered a hard fist to his throat. Gasping, for air, he staggered but still retained a crushing grip on one arm. With strength born of terror, she aimed one foot in a kick to his groin and connected. He released his hold as he went down in a fetal position. She thought he might have been trying to scream but no sound came from his open mouth.

Her first instinct was to get back to the house, but someone had turned on the porch light. Did the man on the ground have a partner? He hadn't seemed to expect anyone. She only hesitated for a moment before breaking for the alley, her pack jouncing loose on her back. Hard footsteps pounded across the yard toward her. There was no time to unlatch the gate; could she clear the fence?

She would never know the answer to that question as two hands grabbed her from behind and she hit the ground. With nothing to cushion her fall, her head hit the ground again. Her ears rang. She shook her head to clear it as she gathered her strength to fight. She tried to roll away but the hands that had brought her down were now lifting her to her feet. They didn't free her though.

"What's the rush, Jen?" Houston's question had her turning toward him with a gasp. "The investigation is just getting started."

"YOU!?" Jen shouted in disbelief. "You scared the crap out of me! What are you doing here anyway!?"

"I told you I had questions."

"Yeah," she snapped. "So did your partner."

"What?!" his head snapped around.

"Behind the tree." she motioned. One of the hands that held her slid down her arm to take hold of her wrist as he pulled her behind him toward the tree. The man wasn't there. On the heels of that revelation, the sound of a vehicle jumping to life some distance away, explained the absence of her proof.

"Who was this 'man'?" Houston listened to the retreating vehicle.

"I didn't have a chance to ask." The adrenaline that had kept her upright now drained away and she grabbed for the rope of the swing.

Seeing her wobble, Houston put his arm around her waist and turned her toward the back door. "Come on. Let's get you back in the house."

"You weren't going for a late night run, were you?" The emphasis was definitely on the word run as he eyed the back pack now laying on the ground. One anchor strap had ripped loose in her struggle.

"What I do and when I do it is no one's business," she snapped, but the terror she'd felt at the man's hands wouldn't leave her and took some of the bite out of her words.

"The law might have another viewpoint on that."

Yes they would. Her argument crumbled. Her hope of making her escape tonight lay in ashes on the ground next to the broken back pack. She frowned. Irene would wait until sunup then leave her another clue to follow to the next rendezvous point.

Resigning herself to trying to mollify Houston by answering what questions she could without giving anything away and lying through her teeth for the rest, she reached for the pack and winced. There were a few new pains but nothing that should slow her down. First, she had to get rid of Houston and get to her bike before her attacker made another attempt. She went back into the kitchen with the backpack dangling. He followed her.

"Why are you here?" she asked. "I mean, why my house? Why this time of night?"

"Questions," he said. "And then I heard a scream. I broke your door lock and came through the house, thinking you might be in trouble, or actually, more trouble than you already were, only to see you running for the gate like an Olympic sprinter. Like I said, Questions."

Getting rid of him wasn't going to be easy. "I'm guessing this will require a pot of coffee." she frowned.

He grinned. Why had she even asked? She set the pack against the closed door, hoping to assure him that she didn't plan to make a quick break out the back again. She dumped the coffee pot and grounds and started a fresh one for him. She opted for ice water. There was no way her stomach could handle more coffee. It growled audibly in response to her musing, and she thought longingly of her apple, now laying somewhere out in the yard.

He heard it. "Something to eat would hit the spot."

"The Big Cup is open 24/7," she growled, every bit as loud as her stomach. Knowing he would be impervious to the hint, she reached up in the cupboard and dropped a bag of chocolate chip cookies in front of him. She thought about grabbing one for herself, but as dry as her throat was, she wasn't sure she could swallow it without choking, so she let it be.

"Thanks," he waggled a cookie at her. "This is the first food I've seen since breakfast."

"If you have questions, ask," she refused to feel any sympathy for his empty belly, "or do you need a length of rubber hose for this?"

He scowled, as he stuffed the cookie into his mouth, chewed, swallowed. "When did we become enemies, Jen?"

"When someone took pot shots at my windshield, and miracle of miracles, you just happened to be at my car door when it happened. Then, you threatened me. And, then I get attacked in my own back yard not ten minutes ago, and, suddenly, there you are, again. In the last few hours, I've been scared out of ten years of my life, dammit. I have some questions, too." She bit down on her lip to stop its trembling.

"I threatened you?" his eyebrows climbed.

"You said you were going to 'Get' answers about why someone was shooting at me," she challenged him to deny it. "It sounded like a threat to me."

"And, I plan to," he shrugged.

"Yet, in your vehicle, you said you couldn't because you were part of the investigation."

"That was then, this is now." he shrugged, picked up another cookie.

"What changed?"

"I'm on administrative leave," he frowned. It wasn't the full truth. It was desk duty. He wasn't barred from working on other cases, just not this case.

"What? Why?" That had to be a slap to him. Disbelief, commiseration and caution tussled in her head.

"I discharged my service weapon. It requires me to turn over my gun and my shield. It's automatic." Another cookie went in his mouth, disappearing quickly.

"You're kidding," she laughed. "No one was shot or killed." When he didn't join her laughter, her humor died. "For how long?"

"Until the investigation is closed and I'm cleared of any wrong-doing. Which brings me back to you," he snagged another cookie, pointing it at her. "If you insist on running, the case won't be closed until someone brings you back. I plan on making sure that doesn't happen."

His job was at stake so she didn't see how she could blame him for that. "I have no intention of running." She turned her back to him. It was easier to lie to him if she wasn't looking at him. Pulling a mug down, she filled it with coffee. Schooling her features, she turned back and set it in front of him.

A scowl creased his forehead. He didn't believe her. "So where are Irene and your son?"

"Link is at a camp out with his scout troop and Irene took the night off."

"Then what had you going off at midnight?"

"He forgot some things he was supposed to take with him. I had to take them to him." Jen's brain scrambled furiously to stay on top of her story.

"How? Your car is in evidence impound." he stared at her steadily. She felt sweat beading all over her body and forming a trickle between her breasts.

"I called a taxi," she snapped defensively.

"To the back gate?" Disbelief added a sharp, acid edge to his words. He struggled to bring his emotions under control.

"Come on, Jen. No one, and I mean no one, calls home after just being shot at and reminds them to check over a bag for a camp out. And no camp out for children starts that late at night," he barked, then his face softened. "Oh, that's right. It wasn't scheduled until tomorrow, was it? Which makes your little jaunt tonight even more suspect." He waited for a response but she remained silent.

"I knew when I brushed the glass fragments off you shoulders, Jen, that you were going to run. I've seen the look in too many eyes to be mistaken about it. God knows, I've watched you ever since I started coming into the café. I've seen the hunted look that darkens those beautiful blue eyes frequently. I'd like to help you if you let me, but I won't go into a situation blind. Tell me what's really going on, Jen."

The compassion he broadcast was almost her undoing. Oh, how she longed to lay this burden on his broad shoulders. And if she had been the only one involved, she would have, gladly, and let the chips fall where they may. But she had to think of Link, and Jill, and Irene. A misstep could cost more than just her life. Steeling herself against the tug of his earnest plea, she put ice in a glass and filled it at the tap.

"I've said it over and over again tonight, 'I don't have any idea who shot out my windshield or who would want me dead'." At least that was the truth. "And, at the risk of repeating myself, maybe he was shooting at you, and was just a lousy shot. You've still haven't explained what you were doing in the employee parking lot at just that time."

His visage turned grim again. "I've been asking myself that, a lot, over the last few hours. And I have to wonder what would have happened if I hadn't been there. Those weren't 'pot shots' Jen. They were three closely grouped shots, professional, right through the windshield, just above the steering wheel," the memory still had the power to raise the hairs on the back of his neck, "right where your head should have been." He unknowingly repeated her own conclusion.

He raked his fingers through his hair, massaging down the hair at the nape of his neck, and sat quietly for a moment, his eyes closed in thought; then he stood up and stepped over to pick up her pack. "Let's go."

"Where?!" she made a dive for her bag which he easily deflected, but their mutual grip swung her body uncomfortably close to his. For a moment her breathing stopped. She dropped her hold and stepped back.

"Why," his confusion was as fake as his damn crocodile smile, "to take these necessary things to the overnight camp-out, of course."

She felt herself deflate like a leaky balloon. Holding his hard gaze as long as she could, she whispered, "Please, Houston, for the sake of my family and our friendship, if that exists anymore, you have to leave. Believe me, if I could tell you anything, I would."

He stared at her silently for a space then slowly shook his head. "It can't work that way, Jen. The only way it can work, is if you tell me what's going on and I do everything in my power to help you through it. Or out of it."

"And you have the ultimate power? You have autonomous control to guarantee that myself or anyone involved will be safe?" she challenged softly, and locked her eyes to his.

This time it was he who turned away, and ran his hands through his hair again before jamming them in his pockets.

"That's what I thought. Anything I told you would have to be run up the chain of command wouldn't it?"

"Dammit, Jen, I have a responsibility to go by the book. That's how it works."

She sat back down at the table. "There's nothing I can tell you, Houston."

He stared at her silently for a space then slowly shook his head. "Dammit, Jen, I have a responsibility to the oath I took. My hands are tied."

"I've told you everything I can, Houston."

He picked up his cup again, drained it, and set it in the sink. He picked up her bag and, for a moment, she thought he was going to open it but then he placed it by the door once again and moved in front of her, so close she was forced to look up into his eyes. When those eyes focused on her lips and his head dipped, her heart stuttered in her chest.

She saw the kiss coming, and a faint voice in her head said, 'turn away, this will not end well', but the heat in his eyes warmed the chills that had gripped her since the bullets had shattered her windshield, and she didn't want to lose that heat. She needed that heat like she needed air. It wasn't smart, but she'd dreamed about his kisses for so long, and if, no -- 'when' – she was able to get away tonight, she knew that this would be her last chance to taste that dream.

She craved the taste.

His lips took hers in a gentle claiming and she couldn't help her response. She opened to him with a welcoming he couldn't mistake. His arms closed around her like banding straps, lifting her from the chair, and the kiss escalated from gentle to ravenous in a heartbeat. His hard body ground into hers, trying to fuse them into one, and all sanity left her mind.

There was nothing but heat, and need, and want, coursing throughout her body. It could have lasted a minute or an hour, she didn't know, and then it ended. He released her and stepped away. The look in his eyes, as though he'd just done something unforgivable, brought back her chills two-fold. She fought the urge to throw herself back into those arms, into those moments of forgetfulness.

"Get some sleep, Jen. You look exhausted. If you run, I, and every cop in Wyoming and all the surrounding states, will be looking for you. It won't go well. Have a good night."

In a few strides, he was out the front door. She watched it close silently behind him before she sat down again at the table, crossed her arms and put her head down on them. Struggling to regain some control over the emotions that Houston had just drawn up from her soul, she blinked back the suspicious moisture blurring her vision. That taste she'd craved, had yearned for, for years, she knew would haunt her the rest of her life, but she refused to regret a single moment of it.

Houston had hit it on the head. She was exhausted. She would just rest for a while. Give him time to think she didn't intend to run.

Yes, the law would be hunting for her, but not seriously. There was no crime involved except gunshots fired inside the city limits, and she hadn't fired them. No, it wasn't the police finding her that terrified her.

She stood up and shut off the light over the sink. Taking the back pack with her, she went to her room and set the alarm to wake her in two hours. It would be enough, it had to be. She fell on the bed and closed her eyes.

CHAPTER SIX

Houston swore and pounded his hand on the steering wheel. What in the hell was Jen mixed up in? What was so serious that even being shot at wouldn't unseal her lips? And for God sake, why couldn't the rational part of his brain quit thinking about that kiss and how her body had felt, pressed into him?

She was right to wonder just what he was doing in the employee parking lot, but he couldn't shake the gut deep fear of what could have happened if he hadn't been there.

The answer of course was that he had hoped to persuade her to go out with him, but could he tell her that, now? He grinned without humor. That goal was shelved until this little puzzle was solved. Maybe even permanently. Dammit, those weren't wild shots. And if the shooter knew where she worked, he'd just displayed that he knew where she lived, too.

He started the truck, sat for a moment, then turned it off again. He couldn't leave her here, but what else could he do? Arrest her? Put her in protective custody?

Maybe not such a bad idea. He considered it further, then pulled out his phone. When his brother answered, grumpy at being woken up at Jesus o'clock in the morning, Houston talked him down and explained the situation. For this to work, he had to have both Hawk and Savvy on board.

Several minutes later, and knowing he was probably making the biggest mistake of his career, even bigger than that kiss, he finally shut off the phone, stepped out of his vehicle and jogged back up on Jen's porch. Sucking in a deep breath, he rapped sharply on the door.

The turmoil in her mind had made rest impossible, as she lay waiting to hear the sound of Houston's vehicle leaving, willing him away but hoping he'd stay. The pounding on her front door jerked her head up, her heart leapt to her throat, and it took a couple of moments to swallow down the panic. If it was someone intent on harming her, it was unlikely they would knock. Besides, the lock was broken. And Houston's truck hadn't gone anywhere. She pushed herself from the bed and moved through the dark house into the living room.

She had a suspicion and a hope, but still looked out the window, just to make sure, and saw Houston lifting his hand to knock again. She had to shove the joy she felt at seeing him again down deep inside the catacombs of her heart and deal with facts. Sighing at the inevitable, she opened the door.

"Did you forget something?" she grumbled, stepping out of the way as he pushed past her and reached around her to shut the door. He left his hand braced against it, as though he expected her to bolt again. She stared hard at his hand on the door until he let it fall to his side.

"You can't stay here. He knows where you live."

That thought had never left her mind since the questioning at the police station. A retort rose to her lips but she bit it back. She could hardly tell him she wasn't planning on staying here after trying to convince him exactly the opposite. Although she was sure his quick once over of her, still fully clothed, when she'd opened the door, made that plainly obvious.

"Really?" she gave him a hard look. "This is my home. Where do you expect me to stay?"

"I have a safe place arranged," he said. "Pack what you'll need for a couple of days. I'll explain it on the way."

"I'm not going anywhere until I get details." Her arms folded firmly around her middle, she stepped away from the force field that was Houston Whitehawk. "And when Link and Irene come back here, what are they supposed to do?"

"Why don't you tell me?" Houston gave her a hard look. "Are you going to try to convince me again that they're at a 'troop camp out' and just 'taking a night off'?" He shook his head, "I didn't believe your story the first time, Jen, so you need to come up with something a hell of a lot better. And, until you do, I'm going to act as though that phone call at your car was a warning to Irene, that she and Link should disappear."

He could have slung her over his shoulder, and the thought did cross his mind, but she still needed to gather some clothes. He tried reason.

"Savanna Mills is going to put you up for a couple of days."

He flipped the light switch behind her, flooding the living room with light, and with her dogging his steps, headed for the back pack he'd set by the kitchen door, snagging up his jacket on the way. When he didn't see the back pack by the door, he headed unerringly for the bedrooms. "Hopefully, we'll have the shooter in custody by then and you can go back to your routine and I can go back to my job."

"If my situation is all that dangerous, why would you put your brother's girlfriend in the middle of it?" She dodged into her room, more to keep him from getting a good look at Irene's dresser than to make his search any easier, and made a grab at the back pack by the bed. His longer arms beat her to it but he didn't fight her for it when she snatched it back from his hands, and set it on her shoulder. "She's recovering from her own troubles. Why would she want to step into someone else's predicament?"

He tapped the back pack on her shoulder, "Does this have everything you're going to need? Work clothes and such?"

"Will you just go away, Houston?" She jerked away from him. "I've been managing my own life for over thirty years now. I can handle this myself." Marching back to the living room, him right behind her, she opened the door, motioned him out, and somehow expected him to leave.

Instead, with a muttered curse, he slammed the door and flipped off the light, plunging the room into darkness again. "Are you trying to get dead?" he snapped, yanking her away from the door. "You might as well glue a target on your head."

Her mind went blank for a moment. She'd been so irritated with him that she hadn't given a thought to the danger she'd put herself in until the room went black. Now, her knees turned to water. To keep from falling, she grabbed for the little table by the door, and the back pack on her shoulder slid down her arm. The bowl set there to hold keys and coins, rattled and nearly fell off. How had she come to feel so safe in Houston's presence that she forgot the jeopardy she was in? That her whole family was in?

Houston's arm went around her, to catch her. She couldn't see his face in the gloom but there was comfort in his touch. And heat. Definitely heat.

"Let's go." He opened the door cautiously and stepped onto the porch, pulling her out behind him. That she had no more objections told them both just how shaken she was. "If you need anything else, Hawk can drive you back tomorrow to get it."

Jen settled into a troubled silence as they drove away, south on Cole Creek Road, to the nearly empty streets of Casper, but her silence didn't mean she'd given in to Houston's heavy-handed orders. In the back pack, she had everything she needed for the road. And, as soon as she had the chance, which actually might be easier from Savvy's apartment, she could slip away. The only problem was that she was a heck of a lot farther from her motorcycle than she had been.

Savvy's sister, Bryn, was just coming out of Savvy's door as Houston followed Jen down the hall. Savvy stood in the open doorway.

Bryn gave Jen a quick smile as she greeted the two of them quietly.

"Bed's all made up with fresh sheets," she said, stepping clear of the door. "Try to get some rest. You look completely drained, hon."

"Are you staying with Lacey?" Houston whispered to her.

"That's the plan," Bryn grinned. "I spend so much time there that I have my own key. Won't even have to wake her up. But I will anyway," she said, with an evil little chuckle. "This is too good to keep to myself for long."

"This isn't for public consumption," Houston scowled severely. "Don't let it go beyond Lacey's ears."

"I won't," Bryn assured him.

"I'm sorry for putting you out," Jen said. There was more she could say but she didn't. Let Houston think she'd accepted the inevitable.

"Don't give it a thought." Bryn smiled at her and moved off down the hall.

"Come on in and let's get you settled," Savvy smiled kindly at her and pulled the door open wider to usher them through.

As Jen entered the apartment, she looked around. Savvy, barefoot and wrapped in a knee length robe, took her hand and gave it a reassuring squeeze. Hawk, bare-chested with a pair of gray sweat pants riding low on his lean hips, was leaning against the kitchen island, a cup in his hand. She knew he'd been wounded in Afghanistan, but she'd never seen the scars on his shoulder and below his ribs. She shuddered as she saw the damage bullets could inflict and remembered the near miss she'd had just hours before. He offered her a lift of his lips as he brought the cup to his mouth. There were no smiles left in her, so she looked around the apartment instead.

A big sectional sofa took up a good portion of the spacious living area and a table lamp sent a warm and welcoming glow throughout the room. Straight ahead, a hall, also lit, lead off to what, she assumed, would be bedrooms and bath. If she could have been comfortable anywhere, this would have been the place but she didn't plan to be here long enough to get comfortable. Just long enough to ease the mind of her guard dog.

"Have you had anything to eat tonight?" Savvy's voice broke into her thoughts.

Jen thought longingly of the bite of apple she'd managed before Houston had forced a change in her plans, but she wouldn't put this couple out any more than she already had. "I had a bite a little while ago." In her side vision, she watched Houston's eyebrows rise.

'Can't stop lying even on such a commonplace, Jen,' they seemed to say as their eyes met. He couldn't know for sure, of course. She could have had one of those cookies still sitting on her table. But somehow, she had the eerie feeling that he could read her mind. He said nothing though, and only moved toward his brother as Savvy led her down the hallway.

"The bathroom is right across the hall from your door," Savvy motioned that direction as she opened the door to the room Jen would be using tonight. Another swift chill ran up Jen's back and she trembled. Savvy noticed. "And there are some extra blankets in the chest at the foot of the bed."

It was a feminine room, white with blue and yellow accents and a mountain of bolsters and decorative pillows scattered across the bed, which Savvy tossed unceremoniously to the floor on the far side in order to turn back the covers. The smell of fresh linens lingered in the air. With the stack of pillows gone, the bed looked as inviting as a cloud to Jen's exhausted body.

"Thank you, Savvy," she dropped the back pack to the floor beside the bed, sat down on the mattress, and removed the shoes that, she suddenly recalled, had probably saved her life tonight. "This feels like heaven." She started to open her bag to get the long t-shirt that she usually slept in but stopped. "I think I'd better use the bathroom before I climb into bed."

"Of course," Savvy smiled and turned to leave. "If you can't find everything you need, just holler. I'll be up for a bit, yet."

Lifting the back pack again, Jen followed Savvy into the hall and went into the tidy bathroom. Shutting the door behind her, she pressed the lock. She dug out a small toiletries case, found her tooth brush, and set about getting ready for bed, knowing she might as well take advantage of her enforced imprisonment. There was no doubt in her mind that this was exactly that. She'd seen the look that passed between Houston and his brother as she rounded the corner into the hall. They would be on guard, expecting her to run.

It was already too late to meet up with Irene and Link tonight and it might be hours before she found an opportunity. 'Take advantage of the opportunity to get some rest' she told herself, echoing her survival instructor of so many years ago. If it helped throw them off-guard, to relax their vigil, so much the better. She debated whether to take a shower but decided it could wait until later, maybe tomorrow.

Taking care of basic needs, she brushed her teeth and wiped down the sink with some tissues before returning to her room. She locked the door behind her. Once changed into the t-shirt, she wedged her pack between the bed and the nightstand, and walked over to the window. It was three floors to the ground. Although she'd noted some small balconies on the building, there wasn't one at this window. It wouldn't do her much good to try to escape out the window if she broke her legs when she dropped.

As desperate as she was to get to Irene and Link, she wasn't desperate enough to rummage through Bryn's personal things. Besides, it was doubtful that Bryn would have ropes or escape ladders neatly stacked in the closet anyway.

With exhaustion washing over her, and the occasional chill still shaking her, she dug another blanket out of the chest and spread it across the bed, then stretched out and pulled the covers up, waiting for warmth to reach her extremities. God, why couldn't she get warm?

It was slow to happen as she shivered in the cool sheets, but eventually the chills abated to the point she could uncurl her body. Her stomach reminded her of it's emptiness, and she thought longingly of her apple. She could have gone to the kitchen and gotten something to eat. Savvy had offered, but it would mean leaving the warmth of the bed, and she would have to put her clothes back on. No way would she wander around a stranger's apartment in a t-shirt. And, for all intents and purposes, they were all strangers.

Determined to ignore her empty stomach, she rolled over and curled into a ball for added heat and closed her eyes. In minutes she was asleep.

CHAPTER SEVEN

Bright sunlight struck across her eyes when she opened them, but that wasn't what had awakened her. The stomach that had growled her asleep now gnawed her awake. The room shifted and she closed her eyes against the mild dizziness as she swung her legs over the side of the bed. She sat still for a moment trying to remember when, discounting the gallon of bad coffee, she'd last had food. Once the dizziness faded, she opened her pack to extract clean panties. Because her wardrobe was limited, she pulled on the black leggings she'd worn last night, picked up her small toiletries case, and headed for the bathroom. Toothpaste might not provide any nutrition but it would give her salivary glands something to work on until she could find some real food.

SAVVY LOOKED UP AS Jen rounded the corner from the hallway, and watched her guest's eyes search the room for any other presence. Finding none, the woman relaxed imperceptibly. She'd heard her stirring in the bathroom and had heated the waffle iron with the full intent of feeding her up properly. That disclaimer last night that she'd 'had a bite' hadn't rung true to Savvy, and it had been easy to see that Jen was hanging on by shear will. To insist she eat, then, could have sent her over the edge. With two places set at the table, it would be easier to persuade Jen to join her.

Seeing the strain on Jen's face and the dark circles under her eyes, Savvy said, "You had one heck of a night, according to Houston. How are you feeling this morning?"

"Like I had one heck of a night," Jen replied but didn't offer to elaborate.

"There are cups in the cupboard above the coffee pot, and it's hot, if you want some." Savvy poured batter in the waffle iron and closed the lid as Jen poured herself a small amount of coffee from the carafe and took a hesitant sip. "Sugar's on the table and there's creamer in the fridge. Juice, too," she added, "just help yourself." She pulled a covered pan of sausage links from the warming oven and set them on the table beside the butter and syrup.

"You shouldn't have gone to all this trouble," Jen said. She found a glass in the cupboard next to the cups and searched the fridge for the juice. "Just some toast would have been fine."

She wanted to leave as little debt as possible behind, but the smell of the sausage was making her mouth water.

"It's no trouble. I enjoy cooking." Savvy's eyes showed her delight. "Would you like eggs, too?"

"No, thanks," Jen shook her head as she retrieved a jar of apple juice and twisted off the lid long enough to pour some in her glass before replacing the jar in the fridge. "The waffle will be plenty. Do you want some juice, too?" she asked before shutting the door.

"I'm good," Savvy said. "I had juice and coffee with Hawk before he left, but I wanted waffles and he didn't so, I decided to wait for you. It is nice, sometimes, to eat a meal without a testosterone infusion," she grinned.

Jen smiled. She hadn't had that problem in years, but Savvy was in a new relationship, navigating new waters.

"I also wanted to make sure you're okay. Have you talked to your son or your housekeeper, yet?" Ignoring the swift intake of breath behind her, Savvy turned as the waffler dinged, as though her subtle probe was of no import. She lifted the steaming lid and forked a waffle onto a plate then poured more batter on the grill. When she turned back around to set the plate on the table, Jen had composed her face. The nerve Savvy had touched had been tucked down under a calm surface.

"Oh! Irene's not my housekeeper. Imagine that on waitress wages! She's Link's aunt and she comes and goes pretty often. She is pretty helpful when she's here, though." Jen cut the waffle in half and transferred the portion to her plate, "I think it'll be better to wait until this afternoon, until they're back. You know, face to face." She cut a slice of butter to spread on her waffle. "So they can see that I'm alright."

"Yes. That's probably a good idea, for them. But, what about you?" Savvy sat down and took the other half onto her own plate and began adding butter and syrup. When Jen didn't respond, Savvy forked a sausage link beside the waffle and started eating.

Jen quickly followed suit, cutting into the waffle with her fork and putting a bite in her mouth. "This is so good," she closed her eyes on a sigh. "I didn't realize how hungry I was."

By the time the waffler dinged again, Jen's plate was nearly empty. Without asking, Savvy split the last waffle and set another half on the woman's plate. "More coffee or juice?" she asked.

"Maybe some juice, if you don't mind. Not that your coffee isn't good," Jen smiled apologetically, "but my stomach is having a hard time recovering from the police station coffee I drank last night."

"I lucked out that way," Savvy chuckled. "All my questions were asked in the hospital. I didn't have to drink coffee all the time."

Jen looked at Savvy, noting the scar on her jaw and the long-sleeved shirts the woman wore most of the time, to cover all the other scars she knew those shirts hid. It had to have been a terrifying experience but Savvy sat across the table talking and smiling like it might have happened to someone else.

Jen took another bite of waffle, "I don't think I've ever said how sorry I felt for what you and that girl, Kristen, went through, and how incredibly strong I think you are. I don't think too many others would have stood it; who wouldn't still be complete basket cases." Jen smiled as she reached across the table and took Savvy's hand, squeezing gently before releasing it to pick up her fork again and cut a bite of sausage.

"Thank you," Savvy's face turned serious as she continued her own breakfast. "Once in a while, it's hard not to let memories of Bass and his warped mind slip into my thoughts. But I have to give Hawk credit for lifting me out of that. When he looks at me and smiles, I don't remember the scars."

"How is Kristen doing?"

"Okay, I think. We talk often. She'll be starting college this fall, majoring in Criminal Psychology. She's still in therapy, and Hawk has persuaded me to go back to my therapist. There's a lot we have to work through. Both of us."

"Where is Hawk, anyway?" Jen asked. "Houston told me last night that, if I needed anything from my house, Hawk would drive me back to get it."

"Hawk is at the office, getting the phone lines set up. If you need something, I can take you over."

Jen collected her dishes and rose to put them in the sink. "I remember a couple of things I should have picked up while I was there, but I hate to put you out. You've already done so much for me." She looked for dish soap and found it under the sink.

"Don't bother with that." Savvy carried her own plate to the sink, gave it a quick rinse and put it in the half-full dishwasher then reached for Jen's few dishes and added them in. "Dishwashers are amazing," she grinned. "And taking you to your house won't be a bother," Savvy reassured her. "I'm at loose ends today. How soon do you need to go?"

Jen returned the dish soap to it's place and closed the cabinet door. She peered at the clock on the stove, which showed 9:45. "If I could get there before noon, I can grab a couple of essentials and try to reach Irene again. Let her know what's going on," she threaded the lie into her explanation. "Unfortunately, I don't have Irene's sister's number and the number I thought I had in my contacts list for the troop leader, isn't there but I know Irene will have it. She can call him and make arrangements to collect Link when they get back into town."

Keeping her back turned to Jen, Savvy tossed a packet of dishwasher detergent into the machine and set the cycle. Her guest couldn't see the skepticism on Savvy's face. Houston had given Hawk a detailed account of the shooting and his suspicions that Jen might be planning to run. Suspicions with which both Hawk and Savvy agreed. The hunted look Savvy had seen occasionally when they ate at the Big Cup, was now a constant shadow at the back of Jen's gaze, despite her attempts to hide it behind that carefully constructed facade.

Jen was obviously terrified of something and she was poised to disappear if given half a chance. The question in Savvy's mind was 'Where were Link and Irene? Were they together and were they also running or did someone have them?' Her heart clutched a little as the questions chased each other around her brain. She knew the futility of trying to do it all on her own, and somehow she had to try to get inside the colossal wall Jen had erected around herself and convince her to let some help in. It would be tricky, knowing that the woman could rabbit in the blink of an eye. Savvy was torn between pressing the issue and letting it play out for a spell. Well, it could wait for a few more minutes, she decided.

"I've got a couple of things I need to do before we leave," Savvy said, walking into the living area and turning on the TV. "Why don't you make yourself comfortable and I'll be quick as I can, then I'll drive you over."

Jen battled down the impatience gnawing at her. "Sure," she answered, sitting on the corner of the sofa, trying to look relaxed. "No rush."

A debate raged in Jen's head. Could she summon a taxi, grab her back pack and be gone before Savvy returned to the living room or should she wait until she was back at the house before making her break? But taxis and Ubers were scarce in Casper and would likely take too long to arrive. And, even if she left now, Savvy would alert Hawk, and probably Houston, before she managed to get back to her place. They could be waiting for her when she showed up. But, if she let Savvy drive her, under the assumption they would both be returning to this apartment, she wouldn't be able to take her back pack with her.

It didn't take her long to decide. Returning to the bedroom, where her things were wedged between the bed and the nightstand, she opened the bag, pulled the papers she had to have, and all the cash, and stacked them on the bed. Stripping off the t-shirt she'd slept in, she distributed the things from the bag across the length of the shirt, rolled it into a tight coil, flattened it as much as possible, and tied the ends together around her slim waist. The waistband of her jogging pants would hold the t-shirt in place. The shirt she'd worn last night lay on the foot board of the bed where she'd thrown it. She slid it over her head and stretched it as much as possible so that the folds hid the bulge under her waistband. Lastly, she picked up the keys she'd dropped on the nightstand last night and went back to the living room to take up her seat once more. Seeing the TV remote in front of her, she flipped through the channels and found a game show.

Savvy returned a few minutes later. "Sorry to take so long."

"Not a problem. Are you ready to go?" Jen shut off the TV.

"Sure am," Savvy smiled and led the way.

Her car was an older hatchback and, Jen noted, there were some chunks missing from the front end. When Savvy saw where her gaze had settled, she laughed. "The deer walked away under his own power."

"They just don't make cars the way they used to." Jen smiled, as though she'd been around before car bodies were molded of plastic. And some days she felt like she had been, too.

"So, where to?" Savvy pushed the fob and the car came to life.

Jen told her to head out to Cole Creek Road and they exited the parking lot.

"Haven't you been able to contact Irene?" Savvy waited at the light.

"It goes straight to voice mail," Jen shrugged easily, as though she didn't know the phone was no longer active. "She probably forgot to charge it."

The rest of the drive was made in relative silence, broken only by off-side comments about other traffic or suicidal pedestrians and once at Cole Creek Road, more directions, until they pulled up in front of Jen's house.

"I shouldn't be but a couple of minutes," Jen said as she opened the car door. She didn't bother with the niceties of inviting Savvy into the house. Darkness would have been better but all she needed was a little head start and she would be gone. Trotting up the sidewalk, she fished her house key out of the pocket of her pants. She knew the door was broken, but if Savvy was watching her, she didn't want to put any questions in her mind. In the front door and out the back.

CHAPTER EIGHT

She knew the minute the door opened that she wouldn't make it. She grabbed for the wall to stay upright. Her lungs emptied of oxygen and her brain turned fuzzy as the level of devastation, of sheer destruction, registered. Drawers dumped, china from the hutch smashed, cushions and pillows spilled their guts all over the living room.

Still, even knowing that the rest of the house would look the same, she moved numbly forward to check the other rooms, ice water flowed sluggishly through her veins and formed ice water tears that tumbled down her cheeks at the sight of what had been done to Link's room. This was no systematic search, she realized. Deep down, there was hatred and rage. Lucano!! The name screamed in her head and she clapped her hands over her ears but couldn't block it out.

Jill's secret was out. The cover Irene had so carefully built for her, new name, new back history, new everything, was all for nothing; Link's grandfather had found them. The house was probably being watched right this moment.

Irene's room had fared no better. The cubby hole behind her dresser had been smashed into a huge and gaping maw.

Though Jen had left nothing of value in it, what she hadn't taken had been flung to the far corners of the room. Even the toilet tank in the bathroom had been smashed and water seeped under the bathroom door, to soak the hall carpet, the filler valve still vainly doing its best to refill the tank that was no longer there. The shower curtain was ripped from the rod. Spare towels, once folded neatly on the shelves beside the sink, were now soaked and strewn on the floor like bodies in a war zone.

In the kitchen, broken glass and dishes carpeted the tile floor. Knives, forks and spoons mixed with food from the cupboards and refrigerator to create a macabre collage with the shattered dishes. No box or canister had been spared. Unable to remain upright, her chest heaving, she sat on Irene's metal kitchen stool. It was the only thing that had survived the destruction unbroken.

SAVVY SAT IN THE CAR and wondered if she should be watching the back door. Jen had clearly not wanted her to come in the house but she couldn't shake the feeling that something was wrong. That odd sensation of evil, not a tingle but a slimy, wiggly thing, crawling up her spine, made Savvy squirm in the car seat.

She hated that feeling. Sometimes it was just a premonition but, other times, it was a prelude to a nightmare. Even as the thought entered her mind, a nightmare started to creep in with it. It was a nightmare that the therapist had triggered during one of their sessions. She quaked as the images took hold of her brain and the scene unfolded. And even as they did, she heard a tiny voice whisper, "It's a nightmare, you have the power to stop it. Don't let it control you."

He was sitting on the bank of the river with his ten-year-old niece, Molly. The niece who was terrified of water. They were waiting for her mom and dad to arrive from a float tube excursion down the river. He'd volunteered to stay with her so his brother and his wife and their younger son could have a relaxing time and, of course he would help load the tubes and drive everyone back to pick up their car.

He and his niece had found sticks and built a small fire and he had cut a couple of willow branches and stripped the bark off to make the sticks to toast some marshmallows. As he pushed the fluffy, gooey balls of sugar onto the sharp points, he noticed, again the soft mounds of Molly's budding breasts and wondered if they would feel as soft as the marshmallows. He noticed a lot about Molly. He imagined even more. Was she getting pubic hair? Was her body already preparing itself for sex? What would it feel like to be her first? He wondered.

"PUSH IT AWAY," THE tiny voice said.

"Do you have a boyfriend at school, Molly?" he asked, and watched her blush. "A pretty girl like you must have at least one."

She giggled. "I like Jeremy but I don't think he even notices me," she admitted.

"Isn't there one who thinks you're hot?" he teased.

"Well, Max called me hot and tried to kiss me," she said, her face flaming.

"That's all?"

At this she halted for a moment and dropped her eyes to her lap. "He touched my," she lifted one hand and passed it in front of her chest.

"What did you think about that?"

"It made me feel funny."

"Good funny or bad funny?"

"Weird funny." She had yet to look at him.

"You can pull yourself out of the dream, Savvy," the little voice said.

"Did he hurt you?"

"A little, but mostly it just felt weird."

"Do you think you would have liked it if it had been Jeremy who touched you?"

Her shoulders lifted in a shrug.

"Would you like to know how it would feel if someone who loved you touched you?" Her eyes rose to his face. "I could show you how a boy is supposed to touch a girl he likes, so you'll know what it should be like for you. It can feel very nice, if it's done right."

Sitting cross-legged on the ground, he patted his knee.

SAVVY YANKED HERSELF out of the nightmare as the therapist had trained her to do. At least, Thank God, this time it worked. It didn't always. And this was an old nightmare. She knew how it ended.

She was glad to be in her car, waiting for Jen to return.

She looked toward the front door, still ajar. It didn't seem like grabbing a couple of things should have taken this long.

Still, she sat for another minute, then, unable to ignore the feeling any longer, she got out of the car and walked up to the door, walked in, and came to an abrupt stop, like running into a wall, as the carnage hit her. Fearing what might lie beyond this room, her first thought was 'Run!' But, of course, fearing what might lie beyond this room, she couldn't. What she could do was get help.

Silently, she stepped back out the door and pulled out her phone. "Hawk," she whispered, "I'm at Jen's place. You've got to get over here. And, you'd better call Houston." Heart in her throat, she disconnected and slid the phone back into her pocket, She heard, but decided not to hear, Hawk's command to get back in her car and lock the doors.

She re-entered the house, ears tuned for any sound. She heard a faint ... something, coming from deeper in the house. Carefully, she tiptoed toward that sound. As she got closer, it began to sound like panting, or gasping. As she neared the doorway into the next room, which was, she saw, no longer a kitchen, the thought crossed her mind that someone must be hurt and unable to call out. She peered cautiously around the door jamb and saw Jen, sitting on a bar stool, staring in a zombie-like trance at the ruins under her feet. Dry sobs pumped from her chest as from a bellows.

"Jen?" she whispered, still unsure if danger was lurking nearby.

Jen's eyes turned toward her slowly but there was no answer. Savvy crunched through the food and broken glass under her feet and touched Jen's hand. She could have been touching an ice sculpture. "Jen, for God's sake what happened? Are you hurt?"

"I think my sister must be dead," Jen said.

The pain, clearly visible in her unfocused eyes, twisted a hard knot in Savvy's gut. An instant picture of Bryn, lying motionless amid the carnage on the floor, jumped into her brain, froze her to the core. Pure instinct made her reach to wrap warm arms around Jen in a hard hug; an attempt to hold together the pieces that might fly apart with the slightest nudge. And to anchor her own thoughts to something solid.

"Is there anyone else in the house?" Savvy whispered.

Slowly, Jen's head lowered to Savvy's shoulder and her arms became a vice, fusing their bodies together. A barely felt head shake was her only response, until the dry sobs became a gusher.

Savvy absorbed the pain until she couldn't stand more, then asked, "Do you have any idea who did this?"

Jen didn't answer but there was a subtle shift in her demeanor. Slowly, she began to release her hold on Savvy and her spine stiffened. Her eyes swept the room and a return of determination brought some color back to her face.

"I've got to try to contact Irene again, but I can't do it in … in here." Her hand motioned around her, then she pulled out her phone and took the few steps to the back door. "I'm just going out on the porch so I don't have to see all this," she said, her voice barely audible.

Savvy nodded her understanding, she was having a hard time looking at it herself.

Debating for long moments, whether to follow Jen out back, she decided against that. She, of all people, knew the need for solitude when you had to pull yourself together.

Making her way back into the living room to wait for Hawk, her empathy for the woman ramped up as she walked back through the chaos, the senseless destruction. Thinking that out the door was actually a great idea, she reached for the door knob then drew her hand back. If she went through any door, it had to be the back one. Jen had needed privacy to deal with what had happened but she shouldn't be left alone too long. Just as Savvy's feet moved toward the kitchen again, she heard Hawk's truck pull into the short drive. Relief coursed through her and she hurriedly opened the front door to him.

"Oh my God, Hawk, it's horrible." she said at his quick intake of breath. Framed in the doorway, his arms closed around her and some of her strength returned.

"Is Jen hurt?"

"Not physically," Savvy stepped back, "but mentally is another question. She went out on the back porch to try to contact Irene again."

"I called Houston on the way here, he won't be far behind me. Jen has to call this in." He gave the room a hard once over then headed for the back. He disappeared into the kitchen just as Houston's red Jeep drove in behind Hawk's truck.

In seconds, Houston mounted the porch steps and Savvy met him at the door. When he walked into the room, he sucked in a deep breath. Having seen this room, clean and tidy, less than twelve hours ago, and to see it now, stopped him cold. But there was no coppery smell of blood, and his muscles relaxed infinitesimally. "No one hurt?"

"Not here, I don't think," Savvy shook her head. "But, oh, Houston, who could do something like this? I can feel the hate seeping out of the walls."

He could have told her he'd seen worse, but at the moment, he didn't think anything had struck him so forcefully. "Where's Jen?" he asked.

"She went out back to call Irene."

"What!?" That one word reverberated through the house.

"It's okay," Savvy tried to insert some calm, "Hawk went out to get her." but she was talking to Houston's back. She hurried after him.

Hawk came jogging across the yard as Houston and Savvy cleared the kitchen door. "Jen's gone."

He turned to Savvy. "Did she say anything to you while you were in the kitchen?"

"She said, "I think my sister is dead," and then she broke down in sobs. I held her for a little bit. Then she said she had to try to get hold of Irene but she couldn't do it inside the house."

"Why not?"

"Look around you, Houston. Even I was having a hard time dealing with all this. Such anger and hate, I didn't want to stay in here either but I thought she needed a few moments, alone, just to process it."

Hawk and Savvy shared guilty looks. They had failed in the job Houston had asked of them. Keep an eye on Jen and make sure she didn't take off.

"Did you check out the back gate?"

"Both directions. And there are no side gates that I could find."

Houston's mind flew back to the night before. If he'd needed confirmation that Jen was planning to disappear, this was it. Son of a Bitch. A cold lump settled in his guts crowding out every other thought.

The first thought that hit him with any clarity, was that he needed to move his car. Relaying that to his brother, he went out front and backed out into the street to find a spot around the corner and down a ways from Jen's house.

In the few minutes it took to get back to Hawk and Savvy, his 'cop calm' took over and he started giving orders. "Savvy, go out, get in your car and lock the doors. Wait five minutes then call 911. Don't mention my name unless it comes up. I'm not supposed to be involved with this investigation. If we're not back before they leave, go on home."

He didn't see her nod as he turned to his brother. "Let's go." He strode down the yard toward the back, Hawk on his heels. "I hope you haven't forgotten everything Dad taught you about tracking," he opened the gate that swung unevenly into the yard. "She will be running and on this hard packed gravel, she won't leave much to follow but you go left and I'll go right. One of us should be able to pick up a sign."

Savvy went back to her car.

EYES AND EARS LASER focused on the weeds and soft dirt that followed a goat track beyond the fence, Houston moved silently and quickly past back doors and cluttered yards. One house had him taking notice. Not just for the tidy lawn and abundance of flower beds, but because an older woman, wearing a house coat and slippers, was watering her petunias. He stopped and called to her.

"You have a lovely garden," he smiled his most disarming smile. "Quite a contrast to some I've passed in the last few minutes."

She smiled back, clearly pleased at the compliment. "The scenery is better if you do your looking on the street side, but thank you. I try to keep my yards looking nice."

"Have you been out here all morning?" Houston asked.

"For a while," was the response.

"You didn't happen to see someone run this way while you were out here, did you?"

"I have a neighbor up the street who jogs often. Sometimes she uses the path back here."

"This morning?"

"Why do you want to know?" In the woman's sudden scowl, it was easy to read her suspicion.

"They were all gone last night and someone broke into her house and wrecked the place. I was hoping you might have noticed a stranger running away."

"Oh no," the woman's hand went to her breast and she glanced toward her own house as though wondering if she'd remembered to lock her door. "It wasn't a stranger, it was definitely her."

Houston whistled hard and sharp. That jolted the woman into action and she dropped the hose where she stood, to hurry into her house and check her doors and windows.

At Houston's whistle, Hawk on the other wing reversed course and ran back down the path, spotting his brother tracking ahead of him. He fell into step beside him when he closed the gap.

"What did you find?"

"An observant neighbor," Houston answered. "She saw Jen running this direction."

Working like a well oiled unit, the brothers took either side of the trail and with sharpened intent followed Jen. Houston stopped for a moment to examine a fist-sized rock that had been rolled to the side, as if from an uneven footstep. The ground underneath had not had time to dry out. If the rock had rolled under her foot, she could possibly be limping.

"She ran down this side," he said, moving on.

"We've got a cross road coming up," Hawk pointed out. "She can go any direction from there."

"Maybe we'll find another observant neighbor."

The path dead ended at the cross street, with no sign of human movement in the vicinity.

Nothing but dirt and sand in one direction. The other way led toward the next cluster of houses, half of which were for sale. One of which was boarded up. He remembered that house well. He'd answered calls to and about it, to assist sheriff's deputies many times over the decade. Behind the houses, high brush and low trees swayed in the wind. A pond, unseen from here, lay a few hundred yards beyond that.

"That way," the brothers spoke and pointed toward the cul-de-sac at the same time.

They set off, shoulder to shoulder, at a slow jog, confident of their direction but still watching for signs along the way. Rewarded by the discovery of recently crushed weeds near one of the houses, Houston motioned Hawk to circle around and he went between two of the houses to check behind them.

In minutes, he zeroed in on the cinder block shed, sitting far back on the lot of the boarded-up house, and the tire tracks leading into it, and out of it. He tested the padlock on the door. Locked solid. He would need a bolt cutter to get inside, and probably a search warrant. Closing his eyes against the gut churning knowledge that Jen had, in fact, disappeared on him, he whistled for his brother who appeared quickly between the houses, three down from where Houston stood. The sound of footsteps brought his eyes back to the present as Hawk approached.

Hawk took in the situation at a glance. "These tire tracks head over the prairie back there."

"Yeah," Houston nodded. "Go back to Jen's place and give Savvy a hand. You might mention the lady with the neat back yard, too. She was quite positive the person she saw jogging behind the house was Jen. They'll want to question her."

"What are you going to do?" Hawk asked his brother.

"I'm going to follow these tracks and see if I can find any other clues." Houston waved as he disappeared into the brush.

CHAPTER NINE

Knowing that the police must already be aware she was on the run and what she was wearing, and far enough, clear across town, from her house, Jen pulled in behind the Family Dollar in Mills just west of Casper proper and quickly dug out some cash from her 'money belt'. It was dangerous to leave the bike, and the bedroll strapped to its rack, behind the store, but back here, there was only one security camera, which, she knew, didn't function. You choose your own devil, she thought. She wished she had her baseball cap to cover her dark blond curls, or even a hoodie but wearing her helmet inside the store would trigger too much curiosity. Best she could do was keep her head down.

Inside, she went to the clothing section and found an over-sized, long-sleeved green t-shirt, a black hoodie and a package of panties and took them to the register. The t-shirt, over top of the black she was wearing, should provide enough disguise to get her out of town. Taking care to keep her head down, although she didn't think it would do much good if any of the cops who frequented The Big Cup saw the video, she paid for the item and returned to her bike.

Her helmet was still chained to the rack and the roll hadn't been disturbed. Good. She slid on her new purchase, and stuffed the rest inside the bedroll. Putting on her helmet, she kicked the bike to life, rolled sedately back onto Highway 20-26 and headed west, toward Shoshoni.

Less than an hour later, she stopped at the Waltman rest area, parked her bike beside a couple of big rig haulers, where it would be harder to be seen by surveillance cameras, and went into the restrooms. A woman was at the sinks, touching up her makeup; Jen locked herself in an empty stall and reversed the order of her shirts, took care of other necessaries and waited until she heard the woman leave the room.

Another group of people had entered and lingered at the information board, chattering. Jen joined the little knot of people at the map, found what she was looking for, traced the route she needed, then followed with the group as they exited. As she went out the door, she pulled on her helmet and dropped the visor. At rest areas across the nation, few people pay much attention to other people coming and going unless the license plates on their vehicles happen to be from their home state.

She swung the bike back onto the highway with a verve she didn't feel and forced her mind to stay focused on the road ahead, instead of what she'd left behind in Casper. The steady snarl of the bike helped her to consider, pack, and shove the shambles her life had become into a different compartment of her brain. It seemed that compartmentalizing was not just a handy tool, but had become vital to her sanity.

Unfortunately, Houston Whitehawk kept popping out of that damned compartment. Whenever he did, she couldn't stop the little ache in her heart that made breathing difficult. Maybe, if she shoved him back enough times, he would stay there. A watery laugh slipped from her lips and fogged her visor. Just stop it! She told herself. You can't let thoughts of him blind you to what has to be done.

With more than three hours to ride before she would get to the first rendezvous point, Jen settled the bike into a ground-eating speed. She wouldn't be able to get there before the sun hit her full in the face as it set to the west. Wherever Irene sent her next, she hoped it wouldn't be straight west. And she hoped she would be able to get there before she had to find another clue.

She took a moment to mourn the loss of her back pack. Especially that drawing of Link's that she'd pulled from the side of the refrigerator, but it couldn't be helped. At least, she could be grateful for those few hours of sleep last night, and the meal this morning, which might be the only food she'd see for the next few hours.

HOUSTON SAT AT HIS computer and watched Captain Bricker approach his desk. With a tap of his finger, he closed the screen.

"I know you are aware that Jen Bradley has disappeared," the Captain stated.

"Yes, I heard the call and listened to the chatter," Houston nodded, his face carefully void of any emotion.

"I've sent out a BOLO on her."

"On what charge?"

"Wanted for questioning regarding a shooting."

"I hope you clarified that she was the one being shot at," Houston allowed an edge into his words. "I'd hate to think of some LEO stopping her, thinking she was the one doing the shooting."

The Captain sat down in one of the chairs in front of Houston's desk, but then, realizing they were set low to allow Houston's tall frame to tower over any visitor, he stood up again.

"Look, Houston, I know you've been interested in her for a while," he walked over to the window and stared out, hands clasped behind his back. "The few times I was in the Big Cup when you were there, you watched her like a puppy watches his mama just waiting for an opportunity to latch onto a tit. I knew that, with the least little encouragement, you would have branded her but she shut you down, just like she did everyone else."

"Yes, she did." Except there in her kitchen last night. The memory of those few moments rushed to the surface. She'd welcomed him so thoroughly that he'd had a hard-on all night. Even now, he felt his cock stir to life at the memory. Only the harsh voice of reality had made him put distance between his actively involved body and hers.

Bricker's voice brought him back to the present. "And yet, last night, after the shooting, she was sitting in your vehicle when I pulled up. Is there more going on that I should be aware of?" He turned and gave Houston a hard look.

"I admit, I wish there were," Houston shook his head, "but, no, there is nothing between us." Nothing but that kiss. God, how stupid could a man get over a female?

"So, you have no idea where she might be headed?"

"None at all. You know as much as I do."

"I doubt that," Bricker snapped. "What I do know is that you were at her house last night after Officer Wells dropped Jen off and you took her to Miss Mills apartment where she apparently spent the night. Why?"

"Captain, you know that wasn't a random shooting," Houston snapped back. "I persuaded her that if the shooter knew where she worked, then he knew where she lived and that her house wasn't safe. I arranged for Savvy to put her up for the night. My brother told me that Jen asked Savvy for a ride to her place and the rest, you know."

"All I know is that we have a female, possibly dressed in black, on a motorcycle of unknown make and model, on the run from something that has her scared spitless. And I don't think it's the police she's scared of. If that were so, she wouldn't have chosen to work in a restaurant where cops hang out." He gave his detective another long look. "Do you have any insights, Houston?"

"Nope."

"Does Savvy?"

"Savvy and I haven't discussed Jen's disappearance."

"I see," Bricker said.

Bricker saw entirely too damn much Houston thought, but they both kept their own counsel.

"If you hadn't put in your request for annual three months ago, I would be suspicious of the timing," the captain turned for the door. "Got any plans for it?"

"I thought I'd visit my parents, in Lander, for a few days, maybe get in some rabbit hunting or fishing with Dad." Not even close to his original plan, which had been to persuade Jen to go out with him and use the rest of his time off to solidify a toe-hold with her. But, the annual might work out anyway. He could follow his own instincts to find where she'd taken off to, unhindered by the investigation and a time clock.

"As far as the investigation into the shooting goes, there was no blood found at or near the scene and there haven't been any reported gunshot wounds since it occurred so you're probably clear. Your administrative leave is still in effect though, so keep your nose out of it. I'll let you know when you're cleared."

Bricker left the office and Houston allowed him a minute to clear the area before turning on his computer again. It had taken a little finagling to get into the traffic cams, but since the department had already requested footage, his perusal was not raising any red flags.

Not wanting to hare off on a wild goose chase, he checked all the routes out of Casper. He eliminated the double riders and the larger groups. It wasn't likely she would be carrying a passenger or that she would join a large bunch with which she was unfamiliar. He concentrated on single riders. Finally he zeroed in on a lone biker on the Shoshoni Highway. Video footage was sparse along that stretch but so were side roads, and there were traffic cams at the junction in Shoshoni. The great news was that, if she got that far, either direction the bike went, it would be traveling through Indian Reservation lands. He had lots of connections there.

He shut down his computer and clocked out, smiling and waving to coworkers as he left the building.

SHE PASSED POWDER RIVER and its lonely Post Office a block west of the "Tumble Inn" bar – once a famous stop for truckers and musicians, but now decrepit and abandoned. Ten minutes later, she zipped past Hell's Half-Acre, where the alien planet battle scenes of "Starship Trooper" had been filmed. At Moneta, even tinier than Powder River, fifty minutes after that, a highway patrol car pulled onto the highway a few cars back. She tensed, watching it carefully, but he seemed content to hold his place and eventually she relaxed again.

When finally, with the westering high plains sun drilling into her eyes, she reached Shoshoni, where Highway Twenty-six splits southwest and Twenty drives due north to Thermopolis through the Wind River Canyon. She threw a big sigh of relief and shifted into the turn lane to catch the truck stop. The patrol car followed 26 on its way to Riverton and Lander. Jen pulled into the truck stop and up to a pump to gas up for the ride north. She looked at the name on the credit card. 'Quinn Messer' it said. Generic enough to not raise any questions, but it didn't matter. It would only be used once.

She'd never questioned where Irene got the credit cards she stashed in their go bags, but as a mental image of the older woman's face flashed into her mind, a new worry settled into her thoughts. She wasn't the only one who felt the stress of their situation. Irene had aged considerably in the last six years. Maybe it was time Jen found out more about how Irene's network functioned. Help her out a little.

Had Irene kept track of all the women she'd helped out of dangerous and sometimes, even life threatening situations? There had been many that Jen knew about but Irene had been doing her work since before Jen was old enough to think about the secrets that kept the woman up nights.

"Well, Quinn," she dropped her face shield in place, and wiped the credit card clean before dropping it into a trash can, "it's time to head north."

Shortly, Boysen Reservoir appeared on her left as the road entered the Wind River Canyon and the Wind River Indian Reservation.

The towering cliffs of the Wind River Canyon rose several hundred feet above the rushing water and its narrowness pinched the river into a whitewater rafter's dream. The fishing was pretty spectacular, too, she'd heard.

In an agreement with the Shoshone and Arapaho tribes, the state and the highway department had been allowed to run a rail line through the west side of the canyon and carve a road through the cliffs on the east side. But the people of the tribe had retained ownership of the waters that flow, or rather, rushed furiously, along-side the road. They owned the fishing and rafting rights to the river, as well, and the income added a little extra to the coffers of the residents.

In some places, the walls of the canyon are so vertical that tunnels were carved through the rock to allow the road to go through. Falling rock was always a hazard, and loose gravel was always a special concern for a motorcycle rider. Rock slides and loosened boulders had caused many accidents and train derailments over the years but the drive was so spectacular that, if an alternate route had ever been debated, it had never been built.

Jen and Irene had taken Link on a day trip through the canyon to the town of Thermopolis, and the largest mineral hot springs in the U.S. They'd played in the hot springs and had a picnic lunch there, followed by a visit to the Wyoming Dinosaur Center. It was one of the happiest times she could recall. The memory brought a smile to Jen's face as she dove through the tunnels.

CHAPTER TEN

"What do you have for me, Arch?" Houston set his phone to 'speaker' and picked his coffee from the cup holder as he ran up the 20-26 exit off I-25 at the west end of Casper.

"Nothing concrete, Buddy." said State Trooper Arch McQuery. "I saw a lone motorcyclist headed west on the highway, definitely female, but I never saw her without her helmet. No way to tell what color her hair was. There was a couple of young males in an old sedan that stayed right behind her for some distance. Looked like they were dogging her for some reason, which I thought was strange. They might have just been looking for a good time, but when she stopped at the truck stop in Shoshoni, they continued on toward Lander. So did I, for a bit."

"Did you see her head toward the canyon?"

"I circled back to the junction but she was no longer at the truck stop and I didn't pass her, so she must have gone north." Arch was silent for a second. "You know, that BOLO didn't sound all that urgent, and the gal I was following didn't seem in any kind of hurry, so I'm wondering... What'd she do?"

"Nothing. All inquiries come up clean." Houston doused the speculation as best he could. "Someone took some shots at her two nights ago and she took off. Her son and the boy's aunt have disappeared, too. It seems like they're on the run. We just don't know why yet. Listen, Arch, can you head up the canyon a ways and see if she's there?"

"Got it covered," Arch said. "I called George Yellowtail at his place in the canyon, and asked him to call me if he sees her."

"That works." Houston thanked his friend. "Let me know, would you?"

"You got it." Arch ended the call. Houston drove on toward Arminto and his brother's Jet Ranger helicopter.

"I'VE SEARCHED FOR a lot of lost people before," Travis Whitehawk grinned at his older brother, "but never for someone who was trying to get lost." He tossed some gear in the belly of his helicopter, which idled on a helipad in front of his private hanger on the Arminto cut-off, about forty-five miles west of Casper.

Houston smiled grimly as he added his own equipment to the load. "Yeah. Me, on the other hand, I'm always looking for people who don't want to be found."

"I picked up your chatter with Arch." Travis's radio was always tuned to the official channels due to his involvement in search and rescue. "What's this woman's thing, anyway?" He stepped up into the cockpit and Houston climbed into the bubble after him. Settling in, Travis checked his instrument panel again while his brother took the seat beside him and shut the door. They buckled in.

"I wish I knew." Houston said. "All I know, for sure, is someone tried to shoot her two nights ago and then waylaid her in her own backyard that same night. She's terrified of something or someone and is too terrified to even tell the police. And she thinks her sister is dead."

That last sentence drew a soft whistle from Travis. He set his head phones over his ears and signaled Houston to do the same.

He did, then waited while Travis finished his takeoff checklist and engaged the copter's rotor. Further conversation would have to wait until they were in the air and on the way.

As the bird lifted into the air, circled the field, then leveled off and headed west, Travis resumed their conversation, crackling through the headphones. "I've talked to people who were mixed up in some really bad shit," he said. "They're convinced that dealing with the police is the fastest way to make their situation, whatever it is, worse."

A fact of which Houston was well aware. His only response was a muttered, "Uh huh".

When Houston didn't continue, Travis did. "So, what's the plan?"

"I imagine she's made it through the canyon to Thermopolis by now, but start there and then follow the highway toward Worland and Greybull." Houston didn't think she'd had time to get any farther than that. "See if we can spot a single rider, and then keep an eye on her without spooking her and see if she leads us to her son and the aunt. It would be really helpful if I could collect all of them at the same time."

"If we don't pick her up before dark, following her is going to be damned difficult."

"Cops, statewide, are on the lookout for a lone motorcyclist," Houston reminded him. "We might be able to pick up some chatter."

"Darken Jones has a little outfitter/guide operation just outside of Worland, complete with landing pad and a half dozen cabins, if we have to spend the night," Travis said. "I can gas up there, too. It's off-season for most hunting though, so I'm not sure if his restaurant is open."

"We can discuss that later, if we need to." The thought of where Jen might spend the night worried Houston. If she truly wanted to stay off the radar, renting a motel room wouldn't be her first choice, but the thought of her sleeping under the cold mountain stars made his jaw clench.

LACEY AND BRYN JOINED Hawk and Savvy for supper that evening. Over spaghetti and garlic bread, around the kitchen table, Hawk filled them in on what they knew so far. Not a lot, but the women voiced their concern for Jen and her son as well as offering a few theories of their own. Bryn, from her studies in northern California and her major in Criminal Psychology, offered the most clear-cut insights into what Jen might possibly be dealing with, if she was mixed up with the mobs or cartels.

"There were many newspaper reports that fed into our class discussions," she gathered a last forkful of spaghetti and used it to point around the table. "If the power brokers have their hands on any member of the family, then they basically control the entire family. And that includes anyone, from the street dealers to the federal officials they keep in their pockets." The spaghetti disappeared behind her even, white teeth. She washed it down with a sip of her wine and stood up. "If someone bucks the system, their, or a family member's, body is usually found with their throat slit very shortly afterward."

"Apparently that hasn't stayed on the west coast or the Mexican border," Savvy pushed her half empty plate aside.

Maybe this talk didn't bother Bryn's appetite but it had certainly put a damper on hers.

"No, it isn't. And that's not the first time that sort of reprisal has been reported," Lacey began to collect the plates from the table. "Okay, you cooked, so Bryn and I will do the clean up."

Since that was the rule of the house, Savvy didn't argue. She picked up her half-full glass of wine and circled the island to take a seat on the living-room couch. As she turned on the TV, she heard Bryn say, "I didn't even know Jen had a sister."

And, Hawk, who had grabbed the last slice of garlic bread before Lacey could carry off the bread basket, said, "I remember her saying something about a sister a while back but it was an off-hand remark and she shut it off pretty quickly. I got the impression that they were no longer close."

"That doesn't surprise me either," Bryn commented.

Hawk polished off the garlic bread and held up the last of the wine as an offering to Lacey and Bryn. When they declined, he emptied the bottle into his glass and left the kitchen to claim his spot on the sofa, close to Savvy. The muscles in her neck and shoulders were still tight from nerves and worry. He massaged them lightly with one hand as the TV provided background noise to the chatter in the kitchen. "Houston and Travis will find them," he said, softly, as she eased back into his hand.

For the second time today, the dishwasher began chugging through it's cycles as Bryn and Lacey dried their hands and entered the living room.

"We're going to the movies," Lacey announced. "Want to come along?"

Most of the movies playing this week were heavy on violence and gore, and knowing Savvy's dislike of them, Hawk gave her a questioning glance. When she shook her head, he declined their offer. "I think we'd prefer a quiet evening tonight. Thanks anyway." He said.

"Okay." Bryn said, "We might go out to the Beacon afterwards," She gave them a bawdy sort of wink, "so I'll just stay at Lacey's tonight."

"Stay alert and be careful," Savvy said as the pair exited. It had become her mantra over the last few months.

"Always," they chorused, before the door closed behind them.

In the vacuum that settled over the room, Hawk drew Savvy against his chest and rested his chin on the top of her head. She let the drone of the rom-com on TV lull her. He didn't much like romantic comedies but he understood their soporific quality and how they could sooth Savvy's mind. Still, her mind wouldn't veer far from their current worries, but he'd let the movie do its work of softening the edges.

"You know," he shook his head cynically, picked up her hand to play with her fingers, and looked into her eyes, "all that angst isn't really necessary. Why not just bonk her on the head with his club and drag her off to his cave?"

That triggered a growl from her and he grinned. "If I had a club right now, that's what I would do."

Savvy laughed at that. "And I would wait until you were asleep and beat you to a pulp with your stupid club."

"Ouch!" he winced. "Without that club, I wouldn't be able to bring a Mastodon back to the cave for you to cook, now would I? Would you be more amenable if I just seduced you and hauled you to bed?" His lips made forays up her neck, toward her ear. Her breath caught and he smiled to himself.

"Not until this show is over," she frowned hard but didn't pull away from his nibbling.

"Not a problem," his words tickled her ear. "I have a couple of new techniques I want to try out anyway." His teeth closed on her lobe and bit softly. "I won't bother you a bit."

That drew a snort. "You're already bothering me."

"Want me to stop?" He nipped at her nape. A shiver ran up her neck.

"If you do," she turned in to his kiss, "I will have to use that club anyway."

All thoughts of the show were forgotten as she melted under the soft, seductive claiming of his lips. He coaxed and coerced, soothed and demanded, played and drove her wild. Soon she was wet and panting but the hand that rested on her waist never wandered to her breasts or her hips.

She shifted to give him more access, her need building. She wanted him to touch her, all over.

Hawk sat back and looked calmly at her rosy lips. "How was that?"

His innocent tone didn't fool her for a minute. There were certain physiological signs that didn't lie. Despite that calm tone, he was as turned on as she was. But she could play the game, too.

"That's all you got, Big Boy?" she asked huskily, and turned back to the TV.

"Oh no," he laughed, "I've got a whole box of tricks to try out," and he began to show her more. And more.

The seduction was slow and methodical and even more effective for the torment of it as their clothes seemed to melt away with each new touch until they were laying on the sofa completely nude. His magical hands and mouth kept up the sweet torture, bringing her close to a climax and then easing off again until she was ready to beg him to finish it. But still, he kept her on the razor's edge.

"Hawk, please," her guttural plea excited him.

"You are so incredibly responsive," he whispered hoarsely, from between her thighs. "You have no idea how hard you make me."

"Oh, God, please. I need you in me, now," she choked out.

"Yes, now," he stood and picked her up, making the way to the bedroom.

All thought left her mind as he laid her down on the bed and slid inside her. There wasn't room for Jen or Houston or shootings or anything else except Hawk and what his hard body was doing to her. She climaxed almost immediately and then, under his powerful drives, yet again before he finally claimed his own release.

CHAPTER ELEVEN

Savanna made her way slowly down the hallway. The thought crossed her mind that the door at the far end loomed like the gates of hell. And that wasn't too far off, because Satan himself sat behind that monstrosity of a desk, waiting for her. Nobody disappointed Satan, and yet here she was, ready to face him and plead for another chance. Convince him that she could still make this right. Just one more chance.

She knew she'd screwed up. She never screwed up, it wasn't an option, but the fact remained, the woman wasn't dead. Neither woman was dead, and she didn't have the kid. No, Satan would not be pleased.

Her footsteps approaching the door were silent in the plush carpet of the hall but she knew he could hear her tread. She kept her pace steady. Don't let him feel your fear, she repeated in her head, you've talked yourself out of tight spots before. Stopping at 'the gate', she raised her hand and tapped lightly. It opened instantly. Of course he would have one of his guards standing by it.

"Come in, Benny," the devil said in a careful and modulated voice. "Please have a seat," he motioned to the chair in front of his desk.

She took the seat. Her knees thanked her. She did a quick glance around the room. Freddy was there. He'd opened the door. Dorf, a big man, not fat, just big, stood on the other side of the door. And then, there was Gull, at his own smaller desk.

Savanna knew that tone. She didn't trust it for a minute but she responded in the same voice. "Good morning, Sir."

He reached for a silver cigarette case on the side of his desk, flipped it open and held it out to her. She knew those cigarettes were made in Nicaragua to his own specifications, his own special blend. He nearly always had one dangling from his lips. She hated the smell of them and suspected they contained some things other other than nicotine. The thought of inhaling the pungent smoke from one of those cigarettes triggered her gag reflexes. She bit it down. She knew better than to refuse.

"Thank you," she picked one out of the case with a smile and slid it into her shirt pocket.

"Aren't you going to light up?" he asked mildly. He'd already closed the case and picked up the matching silver lighter, holding it out with his thumb on the lever.

"I thought I would save it for later."

"You should learn to take your pleasure when it's offered." The silky words sounded sinister to Savanna's ears. "By now, in our business, you must know that later doesn't always happen." He waved the lighter up and down. "Light up," The lighter flamed. "I'll see that you get another one. For later."

She pulled the cigarette out of her pocket and fitted it to her lips as the flame touched the tip. Taking a deep drag, she fought down the clawing rasp at the back of her throat from the acrid smoke.

"You know, I wish I could return your 'good morning' but I find that very difficult to do." Satan said, as he set the lighter neatly beside his golden desk pen set. "I am very disappointed this morning, and that isn't good for me." he continued conversationally. "I woke up early, anticipating having my heir with me, at last, and the two women out of the way. I had big plans for the day. Plans to take the boy places. Buy him a toy and a *hamburger, things like that."* He leaned back in his chair, amiably, *"You know, get to know each other."*

Savanna's throat constricted to a hard knot. The drug laced smoke began to make her breath seep out in audible wheezes. She could see the sound pleased him.

"You can surely understand the depth of my disappointment." His eyebrows rose and he leaned forward. "Can you explain to me why these things didn't happen?"

The cigarette, now between Savanna's fingers on the arm of her chair, quivered ever so slightly. She hoped it was not visible to him.

"No more disappointed that I am, Sir," she started to explain, only to recoil deep into her chair as he shouted.

"I really think. I. Am!" his voice, raspy and hard, his breath, smelling of cigarette and mint, pounded each word separately, "More. Disappointed. Than. You."

"Just … just let me explain, Sir. Please," she hated the whiny sound of her mouth.

Satan sat back in his chair, eyes squeezed shut, and steepled his fingers beneath his chin. He could have been any supplicant at the alter, but the alter Savanna pictured in her mind, had her laid on it like a sacrifice. She steeled her voice to continue, to not waver.

"I had her cold. She was getting into her car and she paused for a moment behind the wheel, but just as I pulled the trigger, perfect shots, she dropped down behind the dash. I was sure I must have hit her because I heard her scream. Then, all of a sudden, a shot hit the garbage bin I was behind. I don't know where it came from, but I didn't have time to make sure she was dead. People started shouting and screaming. I'd parked the car about four blocks away, so I was on foot, and by the time I got too it, I heard sirens so I had to get out of there, fast.

"I thought I could still salvage part of the job by getting the kid, but when I got to the house, it was empty. Not locked. Nobody there.

"They're always tucked away by nine o'clock. Sir, They should have been there. I don't know how they knew to take off, but they did. So I left the house and moved the car into the alley and slid into the yard where I could see the house, front and back. Finally, the woman is brought back by a cop. I waited until she left and made sure there weren't any more coming, then I went around back. I could see the woman moving around in the house, and pretty soon, she came out the back door with a back pack. I was in the perfect position to make another try for her, and I had a hold of her just as another cop showed up. The woman was fighting me hard and I couldn't get to my gun. (leaving out certain details wouldn't change the story, she felt) He came charging into the yard, and I couldn't make it out with the woman, so I dropped her and she took off running. The cop went after her and I went back over the fence, got in the car, and left.

"I don't know where they went but they never came back. I went in the house and searched for the book, and it was a thorough search, but I didn't find it. She must have it with her."

It really looked like Satan was listening. He'd leaned further back in his chair, fingers still steepled but over his lips, for all the world like he was giving Savvy a fair shot.

"With all the cops sniffing around, it wasn't safe to stay in town, so I had to go to ground for a few hours. If you hadn't called me back, I could have found out where they were and still finished the job. Sir."

Satan slowly opened his eyes. They were black and soulless as a shark's. Savanna shuddered and knew he saw it.

"Go on," Satan whispered, as he swiveled his chair around, so that his words filtered from the back of his head, "finish your cigarette."

She looked at the half gone cigarette, still smoldering between her fingers. Flicking off the run of ashes into her other palm, she lifted the butt slowly to her lips and took a deep drag. Whatever drugs he laced through those leaves, now hit her lungs with a welcome shot of anesthetic. Ill advised or not, it gave her a modicum of courage.

"I already have someone else on it, Benny." Satan said, and his tone was regretful. "Someone I trust almost as much as I trusted you."

And, just that fast, her courage fled. "I can still get the boy," she pleaded. "Just give me a chance to make it right. I won't disappoint you again."

"I'm sure you won't," the chair swiveled again, a gun barrel, steady in his hand, pointed at her chest.

Savanna held up her hand, fingers splayed, and tried to rise, but her legs wouldn't obey the command to flee. "No, please!" she shouted as the bullet struck her outstretched palm and entered her chest. A scream ripped from her throat but ended quickly.

Savvy sat bolt upright in the bed, the scream still echoing in her brain and draining from her lips. For several seconds, she felt nothing but numb, then there was such shattering pain in her chest that she couldn't breathe. Gasping against the horrible pressure that twisted her heart and lungs, she tried to throw off the nightmare.

Hawk had her wrapped in his arms, their muscular bands adding to the tightness she was trying to shake off. "Bass again?" he hung on tight, despite her struggles.

Unable to speak, she could only shake her head. When she shoved again to free herself, he didn't try to stop her. She lunged from the bed.

He threw off the covers and followed her.

"If it's not Bass, what is it?" His voice edged toward panic.

She knew he hated the helpless feelings he got when she had one of her nightmares, but with everything in her focused on the pain tearing through her, she couldn't help him at the moment. Usually, they were able to bring each other out of these nightmares by just holding on to each other tight. She held up a hand to stay him, as she struggled to draw air into her lungs, past the pain in her chest. She stared at the hand, the same one the bullet had penetrated before entering her chest. It ached as though the bones had been shattered but the skin was unmarked. She knew there wouldn't be any blood on her but the sensation of being shot still rocketed through her body.

"Tell me," Hawk murmured.

Knowing he needed her to give him something, she moved into him and dropped her head to his chest. She tried to find her voice, but it remained silent. With effort, she took another deep breath that scored her chest. "I've been shot." she whispered, her hand going to her chest again.

"What?!" She needed him calm but the exclamation jumped out of his mouth before he could call it back. Reining in his shock, he guided her gently back down onto the bed. Laying one arm across her shoulder, he rocked with her until she finally settled against him.

"Can you tell me about it?"

She nodded hesitantly and told the nightmare with agonizing slowness, her chest hurting all the while. When she was finished, he just held her. No words, only warmth.

Carefully, she gathered up what pieces of self she could find and started putting them back in place. There might be pieces missing at the moment, but like a jigsaw puzzle, she would find them and begin to return to wholeness, and Hawk would help her put them back in place. For now, it was enough that he held together what she'd managed to gather. Eventually, the quaking that shook her body slowed.

"We should call Houston." he whispered at her temple.

"What can he do?" She looked at the clock: two a.m.

"Maybe nothing, but this might give him information he can use when he finds Jen."

She nodded, and instantly regretted it as Hawk dropped his arms to crawl across the bed to his cell phone. More chills wracked her bones. She pulled the comforter around herself in an effort to ward off the ice that coated her. The smell of Hawk surrounded her, and she felt his warmth begin to seep into her body.

Hawk swore as the call went straight to voice mail. Either Houston was out of range or he had his phone turned off. He sent a quick text message. There was no more he could do until his brother got in touch.

"I don't know about you," he said, "but I think this needs an infusion of coffee," He took her hand and brought her to her feet. Tucking the comforter more securely around her, he led the way to the kitchen where the pot was always ready to go. He pressed the start button and scooted their chairs close together. He sat down and wrapped his arms around her, rubbing his hands up and down her arms and back.

"I'll bring your laptop in if you need to write this down," he offered, although he was positive this nightmare was permanently burned in her brain just as it was in his.

"Maybe later," she shook her head, and instantly, Satan's words about 'later' made her teeth chatter. She stared down into her palm and brushed at the ashes that were not there. And, maybe, like the ashes that weren't there, there would be no 'later'. She looked at Hawk's face. There had to be a later.

"On second thought, that's probably a good idea," she changed her mind. "Transferring them onto paper might help. The therapist said it might be helpful to create a journal of sorts."

Hawk placed a kiss on her cheek and another on her lips before he went back into the bedroom to fetch the laptop. By the time he returned, she had two cups of coffee on the table and was once more cocooned in the comforter. Only her head and one hand, the hand that held her cup, escaped. He set the computer on the table in front of her and took her cup and moved it off to the side.

"Thanks." Savvy sat up and got the other hand uncovered. She lifted the lid and booted it up. For a long moment, she just sat and stared at the screen but then, her fingers began to fly over the keys.

Hawk sat quietly, not interrupting, and willed Houston to return his text.

"YOU MIGHT AS WELL CONTACT Darken, see if he has a spare cabin," Houston finally said to Travis, over the headsets. It was already near dark and that made it chancy to fly low. Flying low enough to single out a specific motorcyclist on the road and follow her would be suicidal. "Hawk sent me a text. Savvy had another nightmare, but he didn't give any details. It must have something to do with Jen's case though, or he wouldn't have texted."

Worry about Jen ate at him, but he could worry just as well on the ground as in the air where it was too dark to see. Travis nodded and sent a call to Darken's base radio.

A light bloomed ahead where Darken had turned on the flood light to guide the bird onto the paved pad. Travis headed them toward it. He set the copter down and climbed out of the bubble to tie down the rotors and secure their ride for the night.

Houston grabbed their gear and made his way toward the office, a larger light glowing amid the smaller door lamps of the six cabins off to the side.

A weathered sign on the door said, "Come In", so Houston entered the office. There wasn't much in the way of amenities in the lobby; two mismatched chairs bracketing a cast-iron stove that didn't cast much heat beyond the edge of the chairs, but then the fire was most likely banked for the night.

A polished wood counter separated a curtained doorway from the lobby. As Houston stepped into the room, a tall man, grizzled gray hair, ropy muscles hardened by years of physical labor, and as weathered as the sign out front, came through the curtain. A mouthwatering smell followed him in.

"You ain't Travis so you must be Houston," he stuck out his hand in greeting.

"I must be," Houston smiled and shook the man's hand.

Darken handed Houston a key with a solid slab of wood attached by a hefty chain. "I filled out a card, just need you to sign."

Houston nodded as he signed and handed the man the cash. He looked over the chunk of wood, near as long as his forearm.

The proprietor saw the look and grinned. "Makes it harder for idgits to lose my keys."

"I'll be sure not to lose it."

"Second cabin from the north, or fourth cabin from this office," Darken said. "Tell Travis to come chat with me if he has a few minutes, will you?" And, with that, he disappeared through the curtain again.

Houston shouldered their gear and left the office for the cabin. Travis met him on the path, and took some of their equipment from his shoulders.

"Darken said you should come up and chat for a while if you have some time," Houston said. "You might ask if he has a vehicle we can rent to drive into town. We need to get something to eat." he added, as Travis piled all the gear back onto him and turned toward the office.

CHAPTER TWELVE

Houston eyed the rough cots with a jaundiced eye. The wooden frames held sagging mattresses, and looked for all the world like Marine cots, although the blankets looked warm enough. He dumped his gear on the one that looked a little less worn. Eldest brothers should have some privileges, after all.

The entire cabin comprised a single room, with a small table and a couple of chairs set below the only window, which had a pull down shade over it. A counter height cupboard was tucked into a corner, with a hot plate and a big percolator on top. The only other 'amenity' was a small, almost tiny, bathroom.

He sat on 'his' bed and returned Hawk's call, listening quietly to what he and Savvy relayed to him. He got confused a couple of times because Hawk had his phone on speaker and they tended to talk over each other, but the nightmare was easy to visualize.

"So, you actually saw the face of the man who pulled the trigger?"

"Yes." She took a shuddering breath. "And the name of the man he shot, plus the names of three others in the room with them. And it was clear that he wanted Link with him and both Jen and Irene dead. Although he didn't actually call any of them by name, just referred to them as the boy and those women."

"And his face was clear enough that you could describe the man to our sketch artist?"

"Yes." she had no doubt.

"Alright. Let me see if Candlemoss is back from Cancun. I'll give him your number as soon as I make contact, then I'll call you back." he ended the call.

Travis walked through the door. "No need to go into town for food," he announced. "Darken invited us to share some of his venison stew and biscuits."

"I could smell that as I picked up the key. It had my mouth watering." Houston said.

"What did Hawk want?" Travis cast a dubious eye to the cot where his gear was piled and sighed. He'd slept rougher.

"Savvy had another nightmare. This time though, it involved the man who took those shots at Jen. A man named 'Benny'. She also saw the face of the man who ordered the hit. The man who shot her in the nightmare. She has three other names of men in the room when 'Benny' was shot."

Travis whistled.

Houston stood. "Yeah," he said. "First, let me see if our sketch artist is back from baking his balls in the Caribbean." He picked up his phone and swiped a few times, found Darrel Candlemoss in his contact list, and the call went straight to voice mail. He left a message.

"I guess we go eat then."

The food, hot and delicious, filled all the empty corners, and the hour spent trading jokes and war stories around the small table flew by. When they mentioned the reason they were out, Darken said he had ears scattered around the area and would let them know if there was any chatter about a blond female on a motorcycle in the vicinity.

"Thanks," Houston said, "that would be helpful." He helped Travis clear the table and wash their dishes, but when Darken invited them to sit by the fire and continue the bull session, even going so far as to bring out a folding chair for himself, Houston declined, leaving the more comfortable chairs to Darken and Travis. He had calls to make.

When Travis entered the cabin a while later, Houston was in sweat pants, something he only wore when sharing a room with someone, and was sitting at the table, phone in hand, a scowl on his face.

Seeing that scowl, Travis asked. "No luck reaching the sketch artist?"

Hawk shook his head. "I know he was scheduled to return today but I don't know what time today. He might still be in the air."

"Well, we might as well get some sleep." Travis began stripping as he headed for the bathroom. "Coffee's on at four a.m., and Darken said he'll have bacon, eggs and leftover biscuits by four-thirty, if you're interested."

Next morning, Houston took the first bracing swallow of coffee before they dug into their food. The phone rang in the office and Darken left the table.

"Do you feed the rest of your tenants like this?" Houston asked as their host stepped back through the curtain moments later.

"Only when the restaurant is open during hunting season but you might be more interested in that call I just got. I might have a line on that woman you're hunting."

All other thoughts flew from Houston's mind. "Where?" he demanded.

"A little motel outside Wapiti, on the road between Cody and Yellowstone. Dub, the old guy that owns it, checked a blond female into one of his bungalows last night just after dark. Name wasn't Bradley though."

When they pushed back from the table. Darken laughed, "No need to rush," he waved them back to their seats. "it's less than forty minutes there by helicopter and she left a wake up call for six-thirty. Let's finish breakfast. Then you guys can clean up the dishes again while I pull the pumper up to the whirlybird and get it gassed up."

Less than thirty minutes later, the brothers stowed their packs into the bubble again. Darken, with a final wave, pulled the truck away from the pad and back into the hangar. Travis clambered into the pilot seat to start his pre-flight check. Houston stayed on the ground and took out his phone to give Darrel Candlemoss one last shot.

"Holy shit, Houston," Candlemoss's snarl spread a balm over Houston's built up agitation, "this better be damned important. I haven't even had time to unpack, and I've had three hours sleep, total, in the last forty-six."

"It is."

"What is it? A lone eye-witness to a mass shooting? And why are you calling from your private number instead of the station?" Darrel wasn't ready to let go of the snarl.

"This is a personal request, Darrel. The police don't know anything about it for now."

"In that case, I'm charging you double."

"That hurts, Darrel." Houston smiled. The helicopter blades made their first tentative rotation and he hunched down. "Listen, this is a convoluted situation and I don't have much time to explain it all to you. Do you have a pen handy? Good. My brother Hawk is staying at his girlfriend's apartment. I'm going to give you her number. Call them. They can explain everything. I'll pay whatever you think it's worth."

He peeled off the number over the increasing noise of the copter and had Darrel repeat it back to him. That done, he disconnected and called Hawk to let him know to expect a call from the sketch artist, before he climbed up beside Travis. He was depending on Darrel's natural curiosity to have him calling sooner, rather than later.

Once Houston had his headphones in place, he stuck his hand in front of Travis and gave a twirl of his finger. In moments, they were air bound.

THEY HADN'T SLEPT SINCE the nightmare, six hours ago. Savvy had resorted to pacing. Occasionally, she rubbed her hand over her chest as though the pain still bothered her. It probably did, Hawk thought. The amount of coffee they'd consumed might have had as much to do with that as her nerves. Even wrapped in that comforter, and Hawk's arms, when she stopped long enough for him to gather her close, he saw the chills wrack her body. He wasn't sure if Houston's call, promising action, had eased her anxiety or had increased it. She wasn't saying much. At least, with her lips. Her body, however, was speaking volumes.

He couldn't say he blamed her. If he hadn't been holding it together to try to keep her calm, he would have been pacing, himself. He warmed the half cup of lukewarm coffee he held with another infusion from the pot and handed it to her as she paused for a moment beside him.

"No," she shook off the offer. "I'm already sloshing."

Seeing the pallor on her already pale skin, he set the cup aside and pulled her close. "Why don't I fix us some breakfast?" he suggested.

"I don't think I can eat," she said, "but you need to. Go ahead and fix yourself something." She pulled away and resumed her pacing. "Houston called more than an hour ago. Why hasn't this guy called yet?"

Hawk had posed that very question, but only to himself. Savvy didn't need his doubts added to hers.

He pulled a quart of juice from the fridge and poured two glasses. The next time she walked past, he would hand her one of them, instead of a cup. She probably wouldn't even notice the difference. He lucked into a package of store-brand cinnamon toaster-tarts in the freezer and dropped two in the toaster. Savvy's sister and her friend, who were in this apartment almost as often as they were in Lacey's place, the next floor up, frequently added things to the fridge and cupboards that they liked. While Savvy, who wasn't big on prepackaged foods, preferred to cook and bake. Maybe that wasn't such a bad idea, his mind latched onto the thought.

"It is pretty early," he said. "I wonder if he stopped to eat on the way over? Should we offer to feed him, if he calls?"

Savvy stopped pacing. "You're right. I should have thought of that." She walked around the island to the fridge and opened the door. "We have plenty of eggs and ham and cheese, if he likes omelets. Or I suppose I could make pancakes. What do you think?"

I think it's great that your mind is on something else besides a bullet to your chest, he thought, but he said, as the toaster popped up, "Omelets are pretty universal, but you can ask him when he gets here." He took a couple of saucers down from the cupboard above the coffee pot and put a hot pastry on each, setting the plates on the island. She sat down. He took his and bit into it and smiled when she did the same with hers. They hadn't finished them yet when Savvy's phone rang, making them both jump. She snatched it up and answered.

In only a few brief sentences, Darrel was intrigued enough to forget his irritation with Houston and tell Hawk and Savvy that he would be there in ten minutes. He tossed his pad, templates and pencils in a back pack and headed for the car. He would draw out the full story as he drew out Savvy's memory. He was very good at digging out details his subjects didn't even know they remembered. He made it to their place in five minutes.

Once Candlemoss arrived, Hawk decided he'd better take over as cook. He could see Savvy's nerves dancing under her skin, and it was plain that Darrel saw it, too. The artist, his voice calm and soothing, talked of the weather and other trivia as he pulled out his tools and templates, setting them ready on the island counter.

Taking a seat, he pulled another chair to his side, and, with a smile to Savvy, patted the seat. She sat down. "It goes faster than you think if you and I are both comfortable."

"HIS HAIR WAS THICK and black," Savvy said, "with a slight widow's peak. And there was silver at his temples and threaded through it."

Darrel concentrated for a couple of minutes, his focus on the pad and pencil in his hand. When she murmured approval of the hair, he sorted through some templates and handed her a sheet of sample eyebrows.

"Which of those looks most like his eyebrows?" Darrel asked, only looking up from his pad where his pencil sped over the paper to see which ones she selected. "Close together? Or farther apart?"

"Farther apart," Savvy looked over his arm as the face took shape. She shivered again. "But I think he must wax them or something because there was a shadowed area around the brows, and in between, where it looked like hair might be starting to grow again."

"How did the nose look?" They went through the same procedure with a new set of templates.

"That one, only the nostrils were flared a bit more and the bridge was narrower." He made some adjustments. "Yes, just like that," she nodded.

He continued to show her templates as the face began to take on distinctive characteristics.

"And the ears? Close to the head or did they stick out some?"

"Close to the head." Savvy squinted. "I remember the left ear lobe was shorter than the right, uneven, almost like it had been cut off or something. He tugged at it a couple of times." Her eyes emptied as the memory rushed into her mind.

"Any other detail that sticks out in your mind? Moles, discolorations on the skin?" Darrel gently coaxed her out of the 'then' and back to the 'now'.

She stared at the face of the man that had pulled the trigger and felt the toaster-tart rise into her throat even as the bullet entered her chest again.

"No," she shook her head and clutched the front of her shirt. "Excuse me, please." she stood up and headed for the bathroom.

Hawk suspected the omelet was cold by now, but Darrel picked up his fork and took a bite while they waited for Savvy to return.

"I can warm that for you, Darrel," he offered.

Darrel smiled. "This is fine. It happens so often, when I'm involved with a sketch, that cold food seems normal."

Hawk picked up Savvy's untouched plate and scraped the contents into the trash. He would get her to eat something after Darrel left. "How much more do you need from her?" he asked.

"Anything else she can remember about the gun, what was on the desk, the designs, if any, on the cigarette case or the lighter. Even details about the desk itself or the chair he sat in, or the faces of the others in the room. It's all helpful in an investigation. And, if she remembers enough details of the witnesses to get a good likeness, the authorities can use that, as well. But we've got the important stuff right here." He swept his hand above the sketch and finished off the omelet.

"I'm not sure there is going to be an investigation," Hawk said. "Houston is going to have to tread very carefully and have more solid evidence than this to lay out, before they will even open a file."

"I can see your point," Darrel nodded.

"Would you like a toaster-tart?" Hawk offered. "Or something else to drink, besides that cold coffee?"

"Sure," Darrel grinned. "Tarts and hot coffee sounds good."

He was happily chewing on the last bite when Savvy, once again composed, returned to the kitchen.

CHAPTER THIRTEEN

Jen opened the door to bungalow ten. Although the term bungalow might be a bit of puffery, the room was better than some she'd stayed in. The bed didn't look lumpy and the cowboy motif wallpaper had faded to the shades of old TV westerns, insured to put you to sleep before the end of the show.

Being on guard for the last six years had honed her sleuthing instincts, and noting the lack of security cameras along the road outside, she'd pulled into the motel, hoping the management felt the same lack of necessity. They did actually have a security camera behind the desk, but the wire hung loose on the wall. Best of all, the bungalow had an attached carport, out of sight of the road. Circling the room, she dropped the key on the night table, her bedroll and the sacks from the Walmart in Cody on the bed, and put the deli food she'd picked up at Albertson's on the stand below the wall mounted TV.

After she had discovered that the bathroom could have been a little bit cleaner, she pulled the lone chair to the counter and unwrapped her cold meal, a hoagie sandwich and a soda, and ate. The sign in the office had offered a "Continental Breakfast" between five and nine a.m. At least the coffee would be hot.

She picked up the remote and found some news, but nothing local. It was unlikely that a house in Casper being trashed would be newsworthy, or even that the three people who had lived in that house were now 'in the wind', and it certainly wouldn't make national headlines, but she had to check.

She shut off the TV and made ready for bed. She hoped that the office remembered her wake up call.

CLEARED TO LAND, TRAVIS set the bird down on the helipad in Cody and killed the engine. "So what's the plan of action?" he asked, as Houston started going through his pack to get what he needed. He stuffed a clean pair of briefs and a pair of socks in his pockets along with the piece of paper with the name and address of the motel.

"I'm going to see if I can get a taxi or an Uber to that motel. If the woman is Jen, then we're going to ride her bike back to Casper. If it's her, I'll give you a call and you can head home."

"So I wait here until you let me know?" Travis stepped out of the copter.

"Yep." Houston looked at his phone. "It's only about 20 miles to Wapiti. If she sleeps 'til her wake up call, that still gives me nearly an hour to get there to see if we've got the right woman."

Houston was just climbing into the taxicab when his phone rang. He handed the slip of paper to the cabbie and asked, "How fast can you get me there?"

"Thirty minutes," the driver answered.

"There's an extra twenty in it if you can make it in twenty." The driver grinned and gave Houston a salute as his fare answered his phone.

"Hey, Darrel," Houston greeted. "Have you talked to Savvy yet?"

"Hours ago. Man, has that woman got an eye for details. I have a picture for you. I'm sending it now. I just wanted to warn you ahead of time, I've seen this dude before. Or a picture of him. Maybe a mug shot."

"I know he shot a man in cold blood so I've probably seen his mug shot, too." He watched the cabbie's eyes rise in the rear view mirror. "Send it on. And, thanks for the help, Darrel. Send me your bill." He ended the call and waited for the message to ping.

He was just buckling his seat belt when the picture came through. Oh, sweet Jesus, yeah, he'd seen that face. Blasted all over the headlines when his son, Antón Lucano, was arrested and sentenced on drug charges seven years ago. Son of a bitch, he swore softly. Not even the noise of the engine and the road or the cabbie's voice penetrated the roar in Houston's brain. Jen, how in the hell did you get cross-wise of the Lucano Cartel?

IT HAD BEEN NEARLY impossible for Jen to sleep, only dozing in fits and starts throughout the night, certain that every sound was someone who had managed to find her. Every voice from the other cabins, every rattle of door keys, every crunch of tires, and every roar and purr of engines had, even with the exhaustion of the long, long ride from Casper, made it impossible to close her eyes for more than a few minutes at a time. When the office put through her wake-up call, she was already showered, fresh makeup on and the darker hair extensions combed and braided into her blond locks. She dressed quickly and repacked her few belongings. Hot coffee and stale muffins sounded very good about now.

She debated whether to tie the roll and helmet on her bike now or take them with her to the office when she dropped off the key and grabbed breakfast. No, she decided, people were starting to stir in the other cabins – sorry, she corrected herself – *bungalows*, and there were things in her roll that she absolutely could not lose. Even tied to a motorcycle, under a carport, the pack would be easy pickings.

She checked the room again to make sure she hadn't left anything, then tucked the roll under her arm and grabbed her helmet. With the key in her hand, she left the cabin and made her way to the office. An older couple, who looked as though they'd already been on the road too many days, were just leaving the office, Styrofoam cups in hand, as she neared. The man held the door for his wife and then, seeing her coming, stayed to hold it for Jen, too. She thanked him and wished them a good day as she squeezed past.

The middle-aged man who had checked her in last night was nowhere in sight. In his place behind the desk, was a lovely young woman with snapping black eyes and straight black hair tied in a tail at the nape of her neck. Her dusky skin covered high cheek bones and a firm jaw line. She made Jen think of Houston. The girl was saved from model perfection by a chipped front tooth that showed when she spoke.

"Did you have a good night?" she smiled politely as Jen handed her the key.

"It was fine," Jen returned the smile.

"The coffee is hot and the cinnamon rolls are fresh," the girl pointed in the direction of the table in the corner, "and, there's a microwave if you want the roll warmed too."

"Thanks," Jen answered, "but I usually just dunk them." Walking over to the 'breakfast buffet', Jen set her things on a vacant chair and got a cup of coffee and a roll and sat down next to her pack.

Eating on the road, while riding a bike, was not an option, so Jen finished her breakfast, wiped the sticky off her fingers with a napkin, and headed back to the carport where the motorcycle waited. Pulling the roll from under her arm, she rounded the corner of the cabin, and came to a screeching halt.

"Going somewhere, Jen?" Houston leaned against the wall of the carport. His words were decidedly less friendly than the first time he'd asked her that.

The air turned into a kaleidoscope as the blood rushed from her head, and everything in her went numb. The bedroll, the keys and the helmet dropped from her nerveless hands which flew to her mouth to stifle the scream that surged up from her soul. Only a harsh cry of, "NO!" escaped her lips as she whirled away.

As hopeless as she knew it would be, she thought of running.

She dissolved into tears. She never cried. Except when she was angry. Right now, she was mad as hell. Mad at her situation, mad at her sister for putting her in this situation, mad at Houston for being so damned persistent, mad at Houston for getting under her skin, and most of all, mad at herself for allowing herself to fall for the most deadly man in her existence. Most deadly, except for Antón Lucano and his father. The tears of anger flowed down her cheeks. She swiped at them with one hand.

"How did you find me?" she snarled.

"I told you, if you ran, I would track you down, Jen. I have a very good network. Those tears aren't going to do you any good."

Grimly, she turned back to face him. "You don't know what you've done, Houston." Hating the weakness in her voice, she took a deep breath. "When you take me back, you kill me."

"I'm not taking you back," he moved forward, took her hand, and led her into the woods behind the cabin, "yet."

"Where are we going?" she pulled at her hand but he held on like a vise. "For a walk."

"Houston, I don't have time for this. Just take me back to Casper and let's get this over with." She continued to struggle for her hand but he refused to free it.

They were two hundred yards into the trees before he stopped and faced her.

"How did you get crossed with the Lucano outfit?"

She gasped. He couldn't possible know. God, not even Frank knew that name and she knew she'd never breathed a word about the Lucanos to anyone but Irene, and Houston had never met Irene.

'You can't trust anyone. They have people, cops and judges, even Feds, in their pockets. For Link's sake, promise me.' Jill's words whispered through her head. Was Houston on the take from the Lucanos? Every fiber in her body said 'no' but how could she really know?

Link! The image of the child she loved more than life, leapt into her mind. If Jill was dead and Houston took her back, would Irene still have the resources to keep Link safe? Without her? The thoughts curdled in her gut. A shudder shook her from head to toe.

"How many times do I have to tell you, I have nothing else to say?" With a look of defeat, he finally released her hand. She rubbed the circulation back into it. "If you're taking me back to the police station, then we'd best get on the road."

"We're not going back to the police station." Somewhere, in the last few minutes, he'd decided not to return to Casper. He headed back to the cabin, his hand once more firmly clamped around her wrist.

"Then why are you even here?" she demanded. "That's what you swore you would do!"

"I'm on vacation for three weeks. I thought we could do the tourist thing." No one who saw that smile spread across his lips, would believe he was happy. "Take in the beauty of this magnificent state. Get in touch with nature."

"I don't have time for this, Houston. Either take me in, or let me go." She didn't bother to fight his hold.

"I'm open to suggestions, Jen. Where do you want to go? Most people on this road are headed for Yellowstone. Is that where you were headed?"

His sarcasm planted an idea in her head. Maybe she could play this to her advantage. She had been headed to Yellowstone, after all. Let him think she'd given up.

Surely, somewhere along the way, she would find a way to ditch him. Her situation was salvageable. She just had to make him think she wasn't going to fight him anymore.

CHAPTER FOURTEEN

He handed her the helmet, and she put it on while he tied her roll to the bike with quick efficiency. He picked the key up from the ground, wiped off the dust, and straddled the seat.

"Hop on."

She did, placing her hands at his waist, just above his belt. A strange quiver settled deep in her stomach as the bike roared to life.

Where her hips pressed against his, a delicious heat spread through her. It would be so easy to wrap her arms around him and truly enjoy the ride. She steeled herself. She had to avoid that emotional booby trap, at all costs. He would be the death of her, she was certain.

Where was he heading? She wondered when he turned back toward Cody. They stopped at a light and she opened her visor.

"Why are we headed back here?" she asked the back of his head.

"I need a helmet," he answered.

He pulled to the curb at Buffalo Bill's Harley-Davidson, and dismounted.

When she remained seated, he held out his hand. "Come on. It's too early in the morning to start the chase all over again. You're shopping with me."

She declined to take the outstretched hand, but reminding herself of her vow to lull him into laxness, she threw her leg over the seat and followed him into the store.

He found the helmet he wanted, then went on to add leather gloves, heavy boots, a gear carrier, a small tent that was little more than a rain repellent; just a tiny nylon bubble, and a black leather jacket. His eyes turned to her, sized her up, and he pulled another leather jacket off the rack and took it over to the cashier.

"Good choices," the clerk beamed.

The broad smile was understandable, Jen agreed, when she saw the total on the screen.

"Don't bother with bags," Houston told him. "Just put everything in the carrier." All the gear went into the carrier, even the leather jackets.

Houston lashed the carrier securely to the tail rack, added her bedroll to it, and climbed aboard, new helmet in place. When she donned her own and took her seat behind him, he kicked the bike to life, popped the clutch and took off with such force she was forced to grab his waist or be thrown off.

"That was unnecessary," she shouted from inside her own helmet, but she doubted he heard her.

He stopped again, at Walmart, where he picked up a few more items from the sporting goods shelves, among them some foil-wrapped field rations. As large as that gear carrier was, Jen didn't see how Houston would get all this stuff in it. He surprised her, yet again, though, when he managed to fit everything, except a pair of saddle bags and insulated mugs, in the carrier, and was able to buckle down the straps with no problem. Fitting the saddle bags over his seat, he settled in and waited for her to climb up behind him.

Their final stop was a convenience store, where he removed the price stickers and rinsed out the mugs before filling them with coffee. Handing one to her, he said, "Add whatever you like," and screwed the lid onto his own.

He watched her add creamer, stir it in, and then fix her own lid in place before he paid for the coffee. Returning to the bike, he dropped the cups into the saddle bags and rolled the bike to the pumps to gas it up. It was disconcerting to realize, when they were once more mounted, that the only way she could get to her cup, was to reach between his legs. She suspected he had planned it that way.

On Highway 14-16-20, once again, he turned the bike west toward Wapiti and the East Gate of Yellowstone. She had to admire the easy skill he displayed on the bike, as he settled it onto the road. But that business of getting to her coffee …

Just to test her suspicion, she slid her hand down the inside of his thigh to reach for her cup. The bike swerved slightly and she stored that bit of information away for future use. At least he hadn't decided to hate her yet. What she refused to store away was the tingle in her hand where it had glided over the muscled thigh. Still, it wasn't long before Jen fell into the easy rhythm of the road as it flowed swiftly beneath them.

When they approached Pahaska Tepee, well west of Wapiti, she attempted to communicate to him that she needed to stop. Even though hearing with a helmet on was hit and miss because of the muffling of the head piece and the roar of the wind, he nodded and pulled up at the green roofed, log-built ranger station, next to the lodge and cabins, which had begun a century ago, as one of Buffalo Bill Cody's early tourist ventures.

"I have to use the restroom," she informed him. He nodded again and put the kickstand down and pocketed the key. She didn't miss the cautionary look he gave her as he did it. She looked for the sign to the restrooms.

There should be an information board and map of the greater Yellowstone area in the visitor center. With luck, she would be able to find the next clue, either here or at another of the information centers along the way. She knew she was on the right road. The tricky part would be doing it without raising Houston's suspicions even higher than they already were. She needed any edge she could get.

Inside the center, she spotted the map on a wall, bolted down under a plexiglass cover. She concentrated on all the park gates, marked boldly in red. And there it was. Irene's mark at the West Yellowstone gate, over in Montana. Pointing west. She ran her fingers over the map, trying to decide which loop of roads would get her there faster.

"It's hard to get lost if you stay on the road," Houston's voice at her shoulder jolted her.

"I was just trying to guess how long it might take." She faced around. He was entirely too close. Afraid her eyes would give something away, she brushed past him. "That muffin at the motel hasn't gone as far as I thought it would."

"We'll find a place to get something to eat on the way," he followed her out.

"You've got food on the bike," she frowned.

"That's for over night camping." His words brought an unwelcome image of campfires and that tiny tent.

She veered away from him sharply, and kept walking toward the bike. As much as her body yearned for just one more of those devastating kisses, she knew she had to avoid them, at all cost. That way was heartache, multiplied.

"There are diners and restaurants at most of the lodge sites. We should be able to find something before the lunch crowds hit," Houston called out.

In Yellowstone, highway 20-14 circled north of the lake and through the huge hidden volcanic caldera before joining with 191 coming up from the south, to continue on north to the West Gate, out of Yellowstone, below the 'chin' of Montana, and on to Idaho. The rough terrain maked it much longer than the straight line distance across the park. "We can stop wherever you want," she said as they stopped beside the bike. She picked up her helmet and slid it over her head.

With Houston behind the handles, and the engine in good voice, Jen took advantage of the freedom to view the fantastic scenery. A coyote slipped back toward the lake, into the trees lining the road as they roared past. A bald eagle watched for dinner from up high in a snag as he guarded his mate on the nest below him. Houston down-shifted and halted with the rest of the traffic to allow an elk and her calf to cross the road just ahead.

Houston had already opened his visor when he jabbed her with his elbow and pointed at a marmot perched on a rocky outcropping across the road, apparently unworried by the eagle's menu considerations. He pulled out his phone and took a quick shot, for all the world just like a real tourist.

Jen flipped up her own visor. "You're really enjoying yourself, aren't you?" she frowned at him. He smiled back.

Her heart stumbled, caught itself. He said, "You only get one trip through life. If you don't make some time to see the scenery, the trip is wasted."

She couldn't argue with that. In two short sentences, he had managed to remind her that for the last six years, her life had been controlled by an invisible puppet master, and that she hadn't had time to be a woman. She'd been too afraid of letting down her guard to pay attention to the scenery, until she had let Houston take control. And that, she knew, was a dangerous analogy.

Her thoughts turned to Link, and how she had failed him. No matter how careful she and Irene had been, it had all come down to this. They were all mice in a deadly cat and mouse game, on the run again, and the cat after them was one of the deadliest big cats in the world.

Houston pocketed his phone and dropped his visor as the traffic began moving. Suddenly missing that smile and the strength he exuded, she lowered her visor and wrapped her arms lightly around his waist. She tried to absorb some of the warmth that radiated through his jacket, hoping it might thaw some of the ice that had settled into her bones.

They'd been on the road a little over two hours by the time they got to Fishing Bridge, on the north end of the lake, in the early afternoon. They found a small general store but no restaurant, and were told that the closest one was at Grant Village, 20 miles on, but it didn't open until 5 p.m.

"Do you want to sight-see until 5, or keep moving?" He asked her.

"We could easily make it to the West Gate before then," Jen checked the time on her watch, "It's only 60 miles or so."

"What's your rush, Jen?"

"I ... I just ... I need ..," her words trailed off.

Houston waited a minute for her to finish but when she didn't, his jaw firmed and his eyes became cop's eyes, hard and flat. "I need to stretch my legs" He walked off.

Catch up, or let him go? Those were her two choices. But he had the keys to the motorcycle. She didn't feel like standing around while he worked off his snit. Reluctantly, she followed his rigid back down the side trail. There were signs warning of bear sightings posted and she was woefully unprepared to fend off a bear. It was doubtful that Houston was any better prepared, but if anyone could face down a bear unarmed, she'd bet Houston was the man. Especially if he looked at it with those eyes. She sped up to match his long stride.

Houston walked on and she followed. After ten or twelve minutes, she figured they'd done about a half mile into the woods, yet he showed no sign of stopping. She jogged up beside him.

"Houston, please," she touched his arm. He stopped and turned those eyes on her. Still cold, still icy, but he cocked his head and raised an eyebrow. "Listen, I'll tell you what I can if we can just keep going west." That hard look didn't waver but the head remained tipped. "Please." she pleaded. "I've got to catch up to Irene and Link."

"Where are they?" He was still in cop mode but his eyes seemed to have softened a bit.

"I don't know." a look of disbelief crossed his face. He twisted around and started down the trail again. She grabbed his arm and pulled him to a stop. "Really, Houston, I don't know where she's headed. She leaves clues for me to find."

"And have you found any clues yet?" he demanded.

"Three."

"Where?"

"The Waltman rest stop, the information kiosk in Thermopolis, and the station at Pahaska. Wherever there's a map of the area, showing the road she's taking."

"How did you know to go north at Shoshoni?"

"She uses a waterproof marker to write the highway number on the wall beside the maps. Even if someone saw it, they wouldn't realize the significance of it and it takes some scrubbing to remove it. If they even bother."

No, they probably wouldn't, Houston thought, "Where did she learn to do this?"

"I don't know," Jen shrugged. "She's been doing it since before I was born."

"Doing what?"

"Helping women get away from violent and abusive situations. My mother helped her before she and dad were killed in a plane crash. Irene became our guardian."

"Yours and your sister's?"

Jen nodded.

"How old were you?"

"Sixteen. My sister was ten."

"Who are you running from?"

Jen turned away. "I can't tell you any more. Either take me to the West Gate or take me to the police, Houston. Irene will keep Link safe, no matter what you decide. He's all that matters." She walked away, back toward the road.

"When are you going to realize that I'm not your enemy, Jen?" he said to her back.

"Everyone is my enemy, including you. I can't afford to have friends." her shoulders were hunched and her hands tight-fisted at her sides.

Houston fell in behind her.

Food was forgotten. The empty feeling in his stomach was nothing compared to the hollow feeling in his chest. Lucano wanted the boy. That had come through clear from the information in Savvy's nightmare. And what book had Lucano referred to? Was Jen's son Lucano's grandchild? The thought scored his brain like coarse sandpaper. And she was afraid her sister was dead. How did that play into this? If he told her what he knew, would that open her tightly zipped lips?

And, just what could he tell her? That Savvy had a nightmare? That source wouldn't be believed by ninety percent; The other ten might be persuaded to consider it. On what side of the divide did Jen fall?

The questions flew around in his brain like cards in a whirlwind. He would grab onto one and then lose it as another one flew by. She was afraid to go to the police. She was positive that if she went to jail, she would die. She'd made that clear from the beginning. There was no reason to put her in jail, and he was beginning to get an inkling about why she feared being put there, but how was he supposed to keep her safe if she insisted on running off? And yet, his duty to his badge was sacrosanct. If she had evidence that might put the final nail in the Lucano family coffin, how could he not bring her in to talk to the people in charge? And, what did that say about any chance they had to explore a relationship?

They reached the bike, climbed aboard, neither speaking to the other. They strapped down their helmets, and he twisted the key. The bike burped and snarled satisfactorily as Jen settled behind. He touched the gas and let out the clutch.

What relationship? The low laugh slipped past his lips but was, thankfully, absorbed by his helmet. She rode stiffly at his back, her hands only touching him when absolutely necessary. He missed the feel of her snuggled against his spine. They started and finished in silence the miles to the West Gate, where he pulled up to the visitor center.

CHAPTER FIFTEEN

Houston followed her into the center to the big plexiglassed map, and, knowing what to look for, found the sign at the same time Jen spotted it, a five-pointed star with one arm pointed toward the words, "Last Chance!".

Jen raised her eyebrows at Houston. He said, "That's a tiny town on the Idaho side, but the star? I dunno. You sure this is the right thing?"

"It's Irene's sort of thing. Pretty sure."

Back on the bike, they rolled on through the center of West Yellowstone, but instead of taking the turn-off, where 20 splits west to Targhee Pass from 191, Houston glided to a stop at a small cafe. He removed his helmet and dismounted.

She leaned back from his boot as it passed in front of her face, and lifted her face shield. "Why are we stopping?"

"*WE* need food. I don't fancy challenging Targhee on an empty stomach. We also should probably find a gas station and fill up. I don't know what services are available, going over the pass."

"Can we still make it through the pass before dark?" she took off her helmet and set it on the back rest.

He chained both helmets to the bike. "It's early enough that the supper rush hasn't started yet, so if the service is fast, we should be back on the road in less than an hour. That should give us about three hours before dark sets in." We'll be at Last Chance well before that."

Entering the cafe, the smell of frying oil and onions tossed her mind right back to Casper, into The Big Cup Cafe. She wondered if they missed her. Maybe Debbie and a couple of the other girls might. Frank wouldn't make any hue or cry about her absence though.

The evening rush, if they had one, was a long way off. They found a booth and ordered. Without much to say, they waited in an uncomfortable silence until their food arrived.

The food was hot, fast and filling but after a few bites Jen's appetite was gone and she pushed the remaining portions of the hot turkey sandwich around her plate until Houston asked if she was ready to go. Eager to be on the road again, she stood and waited at the door as he paid the tab. Still silent, they mounted the bike and found a gas pump.

Houston left her to fill the tank while he went inside to talk to the clerk. She dug out another credit card. This one for Jersey Trucking, and dropped it in the trash bin after it cleared and the pump was running.

When Houston returned, he dug her leather jacket out of the gear carrier and handed it to her.

"The roads are clear but there's still snow in the higher elevations," he said. "The ride is going to get cold."

She took off the gray puffy coat, handed it to him, and he stuffed it in the carrier while she donned the fleece-lined, buttery soft leather jacket. "It'll take about an hour, maybe hour-and-a-half, just to cover the 40 miles to Last Chance, depending on road conditions through the pass. Once we find the next clue, we'll find a place to camp for the night."

The idea of sharing that little tent with him was unnerving, to say the least. "Why not just find another motel?"

"We should save money wherever we can. We don't have any idea when we'll catch up to Irene."

She opened her mouth to tell him she had credit cards but shut it quickly. Explaining a credit card of questionable origin might prove a problem.

It was mid-June, but even in summer, the high Montana mountains are susceptible to snow and freezing temperatures. If it hadn't been imperative to get to the next rest area before Irene's clues could be scrubbed, she would have suggested waiting until morning.

"I didn't think about getting you leather gloves, too," Houston looked her over. "Those light weight gloves you're wearing aren't going to be much protection." he unzipped his jacket pockets. "If your hands get cold, just reach around and put them in my pockets."

Although he'd given her work shoes a critical look, he said nothing else, just threw his leg over the bike and dropped his helmet into place. She followed suit.

The miles drifted away as the elevation rose. The road was relatively clear. Good two-lane, but snow still lingered, dirty and crusted, in the barrow pits. Higher up the slopes, heavier drifts lay protected under the trees. The sun might not be ready to set on the flatter land behind them, but as it dipped lower and lower over the peaks, the air in the early twilight turned cold and colder. It bit at fingers and toes like a rabid wolverine.

Pride be damned, Jen leaned forward and put her arms around Houston's body and found his pockets. Now, protected from the brunt of the wind, her body started to warm. She felt Houston's body relax, a little, as though her body offered him some warmth as well.

He slowed to a stop at a junction, just before they entered the pass proper, where the old Highway 20 had been by-passed by a newer and straighter route. He removed his helmet and waited for her to do the same.

"I don't think we'll find a map anywhere on the old road and it reconnects to this main road just over the top of the pass, but you're the navigator. Your choice."

"Does the old road have any junctions?"

"The guy at the gas station said, 'no', but he couldn't remember if there were any services there."

"Then let's stay on the good road while we have daylight." She replaced her helmet and waited for him to settle in and take off.

The talk of passes had set her a mental image of canyon walls like the Wind River Canyon, but the road over the mountains was wide and flat for the most part.

Even so, ice patches on the road slowed the trip the rest of the way, but Jen appreciated the increased sunshine, and the warmth of Houston's jacket pockets. Her feet told a different tale. Except for an occasional stab of pain, she could no longer feel them or the pegs under them.

As they descended into Idaho, the land along the road spread out into tree-lined flat lands.

She almost sobbed with relief when the first road sign for the town of Last Chance came into view. Somewhere down this road had to be a store, she resolved to buy warmer socks and boots as soon as they reached it.

They rolled to a halt in the center of the only two blocks of Last Chance, Idaho, right in front of the Last Chance Texaco and General Store.

"What's the matter?" Houston barked when Jen stumbled off the bike.

"My feet are frozen." Jen limped toward the building, Houston swearing along behind her.

Some of the expletives, she understood, but there were a couple thrown in that she didn't recognize. She guessed they must be Arapaho.

"Why didn't you say something earlier?" He snarled.

"And do what?" she snapped back.

"I have some warmer socks in the gear carrier. We could have stopped long enough to put an extra pair on your feet."

"These are my work shoes." she pointed out, unnecessarily. He was well aware they were. "They aren't sized for two pair of socks. Besides, I'll get my own soon's I can."

She pushed open the door and the warm air inside wrapped around her with a welcome hug. There were a few other people in the store so their dispute had to be put on hold. But the store had a map! At the map, they found Irene's clue, on the wall at the left side. The number '33+wow' over a scrawl of 'rbug'. Beside it was a sleeping stick figure. "What does that mean?" he whispered close to her ear.

"Rest area."

She traced the highway as it dived south on the map and discovered that highway 33W split off to zip west from 20 at Rexburg as 20 dipped very far south to Idaho Falls, then came up north again, where 33 rejoined it near a place called Butte City. Beyond that, on 20, she spotted the rest area at Timmerman Junction. So 33 was a nice shortcut to the rest area, and it missed the big city traffic, but it was still maybe another hundred-ninety miles from the Last Chance Texaco.

They spent a couple more minutes going over the map, just like regular tourists, before Jen broke off to make use of the restroom. Sitting on the stool, the only sitting place there was, she removed one shoe and examined her foot. The toes were numb and waxy white. Not good. She'd lived in Wyoming long enough to understand the beginnings of frostbite. She rubbed the foot and toes until some feeling returned and then did the same to the other foot.

"Jen?" Houston's loud voice made her jump. "Are you okay?"

"I'm fine," she answered, shortly. "I'm just trying to rub some circulation into my feet."

"Do you need some help?"

"For Pete's sake, Houston, I'm in the women's restroom." The edge in her voice could have sliced tough beef.

"Well, hurry up then. It's a lot easier to set up a camp during daylight."

Still walking with a bit of a limp, Jen exited the building. Houston stood by the bike, waiting. He slid the phone he'd been using into his pocket. Who was he calling, she wondered? She doubted it was the police station since they were headed the wrong way. She hobbled out the door.

If he noticed her slight limp, he didn't say anything. He said, "There aren't any shoes here, but the guy says there's an outfitters store a couple of blocks north. Let's do something about those feet."

After the visit to the outfitters, her new socks and boots were a delight, as she rode the back of the bike out of the parking lot, knee-high bike boots gleaming in the afternoon sun.

She began to suspect he wasn't headed straight to one of the many camp grounds along the road when he took a side road that was posted, 'no trespassing'. The pavement stopped at the fence line, and from then on, it was washboard gravel. The jarring wasn't doing her already travel-weary butt any good and she questioned whether they were even supposed to be here.

She raised her visor and shouted, "This land is posted." His nod was her only acknowledgment. She tried again. "Are we even supposed to be here?" she repeated her previously silent question just as a particularly vicious bump snapped her teeth together with a click loud enough to scare off wildlife.

"I know the owner." his words flew back at her but his concentration was on the tricky road surface.

She refrained from asking any more questions.

As the trees grew thicker, Houston finally navigated a narrow barrow-pit and paused for a moment under a towering pine. He looked around and then rolled deeper into the trees until he found a rocky clearing and stopped. They dismounted and removed their helmets.

"This looks good." He took out his phone and called the owner to let him know where they were. They spoke for a minute, then Houston thanked him and said, "I'll keep my eyes open." He listened some more and said, "Love to, but maybe next time. We're on a tight timeline."

"Why don't you gather some wood while I pitch the tent." He waved his hand in the general direction of the tree line. "There should be some dry sticks and branches close by. Don't go too far though, Craig said he spotted a bear and two cubs the other night that were rummaging through their trash. He drove them off but they might still be hanging around."

She gasped. "And you're sending me into the woods?"

"Just keep the bike in sight and you should be fine."

CHAPTER SIXTEEN

"Why can't we just book it on down the highway and find a cheap motel?" she demanded.

"Two reasons. The one I mentioned at the rest area and the other is, I don't trust you not to take off again."

Well, that was plain enough. His words stung a little, but truth often did. If she'd thought she had half a chance, that's exactly what she would have done. And left him stranded in Bumfuck, Idaho. It crossed her mind that her self defense training had included disabling hits and blows, and she wondered what her chances were of using one on Houston, but she knew she would only get one shot, and if she didn't make it good ... She felt a pang of remorse at the thought of leaving him stranded, but he had 'friends' here. Grumbling under her breath, she went in search of firewood.

When she returned to the campsite, Houston had gathered rocks from the clearing and made a fire ring. He was positioning the tent in the area he'd cleared of stones, when she dropped the armload of wood she'd gathered.

"That's a good start," he told her, then focused on pegging the tent. "but we'll need more to keep the fire going through the night."

"More!? I picked up everything I could find. Why do we need to keep it going all night?"

"We need it to cook our meal tonight, not to mention, keeping those frozen tootsies warm, and keeping that bear from getting too friendly. And, unless you want to collect firewood out there before sun-up, we'll need enough to fix our breakfast. Try again." he said, not bothering to look up.

"This is ridiculous," she snapped. "One more night in a motel wouldn't break me." Or who's-ever name was on the card she used, but he could never know that. "And Irene can't be that far ahead of us."

"You would book separate rooms." His look dared her to deny it. "And you would try to take off again."

She didn't bother to deny it. "If you think I would share a room with you, you're sadly mistaken."

His eyes said, 'Oh, yeah?' but his lips said, "We're sharing a tent tonight."

Her mouth went dry at his words. No retort sprang to her lips.

"We can discuss details when we have camp set up," he motioned toward the trees again, "and enough wood to keep the fire going."

Fuming, she walked off into the trees again. Expanding her search area, she happened on a creek that cut a path through the woods. It was too wide to step across so she didn't bother. She was still worried about running across a bear with her cubs, and a water source, possibly with fish and grubs for food, would be an ideal place for them to hang out. She stared hard at a shadow in the bushes a ways down the other side of the creek, but it didn't move so she decided that she was probably making a mountain out of a mole hill. Hurriedly, she collected another armful of wood, larger pieces this time, and headed back toward the camp.

She heard the roar of a smallish but noisy engine, and a cloud of dust rose on the road. The roar came to a halt by the camp. Was it the owner visiting Houston?

Loaded down as she was, and so far from the clearing, she doubted her chances of getting back in time, still she hurried forward to catch a glimpse of 'Craig'. She could usually assess men easily, to determine whether they would be amenable to aiding her or not.

The dust in the air, however, had not even had time to clear, when the engine roared away again, kicking up another dust cloud, going back the way it had come. "Damn! Damn! Damn!" she muttered under her breath.

As she cleared the trees, she saw Houston, stacking wood in the fire ring. A rifle leaned up against the front of the tent. "Did we have a visitor?" She dumped the wood on top of the pile she'd started a while ago.

"Craig dropped that off," he nodded toward the gun. "Just in case."

Jen wasn't sure if that information eased her mind or added to her anxiety. "Will he pick it up before we leave?" she asked, and wondered what were the odds she could enlist his aid.

"I'll lean it up against a tree. He will find it when he comes by later in the morning."

Her odds just disappeared.

Antsy, and pacing a tight circle off to the side, she hadn't been paying attention to what Houston was doing so it surprised her, when her circle took her toward the front of the camp, that she could no longer see him at the fire ring. When she stepped around the tent, she saw his back disappearing into the woods, the rifle under his arm. Her lips curled in a snarl. He hadn't given her a weapon to carry into the trees. It made no difference that he didn't have a weapon to give her when he sent her to gather fire wood; it was the principle of the thing.

Curious as to his destination, she started to follow him, but soon changed her mind and returned to the tent. Crawling inside the small enclosure, she found that he had unrolled the two sleeping bags and arranged thin blankets between the folds. The space was so tight that the bags actually overlapped each other.

Did he actually think they could sleep like this?

The kiss they'd shared two nights ago came roaring up from her subconscious where she'd tried to bury it. It was no longer buried. It danced before her eyes and touched her lips like Scheherazade at her most seductive. Oh My God, she thought, trying to kill it and shove it back behind the veil. A groan escaped her lips and she backed out of the tent so fast that she almost tripped over Houston who was dropping a tablet into a pan of water.

"What's the matter?" he turned quickly. "Did a snake get in the tent?"

"Snake?!" she gasped, before her mind had a chance to grapple with the thought. She couldn't explain to him what had triggered her abrupt exit. "No ... I ... I thought I saw something move and it spooked me."

Instantly, he pushed her away from the flap and entered the tent, pausing only long enough to pick up a good-sized piece of wood as he did. He left the tent two or three minutes later with the bedrolls hanging from his arm. "I didn't see anything." He was taking no chances though, as he opened each roll and shook them out with a violent 'pop'.

If she had been braver, she would have told him that it had all been in her mind, but she wasn't going to do that. As a penance, she held out her hands for the bedding.

"Give that here and I'll remake the beds."

He hesitated for a moment as though sensing a trick, but then handed the sleeping bags to her. She shook them out a second time and then tossed them through the opening and hunched down to follow them inside.

She took care to lay the sleeping bags so that they opened toward opposite edges of the tent and put the blankets inside them. If they had to share this tent, it was imperative that she put as many physical barriers between them as possible. The mental barriers, hers at least, seemed to be crumbling at a rapid rate. She hated that that kiss had blasted a huge hole in that barrier. One stupid kiss! One careless lapse of judgment! And, even as she battled to plug that hole, her wayward heart yearned for another.

She sat down on the bedding, knees to her chest, and hugged her arms across. How could she be expected to survive even one night laying so close to him, let alone riding pressed up against him for days? She dropped her head to her arms and fought a losing battle to get control. She had to maintain control or risk losing everything she'd struggled for these past six years. Failure was not an option.

Houston stirred the instant coffee into the pot of water when it started to bubble and checked the progress of the other pot hanging over the fire. Jen had been in the tent a long time. He glanced at the closed flap and wondered if she had fallen asleep.

She'd better not be taking a nap because he needed to get some sleep tonight and having her tossing and turning next to him all night would make sleep impossible. He was already having a hard time separating his cop oath from the wants of his body, and to have her fidgeting all night, within touching distance, would make for one hellish night. The motorcycle ride these last several hours had been sheer torture. Feeling her legs straddling his hips had kept the memory of that kiss, and how her body had felt against his, alive and incredibly active. No, she definitely was not going to take a nap.

"The coffee is ready, Jen." There was a soft rustling inside the tent, and her head poked out of the flap. He poured some of the coffee into one of the cups and held it out toward her. She crawled the short distance to the fire ring, stood up, and took the cup from his hand.

"Thanks," she blew the steam away before taking a tentative sip of the hot liquid. It wasn't all that hot though. At this altitude, water boiled at much lower temperatures. He hadn't offered her any creamer so she drank it black. The other small pot hung higher above the fire, lid on. She wasn't sure what was in it but the smell was tantalizing. For now though, the black coffee was enough to fill the empty spots.

The sky was starting to get black now, too. Edging closer to the fire to ease the chill that the light breeze had kicked up, she sat down on one of the rocks that Houston had placed near the fire ring. The fire had warmed the rock and the rock warmed her backside as well. She stretched her feet closer to the flames.

"Drink up," Houston said. "Your cup is also your bowl and the food is almost ready."

"It smells good. What is it?"

He smiled. "Specialty of the house, Chicken and Dumplings, MRE style."

She finished her coffee in a few swallows, shook out the last drops and set the cup on the edge of the stone.

Houston picked up a stick from the pile of wood and lifted the lid off the pot. He spooned some of the food into her cup and handed it to her along with a small sleeve of crackers.

The dumplings were actually chunks of thick noodles floating in the chicken and broth mix but it was edible, and hot. She'd grown very fond of heat. Couldn't quite seem to get enough of it.

If she managed to get out of this mess, she decided, she would collect her small family and move much farther south. And never see Wyoming, or Houston, again. The thought of never seeing Houston again gave her heart a vicious squeeze. But, maybe, if she somehow managed to free herself and Link from the threat of the Lucanos, she would find love someday, and happiness. Surely Houston wasn't the only man who could stir these feelings in her. Surely.

If only he hadn't kissed her. If only she had turned away before he did. If only riding against him for hours today hadn't made her long for him to make love to her. And, even as these thoughts ran through her mind, she felt the tug of arousal start to build.

She looked over at him, watched the firelight play across the strong, bold features that she'd memorized over the last four years. And she locked those features into her memory, the way he looked at this moment. There wouldn't be many more opportunities to gather them. Maybe another day or two, at most.

Did he still have feelings for her or had she killed any chance they might have had together by running out on him? He'd made it very clear, what would happen if she did. But, she had anyway. She'd put his career in jeopardy and he wouldn't forgive that.

"I know it's not haute cuisine," Houston interrupted her thoughts, "but you should eat it while it's hot."

"I was just letting it cool." She started eating. "And, it's not bad." Opening the pack of crackers, she pulled out a couple and nibbled on them between sips of the soup.

"Your face looks a little flushed," Houston said. "You might be too close to the fire."

She sucked in a breath and choked on a piece of chicken. By the time she managed to clear her airway, she had herself under control. "I like the heat," she answered. "And my toes are finally warm."

It had been a thoughtful remark. If he still didn't care, at least a little bit, would he have even noticed?

She finished her food, with the thought running through her mind that he must not totally hate her. Even if she'd destroyed any chance for his love, she was pretty sure he still desired her. That was hard to disguise.

The longing was a physical ache. And she didn't want to spend the rest of her life wondering and dreaming about what it might have been like to make love with him. But, of course, there wasn't any other option.

Houston had felt her eyes on him ever since she sat down on that rock. He could tell her mind had been working something over. Probably how to kill or disable him so she could ride off. A grim smile curved his lips. They hadn't exchanged more than a dozen words since she'd emerged from that damned tent, and those had been stilted and cool. Barely civil. He didn't see a way to change that. No way that would ease the tension between them, anyway.

His own mind had been dealing with the dilemma they were in, as well. The difference was, although there were a number of things he would like to do to her, killing wasn't on the list. Thoughts of laying with her in that tent, and not being able to touch her, were a constant torture. More hours on the bike tomorrow was looming like an imminent execution.

But she was a material witness, and administrative leave or not, he was still a cop. He couldn't tell her what Savvy's nightmare had revealed, and as long as she refused to tell him what she was running from, his hands were tied. And maybe this distancing was the only way to make it through the night with his sanity intact. He prayed that they would catch up to Irene and the boy tomorrow.

She jumped when he spoke. "I'm going to wash the dishes." He gathered the few items that needed cleaning and picked up the rifle.

She stood up, too. "I have to pee."

"I'll be at the creek, so any tree should be fine. There's a small pack of tissues in the gear hauler."

She watched him walk away and quickly took care of her needs. He was only gone minutes, and when he returned, he carried another pot of water, into which he dropped another purification tablet. He put the lid on the pot and sat it near the fire ring.

He moved with such an economy of grace that the ripple of his muscles under his clothes made her mouth go dry. She licked her lips. He looked up as she did and the instant change in his demeanor made a raw curling sensation tighten every fiber in her body. She had dreamed of being loved by him, a hunger that ate at her soul. They had been dancing around this for such a long time. And, try as she might, she didn't want to fight it any more. Maybe, just one time, they could be together. The thought tantalized her. Did she have the courage?

He was the first to look away. Walking to the tent, he leaned the rifle against the flap.

She steeled her nerve. "Houston," he turned to look at her, "could I ask you a question?"

"Like what?" he was instantly wary.

"When you..when you kissed me," she looked away uncertainly, then continued, "did it mean anything?"

Jesus, how was he supposed to answer that? It had been the culmination of a four-year wet dream. Yeah, it had meant something. It had also been a huge mistake.

"Jen, look at me," he waited for her eyes to meet his. "It should never have happened. It was wrong on so many levels, but I won't forget it anytime soon."

"Then, can I ask you one more thing? Since we have to share that tent tonight, would you have sex with me?"

He stared at her as if he couldn't believe what she'd just asked, then he finally found his voice."I just told you that kiss was a mistake. Why would you ask to compound it?"

CHAPTER SEVENTEEN

"Why?" she paused. "Well, I ... I've wanted ... there's been this attraction between us for a long time. It wasn't just one way, either. I felt it when you kissed me." He was staring at her like she was a stranger and she could feel her resolve weakening. She soldiered on. "It doesn't have to mean anything. Just a release of the sexual tension between us. I just ... just ..." she stuttered to a halt.

"Just what, Jen?" he demanded, his visage dark, uncompromising.

"I ... I just want to feel ... to feel ... something ..." other than fear, she bit off the last words. Her brief spurt of boldness died on her tongue and she watched, heart lodged in her throat, as the gears of his mind ran through myriad cycles. His mouth opened and closed several times, but no words came out until, with a string of angry curses, he stepped to the tent, bent down and yanked out his sleeping bag and picked up the gun.

"That's a 'No.'" The words sounded harsh, raspy, as he carried his sleeping bag over to the far side of the fire ring, and spread it out. "Get some rest, Jen. We'll hit the road again at sunrise." He tossed more wood on the fire.

Okay, that was plain enough, she thought, as she felt her heart crumble. Her eyes fell away and heat rushed to her face.

Crushed under the weight of that final straw, and humiliated beyond belief by his flat rejection, she crawled into the tent like a scolded puppy and curled into a ball.

Four years of frustrated sexual longing buried her. She'd thought, just one time, just once, but, it seemed, the kiss had been enough for him. He didn't want her. Four years of repressed emotions squeezed through her tightly closed eyelids as the dam broke. Muffling her sobs in the folds of the bedding, she cried herself to sleep.

He heard the occasional quiet sob and felt like the world's worst heel. At this moment, he wanted nothing so much as to crawl into that damned tent, gather her into his arms, dry those tears and take away the hurt he'd caused. And bury himself so deep in her body that neither of them would see the sunrise. Duty, be damned.

He noted the humor in that thought with a wry twist of his mouth. As if she would even allow him to touch her now. She would be more likely to shred him like a rabid wolf. And he wouldn't blame her.

An audible groan slipped out of his mouth at the thought of tomorrow, when the torture would continue.

Dear God, he prayed, please let us find the boy tomorrow.

It was a long time before the sobs stopped, and it was an even longer time that he flailed himself for refusing what she'd offered. Still excruciatingly hard, he laid down on the sleeping bag and pulled the survival blanket over him. Unzipping his jeans he slid his fingers over his aching arousal, and in a few strokes achieved an unsatisfying release.

Pulling the rifle close to his bed, he closed his eyes, but sleep was a pipe dream. Tomorrow was going to be a hell of a long day.

Jen woke with a crushing headache. The night came rolling back over her, as it had, repeatedly, throughout her restless and intermittent sleep. She didn't have to look in a mirror to see what the last hours had done to her face. Her mouth was dry and her eyes burned as though she'd slept with coals on them. Her face would be puffy and her nose would be red. There was no way she could face him and pretend last night hadn't completely destroyed her. He would see it.

She laid there, wondered what had woken her, until she heard it again. The ting of a pot being stirred. Houston was already awake and fixing breakfast. She groaned. It was still black out. Maybe that was for the best. She might be able to walk down to the creek and splash icy water on her face until it looked half-way normal. She threw back the covers, and forced herself to take the time to fold and roll the sleeping bag and tie the lashes down into it's traveling state.

She saw him sitting, as he had last night at supper, stirring something into the cooking pot.

"Morning," he said, not looking up from his task.

"I'm going to find my tree again." The hoarseness in her voice made her angry. Damn it, she growled under her breath, you threw yourself at him and he rejected you in no uncertain terms. And you did your best to make it impersonal. You're not the first person to make a fool of yourself and you won't be the last. Suck it up, repair the damage, and get on with what has to be done.

The moon had already set but the sun hadn't lightened the sky. It was dark out in the open and even darker under the trees. Trying to remember the route she'd taken to the creek yesterday, she made her way, more or less, in a straight line that direction. Tree roots and broken branches made the going slow, which turned out to be a blessing. Stumbling over a small bush, she avoided a full length plunge into the creek, only by luck.

Soaked in ice water up to her elbows, she slowly backed up onto more solid ground, then cautiously cupped handfuls of creek water and splashed her face. When she ran her hands through her hair, several of the extensions came out. Well, the disguise wasn't necessary any longer. She worked them all out and left them in the bush. Birds or mice might find a use for them.

She was about to rise when she heard a splash some distance down the creek bank. Had Houston followed her? The sky had lightened enough that she could distinguish darker shadows but she couldn't make out shapes. Then she heard a soft mewling sound and a heavier grunt as something moved in the water. Whatever it was, she was pretty sure it wasn't human.

Bear! A Bear in the woods! A scream rose in her throat. She swallowed it. Bears weren't naturally aggressive, but she remembered Huston saying this one had cubs. And Mama Bears could get downright belligerent when things got too near their babies. Did it already know she was here? It must. Had it already scented her? She was down wind of them but their sense of smell, she'd heard, was incredible. If she backed away very quietly, could the she bear still get to her? Judging distance was tricky in the darkness, but maybe fifty yards?

Her earlier excuse for entering the woods was now urgent. She should have done that before she washed her face. Too late now. She moved away from the edge of the creek as silently as a mouse. When she could no longer see the shadow in the creek, she rose to her feet and continued to back away, centimeter by centimeter.

When she judged she was far enough to make it, she started to turn, ready to make a dash for camp when a hand grabbed her arm.

"Shhh," Houston breathed in her ear.

She swallowed the scream that had risen in her lungs. A rush of relief made her knees wobble.

Still holding onto her arm, rifle in the other hand, he backed up, as she had done, until they reached the edge of the clearing then they fast-walked back to the fire. He threw some more wood on the fire and it leaped into a bright blaze.

Putting the fire between her and the creek, Jen sat down, heavily.

"I thought you just had to pee," Houston hissed. His sleepless night was making his temper flare as bright as the flames.

"I still do," she snapped, "but, I needed to wash first."

"You wash before you go to the bathroom?"

"I have hand sanitizer in my gear," she defended.

"Let's go pee," he circled the fire and waited for her to get up. "I'll go with you."

Since he still had the gun in his hands, she wasn't about to object. She headed for the nearest tree, glad he was right behind her. Finishing in record time, while he stood guard on the other side of the tree, she followed him back to the fire where he set the rifle, once again, at his side.

Still simmering at her recklessness, he said, "We'd better eat and pack up before she smells the food." He poured boiling water over some instant oatmeal and handed her a cup and a spoon. "With luck, the bear will keep the cubs clear of the fire, and us, until we're gone." Calmer now, he waited for the oatmeal to thicken. When he judged it ready, he divided it between them.

The bear had driven thoughts of last night to the back of her mind. Almost grateful for the intervention, she ate her oatmeal in silence while Houston dialed Craig.

She listened as he apologized for the early call and explained the bear sighting. Not wanting to risk another encounter, he asked his friend to bring down enough water from the house to dowse the campfire. Assured that Craig would be there in a few minutes, Houston set about breaking camp.

"Will he bring enough water to wash the dishes?" Jen asked.

"There's some hot water in that pan." Houston pointed.

Probably what he'd planned to use for coffee, but Jen rinsed out the cups and two spoons as best she could and turned them upside down to dry on the rocks next to the fire.

It didn't take long to get everything stowed in the gear carrier, and if the cups weren't completely dry, they could be washed again.

Houston was lashing the carrier to the bike just as Craig showed up with a big water can. There was a gun rack in the back window of his truck, and another rifle rested on the top hooks.

Houston introduced Jen to his friend and then they concentrated on the fire. With the advent of the bear, so close to the camp, Huston had built it bigger than was necessary to boil a small pot of water. Pouring the water, a couple of gallons at a time on the fire, they stirred the embers to make sure they were dead. Soon, the flames were reduced to a gray sludge within the stone ring and they decided it was safe.

Jen stood by her bike as the two men talked for a few more minutes, then Houston handed Craig the other rifle. She watched him place it in the gun rack behind the truck seat, then climb inside and wait for Houston and Jen to mount the bike, before he followed them down the road for a couple of miles. Finally, he turned the truck around as he waved them off and headed back toward his house.

"THEY SPENT THE NIGHT on some private property, but they're easy to follow," the gruff voice grunted softly into the phone. "They don't suspect a thing. I can take them out somewhere down the road without a problem." The man listened for a minute.

"God-dammit, I nearly froze my nuts off in the cab of that truck, sitting on the side of the road. Tell the boss that they're following clues that the woman leaves on maps at visitor centers and rest areas. I figured them out yesterday. I don't need these two anymore to find the boy." He held his phone away from his ear at the heated response on the other end. "All I have to do is take out the motorcycle and they're no longer a problem. And the

Boss can call off the other shadow, we don't need the backup anymore. It will be a lot safer for the kid, if I don't have to try to take out all three of them with the kid standing right there ..." He listened to more yammering. "No, I can do the job, I just think it might be easier my way." ... "Yeah, yeah. He doesn't pay me to think." He disconnected. "Fucker!"

THE DIRT ROAD HADN'T improved any overnight, but the return trip to the paved road didn't seem quite as long as before. Traffic was light, this early in the morning, as they headed south toward Highway 33 and points west, unconcerned by the old beat-up and droopy Ford flatbed that chugged along some distance behind them, full of hay bales.

Once they came down off the mountains onto what passes for the flats in Idaho, the highway became a four-lane road, and the truck fell further behind as Houston let out the throttle.

A hundred times, Houston composed an apology in his head and rejected it. He owed it to her, but maybe it was better left unsaid. She sat, rigidly, behind him, not touching him unless absolutely necessary. Maybe that was best, too, but damn, he missed her body pressed against his back. But at least she leaned into the curves properly.

When they rolled into Rexburg, Houston took the Second Street exit into town, which also happened to be part of highway 33, and went in search of coffee, stopping at a McDonald's.

Jen lifted her visor when Houston dismounted and removed his helmet. "Why are we stopping here?"

It was a redundant question when you stopped at a fast-food chain, but he refrained from an eye roll. "I need coffee," he held out his hand for her helmet. When she didn't move, he said, "Come on. I'll buy you a pancake."

Enticed by the thought of hot pancakes and sausage, and unwilling to start an argument this early in the day, she handed him her helmet and followed him.

With the memory of last night's fiasco still nagging in her brain, she couldn't find anything to say. Even the 'almost' bear encounter and

Houston's rescue, couldn't counterbalance that so, she sat quietly while they waited for their food.

The silence had become a wall between them and he decided it had to be knocked down if they were to get anywhere near an answer to his many questions, so halfway through the meal, Houston opened his phone and scrolled through until he found Darrel's sketch.

"Do you know who this is?" he held the picture out to her. Her face paled.

"Of course." Her voice was too calm. "That's Ranaldo Lucano."

"How do you know him?"

"His face was all over the papers when his son was sent up on drug trafficking charges."

"That was six years ago. Amazing recall, Jen." Houston laid the phone down on the table between them where the picture stared out at her. After the first glance she tried to avoid looking at the face, but like a tractor beam, it kept drawing her eyes back.

"Even the highly skilled sketch artist, who drew this picture, thought he'd seen the face before, but couldn't recall exactly where. Why has his face made such an impression on you?"

"Occupational necessity," she glared at him. "When you wait on people, you need to be good at remembering faces."

"So, you served him a meal somewhere, at sometime in the past?"

"No," she snapped, gleaning a look from some men eating breakfast a couple of tables away. She modulated her voice. "As I said, I remember seeing him on the news."

"Is he Link's father?" Her face lost all color and her mouth opened, as though she was ready to scream, then closed again. She pushed her half-eaten breakfast away and stood. The glare she aimed at him could have soured milk.

"No," she hissed. And headed for the restrooms. She couldn't have answered his question any other way without giving away the whole sordid tale. But, little by little, he was digging out the story, and it terrified her. Somehow, she had to find out how much he actually knew. But how was she going to do that without giving up critical information of her own? The food she'd just consumed rolled uneasily in her stomach.

She washed her hands and face and looked at the wild tangle of her hair in the mirror. Her comb and lipstick were buried somewhere in the gear carrier. It was apparent to see why Houston had rejected her offer last night. The memory brought a flush of color into her pale cheeks.

When she returned to the dining area, Houston had dumped their remaining food and waited for her just outside the door. Good. She was ready to don the anonymity of her helmet and get back on the road.

Silent once more, he drove leisurely back to the sporting goods store where they waited another ten minutes for the doors to open.

CHAPTER EIGHTEEN

"Why are we stopping here?" she unconsciously asked the same question she had at McDonald's. "I don't think this carrier is going to hold anything else."

"You need better gloves. And more socks."

His 'isn't it obvious' shrug irritated her. "We're not in the mountains anymore. Let's just get going.

"If we don't catch up with Irene today, we might find ourselves in mountains again before this ride is over," he pointed out.

She had no argument for that, so she subsided and was again silent.

Well equipped with gloves, socks, and ferocious silence, Houston turned right, straight west on Main, and so did highway 33, shortly after nine thirty. They didn't pay much attention to the old truck, filled with hay bales, that passed them a few minutes later. Or the other one sporting a camper shell, that fell in behind them.

There were many junctions, but without finding any clues to change their direction, Houston kept a steady speed heading west toward Arco and perhaps the Timmerman Rest Area. It was looking like Boise was Irene's goal but the interstates would have been a more direct route. Why had she chosen to lead them through mountains and down two lane highways? So many questions and no answers. Frustration mounting, he simmered as the miles rolled by and they found no rest stops anywhere along the route.

Highway 33 rejoined highway 20-26 eight or nine miles east of Arco. But in town, they discovered a major split. North would take them to Mackay and Challis, via 93, but 20-26 headed south again and would take them to Mountain Home, and eventually, Boise,

"What do you want to do?" Houston removed his helmet as he rolled to a stop at some gas pumps. "I'm not picking up a pattern to follow."

Visor up, Jen said, "I think we should stay on 20. it doesn't make sense for her to drop so far south only to turn north again. And there is that rest stop up ahead on 20. Bet that's the one she means."

"Okay." he pulled the insulated mugs from the saddle bags and turned toward the store. "I'll refill these and then we'll gas up and head down the road. It's about a hundred and fifty miles until we hit Interstate 84, then we'll need to refuel. We can check on how far that rest area is inside."

An hour later, they spotted the Timmerman rest area. Inside the building, they found their map alongside a brass plaque that said they were right near the Timmerman cemetery, and these hills round about were the Timmerman Hills. Clearly Timmerman had once been a name to reckon with. A vandal had marked up the plaque with Magic Marker nonsense. But one bit caught Jen's attention, a sloppy but recognizable drawing of a gift package. And a circle with a dot in the middle. "Center – gift" did not tell her much and she found no other symbol that even looked like Irene's work. She pointed the drawings out to Houston, who was not convinced but shrugged and turned to the men's room.

Back on the bike, and seventy five miles later, as the junction onto I-84 at Mountain Home neared, Jen was ready to let Houston have the bike and take a bus. The motorcycle had been bought with comfort in mind, but comfort was hard to come by when you were doing your best over several hundred miles to make no unnecessary contact with the person you were riding behind. The problem, of course, was that she still had no idea where they were headed, and Houston could find the clues faster than she would be able to were she to ride that bus.

At Mountain Home, Houston took the exit ramp and slowed for the light. They both spotted the sign, "Travel Center", or in ordinary terms, a "truck stop", and the smaller sign announcing its gift shop, at the same time. It was a white stucco building, with a green roof, set in a grassy area amid its huge parking lot. When the light changed, they pulled in. A sidewalk circled the building but Jen's focus was on the gift shop.

Saddle sore and grateful to be able to put some distance between her and Houston, Jen headed into the building. Houston followed her.

There were a lot of gifts on a lot of counters and racks, but the only maps she could see were a half dozen of the fold out kind, a rarity in the age of GPS. Irene wouldn't have marked those. Not in the market for key chains or refrigerator magnets, they went back outside.

Following the sidewalk, she found the big map mounted behind plexiglas on a sign board at the side of the building. And, she found what she'd hoped to see. Irene was here.

"What does the 'X' mean?" Houston said, behind her.

"She's here."

"And the other mark is a picnic table?"

"Yes," she nodded her head toward a group of tables under a shelter on the other side of the center. "I'll wait over there. When she drives by and sees the bike, she'll look for me."

"We," he reminded her.

"I," she repeated. "Irene won't stop if she sees you."

"There are other people wandering around here. Why would she be suspicious of one person out of a bunch?"

"The other people aren't following me around as if they don't want me out of their sight." Jen snapped.

Houston looked ready to snarl back, but he finally nodded. "Pick a table. I'll go back in the gift shop." Pulling the key to the bike from his pocket, he dangled it in front of her then returned it to his pocket. "Just in case you decide to take off on your own." He walked away, leaving her seething.

Houston returned to the gift shop and got a drink from the water fountain, but he had a plan forming. He still didn't trust Jen to not take off. If she'd needed any more incentive, he'd given her a bushel full last night. And he had no idea what kind of car Irene would be driving. Knowing Jen would be focused on the traffic, he carefully circled the opposite direction and found a spot, behind some trees, where he could see Jen at the shelter but would be hidden from view. He settled in to wait.

There were two couples sitting at separate picnic tables when Jen entered the shelter, so she chose a spot as far away as possible. She sat, tensely, watching the traffic and trying very hard not to look like she was watching the traffic. It only took a few minutes for her to realize she would never be any good at surveillance. She pulled out her phone as though reading a text or sending one, neither of which was happening. She had no one to contact, but the action eased the pressure behind her eyelids. If she turned just right, she could still see the road without appearing to watch it. Of course, it was possible, given the distance from the road, that Irene would be looking for the motorcycle parked in the lot rather than trying to spot her here, behind the building.

More than an hour passed before one of the couples left, then the other pair shortly after. Finally alone, her nerves eased slightly. Her mouth became cottony, and she wished she had something to drink, but she didn't dare leave the spot to get her thermos from the bike.

A woman with an over-sized tote approached from the sidewalk. Mouse colored hair pulled up in a messy bun, her faded jeans and baggy sweat shirt looked worn, but Jen didn't peg her as homeless. She looked more worn out. Looking around, she took a seat at another table, as far away from Jen as she could get. Jen understood, completely, that need for space.

It didn't take a mind-reader to see that the woman was troubled about something. Her face broadcast anxiety like a bullhorn. A bad breakup? Divorce? A death or serious illness in the family? Jen wondered. Placing her bag on the bench beside her, the woman reached in the tote and pulled out a small bag of pretzels, opened it and began eating them, one at a time, as she watched the traffic. The crunch of the pretzels only made Jen thirstier. She looked back down at her phone. The only thing to read was the slow tick of the minutes on the screen as she pretended to concentrate.

Houston had disappeared. She didn't know where. There weren't that many places someone could hide nearby. She didn't fool herself that he wasn't watching her, though.

She thought longingly, of the drinks in the saddlebag on the bike. Had Houston refilled them at the last stop? She couldn't remember. And she'd absolutely refused to reach down between his legs to see if there was anything left in her bottle as they rode on from Timmerman Junction.

Houston had to keep slapping himself awake. The long, sleepless night and the miles on the road were beginning to take a toll, and, as he sat out of sight, in the late spring heat, it became damn near impossible to keep from dozing off. He wished his hiding spot gave him a better view of the parking lot, but that wasn't possible. The best he could do, was watch the entrance and exits. If something didn't happen soon, he was going to have to change the situation himself.

The woman sharing the shelter with Jen made him nervous. The couples, he'd understood, but the woman had his instincts jumping. The shelter seemed an odd place to deal with problems. And she definitely had problems. Her face was a map of misery and the constant eating while watching the road and her phone, plus the occasional swipe at an escaped tear was a giveaway. Even as the thought crossed his mind, she brushed away another. Her hands visibly trembling, she reached in her big satchel and stayed for a minute before drawing out another bag of chips.

But why stop here? Was she expecting, or hoping for, someone to find her? If the object was to wallow in her own misery, wouldn't a more private place be better? There had to be green spaces, more secluded places, about the town. This place was not secluded. There were travelers coming and going all the time, spending time in the gift shop or getting directions, gassing up. Some lingered, some left more quickly. For some reason he couldn't quite put a finger on, the woman's presence here bothered him.

A bumble bee clambered happily over a dandelion, and he watched it for a moment. Anything to shift his focus and ease the crick in his neck. When the bee flew to another flower, he pressed his fingers to his eyes, rubbed them, and refocused on the shelter.

A dark blue pickup drove slowly by and the woman looked at it with a startled frown before quickly returning to her phone screen. The shake of her fingers was evident, even from where Houston sat, hidden behind his tree.

He thought he'd seen that truck drive by once before. He tried to read the license plate, as it disappeared down the street, but it was too far away.

His instincts were starting to scream like fire engines. There was something very wrong here. If he'd ever smelled 'setup', this was it. He leaped to his feet and in a dozen strides, was over the railing that encircled the picnic tables.

CHAPTER NINETEEN

Jen, phone in hand, let out a squeak of surprise and jumped to her feet when Houston came over the railing but he didn't stop at her table. Instead, he went past her and grabbed the woman's bag. With a heave, he pitched it far out onto the lawn.

The stunned woman gaped at him and let out a scream. "No! No!" she shouted. Rising with lightning speed, she ran through an opening in the railing and aimed for the bag. "What have you done?" she yelled at Houston as she passed him.

He didn't take the time to respond. He grabbed Jen's hand when she, glaring accusations at him, charged after the distressed woman. He hung on, nearly yanking Jen off her feet, as he pulled her down the sidewalk behind him.

"Why did you do that?" she shouted at his back.

He didn't answer. He only stopped at the bike long enough to boost her over the seat like a kid on a pony. Putting a helmet on her head he handed her the key and climbed on behind her.

Why was he making her drive? His body twisted as though he was watching what was happening behind them.

"GO!" he shouted in her ear. "Get the hell out of here!"

His alarm finally penetrated her brain and she kicked the bike to life. Weaving crazily, she managed to turn the bike and aim for the exit, but as she turned, she caught a glimpse of the woman, hands stuffed in her bag. The bag she pointed at them with deadly intent.

Ice filled her veins. In slow motion, survival instinct took over. She took control and slalomed into the street as shots ripped through the bottom of the tote bag and echoed down the street behind them.

Houston shifted positions and leaned heavily on her for a moment then righted himself. "Head for Boise," he commanded, hoarsely.

Jen headed for the interstate, shifting lanes at random, and challenging changing lights. She watched the rear view mirror, her heart lodged in her throat.

How had Houston known the woman had a gun in that bag? She had wondered, herself, why the obviously distressed female had chosen that seat. Most women Jen knew, either called a trusted friend or dealt with their problems privately. But, Jen had thought, maybe the woman hadn't had anywhere else to go or anyone to turn to.

But all her assumptions were blown to pieces by the gunshots. That woman had intended to kill them! That was twice in three days she'd been shot at. She'd been scared before, but now she was getting mad as hell.

In the distance, she picked up the sound of approaching sirens. Of course, someone had called the police. Houston must have heard them, too. His helmet swiveled constantly. Concentrating on the traffic, she didn't have that luxury.

"Get off the highway at the next light and get us and this bike out of sight." Houston's helmet bumped hers as she nodded.

With instructions she had no problem following, Jen took a left at the next intersection and headed into an area of gas stations and strip malls. It wasn't hard to spot a vacant building, and she circled the block to find the alley behind.

There she found a loading dock with short wings built to protect the doors from the wind. She rolled to a stop between the wings. They blocked most of the wind and muffled the sound of the traffic from the street.

She wasn't surprised to find, on dismounting, that her knees were shaky. She leaned against the edge of the dock, took off her helmet and breathed deeply.

Houston remained seated but removed his helmet, too. His head pivoted as his eyes raked the surrounding buildings, looking for curious eyes in windows.

"What's the next move," she asked, still sucking in oxygen.

"Rest for a minute and then you come help me off this seat and dig through the gear hauler."

"What? Why can't you ..." she was already rounding the bike, a sick feeling churning in her gut. She stared, aghast, at the blood soaking his pant leg, from above his knee to his boot, and she knelt beside him there in the loading dock, unsure what to do.

With startling clarity, his reason for tossing her into the driver's seat became obvious. He had put himself between her and the gun fire he suspected was imminent. All her doubts about him fell away like autumn leaves in the wind, and she finally had to admit to herself that she loved him. It didn't make any difference that she'd destroyed any similar feelings he might have had for her. Love was love, painful as it could be, it didn't stop. She tried to tamp down the feelings coursing through her, by reminding herself that he was only doing his duty to protect a material witness, but it didn't help much. She swallowed hard and looked into his face.

"It hurts like a son of a bitch but I don't think it's broken." he said, misinterpreting her own expression. "The slug is still in there though." He put his hand on her shoulder. "I just need to brace myself until I'm sure I can stand on it."

She stood up next to him and lifted his arm over her shoulder, bracing her body to take his weight as he lifted the uninjured leg over the bike seat. He gained his feet with great care. Beads of sweat popped out on his forehead accompanied by soft cursing, but using the back rest of the bike as a crutch, he unbuckled the gear hauler and dropped it to the concrete.

"Open that and find my gun," he hissed through gritted teeth.

"I thought they took your gun." Her eyes were big and her lips wavered, but she tried to act as matter-of-fact as he seemed to expect.

"They took my service weapon," he said. "This is my personal weapon."

She dug into the pack to find it, a Glock 45, wrapped in a lightweight jacket. She also found a bullet hole in the back of the carrier which, if it had not been there, would have entered Houston's back. Nausea rolled in her stomach as she realized how narrow their escape had been. Fighting back the urge to vomit, she handed him the pistol. He placed it on the seat beside him.

"There's a bullet hole in the carrier," she croaked.

"I felt it hit." He didn't seem terribly concerned about it. "See if you can find something that I can use for a tourniquet. And, I'm going to need that knife in there, too."

She returned to digging and found a t-shirt, which turned out to also have a hole in it when she unrolled it. Since it was going to be used to soak up blood, she didn't stress much about the hole. She handed it to him, quickly found the knife, and handed that to him, as well.

He took the knife and gave back the t-shirt. "Roll that, length-wise, as tight as you can and tie a knot in the middle."

While she did that, he used the knife to cut away his pant leg and examine the ugly hole in his leg as best he could. He picked a few threads from around the edges before he reached for the t-shirt.

Placing the knot she'd tied on the small hole at the back of his thigh, he pulled the t-shirt around to make another, heavier knot on the front, above his knee. He stopped, eyes shut, and panted in pain.

"Do you have any acetaminophen in your bedroll?" he asked through gritted teeth.

"Yes," her eyes brightened and she opened her bedroll, found the bottle, shook out two, then another, and handed the three to him. He swallowed them dry.

"I have a dark shirt in my stuff," he said when the panting eased. "Will you get it out for me? And I think there's an empty plastic bag in there, too."

The pack was a mess, by the time she found the things he needed. A deformed slug dropped to the ground as she repacked the carrier. Picking it up, she stared at it with revulsion, then put it in her pocket. He handed back the plastic sack, wadded with the bloody denim he'd cut free, and she added it to the carrier, without question. This, she understood. To some, carrying the bloody denim with them might seem unnecessary, when there were dumpsters up and down the alley but to carelessly leave clues where they could easily be found was the way to disaster. He'd slid the dark shirt up his leg and tied it around the improvised bandage, to hide the blood as much as possible when they took off down the streets again.

He had probably left a blood trail. His boot was resting in a puddle of blood. That would have to be covered, too.

"Can you remount the bike?" she asked, when she'd secured the pack. "If you can get it started and move it a few feet, I'll get some dirt and grind it into that blood." she pointed to where he stood.

He picked up the gun. "Can you handle an automatic?"

"Well enough," she started.

"And so can I." A woman stepped around the wing extending in front of the bike.

Short, wavy gray hair and a face that had seen some wear, Houston estimated her age at near eighty. Dressed neatly in dark blue slacks and light blue shirt with a red jacket hanging loosely from her shoulders, he would have given her little thought walking down the street. Had she been trying to cross a busy intersection, he might even have offered her his arm. The handgun pointed steadily at his middle was not so easy to dismiss. The barrel didn't waver.

"Just toss the gun over here." she ordered.

Houston, his gun still on safety, calculated his chances and found them very unfavorable. He tossed it.

"Irene?!" Jen's gasp behind him, eased some of the nerves jumping in Houston's gut but it didn't lower the gun pointed at him.

'Well, Houston, you anticipated meeting 'Irene' at some point but this isn't the sweet old lady you pictured', he thought to himself. With her gun fixed unwaveringly on his belt buckle, he wasn't ready to breathe easy just yet.

Hearing her name didn't change the woman's focus. "Now, step away from the motorcycle." Her eyes never left Houston as she flicked the barrel of the gun just a little.

"Irene!" The tone of Jen's voice changed. "He's wounded. Can't you see that?"

"I can see that he's still on his feet so, he can walk. Now, move," she flicked the gun again for emphasis.

"Irene, please stop pointing that gun. We've been trying to find you." Jen stepped ahead of Houston slightly. Slowly, the gun, pointed at him, lowered.

"We?" Irene questioned. "When did you become 'we'?"

"It's a long story, but right now we need to get out of here. He's been shot."

Irene raised an eyebrow. "By whom?"

"Some crazy lady at the Travel Center where we were waiting for you," a note of exasperation entered Jen's voice. "We didn't take time for introductions. Where were you, anyway?"

"I pulled in but there were too many people, too many strangers. I suspected you might have been followed. I couldn't risk drawing attention to us together, so I left."

"Then how did you find us?" Houston asked.

"I stuck a tracker on the bike. That's what I intended from the start. That's why I had to stop you there. I planned to find you down the road."

Shit. He hadn't considered that.

"Irene, he has a bullet in his leg," Jen reminded. "We've got to find someone who can treat him who won't report it to the authorities."

Irene turned her gray head toward Jen, her eyes hard. "How much does he know?" she demanded.

"He caught up with me at Wapiti and invited himself along. He knows I was following the clues you left and he figured them out. All I told him was that I was trying to catch up with you and Link."

"There won't be any more clues." Irene stepped over to Houston's gun and kicked it out into the alley where it came to rest in a patch of weeds.

She shrugged the jacket off her shoulders, freeing the hand that didn't hold the gun. But, rather than switching hands to free the other hand, she pulled the jacket off her other arm and over the gun. She wadded the jacket, wrapping it over the barrel. All without losing her grip on the handgun, which was still pointed his direction.

CHAPTER TWENTY

Houston had seen that move before in street fights, and survival mode had him moving. The pain and questionable stability of his leg forgotten, he made an awkward dive for the only protection available, the opposite wing of the loading dock, just as she pulled the trigger.

In one lightning move, she blew out the rear tire of Jen's motorcycle then let the gun drop to her side.

"What the hell, Irene. Have you lost your mind?" Jen stared at the old woman like she was the stranger from the travel center. "I need that bike."

"Not anymore," Irene said. "Get your things from the bike and let's go. I have a car. He can find medical on his own."

"No!" Jen shook her head. "He took a bullet for me. I can't just leave him."

"Jen, get your head on straight. He isn't gut shot. Yet. Get whatever you need and let's get out of here. I'm not going to kill him if I don't have to, I just made sure he won't be following us again."

Houston managed to get his good knee under him. How much mobility it would afford him was questionable though.

Torn, Jen looked from Houston to Irene and back again. "I'm sorry." she whispered to him, as she took the few steps back to the bike and opened the carrier again.

Houston hadn't lost focus on Irene's gun hand, but he didn't think he was in imminent danger.

"I'm not the only one who followed her here." he told Irene. "The woman at the other table wasn't working alone. She was under pressure and being monitored by someone in a dark blue pickup that drove past. Whatever hornet's nest you kicked, they're coming for you."

He watched a flicker of worry darken Irene's amber eyes. Jen, too, hesitated at the carrier, her features paling noticeably.

Irene was the first to recover her voice. She locked her eyes on Jen. "It doesn't matter. The trail stops here. Hurry up, girl. Someone could have heard that shot."

"Are you aware," Houston's voice drew Irene's attention back to him, "that Ranaldo Lucano shot a man named Benny, through the heart, as he sat in front of his desk trying to explain why he failed to kill Jen in the restaurant parking lot? While he pleaded for another chance. Lucano never even blinked; he told him he had others on it already."

He heard Jen gasp but his eyes didn't leave Irene.

Irene's eyes turned icy as she shifted them to Jen. "You said he didn't know anything."

"I don't know where he got this so-called information." The raspy denial didn't sound like Jen at all, he thought, "but that didn't come from me. How would I know anything about that?" A hard shake of her head emphasized her words. "The cops must have an informant in Lucano's network."

Irene turned hard amber eyes back on Houston. "Are you a cop?" She watched Houston's head bob once and her eyes went dark. "Where did you get that kind of information?"

"An informant." he wouldn't elaborate beyond that. "The information that came down was also firm that Lucano wants 'the boy' brought to him and both of you dead. Probably me too, since they now know I've been riding with Jen." He watched as the two women digested that. Then he gave them one more bit to chew on. "He won't stop, no matter how many bodies he leaves behind, until you're both dead, and he has the boy."

He watched the two women's eyes meet, silent messages of fear, worry and anxiety volleying between them like ping pong balls. Irene was the first to make a decision. She walked over to where she had tossed his gun and picked it out of the weeds. Tucking it in the waistband of her slacks, she stuck her own gun in the front and freed her jacket to tie it around her waist.

Walking back, she stopped in front of him and drew her gun again. Pointed, now, at his head, the bore looked as big as a cannon. "Give me your phone." She held out her hand.

He debated trying to disarm her. She was close enough, but he was pretty sure that Jen would wade into the ensuing fight and not to protect him. He wasn't positive he had the strength to subdue them both. He reached in his pocket and handed her his phone.

She put it in her pocket and turned to Jen again.

"Lash down your gear," she said, "I'll be back in a few minutes to pick you up. Him, too," and with a nod his direction, she disappeared the way she had come.

As Jen unbuckled the gear carrier, Houston struggled to his feet. "I'm glad to see she draws the line at cop killing," he said, drawing an angry scowl from Jen, but not before he saw relief wash over her features.

"The day isn't over," she snapped. She tossed the gear carrier over her shoulder. The weight staggered her momentarily until she could brace her feet to counter-balance it.

He looked down at his leg. The t-shirt binding the wound was soaked through and the whole bloody mess looked like he'd been rolled in mud. Infection was a very real possibility if he didn't get the slug out and get the hole cleaned and disinfected soon. How he would accomplish that was the question.

Doctors and hospitals were obligated to report gunshot wounds. That wasn't a route he could take without ripping open the whole can of worms; something he was reluctant to do. At least until he knew more. Which left him to choose between a back alley abortionist and a witch doctor. Hell of a choice.

On the reservation, there had been a woman with some medical training, who treated injuries and kept her silence. Then again, Travis had field training as a medic and Houston would trust his brother with his life. Maybe he was the answer, but as long as Irene had his phone and his gun, Travis was also a non-answer. Shit.

Jen studiously avoided looking at him as they waited, in silence, for what seemed like eons, but was only a few minutes. They watched the alley, as far as they could see in either direction, hoping that no one else showed up before Irene got back.

Irene drove up in a gunmetal gray cargo van with darkened windows and stopped between the wings. Stepping out of the van, she said, "Get into the front passenger seat, while Jen and I load the bike."

"I thought we were leaving the bike," Jen looked confused.

"I changed my mind. Come on, give me a hand." Irene stepped to the back of the van, opened the doors, and dropped a short ramp to the ground.

They ignored Houston, who limped painfully around the front of the van to find the passenger seat had been covered with a plastic trash bag. The two women maneuvered the disabled bike up the ramp and laid it down in the back of the van.

"You sit back here," she handed Jen a gun, "and shoot him if he tries anything."

Considering who they were running from, their paranoia was justified, but he was getting really pissed about being held at gun point. "What is it going to take for you to realize I'm not the person you should be worried about?" Houston turned sideways to ask, as Irene slid behind the steering wheel and put the van in gear.

In his peripheral vision, he noted that Jen held the gun, safety on, aimed at the floor between her feet and her chin rested on her chest. A glimmer of hope teased his thoughts. If she believed he was not a threat, maybe there was a chance to convince Irene, too. "I'm the one who saved Jen's life at the restaurant three nights ago. Did she tell you that?"

"We haven't had a chance to say much. You might be the knight on the white horse, but you're a cop," she scowled, as she entered the street and turned left. She said 'cop' with the same disdain that Jen had used before he kissed her. "Lucano has too many cops, feebees, lawyers and judges in his pocket to trust anybody. Just one word to the wrong ears and we'll be dead. We'll get your leg fixed and then Jen and I will disappear, with Link. You might survive, or you might not, but we definitely will."

"Ranaldo Lucano wants his son."

"Link is not his son!" Jen raised her head and her voice.

"Jen!" Irene barked a warning and Jen dropped her head again.

A memory leaped to the front of his brain. Something Jen had said about 'her husband was dead', and another time, the name 'Antón'.

Antón Lucano, Ranaldo Lucano's son? The one who was in prison? He took a wild stab. "Grandson, then."

The panicked look on Jen's face in the sudden silence was a dead giveaway.

"How long do you think you can run?" Houston asked. "He found you in little ol' Casper, Wyoming. How'd he do that?"

A sick look twisted Jen's face and Irene whitened.

"I've spent forty years helping battered and abused women disappear," Irene said. "No one will find us."

"How hard do you think it is to track two women and a boy?" Houston posed. "You're not dealing with an abusive husband. Lucano's network is every bit as extensive as the word salad agencies in the government. He now knows what you look like. Probably the boy, too. Unless you plan to live in a cave and end your son's education at first grade.

"If his web is as wide as they say, and I expect it is, it's only a matter of time before someone in his network spots you."

"He's determined to get custody and he has the money and resources to win in court," Jen's voice rose from the back. "We only have to stay out of sight until Link is old enough to choose who he wants to live with. And we can home school. Link won't lack education."

"Jen!!" Irene sent a warning over her shoulder. "Don't say any more."

Jen subsided once more.

"Your son loves you. Do you really think he would refuse to live with his grandpa if Ranaldo threatened to kill you, and Irene, as his alternative? Or, if you were already dead?"

"Shut up," Irene glared at him, "or I swear to God, I'll shove you out of this car at the next stop light."

And, Houston believed, she would most likely try, but he had given them enough to consider. He sat back quietly.

They left the city proper, and Irene navigated through winding roads lined with wide spaced ranchettes. Dirt driveways led far back into tree lined properties, sometimes so far back that the houses were not visible. It was at one of these driveways that Irene left the pavement.

Looking out the window, Houston spotted a hidden camera, high in a tree, aimed at the road. There were, no doubt, many more. This must be part of Irene's network. He guessed it had to be sizable.

There was a big bend in the drive, and as they rounded the last curve, he saw a sprawling, multi-winged house, with a three-car attached garage, on the left. Brick and shingle siding in russet and beige, the house said home and warmth. A covered porch ran the length of the front and rockers and a swing invited guests to relax. There was no one sitting there, though. He saw another camera in the shadows under an eave.

Irene pressed a remote control button, and the garage door closest to the house opened. She drove in and closed it behind them.

A window over a work bench allowed enough light to see, as Irene opened her door to get out. Houston followed gingerly. He kept a grip on his door until he got his leg stationary. It throbbed with every pulse of his blood. Just as he got balanced and was trying to decide if he could make it into the house, a door in the wall opened and a big man entered. A really BIG man. Taller than his own six foot two by a good six inches or more, Houston estimated the man must weigh around 400. And it wasn't flab.

"Oh good, Caleb," Irene greeted him as Jen stepped out of the back end. "There's a bike in the back here, with a blown tire. I would appreciate it if you could take care of it for me."

"Of course! Of course, Irene," Caleb smiled at her. Jen climbed out of the back and stepped around the door. Caleb's smile broadened.

"Caleb, this is my ward, Jen." The man nodded at her.

He spotted Houston leaning on the door and gave his bloody leg a hard stare. "Who's the passenger?" he asked, suspiciously.

"He came with me," Jen interrupted whatever Irene started to say.

"Is Abbil in her office?" Irene asked. "He needs to have his leg looked at."

"She was a few minutes ago when I walked by."

"Fine. When you get that bike repaired, will you load it back into the van, please?" Irene moved toward the door.

Jen came around to Houston and lifted his arm to her shoulder. Unconscious of the blood and dirt he smeared on her pant leg, he followed

Irene into the house. He thought he could have made it on his own, but Jen felt good under his arm, so he didn't object.

The woman reaching into the cupboard did a double take when her eyes landed on Houston, and the dish in her hand smashed to the floor. Irene jumped back to avoid flying crockery. The woman ignored the shattered dish and turned an accusing glare on her.

"How dare you bring him in here without clearing it with us first?" she barked, her lips tight.

"He's a cop and he was with Jen when I found them. He'd been shot, Karen." Irene didn't back down. "I couldn't leave him for the police to find. My judgment. My call." She put her thumb to her chest, her face every bit as fierce as the woman's. "Abbil needs to look at his leg."

Houston thought for a second that Irene had said, "a beetle" and shook his head to clear his ears.

The woman wasn't the least bit mollified but she pointed down a hallway, "She's in her office." Careful not to turn her back on them, she reached for a broom and dust pan at the end of the counter.

CHAPTER TWENTY ONE

There were more security cameras in the hall and one, quite obvious, above a door halfway down. Irene stopped at that door and waited for Jen and Houston to make their halting way to her before she knocked.

"Come in."

Irene pushed the door open for Houston to enter the 'doctor's office'. A woman, wearing a hijab, moved unsteadily toward him. A name plaque on her desk spelled out her name, but only the first. Although most of her face was hidden, what was visible was heavily scarred, as were her hands. If Houston wasn't mistaken, they were acid burns. The halting way she moved indicated that more than just her face and hands were heavily scarred.

She assessed his leg with a practiced eye and said, "Let's get him into the surgery." She opened a door behind her and limped through.

And surgery is exactly what it was. Rolling exam table, lights and every tool he'd ever seen in any ER. "My name is Abbil," one side of her mouth moved up in a smile.

"Houston Wh—"

She waved him to silence. "First names only, here," she admonished gently. "Sit up on the table so I can get those rags off your leg and take a look at it." she glanced up, "You two have a seat," she motioned Irene and Jen to a couple of chairs set against one wall, "unless you'd rather wait in the other room."

They took the seats and Abbil set about removing Houston's bandage.

She washed the area with amazingly gentle fingers, but gentle or not, he was sweating heavily and had to suck in a breath or two while she worked.

"Who shot you?"

"I didn't wait for an introduction." He winced when she pressed.

"Why did they shoot you?"

"I don't know, but I wasn't the target. She had ample opportunity to shoot Jen, who was sitting only a few feet away, but she didn't. My guess is, she was waiting for Irene to show up and planned to kill them both."

"And you got in the way?"

"Something like that." There was no reason to explain that was why he'd tossed Jen into the driver's seat.

"There's no exit wound," Abbil commented.

"Nope." Houston agreed.

"I'll need to put you under in order to remove it."

"No."

Abbil raised one eyebrow skeptically. "It's going to be painful. Maybe you'd prefer a Lidocaine nerve block."

Houston vetoed that idea as well. With his leg dead, he'd be at an ever greater disadvantage than he was now.

"It's up to you," she shrugged. It was hard to tell but he though he saw a smirk curl her mouth. "I will deaden the area as best I can, before I start."

"Yes," Houston nodded, "please do." His response earned him another partial smile, or smirk.

He watched her open a small refrigerator and remove a vial of clear liquid then close it and uncover a tray of tools and syringes. She selected one with a long needle, and set it aside while she rolled the vial in her hands to warm it a little.

"If the sight of the needle bothers you, just focus on Jen," there was that lopsided smile again, "You won't even feel it."

Needles didn't bother him, but it was a good excuse to look at Jen. She wasn't quite as passive about needles as he was. She paled a bit when Abbil started injecting the pain killer into his thigh. Their eyes met for a second and he saw the lingering hurt buried there before she looked quickly away. He definitely owed her an apology, but it wasn't going to happen in front of Irene, and it seemed Irene was glued to Jen for the foreseeable future.

Nor could he forget Jen's son. Jen and Antón Lucano's son. The thought made his stomach roil. Where was the boy, he wondered? Was he here also? He hadn't seen a sign of him yet.

Numb or not, he could still feel the doctor's hands as they palpated his leg to locate the exact location of the slug. A lancing pain changed the trajectory of his thoughts as Abbil probed for the bullet. He bit down hard on a hiss of agony as new beads of sweat popped out on his lip. His head swam and he grabbed for the edges of the exam table. Dropping to horizontal to keep from falling off his seat, a harsh groan escaped his lips just as the room faded out.

"I'm impressed," Abbil said, taking a quick glance at Jen before handing her a barf bag and dropping the slug in a metal dish. "He lasted longer than most. Do you need to leave the room?"

"No," Jen shook her head gently but kept a white-knuckled grip on the arms of her chair and the barf bag.

When Houston came-to in the empty room, he was glad to see it remained reasonably steady. Maybe Abbil had given him something to stop the pain anyway, while she worked, but it couldn't have been too strong. What little dizziness remained should go away shortly. A blanket covered him. The foot of the bed had been raised to level, the head had been elevated about ten degrees and the side rails were up.

Throwing back the blanket, he saw that his thigh was swathed in white and that his jeans were missing. He had a brief moment to wonder if the doctor had found it necessary to mention the semen stains in his briefs to the others. He shoved the thought aside. Embarrassment didn't kill you.

For the moment, he was pain free. That wouldn't last long. A bed table had been moved to the side of his bed and surgical pants lay folded neatly on top. There was also a barf bag. What wasn't there, was any sign of Jen or Irene.

Fighting his way through the slight brain fog, he worked the scrubs carefully up his legs before he attempted to sit on the edge of the bed. His bloody socks had been replaced with paper booties. His boots were nowhere to be seen. A pair of crutches leaned in a corner. With the aid of the side rail, he lowered his uninjured foot to the floor.

A wave of nausea hit him as he stood. He picked up the barf bag and waited for the queasiness to settle, happy to see that it did. He set the unused bag back on the table. Hanging on to anything handy, he pulled up the scrubs, tied them around his waist and hobbled over to the crutches.

He hadn't been on crutches since he broke his leg back when he was nine, rock climbing on a dare. He wasn't graceful, getting the sticks under his armpits, but the technique would come back to him.

The first person he ran into was Abbil, coming down the hall toward him. She looked surprised to see him on his feet.

"You continue to amaze me with your resilience and your plain, fool stubbornness," she said, looking into his eyes. "I didn't think you would be awake for another thirty minutes or so. I was just coming to check on you," she reached up to peel back an eyelid, nodded. "Normally, I wouldn't have left you alone but I had an emergency." she didn't elaborate. She did block his way when he tried to move past her. "You really need to rest that leg for at least twenty four hours."

"Maybe some other time," he made an attempt to get around her.

"Any bleeding through your bandages?"

"No."

"Dizziness?"

"It's gone." It wasn't, completely, but he wasn't going to give her any reason to try to force him back onto that bed. "Where did Jen and Irene go?"

"I believe they were going to the kitchen." she sighed and reluctantly stepped aside.

And the kitchen opened into the garage. Panic struck him like a blow. He didn't even have to wonder if Irene would have left him here while he was unconscious, but would Jen? Probably, dammit. If they had slipped away he would have a hell of a time finding them, hampered as he was. Picking up speed as he relearned crutch balance, he raced down the hall, spun into the kitchen and nearly toppled.

Jen and Irene sat at a table about a dozen feet from the wall he had just staggered around, coffee cups in hand, deep in conversation.

"We've got to find out how he found out," he heard Irene say.

Was he the 'he' she meant? Or were they discussing Ranaldo Lucano? Yeah, they were all seeking answers. Him most of all.

Jen spotted him first, spilling some of her drink as she plopped her cup down on the table and jumped up to steady him.

"Abbil said you would sleep for a while," she frowned, her tone definitely accusing. "What are you doing up?"

"I smelled coffee." He grinned.

"Sit down before you fall down," Irene ordered, shifting a chair out for him. Her demeanor didn't say 'and welcome'.

"Thanks, I think I will." Houston balanced on his good leg to collect the crutches in one hand while he placed the other hand on the table and lowered himself gingerly to the chair.

"See if you can find some juice or Gatorade for him," she directed Jen, who started around the long serving island that divided the dining area from the kitchen.

"I would prefer some of that coffee."

Irene scowled at him. "Caffeine increases the chance of bleeding." He matched her scowl and raised it.

"So does getting shot. Just bring me the coffee, Jen."

Houston could modulate his baritone, when he chose, to a level that could not be heard beyond a couple of feet. He chose to now.

"You're going to have to decide whether or not to trust me, and very soon," he said to Irene. "I have risked my career, and my life, by doing what I've done the last two days, and if we continue at cross purposes, Link will find himself an orphan." Their eyes locked over her cup. She looked down into the dark liquid as though seeking answers in a crystal ball. He continued, "If Lucano's network is a wide as you say, and I'm not doubting it is, he already has his people digging out possible places you might be holed up around this town. How secure is this place?"

She glared at him but finally answered, "It's listed in the county records as a private residence but our security is the best. We have cameras and voice and facial recognition monitors all over. We also have security guards if someone breaches the property fences."

"And the locals aren't the least bit curious about what 'private residence' in their midst requires such security measures?"

He went on, drilling his eyes into hers, "Who supplies the medical equipment and drugs for the clinic? Does Abbil order on-line or does someone else bring in what she needs? Every person who delivers supplies or equipment to this house is a weak link. How many people know, or suspect, what you do here?" He leaned in a little closer.

"Your security is sufficient for a wife beater with a restraining order but it won't stop Lucano and you know it."

They hadn't expected Lucano to find them so quickly, he knew. Their very presence here now endangered their whole operation. Jen had mentioned that Irene helped abused or endangered women disappear. This place had to be part of that network.

Jen sat a cup of coffee in front of him. "Thanks." Houston lifted the cup to his lips, but he sighed as she took a seat beside Irene and sat down.

As though he had swallowed a magic potion, an idea began formulating in his mind. "Is there some place, less public than this dining room where we can talk?"

"There are areas on the grounds where we won't be overheard," Irene replied.

"See if you can round up a wheel chair and take me for a walk outside while I shake off the drugs the doctor gave me."

"I'll go," Irene rose from her seat and took off down the hall. Probably to think over their dilemma without listening to other voices, Houston guessed.

"Where's your son?"

Jen's eyes flew to his from across the table.

"He's not here," she shook her head. "We wouldn't be here either if you hadn't needed medical help. Irene knows the danger we've put this house and these people in by bringing you here but she didn't have any other option."

"Don't try to tell me we wouldn't be here if not for me. She came from here," Houston rebutted her words, and downed the rest of his coffee. "She had a remote to the garage door."

"Her car is parked behind the garage," Jen defended Irene fiercely. "She just borrowed the van to pick up my motorcycle."

"Then, where is Link?"

Houston inhaled the heady scent that was uniquely Jen when she leaned in close so that her words barely carried to his ear. The question he'd asked faded to the back of his mind as his body reacted to her nearness with unexpected hunger. Oh, man, he had it bad.

"A woman Irene helped, many years ago, lives in Boise. Link is with her." she whispered.

The wheelchair, rolling down the hall, had a tiny squeak in one wheel that announced it's arrival before it actually appeared. Jen, as though suddenly conscious of how close her lips were to Houston's cheek, sat back in her chair as Irene turned the corner.

Saved by the squeak, the thought ran through his brain, and he resented the hell out of it.

Wordlessly, Irene parked the chair beside Houston and set the brakes. She elevated the leg rest slightly.

"Abbil said it would be more comfortable if you kept the leg up a little bit."

Houston levered himself into the wheelchair and Jen lifted his injured leg onto the foot rest. "Lead the way," he said, reaching down to release the brakes.

They headed back down the hall, past the clinic offices, and turned left into another hall that had other closed doors.

"More offices?" he pointed at them, although there were no name plates.

"Staff quarters," Irene said.

At the end of the hall was an electronically controlled exit. Irene blocked the key pad as she keyed in a series of numbers. The door opened onto a courtyard beyond which lay a grassy area surrounded by a high stone fence. Fruit trees dotted the lawn but he noted another security camera in the branches. He also saw the fine wire running along the top of the fence, just on the inside, where it would not be easily seen by anyone on the outside. He wondered how many volts ran through it.

"Over here," Irene motioned them toward a trio of small concrete benches set in a circle around a fire pit.

Houston rolled the chair between two of the benches where the camera he'd spotted would not have full view of his face. Jen and Irene took seats on either side of him.

"Is this secure?"

"Yes. This area is only used by the employees for relaxation and a cookout on occasion." Irene informed him. "They need to feel free of constant surveillance sometimes, too." She shifted to look him directly in the eyes. "Now, it's time for full disclosure."

CHAPTER TWENTY TWO

Houston sat back, and returned her stare, steadily. He saw the flat challenge in her eyes. She'd probably spent most of her life digging the truth out of any given situation, but he wasn't inexperienced, or intimidated. Folding his arms over his chest, he said, "You first."

There was a lengthy pause. "No." she finally responded, "I've got to know how you know that Ranaldo Lucano shot someone in cold blood."

There were two reasons he couldn't answer her question. One, if she was like ninety-five percent of the population, she wouldn't believe him, and two, he wouldn't breach Savvy's privacy or endanger her life. It was her story to tell.

"I won't compromise my source," Houston shook his head. "I've figured out who, and part of the why, someone wants you dead but there's still a big gap that you need to fill in for me. I need it all, if I'm to have any chance at all of helping you out of this mess."

Jen cleared her throat as though to speak, but Irene waved her off with a slash of her hand. The gesture irritated the hell out of him, but he would deal with Irene's control over Jen later.

"There is an excellent reason we have not gone to the police with any of this. Lucano is a cancer that has metastasized. His tendrils have spread into every local, state and federal jurisdiction west of the Mississippi, maybe farther. And if you haven't already guessed, I happen to be very short on trust. Just how do you think you can help us out of this?"

Houston considered his answer carefully. Irene wasn't wrong. He couldn't guarantee that, if he started sniffing around, Lucano or one of his dogs wouldn't get wind of it and zero in on the location. But he just might have an ace in the hole.

"I have a place I can hide you where Lucano won't be able to find you," he said. "And there will be no trail for him to follow."

"I thought we had a place In Casper," Jen spoke up, "but he managed to track us down. If you take me back there, we'll be even less safe than we were before."

"I'm not talking about Casper." He held out his hand much as Irene had in the alley. "If you want to try it my way, I'll need my phone back."

He could have taken it back but not without destroying the tiny grain of trust building between them. And getting past the security guards, finding his gun, and getting all three of them out of this place would be nearly impossible.

Irene slid her hand into her pocket, gave him a long look and then, with a frown, walked away. Jen ran after her and grabbed her arm. With voices so low that he couldn't catch the words, the two women argued with hand gestures that spelled out the debate.

He wasn't sure what his next step would be if Irene won the argument. His options were limited; he was in the 'enemy' camp and had a bullet wound in his leg, which was protesting loudly, but the decision had to be theirs, for now. Understandable as Irene's distrust was, they were all in a hell of a tight spot, and it was getting tighter the longer they delayed.

Finally, with a moue of disgust, Irene pulled his phone out of her pocket slapped it into Jen's hand and walked away. Circling the benches at a short distance, like a vulture waiting for an animal to die, she rubbed her hands up and down her arms as though staving off a chill.

Jen brought his phone to him.

"If I've made the wrong decision, three people are going to be dead very soon, and one of them is an innocent child." She slapped the phone into his hand just as it had been slapped into hers.

Houston was pretty sure Lucano would not physically harm his grandson but maybe Jen was speaking metaphorically, because being raised by Ranaldo Lucano would most certainly destroy any chance the kid might have at a normal life.

He didn't take the time to reassure her. He punched in a number. When Travis picked up the call, he said, "Is there an out-of-the-way place near Boise that you can pick up me and three passengers?" ... "I'll find it ..." ... "Yep, I remember ..." ... "Will you see that the cabin is ready and stocked for two weeks?" He listened, then turned to Jen.

"Is this place set up to board us overnight?" Finding a motel could create a problem, plus there was that chance of leaving a paper trail again.

"Of course."

Of course it was. Irene must run her network like an underground railroad. Stops and routes orchestrated like a symphony. He wondered, for a second, if the woman who had Link was another stop on the line and decided she must be.

To Travis, he said, "Call me when you're in-bound. We'll meet you there." He shoved his phone back into his own pocket and turned the wheelchair toward the house. Jen walked along beside him.

"We will leave tomorrow morning to pick up your son." He kept his voice low and his back turned toward the camera. "When Travis calls, we'll meet him at the landing site."

Irene was likely following them in, but he couldn't be certain, and didn't want to turn to look. The woman had been running the show for so long that it was almost impossible for her to cede the control to someone else; to a stranger.

He had to bring her around, somehow. They were adrift on a dark and dangerous sea, and as long as Irene was hanging onto the edge of this flimsy 'life raft' he was cobbling together, she could, very easily, dump them all in the drink. Short of handing her back his phone, he wasn't sure how he was going earn her trust. And she had to trust him if he was to have any chance of pulling this off.

He stopped and waited for Irene to catch up.

"Irene," he drew her attention when she walked up beside them, "Will they let you drive the van to Boise tomorrow?"

"We can take my car," she challenged.

"They were watching the house in Casper and your movements before they tried to kill Jen. They have to know what you've been driving. I don't think they will recognize the van. And, unless they spot one of us, we should be able to get out of town before they can find us."

She considered for a moment, then nodded. "Abbil can arrange it, and to have it picked up and brought back."

"Leave Jen's motorcycle here. We won't be able to take it with us."

"Caleb might appreciate it." she said, and punched in her numbers on the door keypad. She opened and held it so he could crank the wheelchair through. "I'll talk to Abbil about the van."

"You might ask her about some Tylenol, too." Houston winced as a vicious pain sliced through his thigh and started nausea churning again.

"You can ask her yourself," Irene growled. "She will want to check on your leg anyway."

The hall seemed longer than it had been. And, maybe, just a little bit less firm, rising and falling in unsteady rhythm. He steered the wheelchair carefully over the tiles as they swam beneath him.

"I'll check with Karen about rooms for us." Jen said. "Do you know where I can find her?"

"Just down that short hallway and to the left," Irene pointed. "She'll be starting supper in the main kitchen."

Jen headed off that direction.

They had more than one kitchen here? Houston had to wonder how many people passed through this place on any given week. Or, maybe one was for staff and the other one for people on the run from whatever terror followed them.

"I'll wait in the dining room." Houston rolled cautiously down the hall that refused to hold still.

"We might as well stop at Abbil's office," Irene advised. "She will want to check out her work. You can ask her about pain meds while she does that."

Abbil ushered them right in. Back on the exam table, Houston was divested, once more, of his pants and given a white sheet to cover the necessities while the doctor checked the bandages for any bleeding. He supposed he should be grateful that there wasn't any need to remove the wrappings.

"The next few days will be critical," she said, handing him back the pants. "I've given you a tetanus shot and flushed the wound thoroughly, but you need to watch for any signs of infection. Normally, I would monitor it myself, but I don't think you will be here that long."

Was that intuition talking or did she know something he didn't? Certainly Caleb and Karen hadn't been happy to see him. They all seemed ready to boot him out at the first opportunity.

When the doctor handed him two plastic bottles of pain meds, one containing two Oxycontin and the other a dozen Tylenol/hydrocodone tablets, and opened the door for him, Irene was nowhere to be seen. He wheeled himself back to the dining room and parked beside a table. The room was unnaturally silent. He didn't like silent rooms. They always made him feel like someone was watching. Which, of course, they were. The fine hairs on his neck rose to attention and he rubbed his hand over his head to calm them.

He'd just about made up his mind to go in search of Jen when she came around the corner. She sat down next to him.

"We have places to sleep tonight."

Wondering how much sleep he would actually get, he asked the question uppermost in his mind. "Do they monitor the private rooms, too?"

"No," she shook her head.

Relief eased some of the tension that had settled between his shoulder blades. Maybe he would finally get some sleep.

"Irene took me to Abbil then disappeared. Do you know where she went?"

"She went back out to the fire pit to make a call." She looked toward the island behind which Karen had dropped the crockery. "If you're hungry, I can probably find something to eat. Otherwise, supper will be in about two hours."

Still fighting back the occasional bouts of dizziness and nausea, he decided food wasn't high on his list of necessities at the moment. "I can wait," he said. "But I would like to see the room."

"Of course. I'll show you where it is." She stood and left him to follow her down a different hallway.

Stopping in front of one door, she pushed it open to reveal a small but tidy room that had been decorated with comfort and peace in mind. She stepped aside to let him enter. A single bed and a nightstand took up one corner and a padded wing chair in a muted floral design, sat in another with a small writing table next to it. One window, laced with security wire, looked out onto an expanse of lawn. A print of a shepherd with a staff, guarding a flock of sheep while an angel watched benignly from above, hung on the wall opposite the bed. A door, a few feet from the nightstand, opened to a small bathroom.

"Irene's room is next door, and I'm right across the hall," she told him. "The doors have security locks and chains. People coming from abusive situations find it comforting."

It was easy to see that a battered woman might find rest here. If he had his gun, he would rest a lot easier, but that was a subject that he needed to deal with when they were on the road tomorrow. He checked the time and the battery on his phone. Unless there was a USB port in the van, he would need his recharging cable before he went to sleep tonight. Or, maybe not. There was one where they were headed. He set the alarm for two hours.

"I plan to rest until supper," he said.

"Do you need help getting into bed?" Jen asked, her spine stiffening, as he saw the memory of the night before playing out behind her eyes. She looked away.

God, had it only been last night that she'd asked him to make love to her? It seemed much longer. And, that quickly, the restraints were back up between them. She definitely didn't want to be anywhere near him and a bed, but she would help him if he asked.

"No," he rasped. Why did the thought of her and a bed instantly fill his mouth with raw oats? He cleared his throat. "I can manage," he said.

He saw relief wash over her, and without another word, she backed out and pulled the door shut. The lock clicked, and he was alone.

Fuck! He thought, rolling his chair to the side of the bed and levering himself onto the mattress. Why had he ever thought that winning her over would be easy? He couldn't have made it any harder for himself, if he had laid out the plan of failure like a battle campaign. And thinking of hard, he felt the erection press against the surgical scrubs. Just, FUCK!

Knowing that the Oxycontin would put him out, he instead took two of the Tylenol, swallowing them dry. Hopefully, once Travis had them in the air tomorrow, he would have a chance to relax and re-calibrate. And he would definitely feel better when he had his gun back. He laid back, fading in and out of a doze, and waited for the Tylenol to work.

Although still groggy from lack of sleep, he came instantly awake when his phone-alarm sounded beside him. He shut it off, and cursing the lack of his crutches and his lack of foresight at not hanging onto them, he managed to hobble his way to the bathroom and take care of needs. He washed his hands and face, and not having a comb handy, ran his hands through his hair. If it got much longer, he would have to start wearing a head band, or braiding it. He frowned into the mirror. At least his Arapaho blood made daily shaving a non-issue, but it couldn't erase the lines of fatigue and worry from his face.

Despite the pain pills, his leg still protested loudly whenever he put weight on it, but he managed to make it back to the wheelchair, raise the leg rest and lift his leg onto it. He was headed for the door when a knock sounded.

"Houston?" Jen's voice followed the knock. "Are you awake?"

Reaching for the door handle, he released the lock and pulled it open.

"They're serving dinner," she said.

"I was just headed that way." He maneuvered the chair through the doorway and let the door shut. As she walked along beside him, he asked, "Have they agreed to loan us the van?"

"Yes," she said, "And Caleb is now the happy recipient of my bike. He plans to ride it over to Boise and haul it back when he picks up the van."

"Neither the bike nor Irene's car should be seen on the streets here for a week or two," Houston warned. "Both could be recognized and bring Lucano's goons back here. I'm pretty sure that's not something they'd want."

"No, they wouldn't, but the bike isn't all that distinctive. Without us riding it, it shouldn't attract any undue attention."

She might be right, he conceded. Still, it bothered him.

Whatever they were cooking smelled really good as they neared the dining room. His mouth started watering. Or maybe it was just that long forgotten McDonald's breakfast from this morning that made the food smell like ambrosia. What a hellishly long day this had been.

He was just trying to decide how to go about getting his food from the serving line to the table, when Irene set a divided metal serving tray on the table in front of him. A big piece of chicken-fried steak, mashed potatoes, green beans with bacon steamed fragrantly and a scoop of some kind of fruit and cake dessert filled the last pocket. Irene put a napkin full of silverware beside it, and Houston nodded his thanks.

He picked up the napkin, and had begun to unroll the utensils when he realized that everyone else at the tables sat, hands in laps, while the last couple of people, Karen and another, carried their plates to the table and took their seats at the head of the table near the kitchen door. So, they didn't eat until everyone was seated?

When they settled into their chairs, he reached for his napkin, then saw everyone bow their heads for grace. Dutifully, he released the napkin and did the same. Karen began blessing the food, the servers, the workers, the recipients, and finally, God.

With the fading echoes of the last 'Amen', he freed his cutlery and began to eat.

CHAPTER TWENTY THREE

Houston managed to stay awake for a while after supper, amid chatter about things he knew nothing of, but he soon bid Jen and Irene goodnight and wheeled back to his room. He was exhausted and in pain. Martyrdom was not a quality he particularly aspired to, so he took one of the Oxycontin and climbed under the covers.

If the two women had enough common sense to see that he was offering them the best option they were going to get, then they would be here in the morning, but if Jen took off while he was asleep, he would follow and find her. It wouldn't be as clean as his original plan, and it would undoubtedly leave a trail that Lucano's minions would eventually pick up, but one way or another, he would find her.

Once the Oxy grabbed his pain, exhaustion took over and he slept.

Sleep didn't come quite that easily for Jen. If she had made the wrong decision when she convinced a very reluctant Irene to agree to Houston's suggestion, then she would be solely responsible for their deaths. And yet, she trusted Houston. With *her* life, anyway, but her life wasn't the only one involved. Not that he had any tender feelings for her anymore. She'd managed to destroy those when she'd run away and then without warning had thrown herself, shamelessly, at him. But he was an honorable man and a straight-up cop. She placed a whole lot of faith in the belief that betrayal was not in his makeup. Still, there was that little niggle of doubt that held her from sleep. The very oath he swore by could crater her plans and endanger everyone she loved.

She knew he was arranging for his brother to pick them up and whisk them away to some secret spot. So secret that he wouldn't even give them details while they were under this roof. Surely, he would be more forthcoming when they got on the road tomorrow. But the fear that everything that could go wrong, would go wrong, was making sleep impossible.

She wondered if Houston was lying in his bed sleepless, as well, but there was no way in hell she would knock on his door to find out. She'd blown that option to smithereens last night when she'd begged him to make love to her. Correction, have sex with her. Right after which, she'd promised him that it didn't have to mean anything. When in fact it would have meant everything to her.

She had no tears left, and with a dry sob, she rolled over and beat the hard pillow into a less hard pillow. She closed the lids over her dry, itchy eyes, and tried, once again, to find sleep.

Houston had no idea whether it was the return of pain in his leg or the anxiety of their situation that had caused him to wake up at three in the morning, but he was most certainly wide awake. Although he still had that last Oxy, he decided he could manage the pain well enough with the Tylenol. His thoughts, though, were more problematic. Why hadn't he thought to ask whether this facility had a regular route schedule that they followed with the van? Did they have a backup vehicle, other than Irene's car, to make pickups and deliveries? He hadn't seen one. Would a change in their schedule trigger questions? These were the questions he hadn't thought to ask in the midst of the pain and the pain-killing drugs. They needed answers before he and the women left.

Perhaps the pain and the meds had blurred his thought processes, but it didn't excuse putting the people here in jeopardy. He had to speak to Irene. She was the one who had broached his request to Abbil and Caleb.

It was less that an hour from here to Boise so he hadn't planned to leave really early, to give everyone, especially Jen's son, time to wake up and have breakfast, but this new consideration might require a change of plans.

The thought of waking Irene at this hour was almost as painful as working his leg out of the bed and over the side, but he managed to get into the wheelchair without mishap. As quietly as possible, he rolled down the hall and tapped on her door.

She opened the door as though she'd been standing on the other side waiting for someone. Her frown said it wasn't him.

"We need to talk," he said, softly. She stepped back to let him enter and closed the door.

"What is so important at this time of the morning?" she growled.

He laid out his concerns. When she confirmed what he'd suspected, that the van was the facility's only mode of transportation, his plans took a nosedive.

"Why not have Caleb drive us, in the van, to Boise?" Irene suggested.

"We still need something to transport us to the pickup point when I get the call." Houston pointed out. "And I don't want anyone from here, or anywhere in Boise, to know where we meet Travis. The more people who know where we take off from, the more chances there are for information leaks to pop up. And more chances for people to wind up dead for nothing but helping us out."

Since she ran her own network on a similar basis, Irene understood that, all too well. She considered for a few minutes as she circled the room.

"How did you plan to get the van from the pickup point back to the safe house?" she asked, as she passed him, without even pausing her circuit.

"The owners of the property that Travis occasionally uses, an older man and his wife, will wait until after we leave and one will drive the van back to the address we designate, the other one will follow in their own car. Caleb can pick it up there."

There was just one minor drawback to the plan though. Whichever one of them drove the van to Boise took the chance of being recognized by any of the mob who might be looking for them.

"Is there a possibility of finding a cowboy hat here?" He asked.

"Why?" Irene stopped near the door.

"If I drive, a hat will cover my head and put most of my face in shadow."

"I'll see what I can find." she said, reaching for the door handle. "What time are we leaving?"

"After breakfast, whenever that is served."

"Breakfast is at six."

Two more hours of sleep, he thought, although he didn't really expect to get any more sleep tonight. "Then seven," he nodded and spun toward the door. "Now, I'm going to get my pack from the van and see if I can find what Abbil did with my boots. I don't intend to arrive in Boise in surgical scrubs."

"It's not wise to wander the halls between lights out and five a.m." Irene shook her head. "It makes too many people nervous. I'll ask Caleb to collect your things and put them in your room before we leave."

He wasn't planning on 'wandering', but she had a point. Although it wasn't obvious, he suspected most of the security were armed. He returned to his room and closed the door. He looked at the shower longingly but the dressings needed to be kept dry and he didn't have anything to cover them with, so he did a thorough sponge bath at the sink, took two Tylenol and stretched out on the bed once more.

CHAPTER TWENTY FOUR

With breakfast behind him, Houston was prepared to return to his room and his gear, but Abbil insisted on checking his wound one last time. On the exam table again, he only winced a couple of times while she examined the sutures.

"Good. I see no sign of infection. But keep it clean and don't do any power lifting for a while." She gave him that crooked smile as she applied antibiotic gel and put a new dressing on it. "It's still going to be tender but it should heal without any problem." She handed him a clean pair of scrubs and with her back to him, stripped off her latex gloves and tossed them in a waste can.

"Irene said you were leaving this morning," she said, "so I'll wish you a safe trip."

"Thanks. I appreciate all you've done for me." He chuckled, "It would have been sort of awkward explaining this at the hospital." He eased off the table and pulled the pants over his hips and tied them at his waist. "I think I can get by without the wheelchair, but if I could have those crutches back again, I'll leave them in the van for Caleb."

"Of course," she left the room for a minute, and came back with the crutches.

"Thanks again," he left through the door she held open and moved down the hall to his room.

The gear carrier sat at the end of the bed. His boots, cleaned and polished to a blinding shine, sat along side. He lifted the carrier to the bed and dug through his things to find clean shorts and socks, a t-shirt, his last pair of jeans and another shirt. There was no sign of Jen's things. There was also no sign of a cowboy hat, or any hat at all. Maybe it was in the van. Irene must still have his gun too, he decided, after digging a little deeper and not finding it.

He repacked his much diminished bundle of clothes and buckled the straps. He was just debating how to haul the carrier and handle the crutches, too, when a tap sounded at the door.

"It's me," Jen's voice seemed wary, uncertain.

He opened the door. She stood in the hall, wearing different jeans and shirt than she'd had on at breakfast, with her few remaining pieces of clothing draped over one arm. She saw the closed gear hauler and hesitated.

"I was going to put my things in that," she pointed.

"Go right ahead," he backed up and motioned her in, letting the door close behind her.

She stiffened at the click but started folding her things with brisk efficiency and stuffing them into the carrier while he watched silently. Shit, he hated the silence that now seemed an integral part of their communication. He had to break through that barrier she drew around herself every time they found themselves alone.

"What's Abbil's story?" he asked.

His question must have startled her because she looked at him, confused, as though her mind had been elsewhere.

"Irene said that she was born into a very wealthy family in Baghdad but her father was too progressive for the politics at the time. He wanted his daughters – she had a sister – to be allowed to get a good education so, when she was six, he moved the family to London. Abbil turned out to be very gifted, academically – in fact, brilliant – and she went to medical school at the University of Oxford. She graduated in the top two percent of her class, then went on to train at Harvard. She met a fellow Iraqi med student there, who shared her passion for medicine, and they fell in love, but he wanted to return to his country and help his people.

"She decided to go with him. The ultra conservative religious factions there, don't like smart, educated women. Especially when, in their spare time, they try to start more progressive educational opportunities for young girls." Jen paused to check a pair of her jeans. If they were the ones she'd been wearing yesterday, they'd been laundered. He saw no traces of the blood he'd smeared on her.

"Some of the more critical zealots," she continued, "broke into their home and attacked her, beat her and left her for dead, then threw acid on her. When her husband tried to defend her, they killed him.

"But she managed to survive. And with the aid of some of her co-workers and friends, she made her way back to Britain. They put her back together and helped her heal, but there was a contract out on her, and she didn't feel safe there. Eventually, she came here. Now, she treats battered women and children and helps them heal before she sends them on their way."

Jen had all her things in the pack and was now refastening the straps.

She faced him for the first time since she'd started the story. "Do you have everything packed?" When he nodded, she added, "I can carry this to the van, if you want. It will be awkward to handle with crutches."

"I would appreciate it," he offered her a smile.

She shouldered the carrier and stepped to the door.

His hope that she would return his smile died as he fell into step beside her. "Is she safe here?"

"As safe as she'll ever be, anywhere."

They passed through the dining room, which was now spotlessly cleaned, and out the kitchen door, into the garage where Irene waited for them. In a hijab.

"I'm driving," she said. "You two will ride in back."

Oh, hell no, Houston thought, taken aback. "Have you ever trained in defensive driving?" He challenged her. Her jaw set into a mulish frown. "Well, I have."

Irene swelled up, indignantly. "I've been transporting hunted people for forty plus years," and I haven't lost a single one."

"I'd hate for Jen to be your first." He barked. "Doesn't anyone here have a cowboy hat? A baseball cap? Any type of head covering?"

There was that smirky smile again, the one he didn't trust any more than her gun.

"I could probably find a Poke bonnet somewhere, if you don't mind waiting."

"It's a good idea." Jen inserted herself into the argument before it could escalate further. "Abbil uses the van sometimes. No one would question seeing her behind the wheel."

Realizing he was unlikely to win this dispute, Houston caved to the inevitable. Irene knew where she was going and he didn't. It made sense, but he still wasn't pleased to lose control of the situation. Again.

"Fine. But, before we leave this garage, I want my weapon back." He stalked to the back of the van. With crutches, his 'stalk' was probably less impressive than it could have been. Jen beat him there and was tossing the pack in the back end when he took the crutches out from under his arms and set them along one side.

He sat on the bed and eased his wounded leg up over the bumper, followed by the rest of him. Since the back end of the van was not carpeted, it made sliding into position much easier, and he slid up behind the driver's seat where a carpet covered tool box was bolted to the floor. There was another one directly opposite him. He stuck his hand between the seats.

"Hand over my gun," he growled.

"It's in the tool box under you."

He growled again as he maneuvered his body back to the floor and lifted the lid. The gun, wrapped in a clean shop rag, was sitting on top. The magazine, wrapped in a separate shop rag, lay beside it. He snapped it into place.

"Adjust the side passenger mirror so that I can see the traffic behind us," he said.

"As the driver, I need both mirrors to navigate traffic," Irene glared at him. "If you haven't noticed, there are no windows out the back."

"Precisely why I need to be able to watch the vehicles behind us." Their eyes met in the center rear view mirror, which was totally useless for the purpose, and the hard stares turned into a brief standoff.

Irene must have decided that, having won the driving debate, she would concede the mirror. She began adjusting it at his directions. Apparently the inside rear view had a purpose after all, because she adjusted it so that she could see him, and Jen, who had set down on the other tool box.

Houston closed his eyes and pressed his head back against a shelf built into the side of the van. It was going to be a long drive.

When they hit the interstate, headed northwest, he opened them again and watched the mirror. If Irene hadn't been within ear-shot, Houston might have offered Jen that apology, but he would find time when they got to the cabin. He would make time. With nothing else to chat about, it was a silent ride.

CHAPTER TWENTY FIVE

Hawk looked around his new office with a glow of pride. It wasn't large, by any means, but there was an adjoining suite that he had his eye on for future expansion. Although it might have been better for Savvy to have a separate reception area, this space worked for them right now.

He watched Savvy at her desk. A glass-topped half-wall divided the small office into two work areas, his desk on one side, hers on the other. She was immersed in organizing the filing cabinets, labeling and inserting folders, making all in her new space neatly tidy. The work seemed to satisfy her on some level he couldn't understand. He needed action. Not that he was idle, but searching for information on the computer was not what he'd hoped to be doing all the time. Even though his current search, into a certain Professor Charles Bickstauffer, was turning up needed background, it was still 'sitting'.

They'd placed the ads for Hawkeye Investigations, online and in the paper, less than a week ago, but the phone remained stubbornly silent. Understanding that the ads in the paper would only trigger limited coverage and the online ads, although they would reach farther afield, would not produce immediate results, he still wished the phone would ring.

Savvy and the girls, her sister Bryn and their friend Lacey Billings, had decorated the office, and although he'd had his doubts, they'd done a fantastic job of it. His desk and the two green leather chairs facing him across it, had been a used furniture find, as was Savvy's desk. All the pieces were in excellent shape and gave the office a professional look. The file cabinet where Savvy worked and the chairs behind their desks were new. It had been mandatory that Savvy's chair be as ergonomically comfortable as possible because of the scarring on her back, but that seemed to bother her less and less. The hurting place on her chest had now superseded any discomfort she might feel in her back.

It wasn't difficult to tell she was still bothered by the nightmare, although she said she didn't let it worry her. Every once in a while, unconsciously, she would rub the place between her breasts where the nightmare bullet had entered her chest.

That night had scared the hell out of him. Not as much as it had terrified her, but she had recovered faster than he had. Of course, she'd been dealing with her strange nightmares for most of her life. He supposed that she'd developed coping skills that helped her recover faster.

His current coping method was to not let her out of his sight if he could help it. For the last twenty-four hours he'd followed her around like a shark on a blood trail. Her boss, Harvey, was okay with him being there, at Vulcan's Forge. Harvey, was one of the few people who knew what Savvy went through when she had one of her nightmares, and he understood Hawk's protectiveness.

Hawk sensed Savvy wasn't happy about his coping method, but she didn't object openly; she seemed to understand how much he needed to be able to just see and touch her occasionally, to assure himself that she was okay. Hopefully, he could learn to give her a little more space, in time.

Fed up with the inactivity, he forwarded the office phone to his cell phone, stood up and walked to where she had her head bent over a file drawer.

"Let's go get something to eat."

She looked up at him. "I just got here."

In truth, she hadn't been all that engrossed with setting up the files. It was the kind of work she did by rote anymore. What had been occupying her mind for the last few days, was Jen Bradley. Where was she? Was she safe? Who wanted her dead? Where were Irene and the boy? Were they together or had they felt it necessary to split up? And the big question, why did seeing all that chaos and destruction in her home suddenly convince Jen that her sister was dead? And who was her sister?

And why had Houston disappeared? He'd told his Captain, when he left on annual leave, that he was going hunting with his brother and maybe do some fishing with his dad, a retired sheriff, on the reservation near Lander. She was pretty sure Captain Bricker had doubts about that.

Savvy knew for a fact that Houston planned to track Jen down and bring her back. Had he found her? They certainly weren't back yet. If he had been in contact with Hawk, she would have known.

Unconsciously, she placed her hand over the spot on her chest.

"We had breakfast at six this morning and it's almost two. I'm hungry," Hawk said. "Since you didn't have anything to eat at the shop, we need to refuel."

She wasn't all that hungry but Hawk's metabolism seemed to burn through calories like setting a match to gunpowder. She thought about ordering something in but she knew he was frustrated by the lack of action on the new business and probably just needed conversation. Which she, busy with the files and her own dark thoughts, wasn't providing. Yes, she could eat a salad with him.

"Where?"

"I know you'll just order a salad, so I'll take you to Olive Garden. You can eat all the salad you want. How about that?"

"How can I refuse an offer like that?" She smiled, offered him her hand, and he pulled her up from her chair, placing a quick kiss on her lips as he did so.

BREAKING APART A BREAD stick, Savvy listened to the noise around them while she and Hawk discussed ways to boost sales. Vulcan Forge's IT guy, Eldon, had set up the Hawkeye Investigation computer system but he wasn't into marketing. Online marketing was now *de rigueur* for anyone looking to build a business.

Savvy had broached the subject of expanding their reach by creating a web page and placing ads that would reach a wider audience, but Hawk wasn't sold on that yet. He said, 'that kind of takes the private out of private detective,' doesn't it?' And he had a point, but word of mouth only went so far.

The server had just brought their food to the table, soup and salad for Savvy and lasagna for Hawk, when a group of four entered. Recognition sparked Hawk's eyes but there was no smile.

Savvy had to turn slightly to see who it was. She didn't know any of them but an eerie sensation started creeping over her skin. A shiver shook her and she turned away. Under the table, she rubbed her hands over the goose bumps that had risen on her forearms.

The hostess led the two couples, to the other side of the room and the moment passed. Hawk smiled at her and returned to his food.

"Do you know them?" she asked.

"I've seen the one guy, the ginger-haired one, hanging with a cop named Jerry, in Houston's department, but no, I don't really know him. I met Jerry at a barbecue that Captain Bricker hosted last summer. He's sort of a jerk, and he seems to get worse when that guy over there comes around the station. Maybe I'm just reading too much into such a brief connection." He shrugged.

And, maybe he wasn't, she thought, returning to her soup. The flavor had gone out of her food but she put a smile on her face and pushed her soup and salad around with her utensils. Something unpleasant had touched her when those four walked in the door. Or, maybe, it was the dregs of that nightmare, followed by the fleeting look in Hawk's eyes when the four had walked in, that were causing a similar reaction in her.

She had long suspected that Hawk's denial of any psychic abilities was a rationalist's rejection of a true clairvoyance. Just little things she'd noticed that he thought nothing of. Like when she'd walked into the kitchen one day, preoccupied, and forgotten why she'd walked in there in the first place and he opened a drawer and handed her a pair of scissors before she even said a word. They were what she'd forgotten she needed. When questioned about it, he simply brushed it off as 'knowing her very well'. Maybe it was, but it didn't explain similar instances with complete strangers.

"Do you want to take that back to the office?" Hawk nodded at her half-eaten food as he pushed aside his empty plate.

She shook her head. "No, we don't have any way to keep the salad cold or the soup hot." She slid her purse strap over her shoulder as he opened his wallet for his credit card. "I need to powder my nose," she said, scooting out of the booth. "I'll just be a minute."

As she walked away, Hawk made a mental note to check into a mini-fridge and a microwave for the office.

Savvy checked her teeth for any food residue and washed her hands before returning to the dining room. As she rounded the corner, the man Hawk had noticed a while ago was just leaving the table where Hawk waited for her. He passed inches from her as he was returning to his own foursome. He smiled at her. It was an ordinary smile, nothing evil or menacing, but that same eerie feeling raced over her body. She had to lock her knees to remain upright and hoped her response didn't give her away.

"What did Jerry's friend want?" she whispered when Hawk stood at her approach.

"I'll tell you on the way back to the office."

In the truck, he continued, "Chuck, that's his name, claimed that Jerry wanted to locate some paperwork that Houston was working on before he went on leave. I told him that Captain Bricker would have access to any paperwork, but he said Jerry told him it wasn't police related. He was hoping I might know how to find him."

"And what did you say?"

"Just what Houston told us to say," he responded, "he's gone to do some fishing with our dad and he didn't specify where."

"And?"

"And, no, I wouldn't call him to find out."

Hawk's words eased a fine tension that had been building in her since 'Chuck's' group had entered the restaurant. Or maybe it was the distance the truck was putting between her and 'Chuck'.

IRENE WHEELED THE VAN through a gate that carried a sign denoting the building behind the fence as a surgical and medical supply house. Rather blatant, Houston thought.

"Medical supplies?" he questioned. "Doesn't that bring out a lot of unwanted scrutiny and greedy drug runners?"

"Not unless a shortage of gauze, sponges and splints suddenly hits the U.S." Irene said, as she rolled down the drive and moved around the building toward twin loading docks. "There are no drugs here. We make sure all the locals are aware of that."

Beyond the loading docks, one garage door on a four-bay garage began to open. Irene aimed for it.

Across from him, Jen's eyes glowed with anticipation. Her son was here. He wished he could share her excitement but he wouldn't rest easy until Travis had them in the air.

A middle-aged woman stood in the shadows at the back of the garage, one arm around a black-haired boy Houston deduced was Jen's son. Jen climbed out of the van quickly and was greeted with an excited squeal as the boy barreled into her arms.

"Mom, Mom," he shouted. "I was getting worried you wouldn't find us." He jumped up and down. "Aunt Irene said we were on a 'venture and we left clues for you. And you found us!"

The woman at the door came forward at a slower pace, nodding toward Irene, who was just leaving her driver's seat.

"Well, of course I found you ..." Jen said, and smoothed his hair back. At that point Link noticed Houston coming out of the van on his crutches and blinked.

"Who's that?" His eyes rounded.

"Ah ..." Jen hesitated, "This is Lieutenant Whitehawk, Link. He's part of the adventure. He's going to help us."

The boy, still clinging tightly to his mom's leg, looked at Houston doubtfully. "How?"

Both Jen and Irene opened their mouths to answer Link but Houston over-rode whatever explanation they were concocting. "I'm going to teach you all survival skills."

Link's eyes brightened. "Are you a scout leader?"

Houston grinned. "Even better, I'm an Indian."

"Really?!" Link looked impressed.

"Really."

"Why don't you come in the house and have something to drink while we wait?" the woman invited.

"Thanks, Betty," Irene said, pulling the hijab off her head and draping it around her neck, "I could use some tea."

Through the door Betty opened, Houston could see a tiny kitchenette crammed into a small space in what appeared to be an office. With the crutches as an excuse, he slowed his steps to look over the garage. Two other vehicles, besides the van, filled two bays; a work truck, that had once been red, with a four by four on the back, and a brown Buick sedan. On the other side of the empty bay was a shop area with tools neatly hung on the walls and a work bench complete with anvil and grinding wheel. A curtained cubbyhole, off to the side, showed a sink that had once been white, and a toilet.

"Can you get in touch with the pilot of the helicopter?" Irene said from behind him.

He hadn't realized she'd lagged back. "Why?" he turned to face her.

"Ask him if he can haul a half-dozen sealed boxes with him when he comes."

"Why," he asked again.

"I have a plan that should work out best for everyone," she said.

Houston frowned. He didn't like people changing plans in the middle of an operation. It automatically created unforeseen problems, but he was willing to listen. "Spell it out," he said

"It will be much simpler if I, dressed as Abbil," she plucked at the folds of cloth she'd just removed, "drive the van to the meeting spot to 'pick up some supplies', we load the boxes into the van while you load Jen and Link into the helicopter, and then I drive the van back here."

"And how will you plan to make it back to the helicopter without causing one heck of a delay?" Houston shook his head at the idiocy of her plan.

"I'm going to drive the van back to Mountain Home and unload the 'medical supplies' we had flown in, then, I'm staying there. You are going to get Jen and Link to safety without me."

Houston mulled it over. It was actually a great plan but it had one major flaw. "Jen will never agree to that."

"Depends on how persuasive you are. Once you're in the air, she will have to listen to reason eventually. My whole life has been devoted to helping women escape the threat of danger, and Jen and her sister have been a main focus since Jen was sixteen. I will do anything to ensure their safety.

And you don't have to fear that I will disclose, to anyone, how they got away."

She would, he knew, if they managed to find her and get her into Lucano's hands alive. When they saw death at the door, they always talked.

"No, absolutely not. You're not dumping this in my lap." Houston shook his head. "I need to have her full cooperation in order for this to work. If we take off without you, she'll think it was deliberate, on my part. She will question everything I tell her to do, read 'lie' into every word out of my mouth. She will grab Link at the first opportunity and find a way to get back here." His dark eyes darkened even more, as he stared into hers. "You know that. And it could get us all killed."

Irene turned away from him and digested his reasoning for a long time. "Why does it matter to you, what she thinks of you?" she said, over her shoulder.

"I just told you why."

"Do you care for her?" she asked. "You must, or you would have taken her straight back to Casper when you caught up with her in Cody. Instead, you came along on her search for me and Link. Why was that?"

"Because I wasn't willing to try to beat the truth out of her. Because I already knew she was entangled with the Lucano mob, and if word got out that she was in custody, I would not be able to guarantee her safety. Because she seemed even more terrified of word reaching Lucano that she was in custody, than she was of giving away Link's location." He closed his mouth and took a deep breath. "And all that wouldn't have mattered a damn except, yes, I have feelings for her. As dangerous as it is for me, a sworn officer of the law, to want a woman who's son is the heir apparent to one of the most powerful drug lords in North and South America, I love Jen."

"Does she know?"

"NO!" he glared at her. "And she won't hear it from me until I get this mess straightened out. I can't have feelings screwing up thought processes, hers or mine."

The kitchen door opened and Jen stuck her head through. "Is something wrong out here?"

"No," Irene answered, "I was just showing him where he could use the restroom and wash up," she pointed in the direction of the toilet and sink at the far end of the garage.

Houston stepped around her and headed that direction.

"I will tell her my plan," she whispered as he passed her, and she turned the opposite direction.

CHAPTER TWENTY SIX

When the door closed behind Irene, he called Travis and made his request.

"I was just getting ready to call you and take off," Travis said. "Where do you think I'm going to find surgical supply boxes and get them sealed up?"

"Any boxes will do," Houston said, "and you work with hospitals and rescue organizations anyway. Surely, some of them have a couple of spare boxes."

"That's going to take some time to round up, dammit. A couple hours delay at the least."

"Just do the best you can," Houston coaxed, and laid out Irene's plan.

"Fine," Travis agreed grudgingly. "One thing you may not know," he added, "Crockett is home on leave and he's staying at the cabin."

"No, I didn't know that." Houston was surprised at first but maybe that could work in his favor, he thought. "For how long?"

"He flew into Lander about the same time we were looking for Jen," Travis explained. "He wanted to use the cabin to decompress for a few days before he dove back into the family routines."

Houston had listened to Hawk through many a session after he'd cashed out and come home. The term, 'decompress' could mean working through several different levels of strain and stress. Would Crockett be willing to go along with the plan or would the appearance of three extra people at the cabin cause conflict? He would have to find out.

"I'll give him a call."

"He told everyone he was shutting off his phone until he was ready to come back."

Well that was just great. Houston grimaced. Imagine Crockett's surprise when three people drop in, unannounced! He said as much.

Travis grinned so big Houston heard it through the phone, "No need to worry, Houston, I can raise him on the base radio."

With Travis on board, he used the toilet and the sink before returning to the kitchen door. The smell of coffee seemed like heaven to him, when he crutched into the room. Betty set a big mug of it on the small counter tucked into the larger office space. The building was much larger than what he'd seen so far, and he guessed, since there was no sign of Jen, her son or Irene, that there must be living quarters behind at least one of the doors he could see on the far wall.

His leg had begun to throb in the van before they had even entered Boise, and now he could see the swelling through his pant leg, so he dug the bottle of Tylenol out of his pocket and swallowed two with his first drink from the mug. He finished off that one and began on another before he asked if there was a place he could stretch out until the pain meds kicked in.

He'd been right about the living quarters as their hostess showed him through one of the doors to a long couch in a study/den and brought him a pillow and a blanket. He thanked her. He wasn't the least bit sleepy, but he needed to elevate his leg for a while. Get the swelling down before they left to meet up with Travis.

Even with the door shut, the occasional burst of childish laughter filtered through and he picked up the sound of cartoons on the TV. Once in a while, he caught the sound of Jen's voice too. The kid seemed to be taking the situation pretty well, for which he was grateful. As long as he could keep everyone calm, he should be able to put the rest of his plan in motion.

Crockett's presence at the cabin worried him. If his little brother needed time alone to 'decompress', the arrival of three people might be a little too much for comfort. He'd seen enough PTSD in vets in the department and on the street not to question those needs, but somehow, he just couldn't see Crockett anywhere near that edge. Still, he had to admit, the blood tie might be a little too close to see the full picture. And, although he didn't want to intrude on his brother, he didn't have many other options for Jen and Link at the moment. Where on earth could he hide them?

These thoughts kept his mind occupied until Travis called to tell him he had to make a couple of stops to pick up boxes but was departing Rock Springs and was on his way. ETA, approximately three and a half hours. It was now after noon. They had plenty of time to get lunch and get to the helipad to meet him. He sat up and reached for the crutches. Jen was standing on the other side when he opened the door.

"I heard your phone," her soft words didn't carry to the rest of the room. "Was that Travis?"

He nodded. "About three and a half hours. We have plenty of time to send for a pizza and get to the rendezvous point."

"Betty has a casserole in the oven. She said there's plenty for everyone."

"That works."

It was an excellent casserole. Betty glowed with pride when Houston asked for the recipe and she wrote it down while they ate.

Immediately after lunch was over, Irene pulled Jen into the same room Betty had given Houston and closed the door. The sound of the argument could be heard over the TV and Link watched the door with wide eyes when it got loud. At least Houston knew that Irene was advising Jen of the change of plans.

CHAPTER TWENTY SEVEN

Houston watched Link as they sat in the van, waiting for the helicopter that would take them to the mountains. He was a cute kid and would be a heart breaker in a few years. Just like his father, Houston grimaced, same dark hair, same brown eyes, and those dimples would draw the girls like flies. Jen must have been twenty-eight or nine when she bore Antón's son. By that age, people generally evaluated others on their character and substance rather than physical beauty but looks still played a part in the assessment. Somehow he just couldn't see Jen falling for the son of a drug lord, no matter how good looking, but he was having a hell of a time getting the image out of his head.

Link's eyes gleamed, he bounced often with excitement and kept looking at the sky through the windshield. Houston knew they'd never ridden in a helicopter before and Travis' Bell 206A Jet Ranger would be a novel experience.

Actually, Houston hadn't flown in one either until Travis had come out of the sky with this one, which he'd bought, used, with his share of the inheritance money from their grandparents. It had been a toss up for several years whether or not any of them would see a dime from their mother's wealthy parents who had refused to acknowledge their only child's choice of life partner until after Crockett was born, but they'd finally come around. He would have liked to have known them a little better. Not because of the money but because he could see little bits of both of them in their mother and some in all the brothers. It would have been nice to explore that connection further. He hadn't known them well enough to mourn their loss, but in a sense, he mourned them still, for what they had all missed out on.

The bird was already settled on the landing pad when Irene drove toward it. A gas truck was parked beside the helicopter, the driver already in the refueling process. Travis was talking to him but broke off as Irene stopped.

"Remember what we talked about," Houston cautioned Link who was ready to jump out of the van and run to examine the helicopter, "we have to wait until Irene backs the van up to the door for loading and unloading."

Jen took her son's hand and gave her head a silent shake, reinforcing Houston's words. Even the supply of Spider Man comics and coloring books, apparently Link's favorite super hero, hadn't been enough to temper his excitement about the new ride.

At Travis' direction, Irene turned the van and backed it up to the door that Travis slid open. He jumped down and opened the back doors of the van. And reached back to start handing down boxes to Houston while Irene got Jen and Link buckled into the passenger seats. When Irene, in her habib, moved away to help with the boxes, Jen protested.

"They don't contain anything," Irene said. "Just sit there and we'll be done in a minute or two and I'll go back to Mountain Home with no one the wiser."

"But you won't know how to find us," Link piped up.

"No," Irene grinned and gave him a hug, "But you'll know where to find me when Houston gets everything straightened out, won't you?" She stepped aside to let Houston toss in their gear carrier and Link's small suitcase. He looked wistfully at the crutches before sliding them back in the van as he'd assured Abbil he would.

"Oh, Irene," Jen's voice cracked a bit, "I still think you should come with us."

Irene shifted her hug to Jen, and patted her back. "I think we can trust Houston," she whispered in Jen's ear. "This will work out for the best and I'll see both of you soon." She backed away and slid the last box to the door of the helicopter for Travis to hand to his brother.

With the box in the van, Houston stood at the doors as his brother climbed into the cockpit to start his pre-flight check. He waited for Irene to lock the doors of the van before she moved to the front to take the driver's seat again.

"Drive safe, Abbil," he called after her. She waved out the window and pulled away. When she was out of the range of the rotors, he saw her window go up and he stepped up into the chopper, sliding the door shut behind him. He checked the seat belts of both Jen and Link, and gave the boy a smile and a thumbs up.

"Ready for this ride, Link?" he winked. Link nodded, his face mixed with fear and excitement as though getting on a carnival ride he'd never been on before. Which probably wasn't far from the truth.

When Travis started the engine and the vibration and noise of the rotors made talking difficult, Houston handed both of them headphones and showed them how to adjust them, then he pointed to the barf bag dispenser, located within hands reach of the passenger seats. He had, on more than one occasion, heard this type of bird referred to as the "Vomit Comet".

"We'll get some turbulence over the mountains," he said, and waited for Jen to nod her understanding before he went up front to take his place next to Travis.

He signaled Travis to keep the channel open so they could talk to Jen and Link. If necessary, they could always switch channels so that their conversation was blocked from the passengers, but by keeping the channel open, they could treat this like a guided tour, pointing out places of interest during the three hours or so of flight back to Lander. He kept an eye on the two seated behind, making sure they were handling the flight well, as the helicopter lifted off and made it's way east, back to Wyoming.

He let Travis take over as tour guide. He handled it as though he was born to the job, pointing out the expanse of the Great Salt Lake some distance south, on the right farther on, the majestic peaks of the Teton Range rising through the wispy clouds to the north, and even from this distance, the tall peaks rising in the Wind River Range.

"Is this where we're going to stay?" Link asked as Travis descended into Pocatello to refuel.

"No, Houston said. "We have to stop to gas up."

The boy gazed curiously out the window at the procedure, but they were on the way again, quickly.

As expected, turbulence hit as they crossed the mountains but Jen and Link handled it well.

There would be more mountains before they got to their destination, but passing over the Red Desert, north of Wamsutter, Travis saw a small band of wild horses and dropped lower to let Link and Jen get a look at them. He kept the bird high enough that he didn't spook the horses but Link buzzed with excited questions about the herd, which Houston and Travis tried to answer, to the best of their knowledge.

Turbulence hit them again but Houston felt it with relief. They were close to the cabin. Travis started his descent and soon the cabin and the red X of the landing pad appeared.

"And, here we are, Ladies and Gentlemen," Travis' voice came through the headphones. "Welcome to Shangri-la. Enjoy your visit." He set the helicopter down gently on the X and started shutting down the bird.

The tall form striding toward them from the direction of the house was Crockett. Houston tried to read welcome on his brother's face, but with him squinting against the afternoon sun and the dust blown up by the blades, it was impossible to tell. Well, he would know soon enough, Houston sighed, as he popped his seat belt and removed his headphones.

Jen had already removed their headphones, freed herself from the seat belt and had Link's seat belt clasp in her hands when Houston lifted himself, gingerly, out of the cockpit. When the rotors came to full stop, he opened the door.

"Ready to check out your new digs?" he aimed the question at Link as he watched Jen through the side of his eye. Link nodded eagerly. Jen didn't respond at all. Houston heaved an inward sigh. She was obviously not happy about this situation. He couldn't say he blamed her. If what he was thinking about doing didn't pan out, she would be in even more danger than what she was running from right now.

He helped Jen from the seat, grabbed their gear and Link's bag and followed them out the door.

Crockett stepped forward. It was hard to read his face, whether he was okay with the additional company or if he wished them all to perdition but he would talk to him after he got Jen and link settled for the night. "Good to see you, Bro." he gave his brother a one armed hug. Travis, right behind them, stepped forward and did the same.

"Jen, this is my youngest brother, Crockett," Houston began introductions. "Crockett, meet Jennifer Bradley and her son, Link."

Jen studied Crockett. Tall, good-looking, brown wavy hair (although it was cut to military length now), more slender than the rest of them, and hazel eyes that seemed to change colors effortlessly. He wore faded and much worn jeans, an olive drab t-shirt with an unbuttoned long-sleeved shirt over that. His feet were clad in moccasins, almost as worn as the jeans.

"Nice to meet you," Crockett stuck out his hand to Jen.

It was big and solid, she noted, as he let his palm linger just a second longer before releasing hers. "I hope we aren't intruding," she said.

"There's lots of room here." Crockett said, and held his hand out to Link, who took it solemnly.

"Are you part of the 'venture, too?" he asked. Crockett winked and that seemed to satisfy him.

"This is the cabin?" Jen asked, taking in the sprawling ranch style house with a loft, and the huge veranda that circled the building some two hundred yards away. The tall glass windows on the western face reflected the setting sun in a blinding display.

"Yep," Houston smiled. "My parents built it when I was about twelve years old. We all use it from time to time." Memories of great times helping build this place and the days spent here, washed through his mind like waves on the shores of Bull Lake where they had played and fished as kids. "Come on, let's get you settled," he said, "so I can get off this leg."

Crockett's eyes narrowed at the leg Houston favored. "What happened?" he asked, as the four of them left Travis behind to secure the helicopter and headed into the house.

"Long story," Houston said. "We can swap yarns after supper."

Crockett took the gear hauler and small bag from Houston as they covered the distance to the back deck. The back entrance was through the kitchen but they continued on through to the great room. Jen and Link stopped and looked at the towering windows in awe. The view was pretty spectacular, Houston acknowledged silently, looking around, as with fresh eyes, himself. The family was so accustomed to it that they seldom gave it much thought. He needed to get up here more often.

Crockett had a fire going in the huge river rock fireplace and the house was toasty. It wasn't cold out but the mountain air would chill quickly once the sun dropped behind the peaks.

"Are you in your old room?" Houston asked.

"Yep."

Jen looked at the doors on either side of this big room. "Which room should Link and I take?" she asked.

The four bedrooms the boys had claimed as their own, two on each side of the living space, where the fire place separated the kitchen and bath from the great room, were all identical except for the color of the quilts on the single beds. The only bed big enough for two was the one in the loft, that their parents shared when they came up here.

"I think the loft is the only bed big enough for two," Houston eyed the stairs beside the fireplace with unease. His leg would not thank him, but he reached for the gear to separate his things from Jen's. Once he had them situated, he could tend his leg. Jen had seen the look on Houston's face when he eyed the stairs and she stepped in.

"Let me get our things and I'll take them up stairs," she said, reaching for the gear hauler. "Your leg isn't healed enough to do stairs yet."

Having also noted Houston's grimace at the stairs, Crockett spoke, "I'll help you up the stairs. Just show me what to carry." Picking up Link's small bag, he waited while Jen and Houston sorted the contents of the gear carrier, which had gotten mixed in all the shuffling, into 'his' and 'hers'. Having fewer things now, Houston stuffed Jen's things back in the gear carrier and handed it to Crockett, who smiled at Jen.

"Right this way."

Jen returned his smile.

It was the first real smile Houston had seen on her face since their lunch in West Yellowstone, up in Montana. He watched the sway of that luscious backside as she mounted the stairs and saw his brother admiring it, too. He envied Crockett's view.

Suddenly, the thought of leaving her alone with Crockett, while he took off to set his plan in motion, seemed like a not-so-smart move. He only figured to be gone a couple of days, at the most, though. Surely, even as unsettled and vulnerable as Jen had to be feeling right now, that wasn't enough time for her to fall for his brother. Was it? He needed more time with her, to offer that long overdue apology and get them back on an even keel. The only thing he had going for him, right now, was that she couldn't accuse him of deliberately leaving Irene behind.

He carried his few belongings into his bedroom and threw them on the bed with more force than necessary. He wished it made him feel better. He went back to the couch.

In the loft, Crockett set the bags beside the bed and turned to Jen. "I have to apologize, the only bathroom is the one downstairs. Never understood why Mom and Dad didn't put one up here when they built this place."

"It'll be fine," Jen assured him as she took in the room.

The queen-sized, polished pine four-poster, sitting on a huge Indian patterned rug, dominated the room with matching night tables on either side. A thick crazy-quilt covered the mattress, and a warm-looking throw was draped over the foot board. Lamps atop each night table promised ample light after the sun went down. A six drawer dresser, and a chair on the other edge of the rug, completed the furnishings.

"I'll let you two decide sleeping arrangements," Crockett winked at Link again and started back down, calling over his shoulder. "We'll have an early supper, just soup and sandwiches, so see you down stairs when you're settled."

Houston ground his teeth, whether it was from the pain that lanced through his leg, or because of the jaunty little whistle from Crockett's pursed lips as he danced down the steps, he couldn't say for sure. But his mood was getting worse as the minutes passed.

Travis came in just then and dropped an armload of wood in the log rack. He nodded at Houston. "Everything's secure," he said, as he went into his bedroom. He saw Crockett stepping off the stairs and nodded at him, too, before closing the door.

Crockett sat down on the couch, close enough to his big brother to talk without their voices being overheard upstairs. "So, what's the story?" he asked, pulling a small hunting knife from a scabbard on his belt and testing the blade with his thumb. "Why are you escorting a woman and her son around?"

Succinctly as possible, Houston gave his brother the story. When he finished, Crockett whistled again but the jaunty was missing this time.

"So, the boy is a drug lord's grandson? Whoa. And you think the grandfather plans to kill the mother to get the boy?"

"That's what my intel, and the bullet hole in my leg, gives me. I've got to leave for a day, maybe two, to contact someone I think can help. If you'd prefer not to have company, I'll try to make other arrangements for them but you're stuck with us for tonight."

"I don't mind a little company," Crockett pulled out his knife and opened a drawer on the end table to withdraw a whetstone. He spit on it and began running the knife blade over it in a rhythmic motion. "The only reason I came to the cabin first was because Dad told me Mom was planning a big 'welcome home' powwow for me. I'm not fond of big parties. I had to give her time and a reason to tone it down to a smaller size."

Houston wasn't entirely convinced of Crockett's disclaimer, but he wouldn't challenge him on it. It was enough that he seemed okay with them descending on him like this.

"Seems an awful waste to kill someone as delectable as that." Crockett continued thoughtfully, setting Houston's teeth to grinding again.

"She's very scared and vulnerable right now." Houston growled, "So, hands off, okay?"

Startled by his brother's comeback, Crockett gave him a long look and a grin started to slowly light up his face. "Holy shit, Bro." Crockett said, and punched Houston's shoulder hard enough to take his mind off the leg for a moment. "I was beginning to wonder if it would ever happen for you. Congratulations. Does she share your sentiments?"

"I can't afford to have sentiments." Houston snapped back. "At the moment, she's just a person of interest. Until I can determine who's on her side and who would happily kill her at Lucano's command, I can't get involved. This is the only way I can protect her and her son. And, no, she doesn't share my sentiments, yet, but I'm still telling you, hands off."

"I tell you what. You're going to take off for a couple of days, so I won't make a move until you get back, but then, be prepared to defend your stake, big brother." The grin spread wide and his eyes glistened in full out challenge.

His stake wasn't looking all that strong right now, Houston considered, but if Crockett tried to muscle in on Jen before he had a chance to smooth things out with her, he would take him out, brother or not.

"Is there any food in this place?" Travis came out of his room. "I spent so much time collecting boxes that I didn't have time to eat lunch and I'm starving."

CHAPTER TWENTY EIGHT

In the kitchen a little while later, Crockett and Travis ladled tomato soup into bowls and slapped the last of the grilled cheese sandwiches onto a platter as Jen and Link arrived. "Have a seat," Travis motioned to the only empty chair at the long trestle table, right next to Houston, and handed Houston a knife to cut the sandwiches before putting them on paper plates. An open bag of chips sat on the table as well as a small jar of dill pickles but they went mostly ignored.

Link sat, unusually silent, absorbing the banter between the brothers like a thirsty sponge. And it hit Jen how much he needed this kind of interaction between males. Other than an occasional sleep over with a friend from school, she and Irene had been his world. Guilt poked at her conscience. She didn't know how she could have made it any different but the guilt still poked at her.

"You're awfully quiet, Jen," Houston tapped her wrist and pulled her from her thoughts.

"Sorry," she said. "I think everything has finally caught up with me. Maybe if I can actually get a good night's sleep, I'll be able to function better tomorrow."

She finished her sandwich and soup and sat waiting while Link polished off another one of his own, then she cleared their dishes and crumbs from the table.

"Run upstairs and get your pajamas and toothbrush. I'll show you where to wash up." she told him.

"Aw, Mom," he protested, "it's too early for bed. The sun isn't even down yet."

She knew he was hoping to 'hang with the boys' for a little longer but she could see the tiredness dragging at his eyes. If she could just get him to wind down for a few minutes, she was sure he would be asleep in no time.

The men smiled as they watched Link silently. Probably remembering their own childhood and commiserating with him.

"Is it too early to read that latest Spider Man comic book?" That question was usually sure to get the response she was looking for so it surprised her when he said,

"Yes."

It left her with two options, cave or put the hammer down. Reluctant to embarrass him in front of the men, she offered a compromise "How about you go brush your teeth and put you pajamas on and you can stay up for another half hour?"

"Hour," he negotiated, his eyes pleading like a puppy.

How could she refuse? "Forty-five minutes," She smiled and ruffled his hair.

"Okay." he grinned, satisfied with his win.

As he raced up the stairs, she turned to the men, "If you'll show me where everything goes, I'll wash the dishes while he's occupied."

"I'll take care of them," Travis said. "Go sit down for a few minutes, before Mom duties call again."

She was afraid, if she sat down, that she would be asleep before Link. "I don't mind, really. I need to stay busy."

Houston stood and rolled his shoulders loose. "Let's go out on the veranda, Jen. The sky is spectacular when the stars start coming out, and the mountain air should revive you."

She tried to decipher his tone of voice. He sounded like he was inviting her for a stroll in the park but she knew she'd killed any inclinations he'd had in that direction. In all the time they'd been on this trip, she'd never heard soft words from him, and she had no doubt that he had buried any feelings for her there at that tent in the woods. She was reluctant, almost mortified, to be alone with him, but maybe he had to tell her something that he didn't want his brothers to overhear.

"Let me get my jacket," she said, cautiously.

"There's sure to be one by the door you can use." Taking pains not to limp, he motioned her ahead of him as he moved that direction.

She stopped in the tiny entry and selected a gray sweater that looked warm. Houston took it from her hand and slid it around her shoulders, then opened the door and ushered her through it.

She tied the sleeves across her chest, and said, "Thank you." in what she hoped was a matter of fact way.

He was right about the sky, she thought, moving to the railing. The sun had just set, abruptly, as it did in the mountains. The moon hadn't risen yet, and only one star glittered overhead, but the Wyoming sky was vast, darkening quickly, and she knew there would be millions more stars later. She focused on the sky and tried to ignore that he was behind her.

"Travis will be flying me back to Casper tomorrow," he said after awhile. "I'll be gone for a day or two. You'll be alone up here with just Crockett for company, but he's thinking to go back home soon. If he decides to leave before I get back, will you be okay up here, just the two of you?"

She felt a frisson of fear at the thought of being alone on a mountain with no transportation and no idea where she was. But she'd been assured that they had left no back-trail and that Lucano could never find them. And it would only be for a day or two.

"We'll be fine," she assured him. "Crockett ... all your brothers, seem nice."

"They are all, or were, soldiers. He will keep you and the boy safe. And he knows this mountain top like the back of his hand. If he gives you an order, follow it."

"Okay." she said, lightly and a tad resentfully.

"Is there anything you need? Anything I can pick up for you while I'm in town?" he asked.

Her face grew warm and she knew a blush was reddening her cheeks. She was glad he was behind her and couldn't see it. Gladder still that the chill in the air helped cool it. She would love some of her clothes from the house, but remembering the destruction she'd walked into, she wondered whether they'd be in any condition to wear. She couldn't ask Houston to buy her clothes. What she really needed was some feminine hygiene things, but she couldn't bring herself to ask outright. "I ... I'll make a list."

Silence fell again as she watched a few more stars start to twinkle to life.

"Jen, will you look at me?" His voice was soft, almost a whisper. She didn't move, for a moment.

When she finally turned toward him, he cleared his throat. "I am sorry for causing you any additional anxiety on this trip and I'm really ..."

"Mom!" Link popped through the door, "I'm done!"

"She'll be right in," Houston answered. He waited for the door to close before he put his hands on her shoulders.

Looking deep into her eyes, his dark and warm gaze searching, his voice still soft, "If I make love to a woman, it means something." He brushed a soft kiss over her forehead, then down her temple and to her cheek where he lingered for a long breathless moment.

Her heart pounded, she held her breath, fearing and yet yearning toward the kiss she felt certain was coming, but he lifted his head and squeezed her shoulders, then released, turned, and walked away. She could only gape after him as he strode off the porch. He couldn't have shaken her more if he'd told her she was on fire. It certainly felt like she was. The chill in the air seemed to have warmed considerably.

"Mom?" The call jolted her back to reality.

"I ... I'm coming, Link." he slowly reentered the nighttime house. At the door, she took off the sweater and hung it back on the peg.

"Where's Houston?" Link asked, at her elbow.

"He ... He had to check on something."

"Come on, Mom!" link begged, "Crockett made popcorn!"

Crockett greeted her with a wide smile. Afraid something in her face would broadcast her emotional upheaval, she headed for the loft. "I'll be down in a minute, Link."

Once away from discerning eyes, she dug out her own toothbrush and a comb, and took a couple of slow minutes to get her thundering heart back under control. Once she thought she could face the men without turning red, she went back down, to find the bathroom.

There, she found towels and face cloths folded on shelves beside the shower. She looked at the shower with longing, but just grabbed a face cloth and gave herself a quick sponge bath. It did a great deal to settle her last small jumping nerve, but she could do nothing about the longing Houston's gentle kiss had roused. It hadn't really seemed like a kiss though, she told herself. It was more a continuation of the apology Link had interrupted, ... wasn't it? She squared her shoulders, brushed her teeth, combed her hair, and carried the toothbrush and comb back up to the loft.

She sat on the edge of the bed trying to understand that kiss. He hadn't mentioned her, specifically, when he made that statement, but she was pretty sure he meant her. Didn't he? Was he telling her that he wanted to make love to her? Sometime? Maybe? It had sounded like it, but for the last seventy-two hours anyway, she'd been convinced that he wanted nothing more to do with her, in a romantic sense. She was just part of his job.

Torn between soaring hope and defeated confusion, she put on the best face she could summon and returned to the kitchen. Just thirty more minutes, then it would be time to put Link to bed, and she could finally seek her own peace under the blankets. ... After she made a list.

Laughter and childish giggles came from the kitchen. Link sat at the table where Travis and Crockett were teaching him the game of UNO. Thankfully, she noted, Houston was nowhere to be seen.

"Holy cow, kid," Crockett scowled fiercely, "I was ready to go out and you hit me with a Draw 4 card? I thought you never played this game before."

Link doubled over with laughter. "Look, Mom, I'm learning to play UNO, It's fun."

His joy was infectious and she smiled. "I can see that."

There was a cork board on the wall by the refrigerator with a pencil on a string pinned to it. A notepad was tucked up at the corner of the board. She pealed off the top sheet and quickly wrote down the things she needed, while the game went on. She grinned a little when she pictured Houston shopping for these things. Something she would lay odds he'd never done before in his life. Folding the note, she stuck it in her pocket.

"UNO," Travis shouted to groans and complaints from the other two, as they tallied up points. They were having so much fun.

"Why don't you play with us?" Crockett motioned her over as Travis began shuffling the cards.

She hadn't played since she and Jill were kids, and the sound of their laughter was much too appealing to refuse. She took the seat across from Link that placed her between Travis and Crockett. Not having to fear dropping a Draw-4 card on Link, she dove into the game feet first. In minutes, they were all laughing like idiots.

Houston walked in the back door just as Jen shouted, "UNO!" and smacked down her last card. He looked at her and gave Crockett a dark frown, then continued on into the living area. He stretched out on the couch, head at one end, raised his injured leg onto the other arm, and closed his eyes. The frown remained intact.

Jen looked at the clock on the stove. "Bedtime, Link."

"Aw, Mom!" he beseeched.

"Nope, that was the agreement." she gave him the 'look', and reluctantly, he subsided. "Come on, or I will be too tired to read Spiderman to you." As she stood to follow Link, she turned to Travis and Crockett, "Thanks, guys. That was fun. Good night." They waved in return.

As she passed the couch, she leaned down and pulled the folded note from her pocket and laid it on the coffee table where Houston couldn't miss it.

"Goodnight, Jen. Sweet dreams." His eyes didn't open and the frown didn't leave his face.

She barely managed to mumble a "goodnight" to him around the sudden hiss she trapped in her throat at that husky 'sweet dreams'. She hurried up the stairs, vowing to herself, with every step, that they would talk. Very soon. Just as soon as she she figured out exactly what she planned to say.

Dammit, she was a grown woman, she knew the difference between scratching an itch and making love, but sleep eluded her for a long time as her mind replayed the kiss, and his words out on the veranda, and the warmth of his breath, over and over. Was it a promise or a warning? The feelings those few moments had stirred up pulsed through her like a strong current through a charged wire, touching the most intimate spots in her body.

CHAPTER TWENTY NINE

Travis settled himself into the big chair at the end of the coffee table and leaned forward, elbows on his knees and his jaw on his knuckles.

"You can stop pretending to be asleep, Houston. Jen's gone to bed and I'm not fooled," he said, gently but with firmness.

"I'm not pretending to be anything but in pain," Houston snarled. "What I am doing, is trying to decide if I'm in enough pain to take that last Oxy Abbil gave me, or hold off in case of future need."

"Since you're not asleep and your mind appears to be focused, what's the plan for tomorrow?"

"Tomorrow, at first light, I need you to take me back to my truck." Houston shifted to his side and leveled his gaze at his brother. "And, then, we, unless you need to take off immediately, will drive to Savvy's apartment where I'll invite them to breakfast. I'll buy you breakfast, too, at the Big Cup if you have the time, before I take you back to the bird."

"I thought you were staying out of sight."

"I'm keeping Jen out of sight. I plan to make myself very visible around town for a day or two before I load some gear in my truck and head back to Lander and the reservation to take Dad fishing at some undisclosed spot. No better way that I know of to kill any rumors about me and Jen disappearing at the same time. Wouldn't you agree?" He swung his leg off the couch with great care and sat up. "And, while I'm in town, I'm going to start setting some traps."

"As much as the offer of breakfast warms my heart, I have to decline." Travis shook his head. "There's already wild fires popping up all over and its going to get worse. They're calling search and rescue units to be ready to roll, and I gotta answer. Refuel, check my equipment, make sure Cale Bone Needle isn't tied up elsewhere."

JEN WOKE TO PALE DAWN light and the sound of the helicopter rotors singing to life. She jumped out of bed and ran to look out the only window in the room. She could just see the tail of the bird and the cloud of dust it raised.

She looked over at the bed to see if Link was still sleeping, only to see no sign of him. Panic froze her for a moment. Was Houston taking her son somewhere? Without her? She raced down the stairs, out the back door, and sprinted toward the landing pad. Squinting, half blinded by the dust cloud, she ran like an Olympian.

Half-way there, she looked up and saw Link, his hand in Crockett's, well outside the sweep of the blades, alternately covering his face against the dust and waving at the occupants of the helicopter as it lifted off into the early dawn sky.

Link was here and he was safe. The relief came so fast that it left her giddy. She slid to a halt. Winded from her mad dash, she stood, one hand on a knee, the other covering her eyes and nose as she gasped for air, coughing as she sucked in dirt and debris with it.

As Jen stared at the ground, she became aware that her feet and legs were bare all the way up to her panties, which the long tee-shirt she'd worn to bed barely covered. Bent over like this, the shirt didn't even cover that. She straightened.

And here came Link. And Crockett.

With as much equanimity as she could gather, she gave her shirt a quick tug and greeted them. "I woke up and didn't see you," she frowned down at Link. "I was afraid you might get hurt when I heard the helicopter taking off."

"I just wanted to say goodbye to Houston and Travis." The boy scuffed his toes in the dirt. "I didn't mean to scare you, honest!"

"Well, you did. Please don't take off like that again without telling me, okay?"

She turned a glare on Crockett, who stood back a few feet. Of course, he wasn't entirely to blame, but she didn't like that appreciative little gleam in his eyes as he watched, either. Reminded again of her lack of concealment, she took Link's hand and turned toward the house. "Let me get dressed, and we'll have some breakfast."

Crockett was right behind them when they entered the kitchen. "I'll start breakfast in a minute," he said. "It should be ready in thirty. Come on, Link. You can help me with breakfast." The two turned toward the kitchen. Jen headed for the loft.

The rocks and gravel she'd flown over, and didn't feel, in her worry for Link, had now made themselves known on the return to the cabin. She sat on the bed and lifted her feet. There were several skinned places, a couple of small cuts, and red marks that might turn to bruises by tomorrow, but they seemed to be otherwise in okay condition. She brushed off a couple of tiny stones that had made places for themselves in the sensitive spot just ahead of her heel. She found a small first-aid kit in the gear hauler, with a tiny foil packet of ointment and a couple of bandaids. She treated the two larger cuts and pulled on a clean pair of socks.

She felt less exposed after she had jeans and a sweatshirt on over the t-shirt, and went gingerly back down stairs to retrieve her boots. On the couch to put on the boots, she listened to Crockett explain to Link how to turn over an egg without breaking the yolk.

Her feet were sensitive and the boots felt snug, but she got them on and laced up before going into the kitchen to help with the meal.

"How would you two like to go on a picnic up the mountain today?" Crockett asked, as he set a plate of toast on the table. "There's a place where you can see for hundreds of miles." Crockett stretched out one leg and reached in his pocket to pull out a Swiss Army knife, a relatively small one. He handed it to Link. "On the way, I'll show you how to mark a trail."

"Awesome." Link crowed, his eyes going round as he examined the knife and opened the largest blade.

"How about you, Mom?" Crockett looked at her.

She thought of her feet. They were tender. Too tender for the run, which she'd considered and rejected yesterday when her feet were uninjured, but she decided that it might be a good idea to get the lay of the land. A hike sounded doable, and she'd be able to orient herself, just in case.

"Awesome," she smiled, to hide her unease.

SAVVY OPENED HER DOOR to Houston. "You are up pretty early."

"So are you," he smiled and she grinned in return.

"Coffee is on. Help yourself while I get dressed. You did mention buying breakfast, didn't you?"

"I did."

Savvy walked off as Hawk walked in. "This must be important, if you're buying!" he said, and led the way into the kitchen. "What's up?"

Comfortable here in Savvy's apartment, Houston opened a cupboard, took down three cups, sat them on the table, and reached for the coffee pot.

"Let's wait for Savvy. Because what I'm going to tell you can't go beyond these walls. That includes Lacey and Bryn," he said, pouring coffee into the cups.

Hawk had no problem waiting for Savvy to hear Houston's news, but Savvy already knew Hawk's own news, so he told his brother about meeting Chuck.

"Savvy and I went to lunch the day after I sent you that sketch, and you remember that cop at the station, Jerry? And his friend, Chuck?" At the dip of his brother's head, Hawk continued, "Well, while we were there, Chuck came into the restaurant with three other people, but as we were about to leave, he came over to our table to ask where you were, and when I told him I didn't know, he asked for your phone number. He claimed Jerry needed to talk to you about some papers the two of you were working on before you left."

Houston's eyebrows lifted with interest.

"Yeah, that's what I thought, too." Hawk continued. "I suggested that he have Jerry talk to Captain Bricker because he would know whatever you might have been working on before you left. Then Chuck said that it wasn't official police business."

"That's interesting," Houston responded.

When Savvy sat down at the table a few minutes later, the topic was fishing for walleye pike at Glendo Reservoir. "You want coffee?" Hawk asked her.

"I'll wait for breakfast." She turned to Houston. "So, what is the reason for this early meeting?"

"As I told Hawk, nothing we talk about here can be discussed with anyone else, even Lacey and Bryn. Are you okay with that?"

"Of course." Savvy had learned early to keep secrets and hold them in her heart.

"Good. Can you make me a copy of the write up on that nightmare? The one about Benny?"

"I have one," she bobbed her head. "I'll go get it."

In less than a minute, she returned with a small sheaf of papers.

"You remember that FBI agent, Special Agent James McCutcheon?" he asked as he spread the pages over the table and took pictures of them with his phone. Click, click.

She searched her memory, back to the dark days in the hospital. "Sort of. Not really." She shook her head. "The dark headed one? He kept asking the same questions over and over, and then he left."

"Yeah, that would be him." Houston confirmed. Click, click. "He called me a few times after I shot Bass. I got to know him a little." Click, click. "I think I can trust him."

He handed back her papers. "I'm going to see if I can enlist his help in bringing down a drug lord."

"And what if he refuses?" Savvy asked.

There was always that possibility, Houston knew. "Since I don't have the resources the FBI does, I'll have to try elsewhere. I hope I'm not wrong about him. One way or another though, Lucano will not get his hands on Jen's son."

Nods of solidarity came from Savvy and Hawk.

Cups drained, they headed for the door, but Houston stopped Savvy. "Could I ask you to do one thing for me?"

"What?" His whisper, secretive, almost sly, made her cautious.

"Do some shopping, just a few things?" he pulled Jen's list from his pocket.

Savvy read it over and grinned at Houston's sudden embarrassment. "Sure," she said. "How soon do you want them?"

Relieved, he bent down and kissed her forehead. "I'll pick them up before I leave town. It depends on how soon I can meet with our Agent McCutcheon." He offered her his arm, gallantly, and said, with some feeling, "Thanks. I wasn't sure how I was going to carry that off, being a bachelor. Sure as hell, someone I knew would see me and get curious who I was buying them for."

THE CABIN, WHICH JEN had thought was on top of a mountain, she now realized was not. The hike took them higher. Much higher. By the time they came to a halt the air and the trees had both gotten thinner and more stunted. Crockett led them out onto a promontory and she caught her breath, as she took in the vista laid out before them.

The mountains, and ridges beyond, rolled away west, in waves to the horizon. The fierce high mountain sunlight caused the navy, the greens and the golds of the hills to appear like a mirage painted with watercolors as far as the eye could see. A long and narrow lake in the canyon below shimmered in its own shades of blue. Even Link had stopped his kinetic activity to stare at the view in silent wonder.

"That's Bull Lake. Long time ago, they dammed up Bull Creek and there it is." Crockett pointed. Us kids used to fish down there every summer when we'd come up to the cabin.

"Used to?" Jen questioned.

"We still do, sometimes, when we come up, but we don't often get a chance to get together like when we were growing up. We used to have a path beaten to the edge of the lake and our favorite fishing spot but it has grown over quite a bit. It's still there, the path, just a little harder to find." A wistful note edged his words. "It's a bit of a hike down to the water," the wistfulness left his voice and he grinned at her,"and the hike back up to the cabin is a lot longer than it used to be."

Jen wondered what he considered 'a bit of a hike', she smiled at the thought, as she looked around. She wasn't sure how high they had climbed, but they were almost to the tree line. From here on up, the trees began giving way to patchy grass dotted with small scrub bushes and large boulders that climbed over the dips and cuts above them.

"What's that mountain over there?" she pointed to the northwest.

"That's Gannett Peak," he said, "highest point in the state. About thirteen thousand feet."

No wonder it was hard to breathe. Jen sucked in air.

He dropped the back pack at the base of a twisted, tenacious pine. "This is my favorite spot to stop," he said.

She could see why. Even the Lucanos seemed very far away, in this place. Gratefully, she took a seat under another short tree, close to the back pack and eased the pressure on her feet, which had grown more tender as they hiked. She wished she had her sneakers, or some moccasins like Crockett wore.

Link had started exploring the area. Crockett called him in to eat.

As he handed out sandwiches and water bottles, he told tales about growing up in the mountains. Some of them were hair-raising to Jen. But Link, round eyed, laughed at the antics of Crockett and his brothers and inhaled them faster than the food.

They cleaned up the area after lunch, loading the plastic and wrappers into a sack which went into the backpack once again. That done, Jen resumed her seat against the tree and let the warmth and the view soak into her soul, and wondered when Houston might return.

"Is it okay if I go look around, Mom?" Link pulled out his pocket knife to make a mark on a tree.

It was on the tip of her tongue to persuade him to sit and rest. They were, after all, on the edge of a sharp drop off, a long way down to the lake. And she was enjoying being off her feet. The thought of following him to make sure he didn't come to harm, didn't appeal in the slightest, but Crockett spoke before she could.

"Why don't we explore some of the mountain together, Link?" he said. "If your mom doesn't mind." His eyebrow rose in question.

"I guess it's okay," she nodded, "as long as Crockett is going with you. I'm just going to sit here and enjoy the view. Try not to fall off the mountain," she called after them.

Settling back against the tree, Jen looked out at the endless horizon and took a deep breath. The vista made her feel very insignificant and far away from the rest of the world. Even thoughts of Lucano seemed to fade into the distance. She let her mind drift and the peace of the moment engulfed her.

A harsh scream brought Jen out of the near doze and to her feet in one move. Heart in her throat, she looked around the area and saw nothing. No Link and no Crockett.

"Link!" she shouted. The mountains and valleys threw her voice back to her. "Link?!!" Her word rose on a tide of panic and once again, the mountains answered. Where were they? She moved in the direction the two had gone. She opened her mouth to shout but a hard knot had squeezed her throat shut. She swallowed hard and tried again. "Link?!"

"We're right here, Jen." With a rustle of low scrub branches, Crockett's head appeared out of a thicket followed immediately by Link.

They were both grinning, and they were both whole as far as she could tell. The adrenaline drained from her brain so fast that it left her weak. She leaned against the tree beside the backpack, and slid slowly to the ground. Shaking, arms wrapped tight around her knees to keep her body from falling apart, she stared at them.

"I heard a scream," she said, hoarsely. "I thought someone was hurt."

"It was an eagle, Mom." Link's eyes glowed with excitement. "There's a tree down below, and the eagles had a nest. We were watching them."

"The one guarding the nest thought we were a bit too close and warned us away," Crockett added. "I'm sorry it scared you." He came over to where she sat and spoke much more softly. "Are you okay?"

It took some effort to stop the trembling but she finally managed. "I will be, in a minute," she nodded. "I just need to get my legs to hold me up."

Crockett turned back to Link. "Hey, Sport, want to try out your echo before we head back? Your mom's was pretty impressive."

He walked out onto the promontory a ways with Link right behind him, and cupping his hand around his mouth, shouted something Jen thought must be Arapaho. They listened to the words die away.

"What did you say?" Link asked.

"I told the mountains and the sky and the sun 'thank you for the beautiful day.'" Crockett said. "Now you say something."

Link thought hard for a moment then cupped his hand as Crockett had and shouted, "Lisa Renee is a dumb GIRL!!"

Even Jen joined in the laughter that this echo caused and the mountains laughed with them.

THE HIKE BACK DOWN to the cabin actually took longer than the climb up, as Link painstakingly followed the trail he'd marked, from tree to agonizing tree. Jen was positive Crockett would have had them there in half the time, but patiently he allowed Link to lead the way, so she didn't object.

By the time she followed the two up the veranda steps, she was limping noticeably. She wasn't aware that Crockett had noticed her limping, but as he held the door for her, he stopped her, cocking an eyebrow.

"Do you have a blister?"

"No, these boots are made for riding motorcycles, not walking. I just need to get them off."

Upstairs, on the edge of the bed, Jen was shocked to see blood stains soaking the sole of one sock when she got her boots off. She peeled off the sock and examined the bottom of her foot. There was more damage than the first examination this morning had indicated. There was one spot, on her left heel, that was currently bleeding, but the rest of the foot was also covered with blood in various stages of decomposition and the whole foot was swollen and tender. Lifting the other leg across her knee, she was glad to see, although there were a couple of blood spots on the sock, the right foot was in better shape than the left.

She needed to get to the bathroom to clean her feet and find some ointment and gauze. How she was to do that without smearing blood across the floor, she wasn't quite sure. Switching the right sock to the left foot, she wadded the bloody sock in her fist, patted herself on the back for the quick fix and headed for the bathroom.

She grabbed a clean wash cloth and set about repairing what damage she could. As she twisted the excess water out of the wash cloth and into the sink full of red, Crockett knocked.

"Are you alright, Jen," he asked through the door. "There's some blood on the floor coming in here."

"Well, darn," she apologized, "I thought I had that taken care of. I'll clean it up as soon as I get my feet tended."

"I'm coming in."

"What? No. I'm fine." she attempted to stop him. "I'll just be a couple more minutes."

He didn't stop, swinging the door open and taking in the problem at a glance. He knelt in front of her, took hold of her ankle and lifted her foot, for closer inspection. "This didn't happen in the boots," he scowled.

"No," she tried to retrieve her foot but he held on. "I skinned a couple of places when I ran outside this morning."

"Why didn't you say something?" his scowl deepened.

"Because it wasn't serious," she was starting to scowl, too.

"Well, it is now," he said angrily, reaching across her, he flipped down the shower seat over the bathtub. "Sit here," he commanded, putting the drain plug in place and turning on the tap. He found a package of Epsom Salts under the sink and dumped a liberal amount in the tub as the water rose.

Link stood at the open bathroom door a worry frown creasing his brow. There wasn't room for him to step inside.

"What's wrong with your feet, Mom?"

"Noth—"

"She cut up her feet when she ran outside this morning," Still angry, Crockett cut off what she'd started to say, "and then she didn't take care of them before we went on that hike."

"Why not?" Both pairs of eyes fixed on her, awaiting her answer.

"They weren't cut, just skinned up a bit." She gave Link a reassuring smile even as she complied with Crockett's order to sit on the shower seat.

"This isn't necessary," she balked. "I just need to wash them and replace a couple of bandaids."

"Didn't you hear what I just said? Look at the swelling," he growled. "This could turn serious, quickly and we're a long way from a hospital."

The voice was a little bit different but the implacable snap of words could have come right from Houston's lips. Reminded of why it might not be in their best interest to be admitted to a hospital, she subsided.

Once Crockett had washed her feet to his satisfaction, he pulled the plug to drain the tub and sent Link to the loft to find a clean pair of socks. He had her feet dried off and some kind of salve from a brown jar in the medicine cabinet applied before Link returned.

She curled her nose at the odor of the opened jar. "What is that stuff?"

"My mom makes this herself, from rendered fat, herbs, and things she gathers," he explained, "I'm not sure what all is in it, but it works like a miracle."

That accomplished, he bandaged her raw soles and handed her the socks Link held out. Then, he helped her out of the tub.

"Now my boots really won't fit," she frowned down at her feet encased in bandages and heavy socks and wondered what she was supposed to wear, instead. She hadn't listed sneakers on the list she'd given Houston but she couldn't have anticipated asking for a larger size, even if she had.

"I need to clean the blood out of your boots anyway," he said, and solved the problem by finding an old pair of moccasins that, although much looser, fit over her bandaged feet easily.

CHAPTER THIRTY

Houston dug the business card out of his wallet and keyed in the number of FBI Agent James McCutcheon. They had only talked, maybe a dozen times, during and after the business with the serial killer and rapist who called himself, "Bass". Once at the prospector's cabin, and then farther up the high ridge where Bass had holed up and where he had held Savvy and a high school girl in chains. Later, two or three times while Savvy was still in the hospital recovering from the wounds inflicted by Bass, and then, a couple of times after that, after Hawk had killed Bass near the cabin.

A mutual respect had developed. When the forensics team closed the investigation of the site, and after what was left of the bodies of the many victims had been recovered, he and McCutcheon exchanged business cards.

Houston liked the man, who seemed to be on the rise in his organization. With a sharp mind, and a code of ethics that rivaled Houston's own, McCutcheon would climb the ladder quickly, he suspected. He fervently prayed that he wasn't mistaken in his assessment of the man's character. If he was wrong, this move could prove disastrous to Jen. But, maybe, what he was about to tell McCutcheon would be the boost the man needed on his climb up the FBI ladder. If he looked at it that way.

Disappointed at the delay when his call went straight to voice mail, he left a short, nebulous message. Waiting never had sat well with Houston, but there nothing else to do. He headed for the police station downtown. Might as well let some people know he was in town.

It was a little quieter than normal, but the blue uniformed bees still buzzed softly. He saw Captain Bricker, caught his eye with a wave.

"Aren't you supposed to be on vacation?" Bricker asked as they turned toward his office.

"I am." Houston nodded. "I came back into town to pick up some stuff from my place before I head out again. Just thought I'd check in and find out if you have anything new on Jen Bradley or the person who shot at her?"

"I was about to ask you the same thing," Bricker looked over the top of his glasses at his Lieutenant.

"I'm off the case, remember?"

"I've never known you to be 'off the case', even if you were off the case. You're still working it over, aren't you? Got any insights?"

Houston grinned. "Nope. I thought I'd buy you a cup of coffee, though, if you have the time."

They made the short drive to the Big Cup and talked about the gallbladder surgery for the Captain's wife, Cheri, and how that went. The Captain said his oldest kid had qualified for the Hathaway Scholarship, so he was trying to persuade the kid that the University in Laramie was the only way to go, what with the cost of college tuition everywhere else. "Kid wants to go to CSU, out-of-state tuition and all. Can you believe it?" Houston nodded and told the Captain about Crockett being home on leave, and the fishing trip he hoped to make with his dad and his little brother while he was here, and the new fly he wanted to try out.

It wasn't easy to curb his impatience with all that small talk, but the goal was to deflect any latent suspicions that might linger in the Captain's mind about what he might know of Jen Bradley's whereabouts. He hoped it worked.

Houston returned to his apartment. No call, no text from the FBI agent. He didn't think McCutcheon would blow him off, but the waiting was not good for his disposition. It would be better if he kept his distance from people for a while.

From his own years behind the badge, he knew that any number of things could keep a cop from returning a call. Especially if the call had been couched to seem less urgent than it was. He didn't want to set off any alarms by calling again, in case the agent was surrounded by a crowd. So he spent several antsy hours in a state of limbo.

SAVVY WOKE IN THE DARK as Hawk's hands made delicious little forays over her waist and hips, but that wasn't what woke her. The clock said it was just after one in the morning. "I just had the strangest dream," she said, as she rolled over to face him.

"A nightmare?"

"Well, no ... or maybe ..." she paused, and he brushed fingers over her forehead. "it wasn't terrifying like some of them are, but Houston should know about it."

"What was it about?" He was fully awake now.

"I was in Houston's office, going through his desk, looking for something, not sure what exactly but not finding it, whatever it might be. I tried to get into his computer."

Hawk's gut started to crawl.

"Then I put everything back," she continued, "very carefully, and started looking at the pictures he has on the desk and on his shelves. I spotted the picture of you kids holding up those stringers of fish. You know the one," he nodded, "and I looked at it for a couple of minutes. Suddenly, I thought 'that's it'. Then I heard someone coming and I ducked behind the filing cabinets until they passed. It was all very cloak and dagger." she said moving his hand, gently, off a breast. "After they were gone, I slipped out of the office, went down the hall and out of the station."

"And?"

"That was it," she shook her head.

In his mind, Hawk could see the picture Savvy had spotted very clearly. He and his brothers, grinning ear to ear, had just returned from a day of swimming and fishing at Bull Lake, a good distance down the mountain from the cabin. Mom snapped a picture of their catch with Gannett Peak rising in the distance. There was nothing in the picture that indicated where, exactly, the picture had been taken, but could it trigger deeper digging? The place where he had shot Bass had certainly made it into the news, although none mentioned the Whitehawk cabin, where Savvy and her sister and friend had been staying before all hell broke loose. But it would be easy enough to locate a largish acreage near that mountain, filed under the name Whitehawk, if a person was determined enough to dig into land records.

The encounter with Chuck rose in the back of his mind, but Chuck would not have been able to just wander around the police station. Which meant someone, who could access it without raising too much suspicion, had to have been in Houston's office. Jerry? He searched his brain for a last name. Jerry ... Jerry ... Officer Jerry DeFerro! That was it. Was he the one, or maybe someone else involved?

He didn't want to raise that specter to Savvy, who was still dealing with the trauma of her previous nightmare. She, unconsciously he was sure, again had the heel of her hand pressed between her breasts.

"The picture doesn't identify anything," he reassured her, looking at the clock over her shoulder. "We'll let Houston know in the morning."

She nodded and settled into his shoulder.

He put his arm around her and pulled her closer, settling his lips on hers, and he moved her hand, gently, from that spot between her breasts. Distraction frequently worked for the both of them, quite well.

A little bit later, with Savvy thoroughly distracted and once again sound asleep, Hawk eased himself out of bed, picked up his phone, closed the door quietly behind him as he left the bedroom and called Houston.

Houston answered on the first ring, fully alert.

"What?" he almost barked.

Hawk, wondered about that sharpness as he related Savvy's dream. "The property ownership is a matter of public record," he went on. "If whoever was in your office is familiar with this state and happened to recognize Gannett Peak from that old photo, it wouldn't take much digging to get an exact location."

"Yeah," Houston agreed, and sounded not at all relaxed. "Thanks for the update." He clicked off.

Houston dressed quickly and went to his ham radio mobile packet rig in the truck. Crockett had to be warned that company might be on the way.

CHAPTER THIRTY ONE

The squawk of the base radio in the kitchen woke Jen. Not that she'd been deeply asleep; she hadn't had an easy night's sleep since the bullets had shattered her windshield.

In the dark, she heard Crockett moving downstairs and his voice, as he answered the radio but was too far away to make out words. It must be important to rouse someone so early. On tiptoe, she started for the stairs but the call ended before she was halfway down.

She stopped him as he headed back toward his room, shirtless, black sweat pants hanging untied on his hips as though hastily donned.

"Is something wrong?" she couldn't help the worry that crept into her voice.

He glanced up at her. "Just Houston checking if everything was okay up here and letting me know that he was still tied up in town."

"At this time of night?"

"Funny thing about my brother," he shook his head, "if he's awake, he figures everyone else must be too." He waved toward the stairs. "Go on back to bed, Jen. That's what I intend to do."

Crockett went back to his room, closed the door and turned on his cell phone. Checking the battery, he plugged in the charging cable and then set the phone to vibrate, as Houston had instructed. He would wait until Jen slept again and then, take a walk down the road a bit before making another call. That call, to his dad, to let him know that it would be a couple more days before he got home.

IT WAS LATE THE NEXT evening when McCutcheon returned Houston's call and agreed to meet with him at the Old Chicago diner.

"Sorry about taking so long, but I've been in meetings in Denver and just rolled back into town," he apologized as they followed the hostess to a corner table.

"Thanks for agreeing to meet with me ..." he started to say 'Agent McCutcheon', but unsure if the man used his official title outside of work hours, Houston amended it to, "James."

"With such an intriguing teaser, how could I refuse?" McCutcheon said as they took their seats. "I know it's a bit late but I haven't eaten all day. That's why I'm letting you buy me dinner."

Houston, didn't object to a late supper if it meant having McCutcheon's undivided attention. He would have preferred to discuss this in a less crowded place, but since the two had to lean in close to hear each other over the music and the noise around them, it would work.

"Busy day?"

"Unusually so," the agent said. "I hope whatever you're going to tell me will make it worth my time."

The server stopped at their table and introduced himself, set out menus and asked for drink preferences. They both ordered coffee.

Houston lowered his voice. "Since you haven't eaten yet, I'll leave it to you to decide if you want to hear what I have to say before or after you've eaten."

Following the cue, McCutcheon lowered his voice, as well. "Well, since I don't see a briefcase or folder full of papers, I'm going to assume what you have is mostly oral. Let's hear it."

Houston pulled out his phone and scrolled through to the sketch of Ranaldo Lucano. He laid the picture in front of McCutcheon. "I can tell by your eyes that you know who that is."

McCutcheon didn't disagree. "Everyone in the agency knows who that is." The meetings in Denver had been a planning session about this very man. The agency was getting ready to move on some of Lucano's main enterprises, a multi-pronged, multi-agency, take down, but local police couldn't know that. He handed the phone back. "How is the Casper PD involved with him?"

"The Casper PD isn't. This is more a personal quest." Houston said.

"Then how are you, personally, involved with him?" McCutcheon looked over the menu, and making a choice, set it aside.

"I'm sure you are aware of the shooting behind the Big Cup Cafe a few days ago." At McCutcheon's nod, he continued. "And, that the target of that shooting, and her son and the friend who lived with them have disappeared."

"How does that make it FBI business?"

The server approached their table and they paused their discussion to give him their order. When he left, Houston picked up the thread.

"I know the name of the shooter. He was a hired thug. A more expendable one apparently."

"Past tense?"

"Very."

"If he's dead, I can't see that it leads us to The Man."

"The Man," Houston emphasized the word MAN and tapped the sketch, making it disappear, "shot him."

"Him? Personally?" McCutcheon's eyebrows rose sharply.

Houston nodded. They both knew that the big bosses of any criminal organization didn't do their own dirty work. Not when you could hire it done and keep your own hands clean. It would take a shattering provocation to have Lucano pull a trigger.

"How did you come by this information?"

"You remember the Bass Volker case?" Houston knew he did. The case was what had brought them together. "Did you happen to see the pages of paper her friend brought to the police when Savvy first went missing?"

"Yes. And I remember thinking, later on, how creepy it was that her nightmares were so dead accurate about Bass's activities."

Houston scrolled through his phone again and found the pages he'd photographed early this morning. Once more, he handed his phone to the agent. As the agent read, his focus intensified and his face grew grim. He didn't bother to look up when their server set their food in front of them.

After the server left, he asked, "This is from her?"

Houston nodded again.

McCutcheon cut a bite of his steak and stuck it in his mouth, chewing thoughtfully, as the wheels turned in his head. He swallowed before he spoke again. "You realize I would be laughed out of the agency if I brought this in as proof of anything."

"You don't believe this?" Houston leveled a look at the agent and calmly took a big bite out of his patty-melt.

"It doesn't make a damned bit of difference what I believe," McCutcheon shook his head. "It's what I can convince my higher-ups to take seriously." He took another, angrier, bite of his steak, chewed for a bit and swallowed. "Why did you bring this to me? How did you think I could use it?"

"It crossed my mind, if you could find where Benny's body has been dumped, then execute a surprise raid on the Big Boss's main office, I'm sure that's where it occurred, find the gun in his desk and match the ballistics to Benny's corpse," Houston trailed off with a shrug, leaving McCutcheon to mull over his words before adding, "How hard could it be?"

The question drew an unexpected bark of laughter from agent McCutcheon, and he pressed his thumb and index finger to the bridge of his nose.

After a few seconds, Houston lowered his voice again and smiled, "How hard could it be?"

"Is Miss Mills okay?" the agent asked.

"Physically, yes."

"Would she talk to me?"

Houston picked up a napkin and wrote a number on it. "You can ask her, yourself."

As they worked their way through their meal, Houston told him about tracking Jen down, the motorcycle ride through the mountains—leaving out some of the more personal details as unimportant to the story—and about Hawk's call in the wee hours of this morning. He also didn't mention being shot. And he didn't mention where he'd left Irene, just in case he'd made an error in judgment and had to take Jen and Link back to Mountain Home and leave them to Irene's network for safe keeping.

McCutcheon was familiar enough with the official chatter about the shooting at the Travel Center in Idaho that he could fill in much of the blank spaces in Houston's narrative without asking for explanations. There would be time for that at a later, more private location.

"You have the family tucked away some place safe?"

Houston nodded, "I believe so, but if anyone has the patience to dig a little …," he shrugged, and didn't elaborate further.

McCutcheon nodded. There was no need to press. He'd been there before.

"Why didn't Mrs. Bradley come to us with this?"

"She said her sister did. And she, the sister, has been on the run since."

"Did she say who her sister talked to or which office she contacted?"

"No, just that she went to the wrong people."

They finished their meal in contemplative silence and then bid each other goodnight. As McCutcheon left, it occurred to Houston that, except for their initial greeting and their parting, their entire interaction had been carried out in little more than a whisper.

The ball was now in the agent's court. Houston prayed it would be enough to tip the scales in Jen's favor. Waiting went against the grain but that was all he could do at the moment. He picked up the ticket and took it to the cashier.

He'd accomplished his main goal and was now eager to get back to the cabin and his guests. It was too late to start back to the cabin tonight. Leaving this late would mean headlights all the way up to the cabin if anyone was inclined to follow him, which, following Savvy's recent dream, was a distinct possibility, so he returned to his apartment and his bed.

He mulled over the puzzle of Jerry and Chuck, as he checked the fridge. He wasn't hungry, but figured, since he might be gone for several days, he should see if there was anything that needed to be thrown out. He couldn't depend on Hawk to do it. His brother spent most of his time either at Savvy's apartment or at his new office.

The shelves were bare of anything immediately perishable, so he shut the door, made a fresh pot of coffee and turned on the TV. Mostly to keep his mind off Jen. He didn't expect it to be a restful night.

CHAPTER THIRTY TWO

Freddy didn't move. No one in the room moved, they barely even breathed. Not Burko, or Gull, the not too bright gopher who danced attendance on the Boss and was always within calling distance to Lucano. Even he sat frozen in place.

Gull was whispered to be a relative of the BIG guy—distant cousin or nephew, or something – although never a hint of it had passed either man's lips. Freddy suspected that Lucano wasn't eager that any blood of his could be connected with someone with a below average IQ. Freddy wasn't certain if Gull knew the exact connection and just chose to remain silent, but at least he had enough sense not to rock his own boat when he didn't even have an oar. They all waited, in the stillness, to see where the ax would fall.

Ranaldo Lucano, the man standing, hands clasped behind his back, didn't move either, as he stared out the tall windows overlooking the city. A stranger might not see the weapon in Lucano's hands but Freddy knew he held the biggest damned ax in those clenched fists that Freddy had ever seen, and he'd seen the man use it, too. Shooting Benny, in this very room, less than a week ago, hadn't made a blip on Lucano's conscience. Just business as usual.

The Boss didn't usually do his own retribution. Instead he just arranged for someone else to do it. Benny had been a cautionary lesson to those in the room with him; Burko, Dorf and himself.

The whisper was already filtering through the organization that the Big Man had actually shot someone, but speculation was one thing, knowing for a fact was something else entirely. It wasn't a good position to be in, being witness to an actual crime committed by Ranaldo Lucano, and Freddy could feel the noose tightening around his own throat.

Dorf had already disappeared. The Boss didn't seem at all concerned about that, either. Freddy wondered if Burko realized that, as the only other two witnesses to the Boss' crime, their unfortunate demise was a foregone conclusion, even if it hadn't been vocalized yet.

The room was eerily silent, all except the faint wheeze of Gull's mildly asthmatic breaths. You could have heard a pin drop, if anyone had dared drop one, as they waited for the Boss to say something.

Lucano had been standing, just so, for the better part of five minutes, leaving the three men to also stand, and wait. Even Gull, the dull, looked uneasy.

Freddy had positioned himself closest to the door, just in case Lucano opened that desk drawer. Even if that happened, and he managed to get out of the room alive, he doubted he would make it out of the building. It was almost a relief when the Boss turned and scowled at the men.

"People don't just disappear without a trace." he snarled.

Freddy hid the astonishment this statement caused, behind his "Office Mask". The face he put on every time he was called into Lucano's lair. People disappeared without a trace all the time, at Lucano's command. Like Dorf, and one of the guys who had been tailing the woman and the man on the motorcycle in Idaho.

And Latrice, who had missed her shot there at the travel center. She'd capped herself, knowing her failure had also cost the life of her husband, who had also 'disappeared'. Latrice's suicide was still under police investigation but the investigators seemed to be leaning toward the missing husband as the reason for the distraught woman's state of mind.

The question of, "Why?" Why she'd been seen firing at two people speeding away from the travel center, was the only point that had kept them from closing the case, but the motorcycle, and its riders, had also disappeared, leaving behind the possibility that the riders had, somehow, been responsible for the disappearance of the woman's husband, and she had planned to kill them. It was a puzzle that might never be answered. Especially if Lucano could find and silence the two women and the man.

"We turned over every damned rock in the state, Mr. Lucano," Burko was unwise enough to open his mouth, "but we're still digging."

The full force of Ranaldo's wrath turned on Burko. "I don't have TIME to dig up the entire FUCKING state of Idaho," he roared. "I. WANT. MY. HEIR. HERE. I want that evidence in my hands, and I want that bastard that decided to interfere in my affairs, *DEAD*!! Bring the women here." The Boss didn't bother to lower his voice at any point.

Good thing this suite of rooms was sound proofed, Freddy thought.

Gull's asthmatic wheezing intensified to a point that even Ranaldo noticed. It was something he usually ignored, but not today. "Get the hell out of here, Gull, unless you've got something to tell me that I don't already know! I can't stand to listen to your warped lungs."

Envy followed Gull out the door. He wondered if Dorf realized their tenuous hold on life, and that they were, even now, circling the drain. Freddy had already made a contingency plan and it was nearly complete, but only 'nearly'.

Agitation rolling off him in waves, Lucano returned to the window. Freddy wondered if he even saw the city lights spread out below, as he turned his back on the two barely breathing statues still remaining.

"Give me details on the women's escape." the Boss demanded, shrugging his shoulders as though trying to throw off a heavy weight.

For a brief second Freddy pictured himself slamming into the back of the Boss and sending him through that window and down the forty stories to the street below. Too bad the glass was made to withstand a bomb blast.

As though he'd read his mind, Lucano whirled around and Freddy nearly pissed himself.

"Tell me what we know." Lucano strode back to his desk and sat down, toying with the handles on the drawers.

What we know? Freddy was too smart to laugh but it was there in his mind. "We don't know what else Benny might have been able to tell us," he said, and saw Lucano's brows knit together in warning. Jesus! Did he just say that? Maybe he really was too stupid to live. He cleared his throat.

"He told you that he went to the house and searched it but didn't find anything. By the time we got Fritz over there, both women and the kid were gone. Fritz went inside the house to check, see if Benny had overlooked anything, but the toss was pretty thorough. He said someone had been in there after Benny tossed the place, though.

"He went back to his car to watch and see if they returned, but when the woman, the young waitress, came back with another woman, the next morning, the older woman and the boy weren't with them.

"The waitress went inside while the driver stayed in the car, but eventually the driver got out and went in the house too. Then, just three or four minutes later two men showed up. He made one for a cop immediately.

"After a bit, the one he pegged as a cop got in his vehicle and drove off. A few minutes after that, the whole place was crawling with cops. Fritz had to move his car."

"How did they pick up their trail in Yellowstone?" Lucano picked up his stiletto letter opener and cleaned a fingernail.

"Fritz said that Benny told him he saw a woman pull up in front of the house, late one night, on a motorcycle, go in for a couple of minutes then leave again. He said he thought that was interesting, and wondered if there was another person in play that he might have to deal with. So, When she came back out, he followed her for a for a ways and saw her turn down a dead end street and disappear behind one of the houses at the end. Shortly after that, she reappeared, without the bike or helmet. Turns out, it was the waitress, herself. She followed a path that runs behind the house she and the kid lived in, went in the back door. Curious! Benny started checking and found the shed where she hid the bike. He told Fritz the make, model and color."

"So, he saw her get on the bike and take off?"

"No, but the old lady and the kid were gone, along with the car she drove, and the waitress's car was in impound after the shooting, so he was sure that's what she'd done."

Freddy shifted, just a little, from one foot to the other and felt the tingle of returning blood flow. "I drew in a favor from one of the locals and had him check some traffic cams," Freddy said. "He made the bike heading west. Lone rider. Looked female but it was hard to tell. It took some time to locate her again but when he did, she wasn't alone."

"And the trap at the Travel Center?"

"You know it failed."

"I don't know why." Lucano leveled his soulless black stare at Freddy.

Burko, damn his eyes, stood as impassive as an Easter Island stone, but Freddy could almost hear his silent prayers of thanksgiving that it wasn't his tit in the wringer.

"When Toolie pulled in to find out what he could, everybody had different versions, from how many shots were fired to who was doing the shooting. All we know, for sure, is that, by the time the cops got there, Latrice was sitting in her car, gun in her hand with brains splattered all over the car."

"What about her husband?"

"Disappeared," Lucano knew damned well what had happened to her husband, he'd ordered it. That wasn't what he was asking, though. "The police are still trying to track him down."

Burko finally spoke up again. "Me and Turk, we was at opposite ends of the street when we heard the sirens so we headed for the place. Then, the pair on the motorcycle flew past Turk. He called me and he turned around and headed after them but we were too far behind. They must have turned off somewhere." He swallowed hard as Lucano's eyes rolled dangerously. "They just vanished. No sign of them or the bike anywhere."

Lucano turned thoughtful. For a few moments, the only sound that could be heard was the occasional, vicious stab of the letter opener through a stack of papers on the corner of the ink blotter. Having reached some conclusion in his own mind, he spoke to Burko again. "Are you sure the man who was with her on the bike was a cop?"

"Pretty sure, Boss." Burko shifted uneasily. "I'm not sure where they met up, but the day after the women and the kid skipped, Officer Whitehawk took a vacation and disappeared for three or four days, then he came back to town for a couple, I guess, then left again."

"I don't want guesses!" Lucano's frown turned deadly again. He made another vicious stab at the papers. "The woman who brought the woman back to the house," he raised a black eyebrow questioningly, "she has to be connected to Whitehawk. Find her, Freddy," the Boss commanded, "and have her brought here." He paused to think. "No, better yet, take her to the warehouse. Contact me the minute she's on the way." The smile that spread across his lips sent chills down Freddy's spine. "I think I'd like to sit in on that interview until the cop shows up with our missing females, and my grandson."

Dismissed and feeling incredibly fortunate, Freddy hastily withdrew from Lucano's web to set plans in motion. As he went through the door, Lucano's hard and heavy roar followed him.

"Gull! Get in here. I need you to print out this stack of papers again."

On his way out of the building, Freddy wondered at the wisdom of taking the woman to the warehouse, a building with a benign look, on one of the lesser used Los Angeles docks, and registered under the legitimate guise of Bali Wind Imports and Exports LTD, where their cargo shipments were housed, with no more than a seventy-two hour turnaround. There was 'cargo' there now, bound for auction houses in certain ports around the Pacific, but they would probably be gone before he could find the women and the boy.

The place had been "inspected" on numerous occasions, but the Boss's fail-safe system had always given them ample warning of any surprises. The system hadn't failed yet. And yet, Freddy, who had resources of his own, knew there would come a time when it would, and he planned to be as far away as possible from the organization and the site when it did.

First order of business was to find out who the woman was. He waited until he was in the elevator then pulled out his phone and called Casper. The call was answered on the first ring.

"Find out who brought the target back to her house the morning after Benny took the shots. Pick her up and bring her to the warehouse." There was a long pause on the other end. "Did you hear me?"

"Yeah, I heard ya, but she's never alone. Since the morning after Benny took those shots, the dude the other female is shacking up with is on her like a leech. It's like he's attached to her with more than his cock."

"Find a way," Freddy snapped. The doors opened to the underground garage and he walked down the row of cars. "And call me as soon as you have her." He ended the call and pocketed his phone.

Now, they waited. If his contact valued his life, he wouldn't have long to wait.

He hummed tunelessly as he got in his car and pulled out of the garage. Making his way out into the desert landscape, he found a turnout and pulled over. As he exited the car, he took out his phone and called Lucano.

CHAPTER THIRTY THREE

Crockett refused Jen's assistance with meal preparation, almost forced her to take a seat at the table and put as little pressure on her feet as possible for a few hours.

"Here, Link," he set a can of chili in front of the boy, who had hopped up beside Jen, and handed him a can opener, "you can help fix our supper."

That started, he found hot dog buns in the pantry and drew a package of hot dogs from the fridge, opened it, dropped them into a pan of water, and lit the burner underneath. He reached for the chili, from which Jen was just lifting the sharp lid, and dumped it in another pan to heat.

"Voilá," with a grin, he made a grand gesture, "your gourmét meal will be ready shortly."

The hot games of UNO that followed cleanup were a bit more complicated for Jen, as she attempted to hold onto the worst cards until Link slapped down a reverse and she could hit Crockett with them. She knew that Crockett knew what she was doing and why she was doing it. He gave her a frown of disapproval, obviously thinking the kid should learn how to lose but he said nothing. By the end of the first game, she'd tallied up so many points that it was a foregone conclusion she would be the big loser of the night.

The games ended early. The long hike and the excitement of the day and night were beginning to tell on Link. Jen watched as his eyes grew heavy, but he hung on doggedly, unwilling to end the fun.

"Last hand. It's time to get ready for bed," she said.

"Aw, Mom," his protest was pro forma, and he couldn't stifle the yawn that followed.

EARLY THE NEXT MORNING, just as the horizon began to show a glow, Houston loaded his hip boots and tackle in his truck, added a couple of five gallon gas cans, and drove to fill up. That done, he headed to Savvy's apartment to pick up the things he'd asked her to buy and pay her for them.

It wasn't yet five o'clock. Few of the building's occupants were stirring yet.

"Is Savvy up yet?" Houston whispered when the door opened. He knew she hadn't been sleeping well since the latest nightmare.

"I was just getting ready to make myself some ham and eggs. Want some?"

The limp Houston had explained to them two days ago, was still noticeable, Hawk observed, as he followed his brother to the kitchen and coffee.

"None for me," Houston said. "I'll eat something at the cabin."

Hawk placed a griddle on the stove and dug ham and eggs from the fridge. "So you're heading back?"

"I loaded up my fishing gear and now I'm off to visit with Mom and Dad for a couple of days. I'm hoping to persuade Dad to go up on the Miracle Mile and catch some trout. And, if anyone should ask .., ."

"That's what they'll be told." Hawk turned the ham slices as the eggs started to sizzle. "You sure you can't take time to have a bite? It's at least a two-hour drive, more if there's casino traffic."

"I wasn't planning to be in town this long. I just came by to pick up the things I asked Savvy to get for me," He handed Hawk a plate.

Hawk set it beside the griddle where the ham slices were beginning to sizzle "So you met with Agent McCutcheon? What'd he have to say?"

"I gave him Savvy's number. He may call. If he does, I'll know he's planning to act on what I told him. As he said, the chances of using what I told him to get the department to act on it, are slim, but they have a thick file on Lucano and his syndicate, so you never know what might just tip the balance in our favor."

Hawk put the plate on the table and dropped some bread in the toaster, got a jar of jam from the fridge, and set it on the table before sitting down.

"I thought I heard your voice, Houston." Savvy walked into the kitchen, her face paler than usual. It was obvious she hadn't taken time to put on any makeup and the scar on her jaw was angry. "I'm so glad you're here. I had a weird dream last night."

"Hawk told me about it."

She nodded, got down another plate, handed it to Hawk.

"I'll grab those things you bought," Houston motioned toward the sack on the table by the door. "If you need to contact me for any reason, call me or leave a message with Crockett and I'll call you back." He finished his coffee and stood.

Hawk waved a fork at the griddle. "Let me throw one of these on some bread for you," he said. "It's a long drive."

"That I'll take," Houston grinned. The smells permeating the kitchen had finally gotten to him. Houston picked up the two sacks and found the receipt. He dug out some bills from his wallet and gave them to Savvy before collecting his sandwich.

"Thanks," he said and took a bite of ham and egg as he turned, once more, toward the door.

"Do you want me follow you to the cabin?" Hawk's voice drew him around.

Houston took a second to consider, "No, I'll call if the need arises." With that, he picked up the sacks and let himself out of the apartment.

CROCKETT HAD, AGAIN, put on his jacket before sunrise and left the cabin, telling them that he'd seen black bear sign in the area and wanted to check it out. He warned them to stay in the cabin or at least very close to it, while he was away. He hadn't mentioned any such sightings on the hike day before yesterday, making Jen suspicious as to just when he'd made the observation. Especially following so closely on the heals of Houston's call on the radio. The hair on Jen's neck had been standing on end ever since. He had been gone for long stretches for the last thirty hours, had returned to the cabin for brief periods to eat, and had slept only a little.

She'd heard bits and pieces of chatter between Houston and Travis, in the helicopter on the way here, about why Crockett was here, about him wanting to have some alone time to de-stress, but she hadn't seen any sign of mental stress in the man. Was he just that good at covering it up and was now making himself scarce as much as possible to handle his demons? Or – and this suspicion was lodged in her brain like a fish bone – were these sudden absences somehow connected to Lucano?

Whatever the reason for Crockett's long disappearances, it was playing hell with her nerves. Too much time to think and worry was really detrimental to constructive planning.

Link was obviously disappointed with not being invited on these outings but Crockett had said "No", in no uncertain terms, leaving the boy blue-deviled and sullen with no one to take it out on but Jen, who was dealing with her own anxiety. Finding things to keep him occupied, while thoughts of Jill and Irene and, of course, Lucano's pursuit, chewed at her mind, stretched her nerves to the snapping point. And this was only day two. How much longer would Houston be gone, she wondered? How much longer before she would have answers? There was also a strong possibility that, when he did return, he still might not have any answers.

Convinced that Crockett's absences were connected to that middle of the night call from Houston, she'd confronted him, but he stuck to his story. She wasn't buying it. She wanted answers, and Crockett was the only one who could provide answers until she could talk to Houston. Where in the hell was Houston?

The urge to go for a run bubbled through her veins. Her feet – although Crockett had insisted she continue to treat them – were fine. Not even a twinge. Whatever was in that ointment had worked like a charm. But with the possible threat of a black bear close by, she'd refrained from exploring farther than the veranda and the perimeter of the cabin.

She'd dusted and polished every surface in the cabin. She'd done all the dirty laundry she could find. She had cleaned all the windows she could reach and would have gone higher if there's been a ladder. Unable to sit still any longer, she rose from the chair beside the couch.

"Want to help me decide what to have for lunch?" she asked Link. She wasn't hungry but the need to move, to stay busy and focus on something other than the morass of worry that continually dragged at her soul, was imperative.

With an eye roll, he said, "We just had breakfast," then shook his head and returned to the comic book on his lap. It was galling to know that if Crockett, or anyone of the brothers, had asked him the same question, he would have been in the kitchen in a flash.

Okay, it was a bit early. They'd just had pancakes a couple of hours ago, but she went to the pantry to check out the menu options anyway. She couldn't plan on Crockett showing up at mealtime, but it didn't take much to heat a can of soup. As though her thoughts had summoned them, she heard the weathered creak of feet on the veranda steps. Crockett was back, earlier than usual.

Okay, that was fine. She wanted answers and she would get them. Preferably without Link's inquisitive ears tuned in to the conversation. She stepped out the back door.

"Hi," Crockett acknowledged her presence with a cock of his eyebrow as he peeled off his moccasins.

"I'm glad you're back," she said, a frown knitting her brow. "We need to talk."

"About what?" He paused, eyeing her, before moving toward the door.

She blocked his way. Both eyebrows went up.

"I don't want Link to hear us." She motioned him toward one of the two chairs sitting a few feet from the steps and when, with a nod, he headed that way, she followed him.

With a sigh, he said, "You'd better just spit it out."

"Alright. I don't believe this taradiddle about a bear," she scowled at him. "This 'whole taking off at all hours and being gone for hours' started right after that call from Houston."

"Taradiddle?" he laughed. "Where did you dig that up?"

"Would you prefer poppycock or tall tale or, how about straight-out lie?" her blue eyes turned icy but she didn't wait for his answer. "If this involves the drug cartel that's not supposed to know where we are, then I have a right to know what's going on."

Crockett turned his head, staring out into the distance and was quiet for so long that she began to think he wasn't going to answer.

"You're right," he said, finally, "Houston has come into some information that makes him believe someone may be checking into this property. I've been patrolling the road until Houston can get back here. It's the only access, by vehicle, to this cabin."

The fear Jen had managed to hold at bay turned her blood to slush. She thought she'd prepared herself for this very possibility, but at his words, her heart stuttered to a momentary halt before kicking into a panicked palpitation. She clenched her hands together in her lap to hide the trembling that shook her.

"Why didn't you say so from the start," she threw her hands up, bewildered. "We could have just gotten in your vehicle and left."

"And go where, Jen? Where would you be safer?"

She opened her mouth to answer, but there was no answer. He was right. If Lucano's men had managed to find this mountain, they could find them anywhere. They could very well be watching the roads leading to this area.

"How are your feet? Do you feel up to a hike?" he asked.

She didn't bother to hide her surprise at the question. "They're fine. Why are we going on a hike?"

"Let's put on some hiking clothes and grab Link. I'll show you the path down to the lake."

CHAPTER THIRTY FOUR

The path down to the lake, nearly a half mile of it, was just as overgrown as Crockett had said, but it was downhill. They rested for a while at the bottom of the path, listening to the wash of waves on the shore. Crockett pointed out where he'd caught the biggest fish of all time.

"Right there, where the sandbar rises sharp and then drops off into that pool. See that?" he said. "The minnows school around the shallows of the sandbar because the big fish don't like to get in shallow water, but they wait for the minnows to get brave, or careless, and then gobble them up if they get out over the deeper water."

"Like Finding Nemo?" Link asked.

"Yep," Crockett nodded. "Just like that."

"Why didn't we bring a fishing pole?"

"Maybe next time," Crockett responded, putting his hand on Link's shoulder. "I just wanted to show you how to get here. Come on. We're going back up to the cabin and have some lunch. Think you can find the path?"

The walk down had been tough but the hike back up the mountainside was an endurance test. Steep enough in some places to require, at least for Jen, the aid of tree trunks and branches.

Crockett went up it like a mountain goat, and Link, not to be outdone, had followed with the energy of a six-year-old. Jen's 'fine' feet, however, were feeling sharp stress well before they made it to the veranda, and the tough six-year-old Link was ready to collapse by the time he got to the couch.

"You need to go in the bathroom and strip, Link," Crockett said. Check yourself for ticks and leave your clothes on the floor so they can be washed."

"Ticks?" Jen looked herself over.

"We need to do the same," Crockett said as Link went to the bathroom. He waited until the door closed before he continued, "I need to say something while he's busy. I'll leave it up to you to whether, or how much, he needs to know."

"What?!" Alarm bells went off in her head and she sucked in a breath.

"I'll grab a bite with you before I go back to watch the road, but if you hear gunshots while I'm out there, I want you to take your son and go back down to the lake ..." He held up a hand when she opened her mouth to object. "It's just a precaution, I'm not really expecting anything, but I need to know that you two can get away if you have to."

He popped into his room and came back a minute later, handing her a belt with a holster and pistol. "Do you know how to use this?" Stunned, Jen could only nod, but that seemed to be enough for him. "I'm going to leave this under that brown jacket by the back door. If you leave, strap it on and get down the path as quickly and quietly as you can. There are several places you can take cover and watch the path. Don't hesitate to shoot anyone who makes it out of the trees."

"Unless it's you or Houston."

He actually laughed. "Yeah."

WITH A SHARP EYE ON the rear view mirror, Houston headed for the cabin, and Jen. There was no proof that Savvy's dream meant Lucano's men were already on their way to his mountain, but then again, he couldn't take it for granted that they weren't.

His foot wanted to be heavy on the accelerator. It was unlikely he would be tagged with a moving violation, but being stopped would cause an unwelcome delay. He pressed the accelerator up to just over the speed limit and set the cruise control. Remembering Hawk and Savvy's lesson from Bass, he also cast an occasional eye to the sky. Nothing but clouds, so far.

The miles of ancient sea-bottom between Casper and Lander rolled under his wheels as his mind grappled with the dilemma of Jen. She was still the mother of a drug lord's grandson and that made her a major threat to his career. The problem was, he was in love with her. Was he willing to shuck his career and everything it meant to him, to protect her and her son? Be with her? Even though honesty forced him to admit that he had already crossed that bridge, the question and the consequences of that answer rolled around his mind. He passed Moneta, cruised through Shoshoni, regretting for a moment he could no longer stop for a malt at Yellowstone Malt Shop – best malts in the Rocky Mountains, they were, until progress wiped 'em out.

And yet, she didn't seem like the type of person who would jump into a relationship without knowing the other person very well. Of course, it was entirely possible she'd gotten pregnant by Antón Lucano before she knew what he was.

At Riverton, rather than going on to lander, he turned northwest with 20-26. There was also the possibility that she hadn't been a willing participant. Maybe that was why she'd kept all the men at the Big Cup at a distance. Then again, being brutalized and raped could turn someone off of intimacy altogether. She'd certainly held him off for a long time—until the offer at the tent, but that, he reflected, had been more like a plea of desperation.

He passed through Kinnear. Morton, the next town, was so small he didn't notice it. And he had refused her. He grimaced. What must it have cost her to ask? And what had it cost him to deny? That thought twisted his guts into heavy knots. He shifted in the seat as pain stabbed his thigh. It wasn't doing his leg any good either.

Finally, he reached the junction with 287 where it joined 20-26. However it was that she'd gotten involved with them, she was certainly running from the family now. And, for better or worse, he was right in the thick of it.

Slowing early to look for the cabin road on the left, he refocused his mind on driving. It was still a couple of miles to the turnoff that would begin the climb up to the cabin. The weather was good and the roads were clear of any snow. He almost wished they weren't. Vehicle tracks were easy to follow in the snow, especially on private access roads. He turned left, off the highway, and watched the graveled road for recent vehicle tracks other than his own. It didn't look like anything had been up here since he left, but not being on foot, he couldn't be positive. He shrugged, and that eased the tension in his shoulders a little.

CROCKETT'S WARNING had lodged in Jen's brain. Years of being ready to run at a moment's notice had prepared her. After he left the cabin, she'd gone upstairs and repacked the gear hauler with clothes for her and Link, before carrying it downstairs. Link might have wondered what she was doing with it, if he'd been paying attention, but she made it into the mudroom without rousing his interest.

She knew there was portable food in the pantry, apples, oranges, jerky, small bags of chips and bottled water. She collected what she though she could carry and added them to the carrier. Then, she set it against the wall by the back door, beneath the jacket that covered the belt and handgun.

The gun made her uneasy. She knew how to aim and fire one; Irene had insisted she learn, but she'd never actually shot any living thing. People who hunted claimed they would be able to go into a battle and kill their enemies, but she'd heard more than one old veteran say that they'd hesitated the first time they aimed at a human and were only alive because of luck.

The prospect of killing another human being made her stomach roll over. She'd always told herself that she could do it to save Link, but now that the possibility might become fact, she had to wonder, would she freeze just that fraction of a second too long?

Prepared as she could be, she prowled the cabin, unable to settle and too wound up to concentrate on anything but the pack and how fast she could get Link and herself to the path.

THE ROAD ROSE TOWARD the last sharp curve where a rocky embankment hugged the edge of the road. Houston slowed to avoid scraping the side of his truck. He suspected Crockett had already seen him coming, so he wasn't surprised when his brother, rifle slung over his shoulder, stepped out in the road a few yards ahead. He brought the truck to a stop and waited for Crockett to climb in and stand his gun between his knees, before he started forward again.

"Everything calm?" he asked.

"Haven't seen a thing. I'm glad you're back though. Travis called me and said that Mom and Dad are talking about coming up here 'to see what ails me'. I'm going to have to leave for home unless you need me here, but if that's the case, we're going to have more company than you want."

"No," with a shake of his head, Houston vetoed that idea. "It's best if they don't know about Jen's problems."

They were approaching the last slope to the cabin when they heard the scream of a big cat, and it wasn't a mating call. Something had threatened the animal, and it had made it's displeasure known. The cat-scream still reverberated in the air when another, much more chilling sound, rang out. A gunshot.

"Jesus, get to the cabin, now!" Crockett swore.

"That was too far away to come from the cabin," Houston said, even as he floored it and the tires dug in, to fling loose scree behind.

"I know, but Jen was getting extremely nervous about your call yesterday morning and I had to tell her what you'd found out. I showed her and Link the path to the lake and I told her if she heard a gunshot, she was to grab her son and the pistol I left her and get down the trail as fast as she could, then find a place to hide."

Another unearthly scream, this one definitely human, overrode the fading echoes of the gunshot even as more gunshots rang out.

"Go," Crockett repeated his order, and Houston tried hard to find another millimeter of travel in the accelerator.

Less than two minutes later, he skidded to a stop beside Crockett's truck, at the side of the veranda. He pocketed the keys and lept onto the grass.

"Check the cabin," he said, as Crockett jumped out of his side of the cab. "I'm going down the path. She can't have gotten far. You follow me as soon as you check that they're not here. Give me a whistle so I know who's behind me."

The leap out of the truck might have been a bit too hasty. His leg sharply protested the abuse after the long hours of driving, but he reached the edge of the path. He paused to listen for the sound of bodies going through the undergrowth. He heard nothing. They must be moving fast.

And why wouldn't they? Jen knew they were running for their lives and they'd been down this path only hours before, but they couldn't be near the bottom yet. He should be able to catch up before they were out in the open.

Now, moving at almost a jog, he rushed up a small hillock instead of going around. A sharp pain lanced through his thigh and he went down on one knee. He sucked in a breath as his vision blurred for an instant. He blinked to clear it. Looking at the spot where his leg throbbed, he saw blood seeping through his jeans. He'd ripped stitches. Swearing through gritted teeth, he stood. Ripped stitches or not, he had to get to Jen and her son before they moved beyond the cover of the shrubs. He hobbled as fast as he could.

A faint bird trill reached his ears and he breathed a sigh of relief. Crockett was on his way. He answered the call but he couldn't let it slow him down, there wasn't time.

A faint crackle of branches ahead and below caught his ear. Jen was close. He still had to get close enough that she could hear him without raising his voice.

It didn't take long. Within a few yards, he caught a flash of her head just at it dropped behind a tall greasewood bush.

CHAPTER THIRTY FIVE

Jen heard something behind her and spun around to look back up the path. Shoving Link behind a large rock, she motioned him to stay down, and she hunkered down as well, while she stared up the hillside, trying to penetrate the shrubs that blocked her view. She pulled the pistol from the holster and released the safety, pointing it up the path they'd just descended. Determination steadied the faint trembling of her grip.

"Jen?" the word came softly.

The familiar voice made her knees wobble in relief. She lowered the gun, her chin quivering as Houston's head came into view and he stepped around the bush.

"Houston!" Link was delighted, not bothering nor thinking to modulate his voice.

Houston stepped down, level with them, and held out his arms, wrapping them around them and the gear hauler.

"Oh God, Houston," Jen whispered, as she buried her face in his shoulder. "I heard a scream and a gunshot, and Crockett told me, if I heard one, to get down the path and hide. And then I heard another blood-curdling scream and more shots."

"I know," he felt her arms slide around his waist and he touched the top of her head with his lips. "That's why I came after you."

"Did you fire the shots? What were you shooting at?"

"We didn't," he said. "I think someone may have crossed paths with a mountain lion."

"So we're going back to the cabin?"

"Yep, just as soon as I can depend on my leg again."

Reminded of where she was, Jen stepped out of Houston's arms.

Reluctantly, He let her go. Those few moments, in which she'd clung to him, had boosted his hopes that he hadn't managed to destroy her feelings altogether. He didn't fool himself that they were over the hump yet, but he could work with that little bit. And if she saw him as salvation for the moment, he could work with that too.

For the first time, she noticed the blood staining his jeans. "Houston," Jen's short gasp drew his attention, "your leg is bleeding."

"I'll take care of it as soon as we get back to the cabin, Jen. Don't worry about it."

There was a rustle behind them and Crockett slid around the boulder they crouched behind. "There's a couple of men headed toward the lake," he said. "It looks like they were up toward the cut. One is injured. He's bleeding heavily. The other one is helping him."

"The cat?"

Crockett shrugged one shoulder. "No mistaking that scream, but they either killed it or scared it off."

"Jen," Houston murmured, "that big spike of granite you passed a ways back up the slope, can you get Link up there and find a spot to get behind it?"

"What are you going to do?" she hissed.

"Maybe nothing. It depends on what our friends decide to do. Crockett and I are going down a bit farther where we can get a better look. If they leave, then we'll come back to get you. If they don't, then we'll deal with them."

Jen didn't like the way he said 'deal with them'. It made nasty little chills dance over her skin. She would have to make sure that Link was positioned so that he couldn't see his idols 'deal with them', but she nodded and pushed her son up the hill ahead of her.

"Stay out of sight," Houston added. "If you can see them, they can see you."

The men waited until Jen and the boy were out of sight before they made their way to the bottom of the path. Once there, they had a good view of the approaching men and of their vehicle by the lake, an older model dark-colored Jeep with a grill guard, basking in the sun like a turtle on the beach.

"Just what is your plan?" Crockett whispered. "Do you think these guys could be some of Lucano's men?"

"It's possible, but my current plan is to not have to explain dead bodies on the reservation if I can help it." Houston scowled. "I'm hoping they'll decide to fall back and regroup. Whichever way it goes, the cabin is no longer safe. I'll have to find somewhere else to hide them. You'll need to leave, too. It wouldn't be any easier for you to explain dead bodies up here, especially if you were one of them."

That drew a black grin from Crockett. "Has it occurred to you that Lucano hasn't sent a professional hit man? I think an experienced sniper could have taken you out in Idaho. And, if these two were trying to get to you and Jen by way of the cut, I don't think they were prepared for the terrain. They would need climbing gear and I didn't see anything like that. Unless they left it behind."

Houston nodded agreement. "He probably thought two women would be easy to take care of, but if these two can't get it done, I'm sure he'll pull in the big guns."

They separated, but stayed within sight of each other as they found cover and watched. They didn't have to wait long. Just as they picked up the voices of the men, two more vehicles drove up to the lake, farther down the shoreline. Not real close, but close enough that they might get curious if they saw someone helping an injured man into a car. Houston recognized the recent arrivals as friends from the reservation. Probably just here to do some fishing. He let out a tense breath.

The duo might not be the most professional hit men, but they had to know that Lucano wouldn't pat them on the back if they started shooting up the locals, he thought. They might get away with one or two bodies, but not car loads.

The pair reached the Jeep, and with the injured man stuffed into the back seat, the other one stepped into the driver's seat, and the Jeep was soon rolling out of sight.

"Looks like we're not going to have a shoot out after all," Crockett said, rising from his spot when the car disappeared down the road. "Maybe we should arrange for our uninvited friends to be pulled over for questioning. It shouldn't be hard to spot that Jeep. They would have a heck of a time explaining the injuries." He handed the automatic to his brother, took back his rifle and headed for the lake.

"Where are you going?" Houston demanded.

"I'm going to say 'Hi' to Clark and his family, see if they will help me look for that big cat, make sure it's dead. The last thing we need is a wounded mountain lion wandering the area." Crockett tossed over his shoulder as he made his way toward the newcomers. "I'll meet you back up top in a while."

Houston's wound sent fresh spears of pain straight to his brain, and he grimaced at the thought of the climb to the cabin. "Later," he nodded at his brother's back and started back up.

Link made the climb easily. Jen seemed to handle it as well, even with the gear hauler, without too much problem, but Houston was sweating through his shirt by the time they reached the cabin clearing. He congratulated himself on making it, as he stood beside her, both of them sucking air into their starved lungs.

Link spotted a friendly ground squirrel on a felled log, near the porch, that was frequently used as a sitting bench. It chattered at him, and he moved closer to watch the little critter. Houston turned to Jen, "Start packing your things. As soon as Crockett gets back, we're leaving."

"To where?" she asked, with a note of defeat in her voice.

"Crockett will be going down to stay with the folks. For us, I'm not really sure," he admitted. "If those men we just saw were sent by Lucano, it's pretty obvious they weren't familiar with the topography here, but you can be sure, the next one he sends will be. I'm flying by the seat of my pants until I can figure out our next steps."

"Alright," she said. Houston opened the back door and Jen called to Link, "Come in the house, Link."

"Okay, Mom."

While Jen climbed to the loft, Houston found some clean sweats and headed for the bathroom to take care of his leg, from which the blood now trickled freely. He thought longingly of the Oxy pill in his pocket but he knew he couldn't take it and drive down the mountain. He took a pair of the acetaminophen/hydro pills instead and set about his task.

"DID YOU FIND THE MOUNTAIN lion?" Houston asked, when Crockett returned some time later.

"I did. She was badly wounded but she managed to drag herself quite a distance before she died. There was still meat and blood on her claws so she got one of them really good before she got away."

"They will be seeking medical, but not on the reservation. Not if they're smart. Still, you should alert the hospital and clinics in Riverton and Lander."

"Already did. And Clark and his brother-in-law said they would take care of the cat," Crockett added.

"PIG, I'VE GOT TO GET to a doctor," Colley moaned from the back seat. "That friggin' cat tore me up bad. Just call Chuck. He's waiting for us in Shoshoni. He'll know what to do."

Pig had seen the shredded arm and the deep furrows across Colley's belly and he knew it was bad.

"We can't go to any fucking doctor!" Pig snarled. "And we don't have time to drive all the way back to Shoshoni. Just find something back there to tie down that flap of skin on your belly and as soon as I find a place to pull over where we won't be seen, I'll see if there's something in here to stop the bleeding."

"Pig, it ain't a flap of skin, it's all the way to my insides and it won't stop bleeding. I ... I'm holding them in as best I can but I'm getting light-headed. I really need a doctor."

"Dammit, Colley, you know if you go to the ER or any medical place, they'll want explanations about where and how you crossed a mountain lion, and we can't tell 'em. Besides, if they heard those gunshots at that house, they could decide to run again, and if they take off, it could be days before we manage to track 'em down."

"Then we can track them down again." Colley's muttered words oozed over the seat back like ground fog. "The Boss will understand."

That drew a harsh laugh from Pig. "Yeah, just like he understood Benny."

Colley muttered something which Pig couldn't make out, and he looked over the seat to see the other man passed out. Good, he thought, that whining wasn't helping his thinking. It was all Colley's fault, anyway. They should have just gone up the damn road but Colley had said that way would be too visible. They'd lose the element of surprise, he said.

Haha. Some surprise.

Some time and much jouncing later, when he spotted a place he could pull off the road and into some trees, he stopped the Jeep and got out. He would get Colley bandaged up and then figure out their next step. He opened the back door and jostled his partner.

"Come on, Colley, we don't got all day. Let's see if we can get you taped up." Jesus, there was a lot of blood. He shook the man again but there was no response. He placed his finger tips to the carotid artery and felt a faint pulse. And, the bleeding had slowed down considerably. Okay, good. Maybe it was better to leave him this way while he figured out their next move.

He smelled gas. Had he hit something, put a hole in the tank? Sonofa.., that's all they needed. He dropped down and peered under the car but didn't see any drips or a puddle. He stood back up and checked the tank lid. It was on solid. Where was it coming from? He desperately needed a cigarette, but with this new development, he didn't dare light up in the car. He'd have to smoke it out here.

He could see part of the road to the cabin from this vantage point so he leaned back against a tree and lit his cigarette.

Who was their closest contact and would they be able to find a doctor who could patch Colley up without filing a report? How long would it take them to get here? Too long, he answered himself. It would probably be dark before they could even get here. Maybe, they could meet somewhere. No, he had to keep an eye on the cabin road, figure out a way to get up there and find the kid. What if he left Colley here and told the contact where he was?

"Shit," he muttered, "like these fucking trees have house numbers."

JEN HAD ALL THEIR THINGS collected into the gear hauler and a plastic bag, which sat at the top of the stairs. Her brain was muddled, fear and anxiety made her thoughts swirl around like cyclonic debris. Shaking it off, she wondered if there was time to wash the bedding. Maybe not, but at least she could change the sheets. She stripped the bed, found clean sheets on the closet shelf and remade the bed. She'd just started down to the washer when Crockett came in the back door and she heard the brothers talking it over. The men saw her coming down the stairs with the armload of bedding.

"If those aren't wet or damp," Houston said, "just drop them in the hamper. They'll keep until someone gets back up here to clean."

Jen, who had spent the two days Houston was gone cleaning the cabin, looked around. It seemed to her that the sheets were the only things that weren't clean, but dutifully, she put the sheets in the empty hamper and shut the lid. Where were Houston's bloody jeans, she wondered?

She pitched in to help Houston and his brother strip the refrigerator and pantry of any perishable foods and place them in a box to go into the bed of Crockett's truck. Houston stopped only long enough to make some sandwiches with the remaining lunch meats and cheeses, which he wrapped and put in a cooler sitting on the counter. He added some mandarin oranges and some pop and closed the lid.

"Link?" he handed him the cooler, "Will you take this out to my truck and put it down between the seats?"

"Sure," the boy said, his eyes gleaming at the thought of new adventure and willing to help it along any way he could.

Crockett went into his room to collect his things, returned minutes later with his duffle bag stuffed, and sat it down by the door. "Dad will be happy to have his truck back," he grinned at Jen and turned toward Houston. "What are you going to do?"

"My current plan is to get everybody off the mountain," Houston answered grimly.

Link bounced back in. "Are we ready?"

"I am," Crockett ruffled Link's hair and shouldered his bag. "Come on out and see me off."

They all went out on the veranda. Link's face turned suddenly serious.

"Will I see you again, Crockett?" he asked.

"I'm sure you will, Buddy," Crockett picked him up with his free arm so that they were eye to eye. "Next time I'm back, maybe you can come to a powwow. How would you like that?"

"What do you do at a powwow?"

"We sing and dance and have a big cookout."

"That sounds like fun," Link smiled as he was set back on the ground and looked up at Jen. "Could we go, Mom?"

"We'll see." What else could she say?

With his arm once more freed, Crockett pulled Jen in close and gave her a big kiss. "I'm so glad I got to meet you, Jen," he said, and released her. It hadn't been a passionate kiss but the emphasis on the word 'so' was enough to turn Houston's scowl fierce.

Crockett winked at him. "Later, Bro," he gave his brother a salute and walked to his truck and tossed the duffle across the seat.

With a final wave, he backed away from the veranda and turned down the drive.

THE CURSES CONTINUED to roll off Pig's tongue as he sucked the cigarette down to the filter, wishing it was something stronger. Maybe one like the boss smoked. He smiled to himself at the memory of the pungent smell of Lucano's special stash. Crushing the butt under his heal, he lit another one. He'd let Colley rest for a bit and then try to get him up again. And if he doesn't get up, what are you going to do? Hell, he didn't know. He wasn't a doctor.

A movement on the road drew his attention and he watched a truck rumble down the mountainside. Only the driver in it as far as he could tell. Did that mean the kid and the women were up there by themselves or did it mean that they weren't up there at all? He swore again. If Chuck had led them on a wild goose chase, his ass was going to be in the can. Let him explain to Lucano what had happened here.

"LINK?" HOUSTON SAID to the boy, who was still watching the back end of Crockett's truck as it disappeared down the road, but he turned when Houston called his name. "Why don't you go up to your room and check, make sure that your mom didn't miss anything. Look under the bed, too. Then bring the sack and the gear hauler out here. Oh, and check around the couch down stairs for any stray comic books or videos that we might have overlooked. Okay?"

"Okay, Houston," he agreed. There seemed to be a note of reluctance in the boy's answer but he went back inside without any hesitation. Jen turned to watch him.

When the door closed behind Link, Houston cupped Jen's stiff shoulders and pulled her closer. "Jen," her eyes looked up at him warily, "I've wanted to tell you something for days but there have been too many people and too much going on. You don't have to say anything, but before we leave this porch, you have to know that I love you."

She sucked in a tiny gasp and something in her eyes melted, making them glow with blue fire but suddenly the fire turned to ice and her palm connected with his face with a hard, open-palm slap that rocked him back on his heels.

Jen hadn't even been aware that the blow was on the way until she felt the shock waves sing up her arm. The disbelief on Houston's face gave her a tiny spurt of satisfaction. She'd been balancing on a razor's edge of fear, humiliation, hope, despair and back to fear for nearly a week now. Houston's unexpected declaration had pushed her over that edge.

"Damn you, Houston." she turned her back on him so he wouldn't be able to see the tears welling in her eyes. She wouldn't cry over him, she blinked them away. Absolutely wouldn't.

"You don't get to say that to me." she said to the wall. "Not now, not ever. A very short time ago, I wanted desperately to believe it, needed to hear it, but not any more. I don't know what your game is but I'm not playing it. Just get me and Link down off this mountain and drop us off at the nearest bus terminal and then go away."

Her words stunned Houston almost as much as the slap had. He'd felt her mistrust of him had lessened, that he'd actually gained back a little of the magnetic pull that had drawn them together from the beginning. Obviously, she didn't share that feeling.

"Jen ..." He began, reaching for her, but she shrank from his touch. His hand dropped. "I haven't lied to ..."

The back door slammed and Link came tottering around the corner of the cabin, gear hauler on one arm and the black plastic bag in the other hand. They both turned as he dropped the stuff in front of them.

"This is everything, Houston," he looked up at them quizzically, sensing the tension, trying to decipher the undercurrents.

"Help your mom put those in the back seat of the truck and you two get in while I lock up." Houston's voice sounded gravelly even to his own ears as he pulled out the house key. Frustration made Houston's response sharper than necessary, and the boy tensed at the tone but both he and Jen complied without hesitation.

Jen got Link buckled into the back seat. Houston had stacked his own belongings on the other end of the seat and tossed his coat over the top. She climbed into the front seat, silent as the Sphinx and her heart every bit as hard and cold.

Houston checked the stove, checked the faucets, shut off the lights, checked the fridge, unnecessarily, locked the metal pantry doors (bears had never gotten into the cabin but there was always the possibility), and lastly made sure all the windows and doors were locked. By the time he finished, he had his body and mind under control again, at least enough that he would be able to make the long drive ahead without snapping anyone's head off.

With Link alert and chattering in the back seat, the subject of Houston's declaration on the veranda had to be tabled. His words, 'I love you' kept repeating in Jen's mind like the impact of a soul-stirring song, that once heard, made a home inside you. But, just like that song, you let it tug at your heart for a few moments and then you had to move on with your life.

PIG COULDN'T BELIEVE his good luck when he saw the second truck come down the mountain switchbacks a few minutes later. He put the binoculars he'd dug out of the glove box to his eyes and sharpened the focus, a male driver and a female passenger. The rear windows were darkened, but from the way the two in front tossed glances to the back, he had no doubt that the other two were in the back seat.

He hurried back to the Jeep. "Colley," he shook his partner, but got no response. "Damn it, Colley, we've got them. They're on the move. Colley," he shook him harder. "Come on, dammit, we've got to follow them." Colley wasn't moving. He pressed his fingers to Colley's throat and felt nothing. Pig cursed, long and loud, as he considered his next move.

Well, he decided, dead was dead. He couldn't drive down the road with a corpse in the back seat so Colley would have to stay here. He dragged his partner out of the vehicle and emptied his pockets of cash, weapons and I.D.s.

Satisfied that he had everything, Pig shut the car door and opened the hatch to get his jacket before he got behind the wheel. The smell of fuel was stronger back here. It only took a yank of his coat to show him the problem.

"Damn it, Colley," he shouted, not caring if he was heard, "You just had to do it didn't you?" He picked the leaking can of charcoal lighter fluid out of the rags his partner had used as a wrapper to hide it in the coats, and threw it as hard as he could into the trees. "That's why we brought coats, you fool! I told you we wouldn't be lighting any fires. You couldn't even get the lid screwed on tight so now everything is soaked."

"Fucking idiot", he muttered viciously, as he started to drag the coats and rags out of the back where they lay on top of a roadside emergency kit. He almost dragged the kit out with them. There were things in those kits that might be useful. Putting the kit back in the car, he stacked the coats and rags on the ground and was reaching for the hatch when a saner thought popped up. Leaving a body was one thing but leaving a pile of clothing was sheer stupidity. The law had ways of tracing everything.

He threw the clothes and rags back into the car and closed the hatch. You could find trash cans along most roads anymore, he could scatter the stuff from here to Las Vegas and no one would give it a thought. He climbed back behind the wheel and backed out of the trees carefully. He turned around to head after the truck. The only major problem was he'd have to get out of the car every time he needed a cigarette.

LINK'S QUESTIONS AND comments about their destination – which Houston nimbly sidestepped – slowed as the miles wore on, until they stopped altogether. Jen looked back to check on him. He had stretched across the seat, and using Houston's coat as a pillow, had fallen asleep. After two round trips down to the lake and back, she was tired too, but there was a question she needed answered before she could rest easy.

"Houston?" she said quietly, her eyes focused straight ahead.

He glanced over at her for a long breath then focused his eyes back on the road. "Yes?" he said cautiously, unsure if he was going to want to hear this.

"Why did you refuse my offer, when we were camped back there in Idaho?" the question came out in a rush of nervous apprehension.

He was silent for so long that she wondered if he was going to answer her, but he finally responded.

"We weren't at what I would call a profound level of trust. I already knew you were mixed up, somehow, with the Lucano mob, and I knew you were planning to run if you had half a chance. I was afraid that if I got in too deep with you, that it might jeopardize my career. And then, you gave it the final blow when you said it didn't have to mean anything, just a release of sexual tension." He reached for a hand which was twisting the tail of her shirt where it lay across her lap. She yanked it back. His jaw tightened and he returned his hand to the steering wheel. "I wasn't about to risk my job just so you could have a few minutes of forgetfulness and move on."

More than his job would have been destroyed if he'd taken her up on her offer. His heart would have suffered serious damage when she found a way to ditch him later on, but she didn't need to know that right now.

"I was frightened." She stared out the window for a time before she spoke again. "We once had some ... some chemistry, but after I ran, I was afraid I might have killed any feelings you had for me so, I left you a way out." she stopped for a moment. "I was afraid that night might be the last time I would ever see you, ever have a chance to feel like we might have made it ... under other circumstances."

That was what he'd feared, too. "I couldn't have given you any other answer that night." he looked at her and the weight of his gaze drew hers.

She nodded and he turned back to the road again.

She blinked back the sudden moisture that blurred her vision and swallowed the lump in her throat.

"Jen?"

She looked over. "Yes?"

"We are going to make it." he promised.

And, against all odds, she really wanted to believe him. She wanted that desperately, but reality forced her to shake her head. "No, we won't."

Her bleak whisper hit him hard.

The miles disappeared under the wheels, as they made their way across the Boulder Flats to Lander.

CHAPTER THIRTY SIX

Once in Lander, Houston thought about taking the scenic highway up and over, through Sinks Canyon, along the Popo Agie. He grinned at that—the name was always pronounced wrong by newcomers, tourists. They would get the Pohpoh right pretty often, but always, always, fell down on "Zyuh". Maybe the still wild and beautiful canyon river would help ease some of the tension between Jen and himself. It hadn't been easy to persuade her to stick with his plan, but she'd grudgingly agreed. Still it would be better if she was really on board with it. He wasn't too concerned about the men at the lake. If one of them had been seriously mauled by the big cat, they were going to be too busy solving other problems to be hunting just now. Still, he stayed on highway 28/287 on the way to South Pass through Atlantic City. If he was lucky, he'd have a chance to show Jen and her son his old stomping grounds some other time.

"Houston? I have to ask you one more thing?" Jen's words, from far over by the door and barely above a whisper, were soft, so soft, he turned and motioned toward his ear. She said, again, "I have to ask you one more thing."

"What's that?"

"What is all this hiding accomplishing? I mean, Link and I have to stop running sometime, get new identities, start rebuilding our lives, and I depended on Irene for a lot of that. Why not just take us back to Idaho? Irene can find us a place, even if she decides to stay there."

"Is that what you want to do, Jen?" he didn't pause for her to answer him. "Now that Lucano knows he has a grandson, do you really believe that he will give up the chase? Jen, that's not going to happen. Eventually he will find you." She heard a definite chill in his voice. "Do you want to be on the run for the rest of your life? For the rest of Link's life?"

"Dammit, Houston, You can't believe that." It was a test of her patience to keep her voice to little more than a whisper, when the urge to shout thrummed in her head.

"Look, I'm working on it, okay," Houston growled. Would she be pacified if he told her he'd contacted the FBI or would she be even more upset? "I'm not going to let anything happen to you or Link."

He slowed as they approached a road-side pull out. It wasn't a big one, just a widening of the shoulder, a scenic lookout sign, and a trash barrel. There were a couple of rigs sitting there plus another passenger car. It wasn't usual for truckers to pull over for a scenic view and this particular spot wasn't particularly scenic anyway, just an historical marker. Maybe there was a road problem ahead. Or maybe the drivers knew each other and had stopped to visit for a few minutes. Houston squeezed into a space behind the last rig, a fuel tanker.

"How come we're stopping?" Link sat up in the back, rubbing the sleep out of his eyes.

"Your mom and I need to talk some things over." Houston opened his door to climb out and signaled Jen to do the same.

Yes, they did, she silently agreed. With an air of inevitability, she got out of the cab.

"I'm hungry," Link complained, "When are we going to eat?"

"Stay in the truck," Jen said, putting her hand on the door to prevent him from climbing out. "We'll be right back. There's sandwiches and pop in that cooler on the floor. Have one of those." She walked away, following Houston

Disgruntled at being forced to stay in the truck, Link lifted the cooler to the seat and opened the lid. He picked out a can of pop first, opened it and took a big drink then got a sandwich and closed the lid. The sandwich was just meat and cheese but it was okay. The pop was much better.

As he munched on the sandwich, he watched his mom and Houston, standing down the slope a little way, hands gesturing occasionally, their faces, at turns, defensive, angry or frustrated. Once in a while, they would wave a hand at the truck. He knew he was part of their argument and the thought made his stomach ache. He was six years old, if he was part of the argument, why wasn't he old enough to be part of the discussion?

It seemed, to him, they'd been down there a long time. And, now that the pop can was empty, he had to pee but he didn't see any place to do that. There was just a trash can sitting at the edge of the pavement. If he got out to pee on their side of the truck, they would probably yell at him, but if he got out the other side, he'd be in full view of the cars going down the highway. Maybe, he could open the door just enough to block himself from view of the passing cars, step down and pee right there. He'd have to be very careful that he didn't get any on Houston's truck, though.

Decision made, he set the cooler back on the floor, unbuckled his seat belt, and crawled across the seat. Houston, not being used to driving with a child aboard, had not engaged the child safety locks, so Link didn't need to crawl over the seat to the front. He stepped down onto the pavement.

It felt good to stretch his legs after being curled up in the back seat for so long. Business taken care of, he zipped up and looked at the big trucks parked there. He wondered what it would be like to drive one of those, traveling all over the country, seeing all the different states. It might be fun, he thought. Yes, he was pretty sure he'd like to travel, but not in the back seat. That just made him sleepy.

The truck in front of the tanker had a really cool design, an eagle and a flag. It made him think about the eagle's nest that he and Crockett had found up the mountain. He walked forward to get a closer look. A car moved over as it drove past them and slowed down. The driver jerked his head around and blinked, almost twisted his head off with staring.

THE LUCK MUST REALLY be with him today, Pig decided, when he saw the truck in the rest area. The man and woman he'd watched make their way down the mountain side had gotten out of the truck to carry on some heated discussion. The kid was wandering around the semis. There was no sign of the other woman.

He debated whether to make his move now or wait until there weren't so many people around. It was a proven fact that, if you moved fast enough, you could snatch things right in front of a crowd and most people wouldn't even be aware of what went on, but you couldn't always count on it, and with the Boss monitoring every move he made, there wasn't room for any mistake.

It was bad enough that he'd dumped Colley's body where, hopefully, it wouldn't be found for a lo-o-o-ong time. That would take some explaining.

No, he decided, there weren't enough people to qualify as a crowd, and sure as hell, someone would get a good look at him and the Jeep. If he failed at this, Lucano would call in Major, to do the job. Pig had no idea if that was his first name, his last name, or a rank, but Major was a known man and rightly feared. After Major brought the kid in, Pig had no doubt that Pig would be the first name on Lucano's cleanup list, so it was best to keep Major out of it.

As he rolled on down the road, he wondered why Lucano hadn't called Major in to begin with. Pig knew that Major earned high six-figures for a job but the Boss wouldn't have blinked at that. No, more likely, the rumors that floated around, that no one knew what Major looked like, must be true. All his jobs were dealt with via phone and overseas accounts. His reputation of never leaving a witness was well known. Maybe he'd balked at bringing in the kid alive.

Pig turned his brain to planning his ambush.

As he searched for a side road which had cover for the Jeep but would allow him to watch the road, Pig gloried in the regard he would earn if he managed to pull this off. What would the Boss do when he returned, with the kid in tow? Maybe move him up into the office and out of this stinking half-desert.

No, he wasn't the office job type, but he'd definitely earn a little respect. Maybe, the Boss would start calling him by his full name, Pigliano, with a silent 'G', like lasagna, instead of the demeaning nickname he'd stuck on him. Pig thought he would enjoy stuffing that nickname down a few throats, when he had the Boss's respect. And his thoughts drifted with gratitude to the late Colley. Pig wouldn't have to share his win with anyone.

He spotted a two-rut track that rose up into the pines and disappeared. He slowed to bump along the ruts and into the cover of the trees. When the highway disappeared behind him, he turned the Jeep around and rolled back down the slope until he could just make out patches of the road through the branches. He stepped out of the car, dug his cigarettes out of his pocket, and walked a few feet away before lighting up. He smiled through the smoke as he watched the road and planned his crowning achievement.

"LINK?" HOUSTON LOOKED into the back seat through the rear view mirror. Jen was silent in the other seat as they rolled past Atlantic City

"What?" Link jerked himself awake.

"We'll be in Farson in about an hour and I know the best ice cream shop in that town. Do you think you could eat some ice cream when we get there?"

"You bet!" Link bounced in his seat.

Jen looked over at him, her head tipped in question, "We already stopped once. Do you think it's wise take the time?"

"One of those guys at the lake was hurt, pretty bad. It would take them hours to find some one to treat him, someone with the training and equipment to do the work, who was also on the shady side of the legal system. We should be okay." Houston assured her.

"Hey, Link? We'll be passing South Pass City in a few minutes," Houston glanced again at the boy. "Have you ever been there?"

"No, but our teacher told us about it one day. There's a mine there."

"Yes," Houston said, "the Carissa gold mine, but it's shut down now. People still live in the town though. One of these days I'll bring you and your mom back up here to visit it and take a drive up Sink's Canyon Road. The scenery is really beautiful. Would you like to see it?" he looked in the mirror again to read Link's reaction.

"Could we, Mom? Huh? Could we?" He unbuckled his seat belt to lean over Jen's shoulder.

"Maybe some day," she tried to sound lively. It bothered her that Houston talked to Link like there was a future, when the certainty of any future for her and Link was questionable.

Houston looked in the mirror again but it wasn't Link he focused on, there was a dark vehicle behind them, closing the distance. Houston had kept his speed at just over the limit. The car behind them had to do lots more to move up so quickly. It might just be someone in a hurry, he thought, but recent events had made him even warier than usual.

Calmly, he said, "Get back under your belt, Link." He put his foot on the accelerator to maintain his speed, and kicked off the cruise control as Link frowned and resumed his place. When he heard the seat belt click Houston dropped his speed a bit at a time to sixty. A minute later he heard the sound of Link's Gameboy.

With one eye on the car closing up behind them, Houston reached his left hand down to the holster attached to the side of his seat and released the lock, easing the automatic loose for quick access. He edged the truck to the right, to allow plenty of room for the car in the mirror to pass, if that was the driver's intention.

Apparently it wasn't. The driver slowed when he got within a few car lengths of Houston's bumper, close enough that Houston could see the vehicle clearly and identify it as the car from the lake, complete with grill guard. Houston's mind went into cop mode. Where was the other man?

Two oncoming cars appeared over a small rise in the road and were soon disappearing behind them. Houston cleared the top of the rise and saw a long, empty straightaway ahead. If the man in the car was planning a move, this would be the ideal time. Houston eased the gun from the holster with his left hand and tucked it under his still throbbing thigh.

Jen, tuned into Houston's growing tension, asked quietly "What is going on?"

"I'm not sure yet," Houston said, "but keep Link down below the seats. That Jeep behind us is the one from the lake." Jen whipped startled eyes to her own rear view mirror. "Tell me when you pick him up," Houston used his driver's switch-pad control to adjust the passenger-side mirror until she held her hand up to stop. He relaxed slightly. With two sets of eyes on the car behind them, Houston could take an extra moment to calculate possible actions and responses.

The Jeep sped up until the headlights and grill guard disappeared behind the tailgate of the truck then suddenly swerved into the oncoming lane, but in the move, Houston felt the jolt as the grill guard kissed his bumper.

He swore in astonishment. Was the damned fool trying a pit maneuver? The tap on the bumper was in the wrong spot and not hard enough to accomplish the goal, but still the truck slewed awkwardly.

"Hang on!" Houston shouted, as he corrected the movement and hit the brakes.

The Jeep shot by and Houston saw a look of surprise on the driver's face when his truck, bucking against the whip fast maneuver, caught the right rear panel of the Jeep, to send it off-kilter into the left hand lane, and off the edge of the road. Houston straightened his truck and passed the Jeep, now stopped in the barrow pit. Pretty good driving to stay on his wheels. He would have tipped his cap, if he had worn one.

"What's happening?" Link, his eyes huge in his white face, leaned over the seat.

"Get down!" "Stay under the seat belt!" Jen and Houston both shouted at him.

With the Jeep now well behind, but pulling back onto the road, Houston held his Glock out to Jen.

"I hear you know how to use this," he said.

"I've never shot anything but targets. You aren't expecting me to shoot him, are you?"

"Of course not, he's only trying to kill you," his smile was darker than she liked, "but if you could manage to shoot out a tire, that might be helpful."

"He's on your side!" she pointed out.

"He's going to be right behind us in just a second," Houston said, "Just be ready." She took the gun.

"Link! Down! On the seat!" they both yelled as the boy's curious head popped up between them, again.

And then the Jeep was back. Jen saw the man's automatic, over the steering wheel. "If he shoots from there, he could hit Link," she yelled.

"That's just what he won't do." Houston mashed the throttle and swerved. "He wants Link alive." He handed his phone to her. "Call 911 while I …" he swerved again, sharply; her head bumped against the window, "… keep this asshole occupied."

With the Glock held between her legs, she punched the numbers in, while Houston weaved and blocked. After a quick discussion, she set the phone in a cup holder, line open. "Didn't even ask questions except where we were! Said they're sending Troopers, up from Farson." She took the gun into her hand and checked the safety. It was off, already. "Is there a round in the chamber?"

"Yep," he said.

As they approached another rise, a big gravel truck popped over the top, and Houston swung violently to the right. The Jeep, his sight blocked, wanted to move alongside. The warning blast from the big truck's air horn was almost too late, but the Jeep veered, and bounced wildly, again into the left barrow pit. They sped away and over the hill.

"That should keep him busy for a while," Jen crowed.

"Not that long," Houston answered, "he can drive. Didn't bother him much." And only a minute later, the Jeep roared up behind. Houston began once again to weave. The center stripes zipped under fast and faster, edging ninety on the long empty stretch of two-lane highway.

"I'm going to move left far enough that he'll try to move up on our right.. Put down your window and show the gun. Should make him hesitate, just long enough. Don't miss."

It happened just that way. The Jeep roared up. She pointed her gun. He hesitated but leveled his own. She started to squeeze her trigger. Houston slammed on his brakes. Jen crashed forward into the door post. She a saw muzzle flash, and the Jeep's back window shatter.

Then came a flash of fire, and the rear of the Jeep burst into flames. Fire engulfed the interior and the driver disappeared. The Jeep veered off the road, bounced high through a fence, and slammed into a tree. Houston followed more slowly and stopped far behind. He and Jen were out and running toward the Jeep when the driver emerged, screaming, a blazing, lurching, torch, and pitched forward, to the ground.

Houston tore off his shirt and threw it over the body, trying to smother the flames. It didn't cover enough and he shouted at Jen. "Give me your shirt."

"What?!" she shouted back, even as she stripped down to her bra.

Houston covered the man's legs with it and started digging dirt to throw on top of it. Jen ran for the truck and met Link running toward her.

"Get back in the truck," she commanded in a voice that Link didn't dare question. They ran back to the truck together. "Toss me Houston's coat," she said when Link was back in the seat.

"What happened, Mom?" Link complied.

"My bullet must have hit the gas tank," she said. The unexpected and unintended results of her actions hit her hard and tears flooded to run over her cheeks. "Stay in here until the cops get here. Do you hear me?!" She waited for Link's nod before running back to Houston.

She handed Houston the coat and he used it to beat out the rest of the flames. The smell of burning flesh seared into her nostrils and brain and felt like something that would be with her for the rest of her life. The man was still screaming, but intermittently now. His lips moved but the words didn't seem to make much sense. She caught "kid" and the word chilled her to the bone. Then, she thought he said "collie" then something else.

"Can you make out what he's trying to say," Houston asked her.

The man lifted his hand imploringly and whispered, "P ... Pigliano."

"What?" Houston said, but the man's hand dropped, lifeless, to the ground.

"Did you hear what he said?" Houston turned to Jen whose tears wouldn't stop.

She shook her head, her eyes awash, pleading helplessly, as her insides started heaving. "I don't know. It sounded kind of like he said piano." she clapped a hand over her mouth, moved away and vomited. She couldn't stop. The retching and gasping went on and on.

In the distance, she heard the approach of sirens. Too late, she thought. There's no one to help now.

The heat from the burning vehicle and the tree it had set afire finally registered, and Jen moved farther away.

"Go put something on before the cavalry arrives, Jen." Houston rose to stand beside her. "Stay in the truck until someone comes for you. This is going to take some time." He moved toward the road to meet the State Troopers.

Suddenly aware that she was still in just her bra and that vehicles were already stopping to see what had happened, she dug out a clean shirt. As she slid it over her head, another hot explosion burst behind her. She felt the blast and the intense heat that followed. A new and large ball of flame erupted from the burning shell of the Jeep, throwing chunks of fiery debris high into the air, and igniting more little fires all around. Where on earth had that come from?

She ran around to the driver's door, noticing the shattered headlight on the way. She yanked the door open, jumped in, started the truck, and backed it several more yards away. She put it in park and shut off the engine. Knees shaky and not behaving well, she held on to the truck as she circled back around to the still open passenger door, and sat down beside Link. She knew he was as shaken as she when she pulled him in tight and he accepted her long hug without complaint.

"Is he dead?" Link whispered into her shoulder.

"Yes," she nodded, "I think so."

A voice crackled from the front. The 911 operator was still on the phone, which Jen had left on and forgotten about, and asking, over and over again, for a response. Jen reached over the seat and shut it off just as the Highway Patrol Trooper pulled up beside Houston.

CHAPTER THIRTY SEVEN

It was after nine that evening before Houston opened the motel room door in Rock Springs and carried their things into a double bed suite. She should probably, for modesty's sake, object to sharing a room with him, even with Link as chaperon, but she just couldn't bring herself to care. All she wanted was to get Link bathed, fed and in bed, so she could try to do the same. Although, she knew that all the soap and water in the world wouldn't be able to wash those ghastly hours on that road side out of her mind. The image of the man trying to communicate through his burned flesh was seared into her brain as though she, herself, had suffered the flames. Her stomach churned again at the memory.

You would think, she thought, as she went in the bathroom to run Link's bath, that something so horrific would be the end of their ordeal, but she knew that it wasn't. Lucano was still out there, still wanted her dead. He wouldn't stop. She wondered if she could survive the next attempt.

"Mom?" Link asked, when she sent him into the bathroom, "are you okay?"

She must look like a zombie, for him to ask that question. She would have to do a better job of appearing normal. She looked around for help but Houston had left the room.

"I guess I'm still in a little bit of shock," she admitted. "It was a terrible thing that happened to him."

"But that bad man was trying to hurt us," he said, with the straightforward logic of a six year old.

She pulled him in for a hug. Something she had repeated often in the last few hours, but he didn't mind, seeming to need the comfort as much as she did.

"I know," she said, "but it was a horrible way for him to die anyway, no matter how bad he was. Now," she released him, "go take your bath while

I find your pajamas. We'll all feel better in the morning." It was a distant hope, but it was all she could offer him for comfort.

A short time later, Houston walked in just as Link was putting on his pajamas, take-out bags in his hands. Link's eyes lit up.

"Wow! Thanks, Houston, I'm starved!" He shared a grin with him.

"Have a seat," Houston said, as he began to spread out the meal on the table near the window. He didn't have to repeat himself as Link plopped into the closest chair.

Jen was glad to see Link's resiliency. She had no appetite. The thought of grilled meat sandwiches made her empty stomach rebel.

There were only two chairs and she saw that as a sign of reprieve. "You two go ahead. I want to get a bath." She picked up the sweat pants and shirt she'd chosen, instead of the panties and t-shirt she usually slept in, and hurried into the bathroom.

She'd had to reheat the bathwater at least two times, that she remembered, before she finally climbed out of the tub, her fingers and toes pruney and rough. As she toweled the water out of her hair, she looked in the mirror over the sink. The face that stared back at her was haunted. She wasn't surprised. The memory of her wild shot, and its repercussions, would haunt her forever.

She was glad to see that Link was already asleep when she walked out of the bathroom. Houston had turned down the far bed and was now sitting in the other chair, TV set to a news channel, the sound muted.

"I brought you a garden salad," he motioned toward a plastic lidded container, "and some juice. Extra dressing, if you need it."

He'd suspected what the hamburgers would do to her appetite. His understanding almost had her tearing up again.

"Thanks," she said and sat down in Link's abandoned seat. He gave her a smile and a nod then turned back to the news as she opened the lid.

She had picked her way halfway through the salad when he suddenly picked up the remote, turned on the sound and sat forward, intent on the activity unfolding on the screen.

"The surprise, joint raids, by the FBI and other arms of law enforcement, on several of the alleged Lucano drug syndicate's warehouses, offices and other holdings, has resulted in the arrests of at least twenty of the syndicate's top lieutenants and fifty or more of the extended cartel members. One of the raids uncovered a warehouse the FBI says was filled with women and young boys, most of them undocumented immigrants. Information currently available alleges that these people were the victims of a sex trafficking ring and were destined for locations in the far east.

"Ranaldo Lucano, the reported head of the syndicate, whose son is serving a seven to ten year sentence for drug charges and tax evasion, was not picked up in the raid, but sources are confident that they have enough evidence to charge Ranaldo with several federal and international crimes. Assurances have been made that he will be picked up very soon." The anchor handed the story to an on-site reporter who closed the segment by saying, "Stay tuned for more. We will update you on this as the story develops."

Jen was having a hard time digesting what she'd just heard. A fine tremor shook her. Did this mean that Irene and she and Link were safe now? Had Lucano's teeth all been pulled? She didn't realize she'd voiced that question aloud until Houston reached over and pulled her into his lap, wrapping his arms around her.

"Until Lucano is in custody, I'm sure he has a tooth or two left," he whispered into her hair. "We're not clear yet, but I think we can breathe a little bit easier now." He muted the TV once more but didn't shut it off. He didn't intend to leave it on all night, though. He was sure her eyes would be glued to it as long as it was on.

Fine tuned as he was to Jen, Houston felt the instant she became aware of her position. She stiffened and put space between them, rejecting the comfort he offered. He was already feeling the loss, but he made no attempt to stop her as she rose, a faint tinge of pink on her cheeks, and moved to the bed where Link slept.

"I'll leave it on for now but we should really try to get some sleep," he told her. "It's been a hard day all around and we still have some traveling to do tomorrow. As soon as we decide where we want to go."

She nodded but made no move to climb under the covers. He hadn't actually expected she would, but he could see the exhaustion dragging at her eyelids and thought, if he could just get her to lay down beside her son, nature would do the rest. He handed her the remote as he walked to his bed and threw back the covers.

"Hang onto that for me, will you?" he said, hoping to coax a smile from her. She just nodded. "I'm going to take a shower." Gathering his own sweats, he went in the bathroom and closed the door.

He'd been on the force for twenty years and had seen his share of severe injuries and deaths so, as horribly as the man had died, the incident had not affected him like it had Jen. After a while, when a person had dealt with serious trauma, the horrifying things one person could do to another, the mind, in self defense, developed a tough skin. An emotional callous of sorts. The pain in his heart was for Jen who, despite her connection with Lucano, appeared unfamiliar with violent death.

He was showered and out of the bathroom in less than six minutes. Jen hadn't moved from where he'd left her. She had, however, turned the sound back on. He took the remote from her hand. "Any thing new?" he didn't bother to specify regarding what, there was only one thing on either mind.

"They showed a long distance shot of them bringing some of the hostages out of the warehouse," she said calmly, as though it was any other news from anywhere else in the world.

"They'll be replaying scenes from this night for the next week," he nodded. Stepping over Jen's knees, Houston reached down and brushed a dark curl away from the boy's eyes. He didn't stir.

"Link never did get that ice cream." Houston smiled at the small figure, sleeping peacefully. He shut off the TV.

He saw the protest leap to her mouth but he forestalled it, "Come on, Jen. It's been a hell of a day. We both need sleep."

After a long silent debate, she finally nodded. "Okay."

He shut off the lamp on the table between their beds and stretched out, his head on the pillow. His back was toward her, but he heard the rustle of the bed as she laid down, face to the TV, light on, with Link and the separation of the beds between them. Soon, he promised himself, there would be no separation between them. All he needed was patience.

Patience wasn't easy to come by, he realized. She never shut off her light and he couldn't sleep with it on. To make matters worse, she wasn't sleeping either. She tossed and turned in the bed like a beached fish. He could think of ways to settle her nerves but his solutions were causing havoc with his libido. The erection was painful but he couldn't put all the blame on her, it was his own vivid imagination that was killing him.

By two o'clock, he knew he would get no sleep that night. He got out of bed and went into the bathroom, splashed water on his face and head, and ran a towel over it. He gave thought to a cold shower, but he didn't think that would help much, and Jen would hear it and wonder. Best to leave that door tightly closed.

He drank a glass of water, then to kill more time, he brushed his teeth again. It didn't help a whole lot but he figured he could fake sleep for another hour or two.

Jen was sitting against the headboard of the bed, remote in her hand, TV muted but tuned to the same news channel. She looked up guiltily, when he walked into the room. Her finger reached for the power button and the light from the set went dark.

"I'm sorry, Houston," she whispered. "I couldn't sleep."

"Me either," he said softly. "Leave it on."

She powered it on again. He sat down at the table and motioned her to take the other chair. She did.

"Have there been any new developments?" he asked.

She shook her head. "Just repeating the earlier footage. I keep searching the faces of the captives when they show that part, wondering if Jill might be one of them. But the video isn't good." A tear slid down her cheek. "I know I'm just torturing myself. They probably don't keep the 'merchandise' locked up very long before they ship them out, but I can't seem to help it. And Jill, even if she isn't dead, hasn't made contact for over two months now."

"They keep the cameras at a distance to protect the identities of captives until they can be processed and family notified, if they can find them." She nodded.

Houston reached across the small table and took her hands in his. It felt like holding ice cubes. He blew on them softly and chafed them. A tiny smile touched her lips.

"I know," she whispered. "My nerves do that to me. I can't get warm."

He raised her hands to his lips and placed a kiss on both. "Jen, come to bed with me." The tension in her body was instantaneous but she didn't jerk her hands away. A bubble of hope bloomed in his chest.

"I c ... can't," she gave a tiny negative shake of her head. "... Link ..."

That her mind had gone immediately to sex was encouraging. He stifled the smile that tried to tug at his lips.

"Link is sound asleep and I don't expect anything from you except sleep." He placed another kiss on her knuckles. "Maybe, if I just hold you, you can get warm and we can both get some sleep. You can leave the TV on if you want, but shut off that lamp. I can't sleep with it on."

"Won't the TV keep you awake then?"

"I'll hide my eyes behind your shoulder," he winked.

He watched as her eyes wavered then warmed. "See, it's working already," his grin increased the heat he saw. "I promise, nothing will happen tonight except sleep." And he'd keep that promise if it killed him.

HE KEPT THE PROMISE, and he was still alive the next morning when the sun woke him, but it had been a close thing. He had tucked her close to him but kept his arm, harmlessly, around her waist. Harmless to her anyway. His body was exhibiting some excitement. It had been, all night, even in his limited sleep. The broad smile that he didn't bother to quantify stretched his mouth to his ears. They'd turned a hard corner, he thought.

He freed his arm, triggering a soft sigh from her but she didn't wake. The TV was on but still muted.

Tucking the blanket around her, he rolled gently out of bed and made his way to the bathroom. He could still feel the shape of that delectable little butt against his abdomen and pressed himself against the hard sink edge in an effort to chase the erotic thought out of his head. His body urged him to go back to the bed and wake her, very slowly. He was pretty sure she wouldn't reject him, but there was Link, and that promise he'd made her last night. His mind pictured her tapping on the bathroom door and walking in. It wasn't likely to happen but the idea of it made his mind do a happy dance. It also did nothing to ease the erection he'd risen with. Damn.

He grabbed his razor and set it on the counter, then squirted a dab of shaving cream in his hand. Working up a foam, he lathered his face. It didn't take much to shave the few patches of whiskers that sprouted on his face but he took his time. He was working up his throat when a soft 'tap, tap' sounded at the door. He jerked and nicked his jaw. His mind instantly recalling his fantasy, until Link's voice said, "Houston?", yanking him back to reality. Good thing he didn't use a straight razor.

He grabbed a tissue and dabbed at the spot of blood that welled. "Yes?" he opened the door.

"I have to pee," Link said.

"You'd best do that in here," Houston told him with a wink. He stepped back and Link walked in, stopping in front of the toilet, waiting.

Realizing the boy expected privacy, Houston quickly wiped the foam off his face and left the room, closing the door behind him. The youngster had been under the constant tutelage of females his whole life. He and Link were going to have to have a discussion on the way males usually handled these kinds of situations. For some weird reason, the thought of discussing this with Jen made him smile, again. In fact, nearly every thought of Jen made him smile.

She was awake when he re-entered the bedroom, sitting in the chair by the window overlooking the parking lot.

"What was that smile for?" she asked him.

"I was just thinking about how much warmer you got when we went to sleep," he grinned and she gave him a wan smile.

Knowing where her first thoughts would focus on waking, he asked, "Any updates on the FBI raids?"

"No, they just keep re-showing last night's footage." she picked at a hangnail. "What is the plan for today?" she asked, as her eyes focused out the window.

"First, breakfast," Houston said, "then find a shop to replace the headlight. Then I have to talk to the sheriff, see if they need any more from me."

"How long before we're on the road again?"

He shrugged, then realizing she was still looking out the window, said, "Maybe late afternoon."

She turned around. "Can you drop me and Link off at Walmart before you take the truck to a shop and talk to the sheriff? I need to get a few things."

His first response was 'no', he didn't want to let them out of his sight yet. Not while the shadow of Lucano still hovered in the background, but immediately he reconsidered. Shopping might be just exactly what she needed to bring some normalcy back to what had been, for all of them, an emotionally wringing week. It might even bring some color back into her cheeks. He also had to try to connect with Agent McCutcheon, and he would prefer that Jen not find out about that connection just yet.

"Do you need some money?"

"No." she shook her head, "I have enough for what I need."

Link came out of the bathroom. "What's for breakfast?"

CHAPTER THIRTY EIGHT

While Link lobbied stubbornly for McDonald's, Houston had been in Rock Springs before and knew where the best coffee was served. Coffee was the deciding factor, as far as he was concerned. He pointed the truck toward the Renegade Cafe, just off of I-80. "They serve really good food there, Link. We can stop at McDonald's for lunch before we leave town," he offered as a sop. "Okay?"

Only slightly mollified, Link sat back in the seat. "Fine." he grumbled.

After a cup of coffee, plus two refills, and five minutes on the phone, Houston found an auto repair shop that had a headlight for his truck, in stock. And they were open. He paid for breakfast and they loaded into the truck.

The Walmart was just across the interstate from the Renegade Cafe and it took less than three minutes before he was pulling up in front of its doors.

"The guy at the auto shop said it would take less than thirty minutes to put in the new headlight and then, maybe an hour at the sheriff's office," Houston told them. "I'll pick you guys up about eleven. Will that be enough time to do your shopping?"

Jen had figured thirty minutes, max, but she nodded her head as she let Link out of the back seat. "That will be more than enough. I only need to get a change of clothes and a some toiletries."

"Okay. Here, at eleven, at this door." Houston called after them as the doors slid open in front of their retreating figures.

Once inside, Jen let Link select a cart and headed immediately for the electronics section. She needed to replace her phone. Nothing fancy. A cheap TracFone with a few prepaid hours on it would be fine.

"Can I look at the laptops?" Link asked.

"That's fine," she smiled, "but stay where we can see each other. This won't take very long."

"Can I have a laptop," he asked, hopefully.

She laughed, the first laugh she'd had in days. It felt good. She felt the tension drain away. "Nice try, Buddy." She cuffed his shoulder lightly.

Finding what she needed, she selected a pay card and had the clerk at the counter load it onto the phone. Phone and receipt bagged, she collected Link and headed back onto the floor to do the rest of her shopping.

She browsed the aisles, killing time, but Link had gotten whiny again to the point she put her hand against his brow to see if he might be coming down with a fever. He didn't feel warm. They still had almost twenty-five minutes before Houston would be back but she headed for the check out. Her open wallet netted two unused credit cards besides her own. It had been necessary to pay cash for the phone but the merchandise wasn't as critical. She aimed the cart for the self checkout counters.

Exiting the building, three bags, not counting the phone she'd just put in her pocket, hanging on her arms, Jen followed along behind Link as he wandered past a row of bicycles chained to a rack, price tags fluttering in the wind. A look of longing crossed his face and she felt a pang of guilt. A six year old boy should have a bike, but giving him the freedom to ride, unattended, around the neighborhood had never been an option with the fear of discovery always on their minds. When would his world ever be normal?

She dug out the phone and sent a text to Irene, trying to let her know that they were okay without actually saying anything. She hoped Irene would understand it.

Still ten minutes until Houston was due to show up.

With a sigh, she stopped in front of risers covered with potted flowers, their bright colors reminding her of the plans she'd had for their yard in Casper. Realizing the fruitlessness of crying over something that probably wouldn't have happened anyway, she blinked away the moisture that blurred her vision.

Remembering the absolute hate and destruction she'd walked in on, there was no way she could ever be comfortable in that house again, even if they returned to Casper. Which, of course, they couldn't do until Lucano had been permanently neutralized. Where they would wind up was anyone's guess.

A big delivery truck, from the Bonnie Plant Company, with flowers painted on its sides, pulled up at the curb beside the plant stands. Two people got out and came around to the back of the truck, opened the doors and lowered a ramp to start unloading more pallets of plants with a mechanical mule hand-truck and pallet lifter. The back end of the truck blocked her view. Jen moved toward the front where she could watch for Houston, and called Link back out of the way.

As she watched the unloading of the new plants, bags of mulch, and fertilizer into the area of the lot already cordoned off, Link watched with her and chattered about how cool the mechanical pallet lifter was, and wondered when Houston would arrive to take them to McDonald's. The local gardeners were already circling the new selections when a white van backed up to the front of the delivery truck and two men opened its back doors. At first, she thought they were looking for plants, too, but they headed toward the doors into Walmart, directly behind them. Jen grabbed Link's arm and pulled him back against her as the two men jostled by them.

Suddenly, Link was snatched from her side and she sucked in a breath to yell just as a gloved hand clapped over her mouth. She saw the man who had grabbed Link toss him, kicking and fighting, into the back of the van and she took a dozen steps toward her son as the doors slammed shut and the man who had covered her mouth jumped in the passenger door as it was moving away. She cried out, or she thought she did, just before the world went black.

IT HAD TAKEN LONGER at the sheriff's office than he'd anticipated, but Houston wheeled into the Walmart parking lot, only a few minutes late, and rolled to a stop in front of the doors. He saw a lot of activity around the Bonnie Plant Co. truck. What he didn't see was Jen or Link.

A man with a name tag declaring him a manager, hurried over to Houston's window. "You'll have to move your truck," he announced.

"I'm just picking up someone," Houston said. "They should be right out." His eyes scanned over the doors, the foyer and the surrounding area.

His heart started pounding when there was no sign of Jen or Link "I'll be out of here in a minute."

"I'm sorry, but you need to move now. The police need this area."

All Houston's nerves instantly jumped to alert. His mind already fearing the worst. "What's going on?" he demanded, ignoring the patrol cars that were already pulling in behind him. He didn't move.

"A possible kidnapping," the manager snapped, "now, move your truck."

"Who saw it?" Houston barked.

"A woman ... A lot of people," he stammered, seeing murder in Houston's eyes. "The police will be questioning witnesses when more help arrives."

The manager had enough sense to back out of his reach and hurried after the two officers who were entering the store.

Houston whipped around the corner and took the first slot he could find, close to the doors, a handicapped space. An ambulance pulled into the spot Houston had just vacated and he felt his breakfast sour in his stomach.

Jogging into the store, he saw the curious eyes and excited buzz that followed the path of the officers. He followed, too. Two paramedics were close behind him.

All the activity coalesced at a closed door behind the service desk, where an officer blocked the entrance. He could hear voices but it was impossible to make out what they were saying.

"You can't go in there," the officer said when Houston reached for the door.

Houston ground his teeth. He knew the procedures, he'd followed them for years, but he had to talk to that witness.

"Look, I'm a police officer, too, out of Casper. You can call the sheriff's office to verify that. I've just been in there on another matter. I was supposed to pick up a woman and a boy out front ten minutes ago and They. Weren't. There. I have to talk to the woman who saw the abduction."

The officer looked like he was going to hold his ground until the paramedics stepped up behind them. When the officer waved them in, Houston went through with them. Before the door closed behind, Houston saw the radio at the officer's ear. He heard more sirens outside.

The small office space was never intended to contain this many people. In addition to the manager, a man in a Bonnie Plants work apron, an older woman sitting in the desk chair, two police officers, the medics, and himself, there was little room to move. But nobody was leaving, especially not Houston, who saw Jen, still as a corpse, on the floor as the medics huddled round. He joined them at her side.

The slight rise and fall of her chest reassured him that she was still alive and a silent prayer of thanksgiving rose in his heart.

"Jen, can you hear me?" he said, loudly.

"You know her?" the officer asked.

"Her name is Jen Bradley," Houston answered, not taking his eyes off her. "We have been traveling together, with her son." he touched the pulse in her throat. He saw traces of white powder on her face and his heart gave an agonized squeeze.

"She was drugged," the man in the apron said, and one of the paramedics working over Jen, caught Houston's eyes, nodding agreement as he went through her pockets. The flip phone he extracted was new, Houston noted. She'd said nothing to him about getting one but they could discuss that later, he promised. As soon as she was stable.

Houston looked over at the man. "How long ago did this happen?"

"Sir, you've got to step back and let us do our job," an officer spoke at Houston's shoulder.

The paramedics were not quite as polite, they just shouldered him out of the way. "You can stay in the room but only if you stay out of our way while we get her stabilized." one of them said.

The man in the Bonnie Plant apron was the only one that responded to Houston. "It happened about twenty minutes ago." he said. "We were unloading plants and a white van pulled up. Two men got out, one grabbed the boy and shoved him in the back of the van. The other man grabbed the woman, put his hand over her mouth and then ran back, jumped in the van and they took off. He didn't even try to put the woman in the van. The woman screamed once and started to run after the van then she collapsed."

"And you gave her the Naloxone?" the officer asked.

"Yeah," the Bonnie Plant man nodded. "My godson died of a drug over-dose two years ago. People were standing all around and nobody could do a thing. I always carry Narcan with me now."

The officer turned to the woman sitting behind the desk. "You saw this happen, too?"

"I was in the garden section," she said, "you know, the one out in the parking lot? I heard someone scream and I looked up just as a white van went tearing by. Then this man," she smiled at the delivery driver, "went running over to the woman laying on the ground. Then all hell, pardon my language, broke loose and some one was yelling to get her inside. I think it was you," she glanced at the Walmart manager who looked away guiltily.

"The confusion was causing traffic snarls," he explained to the cop.

"Everything happened so fast," the woman resumed her testimony, apologetically, "that's all I remember."

She turned helpless eyes on the police officer. "There were other people out there. Surely someone else must have seen it."

The officer nodded. "There are officers questioning a few people, Ma'am, but some don't want to see anything. This woman, Jen Bradley, will be able to give us more when she recovers."

"Did you see what kind of van it was?" Houston asked.

"OH, yes," she turned a broad smile on him. "It was a half-ton GMC. Two thousand and four, I believe. Solid white, but the paint was showing some wear. My husband was a car nut. We were always going to car shows, when he was alive. It rubs off on a person after a while, you know." she finished, half shyly, as though she shouldn't be having pleasant memories in such an awful moment.

"That's very helpful," the officer defused her embarrassment. Putting his two-way to his mouth, he sent out a BOLO for the van, using the woman's description and the details of the abduction.

Houston looked down at Jen and saw her eyelids flutter slightly, and a flood of relief washed through him. She was going to make it.

"GET BACK THERE AND get that kid quiet," Chuck shouted over the piercing screams that shredded his eardrums. "Other drivers are looking." To emphasize his point, he looked over at the car traveling next to them with a 'what can I do?' and an I'm-at-my-wits-end, grimace. He didn't know what they could hear, with both windows up, but they'd heard something. Chuck turned off the main drag and headed toward the city limits. They had to get the van concealed.

"How?!" Vance shouted back, just as deafened as Chuck, as he pulled off the latex glove, inside out, and lowered his window just enough to drop it in the street. "We don't have any duct tape or rags to make a gag. All we got is some of that drug we used on the woman and I don't know how much to use on a kid."

"I don't care how you do it, just shut him up." Chuck swore.

Vance climbed over the seat, kneeling next to the bound boy, and clapped his hand over the kids mouth. His hand was instantly covered with tears and snot. "If you don't shut up," he snarled into the sudden silence, "I'm going to knock you out. Do you understand me?"

Slowly, the kid quit fighting him, whether he understood what Vance was telling him, or he was having a hard time getting air was debatable, but the kid nodded. Vance eased his hold slightly but stayed ready to muzzle the little brat again. He took his hand away and wiped it on his pants. Stupid little germ factory, he shuddered. God, he hated germs. Why hadn't he thought to pick up some duct tape?

"Houston is going to kill you!" the kid snarled, his eyes black with hate and a tinge of fear.

Vance laughed at that. "Wow, kid, you sounded almost like your grandpa, there." he laughed again.

"I don't have a grandpa!" he squirmed against the cloth that bound him. "You'd better take me back to my Mom, right now."

"She isn't your mom," Vance scowled down at the boy. "And, you most certainly do have a grandpa. We're taking you to him."

"I want to go back to Walmart."

"Your grandfather will buy you a Walmart." Vance got off his knees although his upper body still bent at the waist. "Now, I'm getting back in the seat, but if you start screaming again, I'll do to you what I did to the woman with you."

"That was my Mom!" Link retorted, "and if you hurt her, you're going to be dead." Repeating his threat didn't seem to have the effect he hoped for, so he subsided.

Vance ignored the threat, as he climbed into his seat, the woman was no longer a problem, but the kid's words skipped around in his head. The Boss had demanded that they were to kill the woman, if they had a chance. He wanted them all dead. But the Boss wasn't here, at the moment. Actually, at the moment, the Boss wasn't anywhere. He was on the run from a massive FBI manhunt and was, most likely, headed for some place without an extradition treaty. That's why he and Chuck had decided just to grab the kid and let Lucano send out his cherry-picked assassin to take care of the others. They both knew, if they were picked up for murder, Lucano would arrange to have them capped before they ever got to court. Yeah, he'd take his chances with that two-bit cop against Lucano any day. A chill rippled up his spine.

But, at least the kid was quiet, except for the occasional thumps coming from the back end as he fought his bonds.

Link looked around the space. The floor of this car was hard, and there were boxes stacked across from him. One was big but there were some smaller ones sitting on top and around it. Occasionally, when they went around a corner, the smaller boxes would totter and he worried that he would be buried under them if they came down.

He was scared but he wouldn't let them know it. He thought of his hero, Spider Man, but when he tried to picture the face behind the mask, he saw Houston instead. Or, maybe Crockett. Which one would save him? A tear slipped down his cheek as he listened to the men in the front seat.

"Too many people saw this van," one said. "We've got to ditch it and get another ride."

"You think I don't know that?" the other one snapped. "I'm going to walk back into town and find us another vehicle and something to use as a gag, then we're going to put that kid in his 'car seat'" he paused to chuckle at his wit, "then we'll head for the airport as soon as the pilot contacts us."

"What am I supposed to do?"

"You stay here and keep that kid quiet."

THE PARAMEDICS HAD given Jen another shot of Naloxone before they loaded her into the ambulance. And, once they'd brought her into the hospital, the ER doctor had started a Naloxone IV drip as soon as Jen was in a bed. She was in and out still, but she was not coming back as quickly as Houston felt she should.

He stepped outside the ER cubicle and called Travis. His next call was to FBI Agent James McCutcheon. Miracle of miracles, he answered immediately.

AWARE OF NOISES AROUND her, Jen's eyes opened cautiously. She was in a hospital bed. What was she doing here, she wondered? What had happened to put her in the hospital? Her mind swam sickeningly and her stomach churned in wild dis-harmony with it. Feeling the contractions in her belly as it prepared to purge it's contents, she rolled to the side, an IV tube dangling from her arm, and grabbed for the railing that confined her. A plastic bag appeared, miraculously, in front of her mouth and a hard hand guided her head downward holding her hair out of the way.

"She's coming around again," Houston's voice spoke to someone she couldn't see. She couldn't see Houston either, from her current position, but she knew that voice and the touch of his hand as he handed her a wet wipe for her mouth. She wiped her lips and looked at him gratefully. He sat beside the bed, his face a mask of concern.

As though her stomach, in expelling it's contents, had cleared the fog from her brain, the men in the white van came roaring back into her head. "Houston!" she cried out, "They have Link! We've got to find Link!" she tried to get out of the bed.

Her stomach chose that moment to decide it wasn't finished yet. She rolled to the side again and Houston handed her a clean barf bag. Her hands were shaking.

"I know," she heard him say, as her insides heaved. "We've already got people looking for the van. We'll find him."

"He'll be so scared," she grabbed his hand in a crushing grip, tears welling in her eyes and overflowing.

"Probably, but fear won't kill him and neither will they. Remember, Lucano doesn't want his grandson harmed, just you, Irene, and me." a rueful smile curved his lips.

"Then, why am I still alive?"

"We have a very prepared by-stander to thank for that. I managed to convey my thanks and get his name and number for you." Houston stepped away from the bed as a woman in a white lab coat, with a stethoscope and a name tag that declared her to be a doctor, took the hand Houston had just relinquished.

"I'm glad you're still with us," she smiled.

"Were you in doubt?" Jen asked, without any humor.

"Your lab results showed a heavy dose of Fentanyl but a good Samaritan, fearing a drug overdose, gave you Narcan, so, we were cautiously optimistic. How are you feeling?" she clicked a pen light and shined it in Jen's eyes.

The sudden flash of light against her retinas caused her stomach to rebel again and she grabbed for the plastic bag. The doctor handed it to her this time.

"I think we're down to bile now," Jen said, handing it back when she finished. "How long have I been in here?"

"Almost three hours." Houston said.

"How soon can I get out of here?" Jen fixed her gaze on the doctor.

"Your vitals look good." the doctor said. "If you feel up to it, I can sign you out in a couple more hours."

"Can't we do it sooner? I have to find my son."

Empathy filled the doctor's eyes and she gave Jen's hand a sympathetic pat before leaving the room. "That depends on you."

Houston picked up the hand the doctor had patted. For some reason his firm, calloused grip was sooo much more comforting than that gentle pat.

CHAPTER THIRTY NINE

Travis flew his Jet Ranger toward Rock Springs and a friend's vacant field where he could set it down just east of town, and called Houston to give him the address and, just in case, the map coordinates of the place, with his ETA of about twenty minutes.

"Jen and I will be there waiting," his brother answered without preface. "We're on our way, now."

"You're bringing Jen along?"

"He had no choice, Travis." There was enough sting of venom that Travis swallowed any further comments.

"Sorry, Jen. I just thought they would keep you in the hospital a little longer. Bro, you should warn someone when you put your phone on speaker," Travis laughed.

"Yeah. Are you sure of the destination, Travis?" Houston interrupted before the conversation could spiral downward.

"As sure as I can be without exhibiting what you might call excessive curiosity." he said. "The radio chatter says a private jet has radioed the airport there for landing clearance. They're a little over an hour out but it won't be long. The pilot was not real long on details but he said he would need to refuel. So, either an immediate return trip or a longer trip from here."

"Do you have any idea how long a trip?"

"They're talking about a Cessna Citation Longitude, so the flight range is about 3000 miles, give or take. There's a lot of speculation around about who's aboard. The betting says it's a big movie scout checking out possible film locations." Travis sounded a bit doubtful of that.

"If we can't stop them here, they could be well into Mexico before they need to refuel again."

"I certainly wouldn't be able to stop them," Travis said. "How do you plan to keep them grounded?"

"I don't. I just want to make sure Link isn't on that plane when it takes off," Houston said. "Stopping them is the Feds' problem. You know, I don't think Lucano is on the plane. He's most likely already out of the country. This is just to take Link to wherever Lucano decides to go." Houston paused a moment. "Did you bring your long range sniper rifle like I asked?"

"Loaded and ready to go." Travis said. "Gotta get back to flying this thing now."

Houston crossed the cattle guard into the field. Houston and Jen heard the chopper approaching from the east.

The wind had picked up in the last half hour and they watched Travis fight to keep the bird level as he set it down. He didn't intend to stay long, and kept the engine running so the rotor set up a small storm of sage twigs and sand.

"Stay in the truck," Houston said to Jen. "I'm just going to get the rifle and Travis will take off again."

Bent down, Houston ran in, under the blades as Travis opened the door.

AS he handed over the powerful weapon in it's protective case, Travis shouted over the engine whine, "You going to kill them or what?"

Houston smacked his brother's shoulder. "Why do all my brothers think I'm going to shoot someone every time I have a gun in my hands?"

"You shot that Jeep," Travis pointed out.

That's what the sheriff had assumed, also. He saw no reason to correct that assumption, even for Travis. By that time, the two had cleared the rotor and straightened up. Houston saw Jen begin to step out of the truck and waved her back. "Yeah, but the chase was getting pretty hairy at the time. The worst part of the whole thing was that Jen saw a man burn to death," Houston frowned, as the thought sobered him, "and she'll probably have nightmares about it the rest of her life. It's not a pretty way to die and it's really ugly to see it happen."

"Yes it is," Travis agreed. "I heard the bullet hit an emergency flare in the Jeep and that lit some fuel soaked rags before the gas tank exploded. Me, I wondered why he was carrying fuel soaked rags anyway."

"The sheriff mentioned there were traces of strontium and potassium in the vehicle, maybe from a flare, but the investigation is still very preliminary." Houston said, closing off his mind to memories of the fire. He stopped by the truck and willed Travis to turn back to his copter.

When he didn't, Houston said, "To answer your question, Travis, I don't plan to shoot anyone." he slid the rifle into the back seat. "When they get to the airport, the van should slow down as it approaches the jet. Of course, they might be driving something else by now. I'll have to play it by ear." He opened the rifle case and took the weapon out of it. "All I intend to do is get close enough to shoot out a tire or two. Maybe keep them pinned down long enough for airport security to put them in cuffs. They won't even know I'm there until I go in after Link."

Travis nodded as if this was the wisest plan he'd heard all week. "Why don't I drive you, then? I know most of the emergency people in Sweetwater County. Should be able to convince them." He watched as Houston checked the weapon, its magazine and the ammo in it. "Tell you what, Houston. I'll drop you off wherever you want, Jen and I will go back around to the terminal, talk to security, explain what the plan is, and then we, me and security, can go out, while you keep them pinned down, take their guns, and get Link." He shrugged and spread his hand out, palm down, to indicate that it was already a done deal.

Houston considered. "You know they won't give up Link without a fight. You'll be putting well meaning amateurs with minimal training up against men with no morals and no compunction about shooting their way out of a situation. I don't think they're dumb enough to use Link as a shield, but you never know how desperate they might be. They could use him and tell their boss that he was hit by a stray bullet."

"There's a couple of security officers working there who have some military experience. One of them may be working this shift and we can keep the rest out of range. Just a show of force. Make a decision, Bro. You have to be in position before the jet makes its final approach or they could see you."

"Come on, then." Houston nodded. "Grab whatever you need and let's do this."

"Let me lock up my bird," Travis said, just as his radio crackled to life. He hurried back to the cockpit and put on his headphones. He listened for a minute then removed the headphones and shut down his baby.

"You called it," he hollered. He jumped down, locked the door, and ran back as the rotors slowed above him. "They found that van parked in some trees behind an abandoned shop. Empty."

"I didn't think they were entirely stupid," Houston slid the rifle back into its case. "Let's go."

"You okay, Jen?" Travis asked, seeing her face, pale and drawn and the tremors in her hands, as he stepped into the driver's seat and Houston climbed in the back.

"I'm fine," she said, but she didn't turn to speak.

He wasn't convinced. "That's what I thought." Travis started the truck and circled around toward the cattle guard.

The Rock Springs airport sat atop a butte off of I-80, about fifteen minutes east of the town. Travis dropped Houston off with his rifle outside the security fence and drove past the terminal and toward the service buildings beyond.

He rolled down his window to speak to the man who blocked the gate to the hangars. "Hi, Orvis," he said.

"Travis," Orvis Mayweather acknowledged. "Where did you get the new wheels? Did you finally get rid of that old rattle-trap of yours?"

Travis laughed. "Not on your life. My old Bronco has another 200 thousand miles left in it, easy."

"Yeah, right," Orvis gave a bark of laughter. "It can't be easy to find parts for that thing anymore. What do you use to keep it running? Bubble gum and paper clips?" he laughed again.

"I find dental floss and duct tape work best," Travis grinned and set Orvis off again. "No, I just borrowed my brother's truck for a bit."

"So, what brings you up here?" Orvis asked.

"I was hoping to see your chief, Butch." Orvis raised his brows. "Is he working today?"

"Yep, he's on the grounds, but he's pretty busy right now. Got some big muckity-muck flying in soon."

"That's what I need to talk to him about," Travis kept his expression easy. "Could you call him over? Tell him it's important."

"Sure, just park over there by his office." Orvis lifted his two-way to his mouth and pressed the call button.

CONSTRUCTION FOR THE airport had created some dirt piles and ridges, grass and sage covered, around the perimeter, and Houston used the natural cover to camouflage his progress as he looked for a position. Since the airport didn't have a control tower he wouldn't be visible from certain vantage points. He searched for those points. If he was seen with this rifle near the airfield, he knew he would be facing some federal charges and some very unpleasant results. It didn't matter. He would face the devil himself to keep Link out of Lucano's hands so he continued his recon. He needed a position that would keep the terminal and service areas out of the direct line of fire.

Whatever the kidnappers were driving now, they would have to meet the plane at the service area, so he needed to find a place where the field of fire wouldn't endanger too many people. And he needed to be able to identify them. They would only be able to come in through the main gate and they would be driving at a normal speed so as not to arouse suspicion. There were other access points around the perimeter but they were restricted access and it was not general public knowledge. No, they would come in through the gate. He just had to pick out which vehicle they were driving. He wasn't going for a kill shot anyway.

The only clue he had was the Bonnie Plant man had said the guy that got in the driver side of the van had kind of ginger colored hair. Not a lot to go on, but if he took out the wrong tires, he'd buy the innocent driver new ones.

Houston moved toward the terminal access point, found a small pocket in a patch of sage brush, most likely where antelope had bedded down, and cleared the lens caps from the the rifle's scope. From this position, he had a good chance of taking out tires on the kidnapper's vehicle, and with some luck, he should be able to take out a tire on the jet as it sat by the service building.

His leg reminded him that it wasn't healed yet as he settled into the pocket, tested the wind direction, and waited. The wait was shorter than expected. His phone, vibrated against his thigh.

"Change of plans," Travis said, urgently. "The pilot has requested use of the hangar to receive 'cargo'. His ETA is ten minutes. That means ..."

"Yeah," Houston was already on the move, "that means our two guys will be headed for that hanger, inside, off the tarmac. Fewer witnesses, and I've got ten minutes to get there." He slid his phone back in it's place. It was no longer possible to keep the rifle out of sight, he would be running right past the terminal. His only hope was that Travis would be able to alert security and explain the reason for it.

Ignoring his leg's protest, he abused it some more, and broke into a jog. He wasn't worried about the car with Link in it, they wouldn't show up until the plane landed and was taxiing to the hangar.

It took him six minutes to circle the perimeter and enter the service area. Travis met him as he limped up. Outside the building.

"Orvis said you can set up behind that grounds shed over there," he pointed.

"That's handgun range. Way too close," Houston gave a hard shake to his head. "I'll be shooting straight into the building and out the other side, if I miss. Some innocent person could get dead."

"How can you miss at that range?"

"And who could have guessed that a stray shot would hit an emergency flare in the back end of a moving vehicle." Houston shrugged. "Just change guns with me," Houston shoved the rifle into Travis' hands and held out his hand for the pistol at his brother's side. "Where's my truck and where's Jen?"

"Your truck is out of sight of the runways. Jen was jumping out of her skin and wouldn't stay in it, and sneezing like she had hay fever."

"The drugs haven't completely cleared out of her system." Houston guessed.

"Yeah, well, she thought she should stay close, in case, we needed help with Link. I told her it wasn't a good idea, that she was looking too pale. I sent her to the coffee shop to get something to drink and maybe some antihistamine." Travis said. "Butch sent for one of his staff, a female officer, to escort her there and stay with her."

Not quite trusting that solution to hold for long, Houston didn't have time to figure out a better option. He found a position, on the ground behind a detached snow-plow blade, where he could see the open bay of the hangar and still keep an eye out for the car. There was some other tools and equipment that he had to step over to find a good spot. He was barely in position when the deep whine of the jet engines announced the plane's approach. Maintenance was jockeying the last small plane to the other side of the hangar to open space for the jet.

Every eye in the airport was focused on the exciting arrival, except Houston's, which could still see the road entering the service area in his peripheral vision. Wheels down, the plane touched the tarmac and the air brake flaps lifted to engage. The plane ran only to the first taxiway entrance and turned, dangerously fast, Houston thought, toward the hanger. Following ground crew hand signals, the pilot eased it through the wide doors.

From the side, Houston saw the vehicle, a gun-metal blue pickup with a bed full of strapped crates, roll up to the rear of the hanger. The male passenger had a nest of dark hair. The other was Jerry DeFerro's friend, Chuck. Houston cursed under his breath. How in the hell did he fit into this?

The timing of the truck's arrival was too precise to be accidental. They must have been waiting at the bottom of the butte for the pilot's instructions, to ensure that all focus was on the plane and allow the truck to drive up unnoticed.

And they almost managed it, too. Slowly the truck disappeared from Houston's view. He moved to the corner of the hangar where he could see the truck had come to a stop The driver and passenger stepped out of the cab and went in the back door. He caught just a glimpse of the jet's stairs unfolding. He flattened himself against the side of the building until he heard the click of the door.

No one was guarding the truck! Stupid move, or were they just that confident? Disbelief warred in Houston's brain. Was Link stuffed in one of those boxes or had they left him somewhere? Only one way to find out.

He jogged to the truck and hunkered down where he could not be seen from the door. The left rear tire was at his knees. Unscrewing the cap on the air valve, he depressed the valve stem and wedged a small grain of sand to hold it down, listened for the faint hiss, then loosely replaced the cap.

Now, which of those boxes might contain a six-year-old boy? "Link," he said softly, tapping on the biggest box, and was rewarded with a scrabbling thump.

Relief released the breath he'd been holding. "Link? Can you answer me?" Another thump was his answer. The boy was gagged but he was alive.

The crate was cinched with three strands of good Wyoming fence wire, twisted and crimped down tight. And Houston hadn't expected to need his fencing pliers.

"I'll be right back, Link," he tapped on the box again. "I have to get a tool."

"Is that where he is?" Jen's frantic whisper from the back end of the truck nearly stopped his heart.

CHAPTER FORTY

Houston dove back around the bumper, and came nose to nose with Jen. "What the hell are you doing here?" he whispered harshly.

He grabbed her hand, jerked her up beside him, and pulled her, running for the plow blade. It was only a few steps but they had barely reached it when the back door of the hangar opened wider with a reluctant squawk. There was no time to scold Jen but his glare brought a spot of color to her face.

"Just bring the truck around inside and start loading the cargo so we can get refueled and take off before the wind gets any stronger," a voice ordered as 'ginger hair' walked out, dangling a key in his hand.

Jen was yanking at his sleeve and pointing at 'ginger hair'. "That's him," she mouthed as Houston turned. He nodded.

A string of curse words came from the truck when the man noticed the flat. He kicked the wheel and cursed again. Hobbling to the door, he jerked it open, disappearing behind it with only his finger tips still visible.

"The rear tire is flat!" he shouted over the noise.

"You can make it to the hangar doors, Chuck!" the voice snapped angrily. "Just get the truck in here."

The door squawked again, 'Chuck' climbed into the truck and goosed it to life, and with the tire flapping in protest, disappeared around the far corner of the building.

"Stay here, and for God's sake, stay out of sight," Houston ordered. He drew his gun as he ran the length of the hangar to where a small window near the corner of the building allowed him to see the interior.

The pilot stood at the head of the stairway of the jet, flight jacket open, shoulder holster visible. Vance was standing at the base of the steps. Houston couldn't see his gun but he'd be stupid to bet his life on him not being armed as well. Houston had seen Chuck's gun, tucked in the waist band of his jeans, while he and Jen were crouched behind the plow blade.

The truck came around the far corner and pulled slowly into the bay. The pilot motioned him forward until the hood was close to the stairs.

Although the lower half of Vance's body was now hidden by the front end of the truck, Houston knew that all three of them were armed. Were there any more men inside the plane, he wondered?

Vance moved toward the truck, and as soon as Chuck shut off the engine, he dropped the tailgate. His gun winked from under his t-shirt.

Houston calculated his chances of taking all three of them without gunfire and didn't like the odds. The men were in the middle of a kidnapping and Houston knew they wouldn't surrender peacefully. There was a little boy between him and the others and he really didn't like the idea of that box becoming a casket.

"You," Chuck shouted, as he climbed out of the truck, motioning to someone Houston hadn't been able to see, "help me get this into the plane." He put his hands on the box that Houston had tapped and pulled it to the edge. "And, you," he said to Vance, "start loading the rest of these into the cargo hold."

Houston's jaw dropped when Travis, garbed in maintenance coveralls, walked over to the tailgate. Holy shit, Houston's eyes flew wide open and his mind scrambled frantically to remember if Chuck had happened to be in the Big Cup Cafe at the same time that the brothers had been seated at their booth? He didn't think so but was Travis really willing to risk recognition just to get another combatant in the ring? Now there were two people in his line of fire. But at least one of them knew how to handle an emergency situation, and Chuck hadn't blinked an eye at Travis. Houston smiled a grim smile. Maybe they could laugh about it over a beer, later.

He stepped back and his foot landed on something soft, something that made a soft protest. Angry beyond belief, he swallowed hard to dislodge the heart that seemed stuck in his throat as he jerked around and glowered at Jen, who was peering over his shoulder.

"I thought I told you to stay behind that plow!" he hissed at her.

"I flunked obedience school," she snarled back.

He ground his teeth and forced his words out softly, "Keep your voice down."

"They can't hear us over that big engine," she whispered back.

"Jen, for God's sake, there are three armed men in there. I can't take a chance on one of them shooting you."

"Actually, I believe there are more than that. Doesn't security carry weapons, too?" she said. "And that's why I have to be here. My son is right in the middle of it."

"This is Maintenance. Maintenance personnel don't carry firearms. Jen. Please. Go. Back." he pleaded.

"No," she shook her head, mutinously, but her eyes softened "but I will stay behind this corner."

It was the best he could hope for, he didn't have time to argue. He couldn't let them get Link onto that plane.

He poked his head up enough to look through the window again, saw Vance at the tail gate, obviously prepared to help with the unloading but waiting for the other two to clear out of the way. Travis and Chuck were working the big crate off the truck bed with Chuck signaling Travis to handle his end very carefully.

This was not cargo they could put in the hold, and there wasn't room for the two carrying the box to squeeze through the door with the pilot standing there. The pilot would have to either step back into the cabin or come down the stairs. Please decide to come down, he prayed.

"Hey, there's something moving in here," Travis shouted over the sound of the engines.

Travis knew exactly what was in the box. Houston gave him points for the 'dumb' act.

"It's the boss's pet boa constrictor," Chuck answered. "He likes to have it with him."

"I need a distraction," Houston muttered to himself, "but what?"

Jen tugged on his sleeve. She must have heard him.

"Let me get back by the plow blade," she whispered.

"Yes," he nodded, thinking she'd finally come to her senses.

"I can create a distraction."

"What?! No!" The harsh whisper ripped from his mouth as fear twisted his guts. He shook his head in a violent negative.

"Yes." she insisted, just as harshly. "This is a metal building and there is a good-sized rock there by the plow. They can't help but hear it but they won't be able to tell, for sure, where it came from. Since the front is all open, they'll suspect that whatever hit the building, came from around the back door. They will be looking that direction."

She saw the objection leap to his lips and hurried on. "All I have to do is throw the rock against the building hard enough to make them turn. Travis and that other man have their hands full. That leaves just the pilot and Vance for you to handle."

"No," he repeated, "it's too risky."

"Not for me," her eyes held his, a plea swimming in a pool of blue. "I can get behind the plow before anyone can get to the door. You'll have the advantage with their attention focused on the back."

So many things could go wrong with her plan, but it could provide the distraction he needed.

"How hard can you throw?"

"College fast pitch softball league championship team. I was the pitcher."

He couldn't help the smile. He nodded. "Get behind the plow and show me the rock," he commanded, gruffly, "then wait for my signal."

She nodded. Ducking below the window, she scurried to the plow blade.

Houston waited until she lifted a grapefruit sized rock over the top of the blade, then edged his eyes over the window sill again. He had no doubt Travis could, and would, handle Chuck.

The pilot, now making his way down the stairs gave the inside of the hangar a visual sweep. Houston ducked. He gave it a second then looked again. Vance was loading one of the smaller boxes into the cargo hold and making room for the rest before he went back for another one.

When the pilot reached the bottom and stepped aside, he scowled at Chuck and waved impatiently for him to hurry. Chuck and Travis moved forward until they reached the foot of the steps where a short debate ensued over who was to lead and who was to follow. Finally, Chuck backed up the first step and started the climb to the cabin leaving Travis to support the weight.

Houston looked back at Jen and raised his hand like an Indy race starter. He looked back through the window as Travis reached the door but the pilot had started back up the stairs. He didn't dare let the pilot get inside the passenger area before Travis had a chance to take care of Chuck and get turned around. He sliced his hand down sharply and moved quickly around the corner of the hangar. The open bay was one step away when the rock hit the side of the building.

She'd been right about the sound. Even over the steady idling whine of the jet's engines, all heads turned toward the back door.

TRAVIS SAW CHUCK'S head jerk up at the loud bang and made his move. Putting all his weight behind it, he shoved the crate into the man's middle. Off guard and off balance, Chuck's boot caught in the carpeted floor and he went down, the box on top of him and Travis on top of the box. He was scrambling to get a hand on his gun when Travis' fist connected with his jaw. When that didn't quite do the job, Travis hit him again. Chuck's head snapped to the side and his body went slack. Travis relieved him of the pistol, pulled the crate off him, and reached inside his coveralls for the zip ties Butch had given him. In seconds, Chuck was neutralized.

As the building rang with the echoes of the rock, Houston stepped through the bay door and ran at Vance who had pulled his gun but was looking at the pilot who had his hand on the back door handle and his gun at the ready.

Seeing Houston flying at him, Vance started to turn but was a split second too late. Houston hit Vance's gun arm hard enough to knock the gun aside, and in the same motion grabbed the man's wrist and twisted fiercely. He felt something pop as, with a cry of pain, the gun flew out of Vance's hand and slid across the floor, under the truck. With the immediate threat neutralized, Houston leveled a chop at the jointure of Vance's head and neck. The man went down like a slaughter-house steer.

Keeping the truck between him and the pilot, Houston moved toward the plane.

"Freeze," he shouted at the pilot, leveling his gun over the hood of the truck. Alerted to this new challenge, the pilot spun and dropped, firing as he went down. The bullet passed Houston's head close enough to part his hair. Houston fired once in return and flattened himself behind the front wheel. He took another shot under the front bumper but the pilot had found cover behind some sandbags. Houston held his fire. The space where the pilot had taken refuge was in a direct line with the snow plow blade outside. If Jen was behind the blade, as she'd promised, she should be safe.

If she stayed, he grimaced, remembering she had stated adamantly she'd "flunked obedience school".

With the sound of the jet engines muffling his movements, Houston moved toward the back of the truck to get a safer angle, away from Jen's hiding place. And just in time, too, as another shot flattened the tire he'd just left.

Then two things happened almost simultaneously. The jet engines shut off, and whined down. A blanket of eerie silence settled over the scene, and the back door of the hangar gave a raucous squawk as it began slowly to open.

The pilot, separated by only feet from the door, turned his gun on the new threat and fired a string of shots and Houston's heart lodged once more in his throat.

"Jen NO!" With little thought to his own safety, he lunged from his position with a native warrior scream, emptying his gun at whatever parts of the pilot showed, before diving behind a forklift parked against a wall. He dropped the clip and slammed in the other one.

After the initial squawk, the door remained quiet and the silence was even more terrifying than the sound it had made. An agony of panic sucked the breath from his body as ice flowed through his veins. He had to get to Jen.

Another shot ricocheted off the side of the forklift and shattered the truck window. Keeping the forklift between him and the pilot, Houston moved back against the wall.

"Jen," Houston screamed, but there was no answer.

"Go check on Jen, Houston," Travis hollered, from behind the fuselage door. "I've got a bead on him. If he moves, he won't survive." To prove his point, Travis placed a shot into a sandbag just in front of the pilot's hiding place, triggering a spate of curses that would make a stevedore blush. A gun came sliding across the floor from behind the sandbags and the pilot raised his hands, standing up slowly, blinking sand out of his eyes.

Houston didn't hesitate. He was out the bay door in front, around the corner, and nearly knocked Jen off her feet. She was just stepping away from the window they had used earlier. He grabbed on to steady her, and himself, then yanked her into his arms. Crushing her to him, he held on as if his life depended on it. At that moment, he was positive it did.

"Is everyone okay?" she asked, her voice shaking.

He could only nod, not trusting his voice yet. Slowly, he released his hold and led her back around the corner.

Butch, with FBI Special Agent James McCutcheon and another agent right beside him, stalked into the hangar through the squeaky back door, guns drawn. Taking in the scene, McCutcheon relaxed and let his gun drop. He knew Travis and he could see Houston stepping through the bay door

"What have we got here, Houston?"

"There's another man behind that truck, Houston pointed, "he's unconscious at the moment."

"Let's get that man cuffed and Mirandized, Steve," Agent McCutcheon directed his partner.

"There's another one in the Cessna," Travis said, "but he's trussed up pretty good" He gave Butch and McCutcheon a cheeky grin. "You're a little late."

"Our invitation got lost in the mail," Butch laughed.

"We'll have to send them out a little earlier next time." Travis grinned.

"It was pretty short notice," McCutcheon agreed. "I see you started the party without us."

Travis shrugged. "The ice cream was melting."

"Where's Link?" Jen demanded.

"I'm up here, Mom," Link shouted, sticking his head out the door of the jet.

"You can come down now." Travis beckoned Link from the plane. The boy ran down the steps.

Jen met Link at the bottom of the stairs and wrapped her arms around him. "Are you okay?" she fussed, checking him over, rubbing the tape residue from his cheeks and mouth and looking at the rope burns on his wrists.

"I'm okay, Mom. Travis got me out of the box and untied me but he said I had to stay in the plane until he said it was safe to come down."

"Travis took good care of you," she whispered. "We'll have to find some way to thank him properly, won't we?"

Link nodded.

Agent McCutcheon watched the reunion as Butch and his agent gathered the kidnappers. "You saved the boy," he said to Houston. "Good work."

Houston's legs were still quivering from his panic over Jen but he locked his knees and returned the agent's smile, with effort. McCutcheon wasn't fooled, he saw the fine tremors and the lingering trace of fear that was slow to dissipate.

"Butch?" McCutcheon drew the security head's attention, "Mind if Houston and I use that office for a few minutes?" He waved a hand at a windowed door on the other side of the hangar.

"Door's unlocked," Butch said.

Houston could hear Steve, the agent, repeating the Miranda advisement to Vance as Travis pushed the pilot over to join them.

"Hey," the pilot, hands cuffed behind his back, complained, as Houston and McCutcheon walked off, "You got to let me get this sand out of my eyes."

"We'll see you get medical," McCutcheon called over his shoulder.

An official-looking black Escalade pulled into the hangar and another agent got out.

"There's one for you in the jet," Travis said when the agent put out his hands to take the pilot. "He shouldn't be a problem. Just take the tape off his mouth and untie his feet. Oh," Travis took the gun from his waist and handed it to the agent with a grin, "this is his."

CHAPTER FORTY ONE

McCutcheon took the padded swivel chair behind the desk and Houston took the hardwood one at the end. The agent rocked and turned side to side a bit, testing.

"I always try desk chairs whenever I have the opportunity," he smiled at Houston's raised eyebrows. "One day, before I retire, I hope to find a comfortable one."

"I've been thinking seriously about retiring myself," Houston said.

"Really?" McCutcheon's own eyebrows rose. "Since when? I thought you were happy on the force."

"Since about fifteen minutes ago," Houston said, forcing his voice to a calm he was still not feeling. "I'm too old for this shit."

"The agency can always use a good man," McCutcheon said. "If you're serious about a change."

"That wouldn't change anything but the scenery," Houston shook his head.

"Better perks, though." The agent paused, but when Houston didn't pick up on that, he went on. "That was a really neat trick with the back door."

Houston's nerves took another nosedive as those moments of sheer terror shook him again. He cleared his throat. "You'll have to congratulate Jen on that. I wasn't out there. She was supposed to be hiding behind that snowplow blade."

"Really? Wow!" with a fuller understanding of Houston's stress, the agent steepled his hands under his chin and leaned back. "When we got here, the door was ajar, with a heavy cable and a tow hook around the handle. It was fastened in such a way that a person could stand back several feet, pull the cable and it would crank the handle down to release the latch and allow the door to be opened. Although I wasn't here to hear it, Butch said the door has a loud screech when it's first opened. It didn't make a sound when we came through it."

"Yes." Houston didn't elaborate. "Did you find Benny's body?" he changed the subject. "Is that why we're having this private chat?"

"No we haven't found the body yet. One of Lucano's men contacted us a few days ago, offering to turn states evidence in exchange for immunity and a new face and identity. He was able to give us names, dates and, most importantly, some judges and corrupt law enforcement officers who were on the payroll. We were already setting up the operation when you bought me supper the other night."

"So, you know where Lucano is?" Houston asked.

"He's gone dark," McCutcheon shook his head, "but Interpol has their eyes on a couple of places he has compounds. All in countries without extradition treaties with the U.S., of course."

"Of course. Link still isn't safe then." Houston said.

"I don't think there's any immediate danger for a while. Our net caught a mass of smaller fish from his organization so Lucano's resources are limited. It will take him some time to regroup. Hopefully, long enough for Interpol to find him, extract him and return him to us.

"No, why I called you in here is to give you some information about Jen's sister." Houston straightened as though preparing for a blow. "Our mole said she was part of a shipment to Hong Kong, about two weeks ago."

"Alive?"

"As far as we know," McCutcheon nodded. "Interpol is working that, too. They have one of their best men on it. Jill was working with us too, giving us valuable information."

"You let her go back into that, knowing Lucano would recognize her?" For the first time in their acquaintance, Houston lost some respect for the man and the agency.

"She would have, if we'd asked, but we didn't have to." McCutcheon picked up a pen from the desk and twirled it between his fingers. "Did you know that Jen's sister has an eidetic memory?"

"No."

McCutcheon nodded. "Surprised us too. It was a boon though. But we must have gotten too close, or else Lucano just got lucky and spotted her.

She disappeared. I wanted you to know. It's up to you, what you tell Jen, but it can't go beyond her. That's still one of the strings we have to unravel."

He stood, gave the chair a final, regretful spin. "I'll have to keep looking. This one doesn't feel right either."

He walked around the desk and out the door, phone already to his ear, "Okay, guys, let's get those three under wraps so that we can deal with this thirty million dollar prize."

As McCutcheon's voice drifted through the door, Houston rose. He needed to touch Jen, hold her, and figure out what in the hell he was going to tell her. Or not. Then he was going to strangle her for taking ten years off his life.

"Mrs. Bradley," McCutcheon called across the hangar, "I've got a fairly clear picture of what went down today, but I'd like to talk to you and Link tomorrow, in my Casper office. We need to hear what he remembers. Houston has my number. Call to set it up."

Houston heard Jen answer, "Okay."

"Butch?" McCutcheon wasn't through barking orders just yet. "Lucano's plane doesn't leave this building until we get forensics out here to check it out and a man to fly it to the base. Seal it off. Nobody at this facility is to touch anything, including that truck. We should have men out here late tonight or early tomorrow. You can have your hangar back as soon as they leave."

"Got it," Butch saluted the Fed.

With that, Special Agent in Charge McCutcheon climbed into the Escalade for a crowded ride back to the terminal parking lot where his own vehicle was parked.

Butch walked over to Travis. "Are you all through shooting up my place for the day?" The question was asked deadpan but there was a glimmer of humor in Butch's eyes.

"Looks like," Travis draped his arm over the man's shoulder. "Sorry to break up the party so early, but we still have a ways to go today."

Houston walked over to Butch, extended his hand. "Thanks for the assist," he said as Butch took it. "When you have an estimate of the damages, send me the bill. I'll see you're reimbursed." He reached in his pocket for his wallet and handed Butch his business card.

"We had already budgeted to get a new door," Butch said, pocketing the card, "Not much left to patch except a couple of bullet holes in the back wall and another sandbag, but thanks."

"I'm going to talk to Jen and Link," Houston said to Travis, and turned to leave.

"I'll get the truck and pick you up," his brother said.

"We'll meet you out front."

"Hey, Link," Travis called, "do you want to go with me to get the truck?"

Houston, who had been trying to figure out how to get a few minutes alone with Jen, gave his brother a grateful look when Link answered affirmatively. He watched Jen's mouth open in an automatic protest. She wasn't ready to let her son out of her sight, but she closed it again, knowing that the activity would help bring some normalcy back to Link's brain.

As Link trotted over to join Travis, Houston held out his arms for Jen. She stepped into them without hesitation and he still didn't have any idea what to tell her about McCutcheon's news. Either option could fill her with hope or, transversely, increase her fears about her sister.

He held on, tight. The feel of her soft curves pressed to his length, brought reassurance to Houston's soul.

"We're going to make it," he whispered in her ear and closed his eyes.

"What did the FBI agent want?" Jen asked into his shirt front.

"We can talk about it after Link is asleep tonight. Right now, we need to find some dressings for Link's wrists then get Travis back to the helicopter and decide where to sleep tonight."

"Where?" she looked up, troubled. "I don't want to stay here."

"You heard agent McCutcheon. He expects to talk to Link soon, so Casper, or I have a friend in Laramie who would probably put us up for the night. Your choice."

"I can't take Link back to that house in Casper." she frowned as another thought occurred. "Should I take Link to the hospital?"

"Physically, he seems to be fine. He might need to talk to a therapist at some point. That's your choice," Houston qualified, "but that will mean more hours in this town. And sleep won't happen until the wee small hours.

"I have a nice sized apartment," Houston offered an alternative, seeing the instant the doubts clouded her eyes. "Or, I'm sure Hawk and Savvy would let you stay at their place until ..." he almost said 'you' but decided not to let her start thinking of herself as a solo unit too quickly. He changed it to, "until we can make other arrangements." He cupped her cheek in his palm and touched her lips with his. He was grateful that they softened, clung.

"I hate to break up this 'Romeo and Juliet' moment," Butch chuckled, his eyes twinkling from over Jen's shoulder, "but I have work to do here, and your ride just showed up."

Self consciously, Jen stepped out of Houston's arms. He could have held on, and he considered it. He didn't think she would have rejected him if he'd kept his arm around her, but in the end, he let her go. They turned toward the bay doors where Travis waited for them, engine idling.

"Thanks again for your help, Butch," Houston tossed over his shoulder as they left the hangar.

Except for a quick stop at a pharmacy, where they bought gauze, ointment and tape to bandage Link's wrists, little was said on the ride back to the helicopter. There wasn't much left to say, at least in front of Link. They waited to wave Travis off, then Houston got behind the wheel and headed for the interstate and Rawlins, a hundred miles east, where they could leave I-80 and head north again on US 287, toward Casper, another hundred-twenty miles. Jen would have to decide where she wanted to spend the night. Wherever she decided, he would be there with her.

Link was wired and chattering, still not completely free of the fright of the kidnapping and being stuffed in the crate. Houston was glad that the boy wanted to talk about it. It was much healthier than going silent. Jen and he took turns answering the boys endless questions and litany of fears. If it meant he would sleep easier tonight, then so much the better.

Normally, at regular speeds, the drive to Rawlins would have taken an hour and a half, but Houston shaved nearly twenty minutes off, by regarding the 75 MPH signs as a suggested minimum. When the first warning sign for highway 287 appeared at Rawlins, Houston turned to Jen.

"Casper or Laramie?"

"Can we go home now Mom?" Link asked, his face subdued.

"Someone wrecked our house," Jen looked over the seat. "We can't go back there yet." She turned her attention to Houston.

"There are things I have to take care of in Casper. I have to find a place for us to live. A rental maybe." She knew it would be foolish to make permanent arrangements. "Maybe Frank will let me come back to work. If not, I'll have to find another job. We should have a little money in the bank but it won't last long."

"Casper it is," Houston shifted into the exit lane.

IT WAS AFTER ELEVEN when they hit 'The Narrows' and entered the home stretch to the Casper city limit. At the Narrows, the mountains once pinched the Platte River so tightly that the pioneers on the Oregon Trail had to take the long way around, away from the river, to get beyond the high ridge to the more open land on the other side. By now, the passage had been tamed, blasted wider and a road added. The road was a scenic drive and the water below was a first-class whitewater kayak ride at high water. Houston wondered if Jen might enjoy floating the rapids one day, after this was all settled.

Link had finally fallen asleep in the back seat, as they slowed from 75 to 45 and then to 30 on CY Avenue. It was late enough that the usually busy street was nearly deserted. Even the high school kids running the drag had called it a night. Houston pulled into an almost empty parking lot at Poplar Avenue and shifted into park.

"Do you want to stay at my place?" he asked her. "There's two bedrooms. Or I can call Savvy and see if they're up. I'm sure she would let you stay with them."

It was thoughtful of Houston to let her make the choice. She knew that Savvy would rearrange their sleeping arrangements to accommodate her, she'd done it before. And Bryn had been very gracious about being ousted from her bed in the middle of the night, but Jen didn't want to wake anybody up. She certainly didn't want to send Savvy's sister off to another bed, whether it was just for one night or for days. And, in truth,

Jen didn't think she would be able to sleep tonight anyway. Houston would understand that.

"Your place," she said.

CHAPTER FORTY TWO

"Where are we?" Link raised his head when Houston lifted him to his shoulder.

"We're in Casper," Houston said. "You and your Mom are going to spend a few nights at my place until we get some things sorted out. Is that okay with you?"

"Okay," Link's eyelids drifted down as he wrapped his arms around Houston's neck trustingly.

Jen grabbed Link's small suitcase from the floor of the truck and was reaching for the rest of their gear when Houston caught her eye and shook his head.

"Leave it," he whispered a cross the seat. "I'll get all that while you get Link to bed."

She nodded, shut her door, and followed him into the apartment building.

Helping Link into his pajamas spread a thin a balm of normality over Jen's frayed nerves. "Do you need to pee?" she asked. When he nodded, she found the bathroom and then walked him back to the bed. With a hug and a kiss, he soon drifted off again as Jen sat next to him on the bed.

She took in the room. It had all the personality of a guest room, and had obviously been decorated with a masculine eye. Only one picture, a forest scene, hung on the wall. A full bed, a dark blue comforter with matching curtains over the lone window established the dominate color scheme. A walk-in closet, a desk, a chair, a four drawer dresser, a nightstand, and an Indian patterned rug in earth tones on the wood-grain vinyl floor completed the décor. One quick glimpse in the dresser told her that someone, probably Hawk, kept things here, and the closet said the same thing.

Refusing to snoop further, she went back into the living room and found her way easily to the kitchen. With a little bit of searching, she found coffee and filters and started a pot of coffee just as Houston walked back in with the plastic bag and the gear hauler.

"I hope you don't mind," she lifted her eyebrows in slight question. She didn't think he would have any objection to coffee, and she needed it, so she couldn't bring herself to care too much.

"Saved me the trouble," he smiled and handed her the plastic bag with her clothes and the rest of Link's books and games. "If you'd like to use the shower, there's a robe on the back of the door." He didn't mention that it was Hawk's robe, but his brother wouldn't mind, and he was pretty sure Jen wouldn't care either.

The thought of a quick shower suddenly seemed heavenly. "Thanks, I'll leave you some hot water."

When she walked back into the kitchen, wrapped in Hawk's thick terry cloth robe, her hair curling wetly over the collar, Houston handed her a cup of coffee. He had added creamer, she noticed, and was struck again by his thoughtfulness. She took the cup with both hands, lifted it to her lips with a satisfied sigh and sipped.

"Why don't we take these in on the sofa," he motioned with his own cup. "It's been a long day and my leg could use the rest."

She felt guilty that she had forgotten about his leg, what with everything else that had gone on since waking up in Rock Springs this morning. She followed him into the living room. His limp was more pronounced than it had been for days and she was reminded of his trek around the perimeter of the airport and the gun shots that had echoed inside the hangar. He hadn't given any thought to protecting his leg, she was sure.

He sat down on the sofa and patted the space beside him. She sat. He'd taken off his boots, she noted when he lifted his stockinged feet onto the coffee table. There was a trace of sand visible in the wrinkles of his socks. He leaned back into the cushions and closed his eyes. She hoped Houston could get some rest. God knows, he needed it.

She couldn't close her eyes though. Every time she did, she saw the men toss Link in the back of the truck like a sack of mulch, or else she saw the burning man, and, every time, her stomach roiled. She sipped her coffee in silence and wondered what Agent McCutcheon wanted to ask Link about.

Since that brought back images of Link stuffed in a box, she closed off that thought, too. Setting her cup down on the coffee, she rose.

"Are you going to bed?" Houston didn't bother to open his eyes.

"I'm just going to check on Link."

She walked down the hall and peeked through the door. Link had thrown off his covers and had managed to turn sideways on the bed. Even as she watched, his arms flailed as though fighting off some unseen threat. She walked across the floor and pulled the comforter back over him, placed her hand on his back and rubbed lightly. That simple touch had always helped him fall asleep before, and it seemed to calm him now. Tears formed in her eyes. Guilt was hitting her from all sides. How would her son react when, in a few years, he learned his true heritage and just how far from normal his childhood had been? It couldn't be kept from him forever.

She returned to the living room and Houston's eyes opened. "How's he doing?"

"He's restless," she answered, as he lifted his right arm across the back of the couch and patted his shoulder. It was all the invitation she needed. Needing the warmth and comfort he offered, she sat down next to him, and with her head on that strong shoulder, turned into him, seeking to bolster her own strength by absorbing some of his. She needed this more than she needed air. As though he sensed that, his arm pulled her close.

As some of his strength seeped into her, she remembered his words on the veranda of the cabin, just before they fled from his mountain top. 'I love you, Jen'. She hoped he'd meant it because she was about to throw caution to the wind.

"Houston?" His head turned toward her, eyes wide open, curious, "will you make love with me?"

He saw clouds of uncertainty floating across the summer sky blue of her eyes and knew she was preparing herself for another rebuff. Once again he was brought to his knees by the hurt he had caused her and his heart sprang into his throat, a painful lump, around which words would not pass. He cupped his hand around her jaw and tried to give her the words he wanted to say, without speaking.

Houston had fantasized of this moment for years, had prayed for this moment for the last ten days. He looked down into those dark blue pools and saw the troubled ripples in them settle, and grow warm under his gaze. He wrapped both arms around her, shifting her slightly so that her body was aligned with his from chest to knees, his thigh pressing between her legs. And he watched those deep blue pools heat to thermal temperatures. He lowered his head until their lips touched softly, seeking.

He let them linger for a while then lifted his head and traced the outline of her lips with his finger. When the tip of her tongue flicked out to taste him, a dam broke loose inside him. The flood of emotions picked him up and sent him tumbling into an uncharted sea. He closed his eyes in a silent prayer that it wouldn't wash them both away.

With a hunger too long denied, he captured her lips in a ravaging kiss. Instantly hard, his erection pressed into her softness, boldly. He sipped, tasted, savored and explored her lips and mouth. She responded with a matching hunger, opening to him with an eagerness that only added to the turbulence consuming him. Needing more, his hand pushed aside the bathrobe to pillage her body, claiming territory he had craved forever. When he moved his hand over her breast and found the nipple already hard, he squeezed it softly.

She gasped against his lips. Fearing he had hurt her, or that he was going too fast for her, he eased back the kiss and moved his hand away. She grabbed it, moved it back, pressed the softly firm globe into his palm. Her head lifted, reclaiming the kiss, protesting its withdrawal. His body erupted with heat.

Without losing contact with her lips, now as hungry as his, he shoved the robe off her shoulders and down her arms. They were both panting by the time he stripped her down to her panties. Stretching her out beneath him, he returned to plunder the body she offered so willingly. Tormenting her breasts with his hands, lips and tongue, he exulted in the aroused gasps and soft cries that issued from her mouth and his now painful erection was ready to explode. When her hips began a rhythmic grind against it, he nearly lost every bit of control he'd tried to hang on to.

Knowing he had to slow down or he wouldn't be able to last long enough to give her the pleasure he intended to, he lifted off her to stand beside the sofa. Her eyes, still clouded with passion, looked up at him in confusion.

The confusion faded when he picked her up and whispered in her ear, "Some privacy is necessary here," and watched her cheeks turn rosy, as he carried her into his bedroom, closing the door behind them with his heel.

She lay where he put her, eyes following him as he began stripping off his own clothes. Her eyes grew hungrier as she watched. Seeing it, he slowed his pace, doing a little striptease that made her lick her lips and touch a finger to one nipple. He wished he would have been able to strip off the bandage on his thigh too, if it could add to that look in her eyes.

Unbelievably, his cock grew heavier and harder. Coming down beside her, he ripped the panties, satiny, blue briefs, off her hips and replaced the fingertip at her breast with his mouth. His hand cupped her Venus mound, delved, and found her wet, and eager.

Jen started to tell him she wasn't protected but then decided it didn't matter. And it didn't. She would glory in it, if she happened to find herself carrying his child. Her disappointment was a surprise when he opened the drawer of the nightstand and found a condom, ripping the foil packet open with his teeth.

"I hope these are still good," he smiled at her, "They've been in that drawer since I first asked you out." If she'd had reason to love him before, that simple statement sealed it forever in her heart. "Want to help me put it on?" he asked.

She nodded. "It's been a while," she whispered, her hand touching his tip.

"Yeah, me too, but it's sort of like riding a bicycle, I think."

He handed her the condom. There were beads of sweat on his upper lip before she had it in place.

JEN SLEPT BESIDE HIM, the sleep of the thoroughly sated. His phone showed the time as 4:45, the sun would be up in an hour. Link would probably be up soon.

They had made love twice, before she fell into an exhausted slumber. If things went the way he hoped, he would need to buy more condoms soon.

Houston thought, selfishly, of waking her again, of resurrecting that hot passion, but he shut the thought off. The dark circles of stress and worry still bruised the soft flesh under her eyes. She needed the sleep.

He pushed off his covers and climbed gently out of the bed, and collected his clothes as he made his way to the bathroom. He shut the door quietly and splashed his face with water, got dressed and went into the kitchen to start some coffee. He would shower later.

As the coffee gurgled, he gathered the cups and Jen's t-shirt and robe, taking the cups to the sink and her clothes to the bedroom. If Link woke before she did, she would need them. Back in the kitchen, he rinsed out the cups and set them on the drying rack while he pondered breakfast. He'd stripped most of the perishables when he'd left ... had it only been two? Three days ago? Not much to make a breakfast with, unless they could be happy with ancient Pop Tarts. He double checked to make sure the box was still in the cupboard, where he'd last seen it, and finally concluded that they would have to eat out until he had a chance to do some shopping.

Remembering Link's breakfast disappointment in Rock Springs, and suspecting that Jen wasn't ready to walk into The Big Cup just yet, he decided that McDonald's was the wisest choice. The coffee maker dinged, he picked up his cup, filled it, and headed for the sofa, turning the TV on to a news channel. He muted it and drank his coffee as he watched more coverage on the raids of Lucano's holdings and offices, but there was little additional information.

He was headed back for a refill when Link walked out of his room, his face streaked with tears. Seeing Houston standing there, Link let out a muffled sob and ran into his arms. Houston lifted him up and the thin arms wrapped around his neck.

"Where's my mom?" he asked.

"She's asleep in the other bedroom," Houston told the boy. "I thought I'd let her sleep for a while longer. She was very tired."

Link nodded a child's solemn nod. "I had a bad dream," a sigh shuddered out of him.

"That can happen to anyone. I have them sometimes, too." Houston hoped his words would reassure Link. "Want to talk about it?"

Link shook his head, but squeezed a little tighter. "It's better now."

Carrying Link in one arm and his coffee in the other hand, he returned to the sofa. It was too early for cartoons and the news was just fodder for more bad dreams, so he shut off the TV and sat down with Link by his side. Inside him, there had always been a place where he thought that a child of his own might settle. Link, it appeared, had taken over a big part of that space.

Houston looked at Link's pajamas. "Who's your favorite super hero?" he asked, already knowing the answer.

"Spider Man," Link answered without hesitation.

"And, who's your next favorite?"

Link shrugged and thought hard for a few moments. "Wolverine is okay. And I kinda like the Hulk, too, but Spider Man is the best."

"Maybe we'll have time to stop by a store and pick up a comic book, today." Houston offered, and was rewarded with a wide smile.

"I have one," Link said. "Do you want to read it with me?"

JEN WOKE TO THE SOUND of Link's laughter, coming from the living room. A moment later, Houston's baritone joined in. The bedside clock told her it was just gone six.

She stretched luxuriously. A few twinges reminded her of the unaccustomed and unusually vigorous activity of the night before, but they didn't dim the glow suffusing her body. Feeling gloriously happy and stronger than she had in weeks, she got out of bed and went into the bathroom to shower. Even the pending interview with McCutcheon didn't splash cold water on her euphoria. Best of all, the two men in her life were sitting in the other room laughing. Her world had righted, finally.

She had just started to strip the sheets from the bed they had really destroyed last night, when Houston tapped on the door and walked in. Looking at the rumpled chaos still clutched in her hand, his eyes warmed and settled on her.

"Leave them," he said. "Sylvia will be in this morning to straighten up."

"Sylvia?" she cocked an eyebrow.

"She comes in twice a week."

"Are you sure you want her to see this?"

He came over and put his arms around her, pulling her tight against him. "Jen, I want the whole world to see this." He took her lips and kept them for a good while. "Come on." he said, with a final peck. "Link is eager to get to McDonald's for breakfast.

She released her grip on the sheet. She wasn't sure if she was ready to make an announcement to the whole world just yet but starting small was a good step.

CHAPTER FORTY THREE

It was a beautiful early morning in Casper, so they bought breakfast take out from Link's favorite eatery and found a picnic table at Cottonwood Park, up close to the Platte, where they ate their egg McMuffins and pancakes. A seagull landed a short distance away and began to move in hopefully.

A nest of squirrels overhead watched the bird suspiciously, chattering angrily when he flew up into the branches, too near their new brood. Houston threw a chunk of hash brown the opposite direction of the tree and the seagull flew after it. When Houston threw another piece even farther, Link saw what he was doing and got into the game. A piece of sausage – not his favorite part of the pancake meal – landed very close to the hash browns.

"You've got a pretty good arm there," Houston told him. Link beamed. "We should get a couple of mitts and toss a baseball around later." The boy agreed eagerly.

Jen reveled in the quiet domesticity of the scene. The night in Houston's bed had triggered old dreams of happily-ever-afters, and that could be very dangerous, she reminded herself, as she watched the passing motorists and dog walkers with a guarded eye.

Thinking back to the years when sitting in a park, having a meal, had been a cause of so much anxiety, always aware of the threat, even while cloaked in their invisibility, Jen sighed. That peace was gone now. Lucano was still out there somewhere, and now they were no longer invisible. It would be foolish to think he would give up. She felt vulnerable. They were exposed here, but Link was so happy, she was reluctant to cut the time short, so she watched. She was positive Houston did too, although he was much more circumspect about it.

"It's almost eight," she started collecting the remnants of their food, "do you think McCutcheon's office will be open yet? I'd like to get this over with."

Houston shrugged and drew the business card from his pocket and handed it to her, backside up. "He works all hours. Give him a call. If you get the answering machine, that means he's either with someone or he's out in the field. Just leave your phone number. He'll call you back."

"He won't know who it is, will he?"

"He knows the people he gives that number to."

Houston had been right. McCutcheon answered on the second ring.

With the meeting set for nine, they headed for the truck, dropping their trash in a barrel on the way. "I need to stop at the bank," Jen told Houston. "It shouldn't take too long." She lifted the strap of her new purse over her head.

"The day is yours," he said. His smile melted her heart.

It was Thursday, and the line at the bank was long. Even though they moved along fairly quickly, there was still some jostling as the bank patrons worked their way forward. Or maybe she was just super sensitive of her personal space after her close encounter at Walmart. She gritted her teeth and fought down her nerves. This is a bank lobby for Pete's sake, she scolded herself. Security cameras everywhere. Quit being a ninny.

Once at the window, she handed the teller a withdrawal slip with her password written below the account number, and driver's license on top. In a few minutes, she was headed out the door with the money in her purse and the receipt in her hand.

She paused in the foyer to verify the account balance and frowned. Yes, she definitely had to find a job. Another depositor bumped her as he moved to get around her and disappeared out the door. A chill went up her spine and she jumped as though burned.

"Get a grip," she muttered to herself. The world was crowded. People bumped each other all the time. She'd wind up a basket case if she panicked every time someone got close to her. Then again, maybe she was already a basket case. She grimaced and hurried out the door where Link and Houston waited in the truck.

"Sorry to take so long."

"They were busy," Houston shrugged. "Link and I have been talking about seeing a movie. You game?"

"We'll see," she responded, "but in the meantime, we should probably see what Agent McCutcheon wants."

She watched as Link's eyes grew round and apprehensive, as though they were being summoned to the principal's office. Opening her mouth to reassure him, she realized she wouldn't be able to give him those reassurances because she was feeling much the same. She remained silent and buckled her seat belt. Houston drove the few blocks to the Federal Building, next to the downtown Post Office.

THE OFFICE MANAGER met them at the door and called McCutcheon, whose instant response made Jen suspect that he'd been standing right behind the door to his office.

"Come on in." he ushered them to seats in front of his desk.

Before taking his own seat, he offered his hand to Jen, then Houston, and finally, to Link. "How are you doing today, Link?" he asked.

Link looked at him. "Fi ... fine." he stammered and quickly looked away.

"Do you know why I asked to meet with you and your mom today?" McCutcheon asked him.

Link's nod turned into a slow shake of his head. "You want to ask me about the m ... men?"

With the perception of a man who had interrogated scores of witnesses, possibly other children, McCutcheon must have recognized Link's nerves. "Why don't we take this into our lounge?" he said. "It's much more comfortable there."

When Link nodded mutely, the agent led them back through the door. "Cammie, we're going to be in the lounge for a bit, will you see that we're not disturbed?"

"Of course." Cammie answered, not bothering to look up from her computer, where her fingers on the keyboard were rapidly filling space on the screen.

"Houston," McCutcheon refocused his attention briefly, "there's a new Wyoming Wildlife magazine by that chair that you might find interesting."

Houston scowled at McCutcheon darkly. "Don't you need to ask me some questions?" The agent's dismissal pissed him off.

"No, just Link and Jen right now. I may need to talk to you later."

With a mutter it was probably better no one could hear, Houston sat down to listen to Cammie's fingers fly over the keyboard.

"This way," McCutcheon led Jen and Link down the hallway where he paused by a vending machine. "Would either of you like something to drink? Water? Pop? Juice?"

Jen shook her head but Link asked if he could have a Coke. Once that was supplied, McCutcheon led them into the lounge.

A comfy sofa with end tables and two over-stuffed chairs surrounded a circular coffee table on which a puzzle was in the works. A half-full urn of coffee sat on a counter on the far wall with a basket of add-ins beside it. A bottled water unit completed the furnishings. Sunlight through the vertical blinds highlighted a few dust motes.

"Why don't you two sit on the sofa?" McCutcheon smiled as he took a chair facing them.

As they settled, he picked up a puzzle piece and looked it over, trying it in a couple of positions before setting it down again. Link watched him carefully.

"That's part of the fireplace," he said to the agent.

"You know, I think you're right," McCutcheon picked up the piece again and tried another area. "Do you like puzzles, Link?"

"Sometimes," Link answered. "but this one looks hard."

"All puzzles are hard until you get all the pieces together. That's what we do here, find all the pieces and put them together so the whole picture is clear."

"Why not just look at the box?" Link looked for it but didn't see it in the room.

"Sometimes you have a box to look at and sometimes you don't." The agent set the puzzle piece in place with a satisfied "Hmmm". "But you recognized this piece," he tapped the one he'd just put in place, "as part of the fireplace even without the box. You have a very good eye."

Smiling, Link got down on his knees by the table and found another piece. "How do you know what the puzzle's supposed to be if you don't have the picture?" He looked at the puzzle and the piece in his hand.

"Well, we have to ask a lot of questions. That's why I needed you in here today, so I could put together more pieces of my puzzle. Part of the puzzle is the time those men had you in their van. Can you help me with that?"

"Okay," Link nodded.

Jen had been left entirely out of this conversation. Even knowing what the agent was doing, putting her six-year-old son at ease, didn't negate her tension. It dawned on her that she wasn't worried so much about Link's distress at being questioned by the FBI, but about her own anxiety. She wasn't sure she could, or wanted to, hear this.

Picking up on Jen's increasing agitation, McCutcheon glanced over at her. "Are you okay too, Mom?"

She looked at him for a long moment, then nodded. "Okay."

She sat, twisting her purse strap, for the longest thirty minutes of her life, as the agent gently talked Link through his experience. Some of Link's words sent chills throughout her body. Unable to listen without reacting, she got up and went to the water dispenser and filled a Styrofoam cup, drinking it down while trying to stop the trembling in her hands.

It helped, but not much. She filled it again and returned to her place beside Link, hoping they were about finished. Taking another swallow, she set the cup on the coffee table where, when her hands again shook, a bit of water sloshed over the edge. Not enough to endanger the puzzle but she reached in her purse for her packet of Kleenex.

She had to dig a bit, but finally found it and pulled it out. As her grip shifted to pull out one, a small fold of paper fell to the floor at her feet. Wondering where it had come from, she picked it up and opened it, staring in disbelief at the words written on it.

The paper dropped from her nerveless fingers as the room began a slow rotation around her. She grabbed for the solid arm of the couch, an anchor.

McCutcheon looked up as Jen reached for the square of paper between her feet again and watched the color drain from her face. Her fist closed around it. She wasn't breathing.

"Why don't you go find Houston, Link, while I talk to your mother for a bit? Okay?" he urged the surprised boy out the door and hurried back to Jen's side. He pushed her head down between her knees.

"Breathe, Jen." he said, as he gently removed the wad of paper, she released reluctantly, from her hand.

One handed, he spread it out on the table, and his own breath caught as he read the words.

> *If you want to find out about your sister, get rid of the cop, tell no one. Go to the empty Macy's store at the mall and wait for further instructions.*

The message was typed. No possibility of checking handwriting but that didn't mean the note was untraceable.

"When did you receive this?"

Jen sat up, her haunted blue eyes dry. "It had to be at the bank," she said, her voice raspy. "That's the only place I've been before we came here. This purse was in my gear before that."

"Did you happen to see who might have put this in your purse?"

She shook her head. "The bank was crowded."

He would pull their security feed. "You realize that this is probably just an effort to get to you?"

"That doesn't matter," she said, "I have to go. I have to find out."

"Your sister was last reported as being shipped out with cargo destined for Hong Kong, a few days ago." He watched her eyes flash with surprise.

"How do you know that?" she demanded fiercely.

"A confidential informant." He handed her the cup of water again. "Jill was working with us."

"She wouldn't!" Jen snapped. "She didn't trust any of you. Why would she agree to work with you?"

"She thought Lucano was getting too close. She wanted to protect her family."

"That worked out well, didn't it?" She stood to pace the room.

"Didn't Houston tell you anything?"

"He KNEW?!" she spun on him, not bothering to lower her voice in the face of this sudden, painful revelation.

"I mentioned it to him at the hangar," he said.

He watched her pace a couple more laps. Finally, he saw the moment she made her decision. She faced him again.

"Is there a back way out of here? Some way that I won't have to see Houston?"

"Why? What are you thinking, Jen?" He didn't like the turn this conversation was taking. "Don't do anything ..." he paused, rethinking the word that popped into his mouth, "unwise. Wait until your anger cools and then work with us. We'll find whoever this person is and see what he knows."

"Working with the law has gotten my son kidnapped, myself nearly murdered and any number of people killed. No, I think I'll do better on my own. If you want to capture the man who left the note, you have about an hour to get agents to the mall," her lips curled in a feral snarl.

"I don't want to have to arrest you."

"You suggested I was being stupid, ... excuse me, ... unwise," she laughed humorlessly, "and I don't think stupidity is an arresting offense so, I'm leaving, Agent McCutcheon." she already had her hand on the door when he made it to her side and laid his over hers. She gave him an icy glare. "I just have one request, will you make sure Link gets to Irene? Houston knows the way. Now, which way out?"

"I can have you detained for interfering in an ongoing investigation," he tried to insert a note of rationality into her heated thoughts.

"I haven't interfered yet."

She yanked open the door and came face to face with Houston, just reaching for the knob.

CHAPTER FORTY FOUR

The look of pain, hurt and betrayal on Jen's face had him reaching for her but she stepped back out of his reach.

"Don't," she said harshly. "Just don't." She walked around him, careful to stay beyond his reach.

He gave McCutcheon a bewildered look, his hand still reaching out toward Jen in supplication.

"You should have told her about her sister," McCutcheon said slapping the piece of paper into his palm. "Right now you have to keep her away from the mall at all costs. Give us time to set up the take down."

Houston read the note and crumpled it in his fist. Swearing roundly, he tossed it back, bouncing it off McCutcheon's chest.

Turning back the way he'd come, he jogged after Jen and caught up with her and Link outside the front doors. She had her phone to her ear. He grabbed it, but she refused to relinquish her hold.

"Damn it, Jen! Will you calm down for just a minute? You're not thinking straight." The tug of war over the phone brought Link running to his mother's aid, a protective scowl screwed on his face.

Link aimed a round house kick at the most sensitive part of Houston's anatomy but Houston managed to turn away so that, unfortunately, the foot landed on the next most sensitive part of his anatomy, the gunshot wound in his leg. His knee threatened to buckle as the pain swam redly behind his eyes.

"Son of ..." he glared at the boy. "Link, stop." Houston shouted at him, just as the phone broke in half.

Staring in disbelief at the broken piece of merchandise, Jen wound up and threw her half of the now useless phone into the parking lot.

Houston pitched his half after it. No longer having to battle Jen, he turned his appeal to Link. "Your mom is getting ready to do something really stupid. I'm trying to protect her."

"She doesn't do stupid things, and that's a bad thing to say." Link jumped to her defense.

'Oh child, if you only knew', the thought raced through her mind as memories of the previous night flashed in her brain.

"You're right, that was a bad word to use. I'm sorry. But she wants to go after a bad man by herself, Link."

The boy cast a look of doubt at his mother."Is that true, Mom?"

He wrapped his arms around Jen's legs. "You can't go by yourself. I'll go with you, Mom. I can help."

Jen glared at Houston over the top of Link's head and he saw the fight drain out of her.

"Damn you, Houston!" she mouthed as she enfolded Link in a hard hug. The fight might be draining out of her but the hurt and betrayal in her eyes was an impenetrable wall. It appeared he was destined to go through life breaking down Jen's walls.

Some curious onlookers had gathered. Cellphones were focused on them. "Let's get out of here, Jen." he said softly, "we're attracting a crowd."

She looked up at the gawkers, then nodded. As they walked to the truck, a woman trotted over, the two broken phone halves in her hands and gave them to Jen. "Thanks," Jen mumbled.

Giving Houston a dark look, the woman asked, "Are you okay, Miss?"

"Everything is fine. Just a misunderstanding," Jen assured her.

Houston might have almost believed her except for the look she aimed at him. With a suppressed sigh, he hit the remote unlock on the truck. When Jen got in the back seat with Link instead of the front, beside him, Houston's jaw clenched so hard he was afraid a tooth might crack but he didn't say a word.

"Take me to Savvy's apartment, please. I left some of my things there."

Houston wasn't sure that was a good idea, but taking a clue from Link's silence, he kept his mouth shut. She had reached a breaking point. He could see her simmering in the rear view mirror. Anything he said would be the wrong thing. And, maybe, a few minutes with Savvy would pour some oil on the water. If anyone could make a crack in the wall Jen had built up around herself, Houston would have put his money on Savvy.

He called ahead only to find that Savvy was at Vulcan's Forge, where she worked from nine to one, five days a week but she said Bryn was at the apartment and would be happy to see them. Thanking her, he put his phone in his pocket and relayed her message to Jen. Jen bobbed her head. But the icy silence held.

AT THE APARTMENT, BRYN welcomed them into the sweet smell of baking, gave both of them a hug, and smiled warmly at Jen's son.

"And you must be Link," she greeted. "I've heard so much about you."

Link nodded shyly but a little smile touched his lips. Bryn was such an outgoing personality that it was hard to resist her when she set out to charm. Houston knew that she could be fierce when the occasion warranted; he'd seen her advocating for her sister when she first arrived at the hospital following Savvy's near-death experience at the hands of the crazed and murderous Bass Volker, over a year ago, but that fierceness was only a part of her.

A timer dinged in the kitchen. "Oh, the last batch of cookies are ready," she said. "Does anyone like warm Snickerdoodles?" she asked, and hurried to the kitchen where her potholders sat on the counter.

"I do," Link piped up, over riding Jen's automatic negative.

"Oh, good. Come on in the kitchen," she pulled the cookies from the oven and shut off the stove.

Link was already there, Houston was headed that way and politeness forced Jen to follow.

"Let's let those cool for a bit while I get us something to drink. What would you like, Link? Milk? Juice?"

"Could I have milk? ... please?" he added when Jen gave him a look.

"I know what you want, Houston," Bryn laughed and motioned to the coffee maker on the counter. "I started a fresh pot when Savvy called me. How about you, Jen?"

"Milk, please,"

While Houston got down a mug and filled it, Bryn poured three glasses of milk and set them on the island. She figured, with the icy currents flowing between Jen and Houston, the cookies should already be cool enough. She smiled as she used a short spatula to lift some cookies onto a paper plate and centered it between the glasses.

Her training and personal experience made her suspect a much deeper connection between the two than mere cop and witness. Only strong emotions could create that kind of permafrost. Her suspicions were confirmed when Jen took pains to sit Link between herself and Houston. She hid the frown that itched at her lips. It wasn't fair to a child to be used as a buffer between two warring adults.

Link reached for the first cookie and bit into it with delight. "These are really good," he smiled at Bryn.

"They are," Jen agreed, sharing a small smile, too.

"I've been making Snickerdoodles for the last couple of weeks because one, I really like them, and two, because our friend, Lacey, has a new puppy she named Snickerdoodle," she chuckled. "Now, she just calls him Snickers."

Link laughed with her as he made short work of the cookie and reached for another.

"Do you like puppies, Link?"

"Yes," he said, some of the smile slipping. "I always wanted a puppy but we can't have one because Aunt Irene is allergic."

"That does make it harder," Bryn agreed. "When we finish our cookies, would you like to go upstairs and meet Snickers?"

He spun to Jen, "Could we, Mom?" he pleaded. "Please?"

"Link," Jen's features changed subtly, not quite a frown, but cautioning, "we just stopped by to pick up some things I left here. We don't really have time to visit."

Bryn saw empathy for the boy in Houston's eyes, but he refrained from comment. Yes, Link definitely needed a break from the tension between these two. And maybe, a few minutes alone together would give the adults time to iron out a couple of wrinkles.

"I could take him up to Lacey's apartment while you gather your stuff," she offered, aiming a broad smile at Jen. "It would only take a few minutes. If it's okay with you."

"Please, Mom?"

It was easy to read Jen, Bryn thought, as she watched the struggle in Jen's eyes. She considered two against one was unfair, but she gave a small inward sigh when Jen finally caved.

"Okay, but only if you don't take too long."

"Thanks, Mom," Link gave her a grateful hug.

"Have another cookie, everyone," Bryn grinned, passing the plate around the table again. Houston and Link both took one.

"I have my degree now," Bryn told Houston, "and I may have a job lined up at the Re-entry Center. Full time. I'll actually be able to pick up my share of expenses. Money has been tight but Savvy has never said anything. I'm sure she's relieved though."

"That's good news for both of you." Houston took a bite of his cookie.

They talked for a couple more minutes until everyone was finished, then Bryn cleared the island and put the glasses in the sink. Houston refilled his cup.

"Are you ready to go, Link?" Bryn asked.

He was already off his chair.

When the door closed behind them, Jen stalked silently down the hall to the room, Bryn's room, where she'd left her pack. It wasn't there. Where had they put it? She checked the closet, then the hall closet. Surely Savvy wouldn't have put it in her closet, would she? With a sinking sensation, the answer came to her, the coat closet by the front door. Where Houston would be able to see every move she made.

'Well, tough cookies, Houston,' she said to herself. She no longer cared what Houston saw or thought.

He was looking out the window, arms crossed, drinking his coffee, when she entered the living room. He looked over.

"We only have a few minutes, Jen," he walked over to the coffee table in front of the big sectional and put his cup down. "I think we should try to clear the air."

"You lied to me!" she snapped. "Is that clear enough?"

"No, I didn't. I was going to tell you, I just didn't know how."

"So you withheld it from me. Same thing, Houston."

"I planned to tell you after Link was asleep last night. Then things got in the way."

Remembering the 'things' that had gotten in the way made her face flame. "That's no excuse. There was time before those 'things' happened. Why was it so hard to just come right out and say, 'Jen, your sister isn't dead."

She fled across the room and yanked open the coat closet, searching for and finding her pack. She pulled it out and shut the door harder than necessary. Then tossed a mental apology to the sisters. She stood to take the pack to the sofa and was stopped by the body of Houston right behind her.

"Would it have eased you mind to know that, instead of being dead, she was being shipped to whorehouses in Hong Kong? I wasn't sure. Tell me I was wrong to worry how it would affect you."

The color that had infused her face only moments before, drained so fast that she saw Houston's hand reach out as though expecting to have to catch her. She stiffened her legs. She. Would. Not. Faint. Dammit. She made the few steps to the sofa and sat down, dropping her head to her knees.

"It would have eased my mind to hear the news from someone I thought gave a damn rather that on a scrap of paper some faceless stranger dropped in my purse."

Houston's hands settled on her shoulders, massaging gently. "If you don't believe anything else, Jen, believe that I give a damn."

After a long breath, she nodded and sat up. When she didn't turn in to his ministrations, he picked up his cup and took it into the kitchen and busied himself at the sink, rinsing the cup and their glasses and sitting them on the drying mat. She took the opportunity, while his back was to her, to find what she needed in the pack and put it in her purse.

NOT CONTENT TO JUST visit the puppy, Bryn and Link came through the door, Snickers wagging ecstatically in Link's arms, a leash hanging loosely from Bryn's hand. "Look, Mom. Isn't he cute?" he set Snickers in her lap.

And he was. At least part Chihuahua with maybe some miniature poodle or Pomeranian thrown into the mix, he was a furry bundle of energy and completely adorable. He covered Jen's face with kisses when she lifted him onto her shoulder for a hug. She smiled, remembering the dog she and Jill had before they went to live with Irene. "Yes, he is," she agreed.

"I see you found your pack," Bryn said, noting the lessened tension in Jen's body. "I should have told you where it was before I left. Sorry."

"Yes, I found it," Jen handed Link the puppy and stood. "Thanks for hanging on to it for me."

"It wasn't a problem," Bryn assured her.

Jen looked into the kitchen just in time to see Houston put his phone back in his pocket. He must have had it silenced because she hadn't heard it ring. She wondered who had called him or who he had called, but she didn't ask. She had things she had to do and it was time to leave here.

"You'd better give Snickers back to Bryn," she told Link. "We have to be leaving."

"Actually," Houston cut in, "would it be all right if Link stayed with you for a little while?" he asked Bryn. "Jen and I have something we have to do and Link would be bored. Maybe he could help you take Snickers for a walk and have another cookie."

"Absolutely," Bryn agreed, catching the surprised look on Jen's face at Houston's request. "If it's okay with Mom? I would love the company."

Jen had been wondering what she was going to do with Link while she went to the mall but she hadn't expected Houston to solve her problem so easily. He and Agent McCutcheon had been set against her going at all so she had to wonder what Houston was thinking.

After a brief hesitation, Jen asked, "Is that okay with you, Link?"

"Wow, could I?"

CHAPTER FORTY FIVE

What Houston had been thinking became clear when they got in the truck. "McCutcheon has the trap set," he said grimly, as he drove down Second Street toward the mall. "Now, all he needs is the bait. And let me make this very clear, right here and now, I've been against this whole idea from the beginning."

Hearing the word 'bait' stated so bluntly gave her heart a little hitch but wasn't that what she'd decided to do, herself? No, she had no intention of backing out now. And she had no intention of leaving Link an orphan.

"Houston?" she drew his attention, "I asked Agent McCutcheon and now I'm asking you, if this all, somehow, goes south, will you make sure that Link gets back to Irene? She'll be able to hide him where Lucano will never be able to find him."

Now, it was Houston's heart that stumbled over his ribs. "We can't think like that, Jen," he answered, his voice gravelly.

"Promise." she demanded.

"Alright, I promise," he looked at her, "but it's not going to go south."

"There's the mall entrance," Jen said, as the truck cruised past it, toward the Wyoming Boulevard stoplight.

"We're going back to the Federal Building. McCutcheon wants to put a wire on you before you go in."

Jen drew a quick gasp. "What if they suspect that?"

"I don't think they're dumb enough to make you strip off your sweatshirt in the middle of the mall and the agents won't let them get you out of there." Houston assured her. They were silent all the way back downtown.

THE PROCEDURE WAS A little more involved than a wire. Aware of the death threat to Jen, the FBI agent, Celine, put a bullet proof vest under her sweatshirt and fixed the wire over top of it.

"That should do it," Jen said fatalistically, as they tested the sound, "unless they shoot me in the head."

"We've got that covered too," the female agent said, handing Jen what looked like an over-sized black handbag. "There's a small ballistic shield sewn into the lining of this bag. If you see a gun, grip this strap,"—it was a black strap, disguised as a continuation of the over-arm carrying handle—"and hold the bag in front of your face." She demonstrated, "Like this. Hold it close but relaxed or any bullet that hits it will break your arm. Got it?"

Jen swallowed hard. "Got it." She emptied the contents of her purse into the bag, all except one item, which she dropped in her pocket. She pulled her sweatshirt down over the armor so it hung loosely to her hipbones. Picking up the bag, she felt the reassuring weight. "I guess I'm ready."

"A couple of other things," the agent held up a staying hand, "There was no date or time stated in the note so it's possible nothing will happen today. We are reviewing the security video from the bank lobby and have isolated a couple of faces that we will be watching for today. If either of them approach you at the mall, we will take them in for questioning.

"There are benches in the hallway. Take the one closest to Macy's doors. The store has been closed for some time now, but they will have to come around a corner to get a shot at you, if that's their intention. Sit so you can see into the main hallway and see both corners."

"Is that everything?"

"I think so." The agent handed her a key fob. "There is an older green sedan in the employee parking lot behind this building. You're not alone, Jen. We will have eyes on you the whole time and there will be agents inside the mall, and out, but you won't see them unless someone approaches you."

Speech was beyond her at this moment so Jen nodded, and the agent escorted her to the back door, pointing out the green sedan through the small window.

As she walked alone to the car, Jen wondered where Houston had gone. Even though she still hadn't forgiven him for lying to her, his solid presence might have settled her nerves a bit.

SHE PARKED THE GREEN sedan near the entrance closest to Sears and entered the mall. Turning left at the corner, she made her way toward the Macy's store, window shopping as she went, trying to look like anything but the basket of nerves she was. She also watched the people she passed. Not that she would recognize anyone, she hadn't been paying that much attention as she stood in line at the bank, but wondering if something about them could tell her if they were capable of murder.

The same feeling she'd experienced at the travel center in Idaho, where she'd tried to be observant while looking anything but, crept over her. Houston had had her back then. Who had it now, she wondered? Where were the agents? She tried to pick them out, but couldn't.

There was an old man at a table in the food court, a drink in his hand and a paperback book open in front of him but he seemed distracted by the number of people, many of them school kids, who were moving into the area, and he closed the book and stuffed it into the pocket of his ratty sweater. He left the table and headed toward Target, his shoulders stooped and his gait halting. An agent? Or the man she was supposed to meet?

For several yards, he somehow stayed even with her on the far side of the hall, but he never looked up, only reaching up to fiddle with his hearing aid as he shuffled along. She paused to look at some jewelry displayed in a store window. The old man wobbled on, unconcerned.

Rounding the corner to the old Macy's store, she headed gratefully toward a bench facing the Navy recruiting office and took her seat, turning to face the center of the mall and the Target store entrance across the hall. The old man had disappeared.

Her body was so tense that, had someone struck a high note, she was positive she would have shattered like crystal. Setting the large tote between her and the busy center of the mall, she took a grip on the handle and waited. It seemed a long time, long enough that discomfort had invaded her lower extremities, when a boy of about nine or ten, maybe a little older, approached her, a small clutch of flowers in his hand. She had to wonder where he'd gotten them. The nearest flower store was down the hill and across Wyoming Boulevard, at a grocery store a quarter mile west.

"A man paid me five dollars to give you these," he said, pushing the flowers into her hand.

"Wh... what man?" Jen gave the boy a startled look. She scanned the people within her line of sight to see if anyone was watching.

The boy shrugged and trotted off, his five dollars earned.

She looked down at the flowers in her hand and saw a note card stuffed into them. Fingers shaking, she pulled it out and lifted the flap. The breath left her body.

> "I told you to ditch the cops. Leave now. Don't speak to anyone. Use the service exit directly in front of you. Get in your car. Go to Menards. Stop near the garden center, beside the gray Honda. You will be met."

When her mind began functioning again, she crumpled the note in her fist, dropped the flowers on the bench and went down the short hallway between Macy's and the recruiting office and out the maintenance entrance, digging for the key fob as she jogged.

A gardener was trimming some shrubs just outside the door. She didn't pay any attention. Tossing the wadded note in his wheelbarrow, she focused on the green sedan, three rows away.

The old man in the sweater ran toward the bench. "Does anybody have eyes on that exit?" he shouted, finger on his hearing aid.

"She's headed for the car," the gardener answered, dropping his nippers in a barrel "but she threw a piece of paper in my barrow. She's headed for Menards."

SO WAS HOUSTON, ALTHOUGH he didn't know the exact destination. He would have been inside with Jen except for the fact that whoever had written the note McCutcheon had shoved in his hand knew him for a cop.

He had been shut out of the fed's plan for that very reason, but he'd been following the green sedan since it left the Federal Building. So, he'd waited, engine running, hoping the first thing he would see was agents escorting a suspect out of the building. He didn't know which door they would come out of though so he kept an eye on the green sedan.

Perspiration made his shirt damp and uncomfortable. He strained his ears for the sound of gun shots inside the mall. The chances of a gun battle in the middle of so many bystanders was not a high possibility, but shit happened. It had almost been a relief when he'd seen Jen jogging to that green sedan with the gardener trying to catch up. Something had gone wrong but Jen was whole and healthy. When she peeled out of her parking slot, he gave her some distance until she was at the intersection and had turned east on Second Street. He didn't need to be close. That green stood out like a beer sign in a bar window.

THE LIGHT AT THE TOP of the hill by Home Depot stopped Jen and gave her a moment to think. Why was she in such a rush to get to the next assignation? She already knew that her sister had been shipped out of the country. What could the note-dropper possibly tell her that would add anymore information? Was someone waiting for her with another glove full of Fentanyl? Or a bullet? She felt fairly safe from a bullet but there were other ways to kill someone. Were they planning on kidnapping her and putting her on the next shipment out of the country? She didn't have any backup where she was headed but she wasn't entirely helpless. Reaching into the tote she felt the reassuring coolness of the brass knuckles, and the self-defense moves she'd practiced religiously for six years hummed a comforting tune in her head.

When the light changed, she moved forward at a slower speed. It gave her time to think. Had she over-reacted to Houston's deception? What would have been her response, if he'd told her about Jill before they made love? She was positive they wouldn't have wound up in bed, and that thought caused her heart to squeeze into a tight ball of pain. The night before had been the most satisfying culmination of a dream she'd nurtured for four years. Thinking it might never have happened was unthinkable. Houston was a wonderful lover. The memory, even now, made tingles of anticipation race through her, lighting fires wherever they touched.

Distracted by her thoughts she almost missed the turn lane, eliciting an angry honk from a like-minded driver by her quick shift left just as the light turned red. She waved a *mea culpa* at him and then wondered if he'd interpreted her message the way she'd intended. She wondered that a lot when she was driving.

She made the turn and the short drive to the store where all her focus turned to finding the gray Honda. The right gray Honda. Cruising cautiously along the front of the store, she approached the garden center entrance. It was busy. But then, it was early June. Of course it was busy.

It soon became obvious that just circling the perimeter of the lot was not going to help her find the gray Honda. There were several gray cars but finding the correct one required going up and down each row. On the second row, the Honda found itself.

As Jen turned to make a pass on the next row, a gray car that had been sitting two rows over, apart from any other vehicles, pulled out of its slot when another vehicle pulled in beside it. The driver re-positioned himself to a sparsely populated space in the last row of cars. Plenty of room on either side.

The move gave Jen clarity. The note had said to park next to it. The driver must plan to make a fast getaway. Maybe she could slow him down. She circled the next row to approach him from the opposite direction. She rolled cross-ways in front of the gray Honda, her passenger door inches from his front bumper and taking up three parking spaces with the green sedan. A move guaranteed to trigger some withering comments and a snapshot or two on Facebook.

The sun reflecting off the windshield of the Honda kept the driver's face blurry but Jen had no trouble seeing the hand out the window, waving insistently for her to move to the side. Instead, she got out of the sedan, tote hanging from her trembling arm, the handle gripped firmly in her equally shaky hand, and circled toward the driver's window, intent on calling his bluff.

The nylon stocking over his head explained the blurring she'd thought was caused by sun reflection.

"Get you car out of the way," the angry demand was punctuated with a gun barrel pointed at her.

She prayed that the vest and shield were as good as promised. "No," she refused. "I am tired of your game. You either shoot me right here, while cellphones take pictures to post on Casper's Finest Drivers, with your car and that gun in plain sight, or you tell me what you want for your information."

His head did a quick scan and did spot a cell phone aimed their direction. With a nasty snarl, he jerked the gun back and down. He glared at her, or at least she thought he did. With the stocking distorting his features, it was hard to tell.

He finally made a decision. "I want two hundred thousand dollars, in unmarked bills," he snapped. "Put the money in a brown paper bag and drop it in the trash barrel at Crossroads Park at nine p.m. tomorrow night. When I have it, I'll leave an envelope somewhere on the playground, with further instructions where to go to find out about your sister."

Jen laughed. "I'm a single mother working as a waitress. What ever gave you the idea I could come up with that kind of money?" She heard the gun cock as it reappeared through the window and her tongue froze.

"You'd better figure out a way," he cursed. "They left me hanging here with no way out. Even Chuck has disappeared. I have to have the money."

"Your financial problems are not my problem." Jen shook her head. "I already know that my sister was loaded onto a transport headed for Hong Kong so, unless you have something else, you've just wasted a lot of time for nothing."

His next words stunned her to silence.

"I know the name of the house she's going to."

A hard hand grabbed the gun, and wrist holding it, yanking the attached arm into the door post with enough force to crack a bone. The man screamed in pain. The gun discharged, the bullet glanced off the shield stitched into Jen's tote. Had she been braced for it, she thought it wouldn't have been such a hard punch but the impact was enough to knock her on her butt. She gasped for breath and looked up into Houston's fierce scowl as he wrenched the gun from the man's hand and snatched the stocking off his still screaming head.

Jen realized she knew the man, a new hire on the Casper PD, he'd started hanging around the cafe a few months ago. It was obvious that Houston knew him, too.

"Well, Jerry, that's good to know," he growled. "I'm sure the feds will be glad to hear that."

As if on cue, a black Escalade pulled up behind the gray Honda and Agent McCutcheon got out followed by two other agents. They circled the Honda, guns drawn.

"You seem to have difficulty getting to the party on time, agent." Houston grinned at McCutcheon.

"I don't think we missed anything," the agent responded. "She was as safe as we could make her and we got the information we needed, thanks to Jen's wire, and I'm sure Jerry will be happy to fill us in on the details back at the office. Won't you, Jerry?"

Jerry sat mutely.

Houston relinquished the arm he still held and handed the gun to McCutcheon. He reached to help Jen to her feet and gathered her in his arms.

With the already swelling arm cradled to his chest, Jerry swore and demanded to be taken to the hospital.

"Your arm is the least of your worries," McCutcheon gave Jerry a dark look before turning to Houston.

"If you'll drive Ms. Bradley back to the office, we can get our equipment off her and you can take her home."

Jen motioned toward the green sedan with a questioning look.

"We'll take care of the cars." McCutcheon smiled at her. "You've been a tremendous help. Thank you." He pulled a business card from his pocket and pressed it into her hand. "If you need anything, call me."

CHAPTER FORTY SIX

After a brief trip west to the Federal Building on Center Street, followed by a longer visit to the grocery store back east at Hilltop, they picked up Link and headed back to Houston's apartment. By the time Jen walked in, she was ready to drop from fatigue. The emotional roller coaster she'd been on since early this morning had sapped all the strength from her body. She could, happily, just sit down on the couch and never move for hours, but she still had to feed Link and get him to bed. Link, on the other hand, was wired with excitement, both from the puppy and from the much redacted version of the sting operation with the FBI that Houston had relayed to him, making her the star of the story.

"I'll put this food away and then I have to go to the station for a bit." Houston said.

"I'll fix something for supper," Jen offered, halfheartedly, as she followed him into the kitchen. Food was way at the bottom of her list of important things, but she didn't think Link had had anything to eat since the breakfast at the park except Snickerdoodles.

"No, I'll pick up something for supper on my way back," he started emptying grocery sacks.

Since she didn't know where things went, she handed him items and watched him put them away.

"Mom, can I watch cartoons?" Link called from the living room.

"Sure—" she started, but Houston had an alternate suggestion.

"Would you like to see the police station, Link? I have to go in for a bit, if you'd like to ride along with me. Then we can pick up something for supper on the way back."

"Big Yikes! Can I go with Houston, Mom?" Link said, excitedly.

Jen blinked at the new phrase. Where on earth had he picked that up? "I guess it's okay," she said, "as long as you behave and do as you're told."

"I will!" he was already headed for the door.

"Why don't you try to catch a nap while we're gone?" Houston suggested, following her son to the door. "A couple hours rest seems in order."

Her answer was interrupted. "Can we see some prisoners, Houston, do you think?" Link wanted to know.

She watched Houston's eyebrows lift at this request but his answer was blocked by the closing door. She hoped Houston nixed that suggestion. She couldn't see any good coming from Link walking past a row of cells like a visitor at the zoo.

Quiet settled over the apartment. As tired as she was, she didn't think sleep would come easy but she sat down on the sofa and turned on the TV. The news was on but she couldn't handle any more murder and mayhem so she found an old movie, a western, where, when someone was shot, you seldom saw blood. She lowered the volume, wrapped herself in a throw from the back of the sofa and leaned back into the corner.

"SHHH," HOUSTON CAUTIONED the boy as he dug out his key. "If your mom is asleep, I don't want to wake her up."

Carefully balancing the two pizza boxes in his hands, Link nodded.

She was asleep. Curled up on the sofa under the afghan like a kitten, Houston thought she looked very much at home. He hoped she felt that way. He held the door for Link and set his key by the door.

"Put the pizzas on the table while I carry your mom to the bedroom, okay?" he whispered.

Link nodded again and headed for the kitchen.

Houston walked over to the sofa and took a minute to look down at Jen. Even relaxed in sleep, the lines of fatigue still creased her face. He leaned over to pick her up, only to have her stiffen and immediately start to fight him.

"Jen, Jen," he said softly in her ear.

Her eyes opened and she saw him. Immediately, the fight drained away and she sat up. "I must have fallen asleep," she said, muzzily. "What time is it?"

"Seven or so," Houston sat down beside her.

Her nostrils twitched. "Is that pizza?"

"Your supper awaits," he smiled, untangling her from the afghan. When she stood, he followed her into the kitchen where Link was already setting out paper plates.

"Two large pizzas?"

"Houston and I wanted sausage and pepperoni but I told him you always put a lot of veggies on yours so we got you one too," Link beamed proudly.

Jen sighed. There would be a lot of leftovers. Good thing they both liked cold pizza.

Along with the pizza, Houston had also bought drinks. Jen set out the cups while Link put a piece of pizza on each plate. By pushing the two boxes to the far edge of the table, Houston made room for everything and soon, with very little prompting, Link was regaling her with his visit to the police station. She was happy to hear that Houston had managed to steer him away from the cell block.

When she reached for a third slice of pizza, Jen was surprised to see just how hungry she'd been. As Link pushed away his plate and yawned, Jen started clean up.

"Can I watch some cartoons?" Link looked toward the living room.

"Bath first," Jen said, "then Pjs and then, if Houston has no objection, you can watch cartoons until eight thirty."

She had expected a minor protest, but Link only scowled. He was still staying on his good behavior in front of Houston.

"Okay," he yawned as he gave in reluctantly, and went in search of pajamas.

From the size of that yawn, she didn't think he would make it past eight, but it was always wise to set the ground rules in advance to save an argument at the end.

With Houston's help, the kitchen was spotless in minutes, and while he hauled out the garbage, she found her own night-wear and the robe she'd worn the night before. Burying her face in the thick chenille, memories of the night rushed back and she felt her skin grow warm. She couldn't let it happen again. Not because she was still angry at Houston, that had long since been resolved in her mind, but there were still secrets between them. Secrets that could tear this fragile truce to shreds. Her secrets. Secrets she'd sworn to never tell another living soul. Secrets that had already doomed her to a half life she'd never believed she would be forced to live.

She set the robe and her clean t-shirt and panties on the corner of Link's bed, her bed also, for the rest of their stay in Houston's apartment. She prayed, for her own sanity, that it would be brief.

Tomorrow she would see about getting her old job back, then strip her savings to rent another apartment. Dealing with furnishing it was another problem, but that would have to come later. Maybe she could salvage some things from the old house. The memory of the last time she'd seen it brought tears to her eyes. She brushed them away angrily. She would need transportation. Her old car was driveable, but were the police done with it? She would have to ask them. Another thing on her rapidly filling 'to do' list.

She heard Houston come back in and she stepped to the bathroom door to hurry Link. She needed to get a bath too and Houston might also.

"Anything you want to watch before the cartoons start?" Houston said, handing her the remote and patting a spot on the sofa beside him.

She shook her head and set the unit back on the coffee table, taking the chair at the end instead of the place on the couch. He frowned but said nothing. Knowing it would hurt him but not knowing how to prevent it, she said, instead, "I want to get my car back, if they're done with it. I'm going to need it."

This time he didn't bother to mask the hurt. His jaw tightened. "My Jeep has been in the shop for the last several days," he answered, tersely, "but they should be done with it pretty soon. There's no reason you can't use it if you want wheels."

"My world is twisted completely out of any known reality. I prefer to get back on my own feet as quickly as possible." she said firmly. "It's important for me and for Link to get back to normal."

"I'm done, Mom." Link skipped into the room and grabbed the remote.

Their discussion had to be shelved.

"Did you brush your teeth?"

He gave her an exaggerated grin showing twin rows of sparkling tooth enamel.

"Did you leave me any hot water?" she poked gently at his stomach and grinned when he giggled.

They watched TV for a little bit before Jen excused herself to draw her own bath. She planned to soak until time to put Link to bed, at which time, she felt she would be ready for bed too. Or, at least she would pretend to be asleep should Houston happen to look in on them.

Her plan to avoid an uncomfortable meeting with Houston went sour when she walked out of the bathroom to find that Link had fallen asleep on the sofa and Houston had already put him to bed. He was just coming out of the bedroom when she approached it.

"He's asleep." Houston headed back down the hallway.

"He was so excited about all he did today that I was sure he would give me a battle about bedtime." Jen said, trailing him. "You must have a magic touch."

"High excitement tends to cause fatigue faster than usual," he answered.

"That would explain why, even after a long nap, I'm ready to join him," she said lightly. She picked up the afghan that had been wadded into the corner and began folding it.

Houston caught her hand and tossed the afghan over the back of the couch. "Jen, what's going on? Are we not past my screw up yet? I thought you had sort of forgiven me."

"I have … I mean, I know I overreacted, and I'm sorry about that, but what I was saying before Link interrupted us is still valid."

He sat down, still holding her hand, and pulled her down beside him. "No, it's not." he kept his voice calm but she heard the faint hint of distress in his words. "You asked me to make love with you, and I did, we did. And it was fantastic, at least I think so. But now, you're putting distance between us and I need to know why." His other hand pressed the bridge of his nose for long moments before he continued. "Talk to me Jen, please. Explain to me that I'm not hearing what I think I'm hearing."

She pulled her hand from his and came to her feet. Wrapping her arms around herself, she paced a ways then returned to face him.

"Listen to me," she pleaded. "Ever since those gunshots behind the cafe, my life has been teetering on a very narrow ledge. Everything is unbalanced. I feel like one wrong step will plummet me over that ledge." Searching for the right words and knowing there weren't any, she continued her pacing. "You don't even know me ..."

His muttered expletive spun her around. "We've known each other for four years, Jen."

"No," she slashed her hand at his words, "we flirted and imagined vivid 'what ifs'. We've only known each other for less than two weeks. And those few days have been an emotional roller coaster that I still can't get off of. This whole thing is moving too fast for me." She leaned on the kitchen counter, gulping huge breaths. "I've got to get my normal back."

"I've already told you, more than once, that I love you and you've said those words too. Tell me now if that wasn't the truth."

She tried to meet his eyes and couldn't. "My feelings can't factor into this."

"The hell they can't!" he said hoarsely, rising from his seat and coming toward her. "This is all about feelings. Yours. Mine. I know what I'm feeling but you've got me confused as hell about yours." He scrubbed his hands through his hair. "And if told you I want to marry you and adopt Link? Would that give you any balance?" he snapped and began his own pacing.

He was offering her everything she'd dreamed of for four years but she'd known from the beginning that it was just a dream. "No," she whispered, miserable. "That can never happen."

Her words hit him like a gut punch and he sat down again. "Are you actually married to Link's father? Is that the reason we can't get married? That I can't raise Link as my own son?" He looked at her, imploring. "I love you. You said you loved me. Isn't that enough to work on? We can figure it out as we go along, Jen."

"No. I've never been married. And up until two weeks ago, I didn't think the Lucano family even knew about Link. But they do, and they're still out there."

"That has nothing to do with this, I just need some space to find my equilibrium."

He looked at her for a long time then, in defeat, he went to the door, and opened it, grabbing his keys as he passed. "I think we both need some space. If you can't get your car back tomorrow, you can use the Jeep as soon as it's available. Sweet dreams, Jen," he added bitterly, and pulled the door closed behind him.

Her life had just walked out the door. Correction, she had pushed her life out that door. And yet, she couldn't change the facts. She'd always known it had to end, couldn't have ended any other way. As much as she loved Houston and had dreamed of an 'ever after' life with him, Link would always be between them. And it would be that way until all the Lucanos were dead. Even if the law managed to catch up with the head of the ring, nothing would change when Antón finally got out of prison.

She had played this charade for six years, ever since Jill had placed Link in her arms and begged her to protect him until she came back. Thinking short term, Jen had agreed to keep her sister's secret. Now, the BIG secret was out but she still wasn't free. Jill might never be able to come back and claim her son, so where did that leave them? Without proof of death, Jen couldn't even legally adopt Link. If anyone found out that Link was not her son, that she had less right to fight for him than his biological parent, it would take a mere scrawled signature to rip him from her. Aside from the fact that she couldn't reveal Link's true parentage to anyone, even Houston, how could she ask him to adopt the child knowing that there was no legal standard that would support his claim. Her own feelings didn't matter, but to allow Houston and Link to develop a deeper relationship would tear them both apart. She prayed it wasn't already too late.

Link had no memory of his real mother. In every real way, Jen had been his mother and he was her son. Eyes burning, Jen walked to the sofa and sat down.

She wouldn't cry, couldn't cry. There were no tears left. Pulling her feet up under her, she wrapped her arms around them and dropped her head to her knees, pressing her eyes to them.

She was cold again. Reaching for the afghan gave her a moment of comfort. Draping it over herself, she pulled it over her head. A makeshift blanket fort, akin to those of her childhood, but unable to protect her as they had once done.

CHAPTER FORTY SEVEN

After driving around for hours, Houston, thoroughly bored with the streets of Casper, rented a motel room. He could have gone to Savvy's apartment, he guessed, but offering some explanation that he couldn't even explain to himself felt beyond his capabilities. Even the brief chatter of the desk clerk when he checked in tested his limits.

So here he lay, on top of the bed, fully clothed, no closer to understanding what had just happened than he had been when he left Jen staring after him as though he'd ripped her heart out, when in fact, it was she who'd done the ripping. Ribbons of hurt, guilt, anger, disillusionment danced a dark weave through his head, each one tugging at his brain until the knots tangled all thought into a tight ball of misery. He closed his eyes, but sleep was beyond him.

It wasn't hard to go over what she'd said, the words were scored in his mind as though chiseled in stone. 'She needed space', 'everything was moving too fast', 'she needed to find her balance again'. Four years didn't seem all that fast to him but the last two weeks had certainly been crazy. And, although he was used to dealing with a lot of crazy on a daily basis, he had to believe she wasn't. Maybe she wasn't wrong to feel like her world was distorted to the point of unrecognizable. But damn it, he didn't know how to fix it.

One thing he did know though, was that he couldn't begin to fix it if he wasn't there. In the morning dark of four o'clock, and unable to sleep, he showered, and left the motel, headed for his apartment. He wasn't ready to throw in the towel just yet.

Her car would never leave impound until Benny's body was found along with the gun he'd used. Which was unlikely to happen in this lifetime. He calculated it would take her at least three or four days to find a job and another place to live. That gave him at least three or four days to get to the heart of the matter, and hopefully, to change her mind.

Walking back into the silent apartment was a little unnerving. He couldn't picture her picking Link up in the middle of the night and leaving, but she'd done it before. He peeked into the bedroom where he'd put the sleeping boy to bed, and let out a sigh. She was there, curled in a fetal position on the edge of the bed, her eyes, even closed, showed the ravages of tortured hours. Somehow, it was no comfort to see the same effects on her that had kept him awake all night. He shut the door quietly and went into the kitchen to start a pot of coffee.

When Link walked in a couple of hours later, Houston started breakfast and they talked quietly as they ate bacon and scrambled eggs. Enlisting the boy's aid with the cleanup, they had the dishes done and the counters wiped in minutes and then went into the living room.

"You can watch cartoons if you want to," Houston said. "I imagine your mom will expect to hear the TV when she wakes up, but if you'd prefer, we can read some of those comic books we bought yesterday."

"Do you like comic books?" Link asked.

"Absolutely," Houston ruffled the boy's hair. "I have a great respect for super heroes, you know."

It was close to nine when Jen walked into the room, wrapped in the robe again, her feet bare. Usually good at reading people's reactions, Houston saw myriad thoughts race across her face when she spotted the two of them, feet on the coffee table, sharing the stack of comics piled between them on the sofa cushions. First was instant relief at seeing her son, busy and content, second was surprise at seeing him, followed quickly by happiness, wariness, guilt and self-consciousness but it was the sadness that lingered just below the surface that made him hopeful that there was still a chance to work out their problems.

"The coffee is hot and we saved you some breakfast," he told her, in his best butler voice, keeping his words short and unconcerned. It felt strange, treating her like they had never shared the earth-changing moments of the last couple of weeks, of two nights ago, but he sensed that she would have instantly thrown up her guards again if he'd put his words on a more intimate basis.

"I put it in the microwave, Mom," Link added. "You just have to warm it up."

"Thanks, that was very thoughtful. I'll just get dressed first." She turned back down the hall and into the bedroom.

"Mom looks awfully tired," Link commented, a troubled frown on his face.

"She has a lot on her mind right now," Houston nodded, "and she isn't sleeping well. She'll be better after everything settles down." He hoped.

Closing the comic he'd been reading, he picked up his phone to call the garage where his Jeep was being serviced. He was disappointed to hear that it should be ready to pick up later today. Well, he consoled himself, she still had to find a job and another place to live.

When Jen returned to the kitchen, dressed and brushed but without energy, and set the timer on her food, Houston, in the same tone he'd used before, offered to drive her wherever she needed to go today. She declined. He didn't push. He had no idea what her plans were for the day, and apparently, she preferred it that way. Even knowing she would reject the offer, he offered to take Link with him while she did whatever she had to do. Once again she declined.

Accepting his defeat with all the grace he could muster, he changed clothes and left the apartment. He put the spare key on the table by the door, telling her to use it if she left so she had a way back in, then he gave Link a fist bump and a wink and headed out.

With no clear idea where he was going, he was surprised to find himself standing outside Hawkeye Investigations. The neat and crisp black lettering under the glass covered name placket beside the door was so fresh that the scent of printer's ink still lingered. He knocked and opened the door.

Savvy looked up at him with a smile. "It's good to see you, Houston. What brings you to our office?" she walked up to him and gave him a hug. "Hawk just went out for some coffee. Should I have him bring another cup?" she asked, reaching for her phone.

He returned her hug as he shook his head. "I just finished off a pot before I came over here. Thought it was time to see your new office." He looked around. "This is a good place. Lacey and Bryn did a nice job on the decorating."

"Yes they did," she agreed, but she noted that he wasn't paying much attention to the décor. Something was bothering him.

"Thinking of throwing some cases our way?" she chided. "Do you need us to stalk someone for you?" That brought a grin to his face.

"No, just at loose ends right now."

His words, as lightly as they'd been said, made speculation bloom in Savvy's mind. Something was troubling Houston, and she would bet that 'something' involved Jen.

"WE'VE NEVER RODE ON a bus before," Link said, as they made their way on her errands.

"Ridden, not rode," Jen automatically corrected. "Where I grew up, we rode the bus everywhere."

"You said 'rode.'" Link scowled at her.

"It's a difference in tense," Jen smiled at him. "Maybe we can work on tenses later on. Riding a bus is an economical way to get around town," she added.

"What's economical?"

"It means, 'to save money.'"

Link's chatter was helping Jen focus on something other than the crawling feeling that she was being watched. She never saw anyone looking at them, but that didn't dispel the paranoia. And without Houston's solid presence at her side, the feeling intensified when they left the Walmart checkout, new phone—this phone thing was getting expensive—in hand, and waited for the bus again.

They stood, back to the wall, as she called the police station. Hopefully, her car was ready to be released from impound. They wouldn't have had to do much except dust the door handles for fingerprints, would they?

Even before the gunshots, the need to be alert to her surroundings and the people in them had always been at the back of her consciousness. It surprised her to realize that, for the last couple of weeks, when she had been with Houston, except for a couple of notable instances, that feeling had been absent. It was back now, ten-fold. The correlation wasn't lost on her. She pushed the thought away. Having fallen into the velvet trap of Houston's strength, she'd started depending on him to protect her and Link, and she had to break that habit.

After a couple of hand-offs, her call landed on Captain Bricker's desk. He picked it up. She was disappointed to learn that her car could not be released until the case was closed, and since the shooter hadn't been found yet, they couldn't close the case. She wondered if they ever would.

She closed her eyes as the disappointment washed through her. Add another vehicle to her list of needs. Another expense she couldn't afford.

She really had to look for a job. If her car wasn't going to be available, ever, she'd have to get another. And no one was going to sell a car to a homeless, unemployed woman. It was unlikely that any landlord would rent to her either, for the same reasons. Glumly, she acknowledged that she could be dependent on Houston for some time.

Her mind went back to Houston's words yesterday, 'And if I told you I want to marry you and adopt Link? Would that give you any balance?'. It would certainly answer all of her immediate problems, and God knows, it would ease the pain in her heart but it still wouldn't resolve the major stumbling blocks to their happiness. With Jill's very existence in question, even she, herself, couldn't make a claim for the boy who called her Mom, and until Lucano and his son were completely out of the picture, Jen's legal standing in Link's life was on really shaky ground.

She made the decision to ask Houston to watch Link while she looked for work. It was embarrassing to have to ask after telling him she needed space and repeatedly refusing his earlier offers, but she didn't have a lot of options at the moment.

Agent McCutcheon's last words to her, as he'd handed her his card, came back to her. Perhaps he would be willing to pull a few strings for her. She'd never gotten too close to the people she worked with, closeness invited sharing secrets, and she had none she could share with them. But McCutcheon knew all her secrets, or most of them anyway. Would he be amenable to assisting her? Would he do it without alerting Houston?

Feeling slightly traitorous, she pulled out the card and placed the call, only to be informed that Agent McCutcheon was out of the office, and Cammie didn't know when he was scheduled to return. Asking Cammie to leave a call back for him, she hung up just as the bus arrived.

It was two tense days later that McCutcheon called her, and said he would meet with her the following afternoon. The tension was more because of her struggle with emotions prompted by the proximity of Houston than the wait for the agent's call, but some of her angst abated with a set time for the meeting. It wasn't until she ended the call that she thought to wonder why McCutcheon hadn't asked the reason for Jen's request.

At two o'clock the next day, Cammie welcomed Jen into the office with a smile, and with a tap on the inner door, ushered her into McCutcheon's office. He rose from his desk and offered his hand. She shook it.

"Can I get you coffee or tea?" Cammie asked, hand pulling the door closed as she did. Jen shook her head. "Some bottled water?"

"No, I'm good, thank you."

The door closed silently, and Jen met McCutcheon's direct look. "I know I left rather abruptly after our last meeting," she started, "but I have a couple of problems I was hoping you might help me with."

"Like what?"

He listened with unnerving calm as Jen explained what she was facing. When she finished, he leaned back in his chair.

"You do realize that to do what you ask, I would have to create false papers for you just as Irene did; lie to a landlord, lie to a prospective employer. It would only prolong your problem and not solve a thing." He paused, watching as she nodded, her eyes downcast.

"I will see if I can help you without exacerbating your problem," he reluctantly agreed, settling back in his chair hands laced together across his middle.

"Thank you," Jen started to rise. His next words stopped her exit.

"We believe we have located Lucano, though."

Jen dropped back down into the chair and sat forward, alert. "Where is he?"

"He has three compounds in different countries but there has been increased activity near his place outside La Paz, Bolivia, leading us to believe that he has landed there. Digging him out will be tricky though."

"Can't you just go in and get him?"

"Sad to say, Bolivia has no extradition treaty with the U.S., and because of the revenue that Lucano's operations feed into the government there, they protect him. We can't risk an international incident."

"Why isn't Lieutenant Whitehawk sitting in on this conversation?"

"He asked to remain informed. I spoke to him a couple of hours ago."

Houston might have told her, she thought, but she hadn't seen him since she left the apartment this morning.

As if he'd read her mind, he spoke. Leaning forward, he opened his desk drawer and reached in. "The reason I agreed to this meeting is that I was asked to give you this."

He leaned across the desk and dropped an origami dove in front of her. The breath left her body. She couldn't seem to get it back.

Irene had taught her and Jill to make these when they were kids and the sisters had made a game of them. Passing secrets and codes via the tiny pieces of folded paper. It had evolved into a game of hide and seek. The note, when found, had usually said, 'Tag. You're it.' and the recipient had to find the sender. She whipped her head around, looking for Jill. Of course, the room was empty.

"When did you get this?" her voice was barely audible as Jen picked up the dove and carefully unfolded it. "You said my sister had been shipped out of the states to somewhere in Hong Kong weeks ago." 'Tag. You're it', she read.

"I also said that Interpol had their best team on it. With Jerry's information, we were able to pinpoint an exact location and we got it to the head of the team who was searching for your sister. He managed to locate Jill quickly, and with the aid of a substantial cash outlay, extracted her in hours. She's here."

"HERE, here?" Disbelief rang in her words but his steady gaze made relief course through her body. Her joints felt like gelatin. She was glad she was sitting.

He nodded. "In the break room. You remember how to get there," he smiled. "I told Cammie that you were not to be disturbed."

Finally, she was going to get some answers. Stiffening her knees and her resolve, she rose.

She stopped in front of the break room door her hand halfway to the handle. All the anguish, all the fear, all the worry about Link's future, all the sleepless nights came down on her in a flood, washing away the eagerness of seeing her sister again. Apparently Jill was still in hiding or she would have called or just come to the door. So, what were they supposed to accomplish with this meeting? Grim faced, she entered the break room.

CHAPTER FORTY EIGHT

Jill looked older. Even older than herself, was Jen's first thought on seeing her sister for the first time in years. There were deep lines in her face, the beautiful face that had persuaded the star-struck girl to seek the bright lights and glamour of the stage, lines that hadn't been on the twenty three year old that had walked away from her family, her son, and never looked back.

From the hesitant look in Jill's eyes, these same thoughts had been running through her mind as well.

"Hello, Jen," she said, standing at the chair from which she'd risen, her lips trembling.

Long gone were the days when they would have run into each other's arms. A lifetime ago. Her heart breaking at this new twist, Jen closed the distance, and wrapping Jill in a hug, dropped her head on her sister's shoulder. And cried.

"Hello, Jill," she wiped the tears from her cheeks, "I've missed you so much. Where the hell have you been?"

A short chuckle was her answer. Jen stepped back and dropped her arms, as Jill, looking almost frail, resumed her seat in the chair, leaving Jen to choose either the couch or the other chair. She took the other chair, the length of the coffee table separating them. Jill acknowledged the distance with a wry smile, swabbing her own tears with a tissue.

Reaching in a small handbag, Jill pulled out a pack of cigarettes then, as though just now realizing there were no ashtrays, put them back in her purse. "Filthy habit," she said. "I should quit."

"I'm confused, Jill. Why are we meeting? I mean why now? Why here?"

Jill eyed Jen intently, as though she had to absorb everything about her in a very short time. A frisson of fear shivered up Jen's spine. Something was very wrong.

"I guess I just wanted to see your face and apologize to you for all you've been through," Jill settled back in the seat. "James, Agent McCutcheon, filled me in on what happened. I'm so sorry for putting you and Irene and my son in danger. I thought by separating myself from you I could keep you safe."

Jen froze when Jill so self-confidently referred to Link as 'her son'. Link wasn't her son. Not any longer. Not in any real way.

"Your 'son' calls me Mommy." The chill in her blood came through in her voice.

"You've never mentioned me? Told him about me?" Pain swung wildly on the question.

"What was I supposed to tell him, Jill?" Jen stood and stepped to the window. "Children aren't big on keeping secrets." Facing her sister again, she let the anger flow out of her. "I've already told him his father is dead. A big lie. I couldn't tell him that his mother was dead when there was a chance you'd walk back into his life at any time.

"Because of the situation we were in, because of our fear that the Lucanos might somehow discover his existence and find us, Irene and I had to keep him out of normal activities that children have a right to expect. A right to participate. He's never really had a normal childhood."

Jill sat and absorbed the blows without flinching, but the brief gladness at their reunion had been replaced with regret.

"That fear was justified with bullets through my windshield. Now, we're homeless, I'm jobless and I am faced with the task of rebuilding a life for us, for me and Link, with little money and without Irene."

"I know," Jill dropped her gaze to the hands knotted in her lap, "That's why I had to apologize. I understand how hard all of this has been on you. Believe me, I am so incredibly sorry, Jen."

"Agent McCutcheon told me that you helped them set up the raids on the Lucano operations. Is that true?"

"I actually work with the DEA, the Drug Enforcement Agency, but it was a joint agency operation. I was able to give them details they needed."

Jen couldn't quite decide if that was a wry smile or a grimace on her sister's lips. There was a time when she would have known. Depression settled deep in her chest.

"So, you've apologized," Jen said. "What's next? Where do we go from here?"

"I was sort of hoping Link would be with you but Agent McCutcheon said that wasn't a good first step. That that decision had to be up to you."

Jen turned back to the window and silence fell over the room. As soon as she'd seen the origami dove, she had suspected this. A fierce protectiveness hardened her heart. Whether she was protecting Link or herself, was the big question. A sparrow landed on the narrow outer sill and looked at her through the glass, his black eyes commiserating with her briefly, before flying away again. 'God', Jen thought, 'to be so free'.

"And what would you tell him, Jill? I haven't even told him I have a sister. He has asked me about family in the past. The only truth he knows is that our parents, his grandparents, are dead. Everything else he knows is false. One day he will have to be told the truth but not yet. He's just a little boy." Her hands waved helplessly at the small green space where the sparrow now searched the lawn for edibles. The little bird looked up at her startled by the motion but then went back to his hunt.

"No, Jill, I love you but I don't want you to see him." She heard an in drawn breath behind her but she didn't turn around. "I'm tired of lying to him. I have been his mother for six years without ever experiencing his birth or having had the chance to fall in love or get married, all because of the lies. No more lies, Jill."

"Please, Jen," the watery plea almost undid her but she refused to back down as Jill continued. "I just want to see him once. You can tell him I'm an old friend from school or whatever you want. The truth can come later. That will be up to you."

Whatever she wanted. The words echoed in her head. What did she want? She didn't want to hurt her sister, although she knew there was no way she couldn't and protect Link at the same time. Wasn't that what Jill wanted too? To protect Link? Wasn't that what had started all this? She turned around and went back to where Jill sat, this time she sat at the end of the couch, their knees almost touching. Her pain as deep as that on Jill's face. She reached for Jill's hands and then stopped.

"I want full custodial rights to Link. I want him to be mine by law. I want to be able to hear him call me Mommy and know it's not a lie. Not the false documents Irene produced to get him into school or to file medical claims; real, legal papers that say he's my son. With your connections, you should be able to make that happen."

The instant denial trembled on Jill's lips but Jen pressed on.

"There is a man, a good man, a wonderful man, who wants to marry me and adopt Link. I want to marry him, but he doesn't know that Link is not my son and that I have no right to enter into a legal adoption with him." Jen rose and went back to stare out the window. The bird was gone. Jen continued on.

"I'm thirty six. The odds of finding someone I could love as much as I love him are astronomical and the odds of having a child, a brother or sister for Link, for him to have what we used to have, are getting slimmer by the year. I love Houston in ways I never thought were possible but I can't marry him without telling him the truth. You swore me to secrecy. Do you understand my problem, Jill?

Jill's head dropped to her chest but she didn't answer for some time while her chest rose and fell with agitation.

"Antón gave me more than Link," the whisper spoke of agony. "I can't have anymore children, Jen. Do you understand my problem?"

Jill's pain stabbed Jen's heart but she couldn't back down on this. Too much depended on it.

"I'm sorry for that, I truly am." Jen said, and meant it. "It seems we both have a problem, but those are my terms. I have a right to a life too, not this shadow life we've been forced to live for six years. What we'll have to continue to live with until Lucano and his son are dead or in prison for life and unable to press a claim for custody. I need to be able to share this with the man I love." she paused for a breath.

"You can force the issue, take him away from me, keep him with you in witness protection or whatever lifestyle you've arranged for yourself, if that's what you decide to do, but Link will probably hate you. Maybe I will too, in time. It's your choice, Jill."

Jen walked to the door but Jill's words stopped her.

"If this man is the one you want, then you have to tell him," she said. "The promise I asked of you was never meant to take away your choices, only protect Link, and now that Lucano knows of his existence, Link is my only concern. We have to keep him safe."

Jen looked over her shoulder at her sister, nodded, opened the door and walked out of the building.

Too shaken to even think about job hunting, or driving Houston's vehicle, she walked up the block and crossed 'B' Street to tiny Pioneer Park, facing the county courthouse and found an empty bench where the tears fell unchecked. The ultimatum had torn out her heart but she wouldn't take it back. She realized that she had been preparing for this for a long time as her resentment of their situation grew. Jill had chosen a path six years ago and forced the rest of her family to follow her down it. It had to end now.

After a while, the tears dried up. She dried up. She was shriveled to a husk of a human. She felt so old. Jill had freed her from the promise but Link's future was still in limbo. Until Lucano was either dead or in prison for life, none of them would ever be truly free.

Digging out a pair of sunglasses to hide as much of the damage as she could, she slid them on and rose from the bench. Walking up the street until she found a coffee shop, she went in and ordered a latte. It kept her mind from a complete collapse for a few minutes, but eventually, she finished and went to the restroom to repair what damage she could before returning to Houston's Jeep.

HOUSTON AND LINK WERE in the kitchen fixing pancakes and bacon for supper when she let herself into the apartment.

"We're fixing supper," Link crowed, proudly, carefully flipping a pancake on the griddle. Houston manned the skillet with the bacon.

Jen smiled at him. "They look really good." and she would get one down whether her appetite said no or not.

"Any luck?" Houston tossed over his shoulder.

"No." She shook her head as she put her purse down and started down the hall to the bathroom.

One look in the mirror had her reaching for her makeup kit. She might not be in a good state emotionally, but she absolutely refused to sit down at the table, looking like road kill.

Carrying it off turned out to be easier than she expected. Link was so excited about spending the whole afternoon doing 'guy things' with his new idol that he didn't notice Jen's quietness, and Houston, although he was pleasant, even talkative, barely even looked at her. When supper was over, Jen insisted on doing clean up, sending the guys into the living room to watch TV. Houston found a baseball game and began pointing out the finer points of the game to the youngster.

Listening to him added a layer of guilt to Jen's already burdened psyche. She could have shared that with Link, she had some sports background, and the ability, but now, as Link approached the age where he could join organized youth sports clubs like Little League, actually Casper called it Junior League, was not an option for her son. Every layer of paper work added a new, traceable trail for Lucano to find and follow. Was that about to change? Did it even matter now that Lucano knew about his grandson? Would McCutcheon, or whatever agency was involved with tracking down the criminal, be able to neutralize the criminal enterprise and free Link from the threat? He seemed confident, but only time would tell. She was so sick of secrets, and sick of feeling paranoid, but that ended tonight. When Link was asleep, she would tell Houston everything.

THE STRUGGLE TO GET Link bathed and ready for bed by eight tested her limits. It didn't help her state of mind when it only took a lift of Houston's eyebrow to send Link off to do the very things Jen had been struggling with for the last half hour.

Her mood grew darker as the time passed until she could get him to sleep, so she shouldn't have been surprised when Link asked, "Why are you so grumpy, Mommy?"

She pasted a smile on her face as all the reasons crowding in her brain tried to rush out of her mouth but she just said she was tired, and apologized to him.

The final straw was when Link shut her out of their bedtime ritual by asking Houston if he would read his latest Spider Man comic to him tonight. With a shrug of defeat, Jen ran a bath for herself and tried to soak the pain in her heart away.

CHAPTER FORTY NINE

Houston was sitting on the couch when she came out of the bathroom, the thick robe tied at her waist. He looked up as she sat down in the chair closest to him, his dark eyes giving away nothing of his thoughts.

She cleared her throat. "I went to McCutcheon's office today. I called him yesterday to see if he could lay some ground work for me to find work and a place to live but he had a surprise for me as well."

"What?"

"He had some news about my sister. The information they got out of Jerry enabled their Ops team to find the place and extract her quickly. They brought her back."

Jen thought she saw just the slightest chink in his wall of stoicism. "Stateside? And he couldn't share that with both of us?"

She shook her head. "She's here. She was in his office. In the break room," she amended.

Starting off slowly then picking up speed, she told him everything. He listened, focused on her face and words, only interrupting once to clarify a point.

"You told her you wanted to marry me?" his words softened to a seductive level and he reached for her hands, pulling her up and into his lap.

"Yes," she said against his jaw as she snuggled into his arms. Her eyes sought his and held there. "Yes, I do, very much."

When his lips claimed hers in a gentle welcome, she walked into his life without a qualm. They came up for air a few minutes later, holding each other as if the bond now forged between them was of the strongest steel.

"That still doesn't solve the problem of Link," she spoke under his chin.

"We will deal with any problems," he lifted her face and probed deep into her eyes with his inky gaze, "together."

"Our name isn't Bradley, it's Collier," she clasped her hands together and laced the fingers.

"I suspected as much."

"How?" she asked, startled. "When?"

"I had some time while you were out looking for jobs so I searched old news coverage from around twenty years ago, where both people died and left children," he smiled at her. "The Colliers were the closest match for time and circumstances and ages of survivors."

Of course, she acknowledged, anything and anyone could be found given enough time and internet access.

"I'm glad you know."

"No more secrets," he whispered as he pressed his lips to her temple and cuddled her closer.

"No, no more secrets," she agreed.

"Thank you, God," he said with a laugh. "These last few days, giving you space to get your life in order, have been pure Hell."

The lips that captured hers this time were far from gentle. Heat and fire swept through her, ignited by the hunger of his mouth as he dove deep into her heart and soul. A hand found her breast and kneaded urgently. The breast responded with needs of it's own and the other begged not to be left out.

He lifted his mouth long enough to whisper that they should take this to the bedroom. She had no argument for that. When she stood up to move that direction, he simply scooped her into his arms and carried her to his bed.

"Your leg ..." she started to protest but he cut her off.

"My leg is fine," he smiled. "It might tell me differently in the morning, but tonight, there is only one thing on my mind."

MEMORIES OF THE NIGHT hummed through Jen's body, rousing little fires of need in her that she tended lovingly; already anticipating the nights to come. She was grateful that, with the lessening of tension in their lives, Link no longer woke at the smallest disturbance.

The apartment was spotless. Link was engrossed in a comic book. Houston had left for the station shortly after a late breakfast. He started back to work on Monday, three days. A brief honeymoon, she smiled.

But she still had to carry her own weight. By the time she closed the laptop, she'd already filled out four employment applications hoping for interviews and her eyes were going crossed. Time to think about supper.

A quick check of the fridge didn't look promising but she had time to hit the grocery store. "Link, put your shoes on, we're going to the store."

While Link worked at tying his shoelaces she left a quick note for Houston, in case he got back before they did, and minutes later they were pushing a shopping cart up and down the aisles of Walmart.

"Can I have that Spider Man t-shirt?" Link tugged on Jen's pant leg.

"You have a drawer full of Spider Man t-shirts."

"But I don't have that one."

"You have enough," Jen put her hand on his head. "We can check out the comics though," she offered an alternative, "see if they have any new ones out."

A sack with two new comic books dangled from Link's arm as they exited the store and headed to the Jeep. Jen helped him in his car seat and got it buckled then unloaded the groceries beside him.

She'd found a parking spot next to a cart return. She climbed into her ride to start the engine and the AC. As she waited for the cool air to kick in, she looked up and her breath caught in her throat. An origami dove, larger than the ones they generally made, was stuck under the windshield wiper.

She scanned the area knowing, even as she did, that Jill was long gone. She opened the door and stood on the running board to retrieve the dove. It was unnerving that her sister was able to slip in and out of their lives like a ghost leaving little smears of ectoplasm on a seemingly normal day.

"What's that, Mommy?"

Jen summoned a smile for him in the rear view mirror. "Someone ... left a pretty little bird on the windshield."

"Miss Harper," he summoned the warnings of his first grade teacher, "said you shouldn't pick up things that people leave. They might have bad stuff in them."

Miss Harper wasn't wrong, Jen thought. This little bird could be the answer she'd prayed for or the nightmare she'd dreaded. It had some weight, a bit more than a paper dove would usually carry. Indecision kept her frozen for several seconds. Open it now or wait until she was with Houston?

"Miss Harper is very smart," Jen agreed, setting the bird on top of her purse as her mind debated how to handle it.

"I bet Houston could tell you if there's something bad in it." Link stated confidently.

"Good idea." She put the Jeep in gear and backed out, to head for home.

"I got two new comics, Houston," Link waved them excitedly as they walked into the apartment to find Houston unloading sacks of his own.

He looked up and smiled at the boy. "Why don't you take them to your room and put them up for now. We can read them later." As Link ran down the hall, his eyes settled on Jen.

"What's wrong?"

It didn't bother her as much as it used to, that he could read her so easily. Maybe, in time, she could learn not to be so worried about how easily he could read her, but right now, she was grateful that she needed no explanation. She set the groceries on the counter and fished the paper dove out of her purse, handed it to him.

"What is this?" he turned it in his hand, looking at it from all sides.

Realizing he hadn't ever seen one before, she said, "A message. From my sister."

"And what does it say?"

She shrugged and added a negative shake of her head. "I wanted to wait until I got here since, whatever it says, will affect all of us."

He looked it over again then handed it back to her. "I don't want to tear it."

She took it back and began to carefully loosen the intricate folds. A key fell to the counter. Houston picked it up, looking over her shoulder as she smoothed the note.

> *"Agent McCutcheon has the paper work you need. It should be easy to finalize the adoption within a short time. I still want to meet Lincoln, as his 'aunt' but I will leave the time and place up to you.*

I will continue to work with the DEA, the FBI and Interpol to bring down the Lucano crime network; all the branches. I know that Link will be better off with you. Use the key to open locker 218 at the Reno Sports Fitness Center. There is a book in it. Should anything happen to me, take it to Agent McCutcheon, it should provide him additional useful information. I love you, Jen and, and I hope in time, Link will come to love me as part of his family."

It was a bittersweet victory. Link would truly be hers but at a terrible cost to Jill, and to herself as well.

Jen wasn't aware she was crying until Houston turned her into his arms and pressed her wet cheeks into his chest. When he kissed the top of her head, she felt the cracks in her heart start to mend. It was a slow and painful healing, but in Houston's embrace, the jagged edges were smoothing out.

"Do you still want to marry me?" he murmured.

"More than ever."

"How soon?"

"As soon as the papers are signed and Link is my son, for real." Her eyes watched his face, testing. He'd claimed he wanted her son as his but that was when it was still a theory. Now it looked like it was truly happening. Would it make a difference to him?

"How long will it take you to plan a wedding?"

"A couple of weeks after that." The relief was overwhelming and her smile trembled slightly. "That is, unless your family wants a big event. I don't even know if your parents will like me. They might not, you know."

"Are you ready to find out?"

Her startled eyes blinked at him. Nerves she hadn't expected began jumping through her like grasshoppers. "When?" she whispered hesitantly.

"This is Crockett's last couple of days before he returns to base. The folks are having a big send off for him. And he did promise Link a powwow," he smiled as he placed a kiss on the tip of her nose. "What do you say? Are you up for a big-ass barbecue?" He grinned, "And I promise, there won't be a bear for miles."

Also by Lois Jaye
Raptor's Kiss
Dragon's Eye (forthcoming)

Acknowledgments

Although writing is thought of as, and is for a great deal of the time, a solitary effort, it is never done in a void. So many people become involved in a manuscript along the way that the hard part is remembering to thank everyone who has contributed to the process.

First, I need to give a heartfelt thank you to the constant and supportive people of my writing groups: Neva Bodin, Gayle Irwin, Leslie Colburn, Alisa Cochrane, Carol Chapman, India Hayford, Guyla Greenly, Sharon Obert, Marion Sisneros, Rachel Brooks, Gina Holder, Darcie Gudger, Debra Moerke, Nicole Jaramillo, Marie Scott and... so many others. Thank you all for your help and your encouragement.

Second, I have to mention my kids, Merri, Dave and Eric, who are always there for story guidance or a listening ear. They are, and always have been, the inspiration for all my creative endeavors. Their smiles, advice, including the eye rolls, always keep my rudder on a straight path.

Last but not least, I need to give a mountain of credit to Walter Hawn, the voice of my audio books and my right arm. He has helped me in so many ways they would be hard to enumerate, from his assistance navigating through the maze of the internet, which I'm about four decades behind the loop there, to his invaluable input on book cover design and on and on. One of these days I will make a comprehensive list of his talents, when I learn them all.

And then, to my readers, I would probably still write but it wouldn't be nearly as rewarding as knowing that you are there to read my stories. From the bottom of my heart, THANK YOU ALL.

Read on for an exciting excerpt from
Raptor's Kiss
the First Book of Raptors!

Excerpt from *Raptor's Kiss*
by Lois Jaye
from Chapter 21

Savvy held her breath until she thought her lungs would explode, waiting for their captor to make a move. The agony in her foot radiated hot spears of pain throughout her body. She bit down on her lip until she tasted blood, stifling the whimpers that might draw his attention back to them. How long had they been frozen like this? Finally, he moved on up the stairs and she heard the faint click of the door. He was gone.

He'd forgotten to turn off the light, Savvy realized, as the first full breath seeped back into her lungs. Or was he planning to come right back? She looked around the windowless room. Besides the plastic-coated mattresses they were on and the remnants of their clothes dumped on the floor, there was a small wood stove in the corner, a low table near it. The chimney bored through the ceiling behind the stairs, possibly connecting to the cook stove pipe upstairs. A small curtained closet, the curtain hanging in ragged strips on one side and empty of any clothing, gaped on the other wall, completing the sad inventory, although, there was an outline on the wall where something had once hung. A first aid kit?

Savanna shivered, violently. Cold or shock she wasn't sure but, her clothes, even if she could reach them, were useless for warmth now. Agony in every move, she pulled herself to a sitting position and pulled her knees to her chest to conserve what body heat she could. Kristen, still shackled, was shivering as well but was unable to change her position.

If their captor hadn't been distracted, Savvy was positive she would once again be trussed the same. That he would return was a given; how soon, was the question. They had a very small window to find a path to freedom. The memory of the sound of helicopter fading into the distance didn't bolster her level of hope and the pain in her foot sucked that level even lower.

With her hands and feet no longer tethered together, she managed to flex stiff muscles but there was no way to check her foot. She might, however, be able to break the ties on her ankles if she could get to the can opener. She looked over at Kristen who watched her with eyes suddenly much too old for her age.

A plan began forming in her mind. "Can you move a little closer to the eye-bolt above you? See if I can get a little slack?"

"What are you going to do?" Kristen asked.

"I'm going to try to get us out of here."

"How?" Hope sparked in those brown eyes but it didn't spark her to immediate action.

Irrationally irritated, Savvy snapped, "Can we hold the twenty questions and just do as I ask?"

Chastised to silence, the girl started inching her way toward the bolt. Remorse kicked Savvy hard as silent tears rolled down Kristen's cheeks, but the cable loosened. Savvy lowered her hands toward the mattress but still inches short. Silently digging up every curse word she could remember, and there were plenty, she considered her options.

"Can you get up on your knees with your back against the wall?" Knowing that the maniac could return at any minute lent a sharp edge to her voice she couldn't help. In a manic rage, their captor wouldn't hesitate to kill one or both of them but, if he chose to do away with just one, she knew who he would pick.

"I ... I'll try," Kristen sniffled.

As the girl squirmed to comply, Savvy gritted her teeth against the yanks and jerks on her injured shoulder but, at last, Kristen was in position and the relief she felt as she lowered her hands was exquisite. Her fingers could just lift the edge of the mattress. She could have cried herself.

Praying she hadn't shoved the can opener too far under, she ran her fingertips along the edge as far as she could, then back again. Her fingers came up empty but there was a suspicious lump under her butt. Putting her weight on her undamaged foot, she pushed herself up the wall and, ignoring the pain in her heel, worked her toe under the mattress until she felt the metal. Using her feet like flippers, she managed to trap the opener and turn her feet toward the wall, clear of the pallet. A cry escaped her lips as fresh pain lanced through her foot like an electric shock, and every nerve in her body jolted. She crumpled back to the floor in a fetal position and, after taking a moment to let the pain ease, she picked up her prize. Kristen maintained the awkward position which allowed Savvy a lot more movement. But how long could she hold it?

Using another precious moment to work through the pain and catch her breath, Savvy considered how best to use the 'church key'. Her hands were still bound behind her but she had managed to get them under her butt once, she could do it again. If she could break the cable ties holding her ankles then, with her hands in front of her, it would be easier to snap the ones on her wrists. Hiding the can opener again was a waste of precious time so she twisted until she could place it closer to her feet.

Unhampered by the drag of clothing, the fresh blood adding a minute dollop of lubrication to her skin and emboldened by her earlier success, she managed, finally, to get her hands behind her knees. The tether he'd cut to free her feet, dangled loosely from her wrists but she was still tied to the cable. She flicked her fingers to revive her now dead hands. It had cost her more blood as the thin slices 'Old Craze' had carved into her abdomen reopened and the trickles of blood pooled in the crease of her stomach but she was able to pick up the key to their freedom in her numb fingers.

Working the point of the can opener under the ratchet point on the cable tie she began to wind it like a rubber band. It wasn't speedy and every fiber of her body protested, but she thought it was loosening. Just as she thought it was about to give, the can opener slipped from her fingers and flew to the patch of floor between the two mattresses. Just beyond her reach. Hopeless tears filled her eyes and she dropped her head to her knees with a moan, to stop them. Tears didn't help anything.

"I think I can reach it," Kristen's tremulous voice drew Savvy's gaze.

At some point, the girl had managed to turn on her side and had been watching her. And, she was right. If Savvy could give her enough slack to turn over, Kristen might just be able to reach it. She didn't have a clue what the girl had in mind but she was willing to try anything.

Listening so hard for footsteps overhead, she was surprised her ears weren't bleeding, she butt-walked toward the wall. Kristen scooted over until she was half off the bed then maneuvered to her knees with her back to the key. She inched sideways until she felt her toes touch it and then, with a move that left Savvy in awe, she picked up the can opener between her feet and bending backwards, plucked it up with her hands.

"Catch," she said over her shoulder, flipping the can opener into Savvy's lap.

"That was...amazing," Savvy grinned. "Where did you learn a trick like that?"

"I've never tried that before, but I play a lot of sports," she smiled back, "and I'm pretty limber."

"I hope you can run, too, because if we manage to get out of here, we're going to have to."

"Cross-country, All-State," her grin widened, "but how can you run with your burned foot?" Savvy didn't bother to answer and the smile dropped from Kristen's face.

Savvy went to work on the cable tie again and was rewarded, a couple of minutes later, with the snap of plastic. Working her feet, one at a time, through her arms, she took a minute to examine the burn on her heel. It was red, angry, and throbbed like the devil, but it didn't look infected. She stood up against the wall and. Lifting her arms as the self-defense instructor had demonstrated, and she'd practiced on numerous occasions, brought her arms down with a sharp twist and snap. Or tried to, but the pain in her shoulder nearly made her pass out. The cable stretched a little, she thought, but it didn't snap.

Swearing like a section hand, tears streaming down her face and sweat dripping down her body, she lifted her arms again. It had to work. It had to. It might damage her shoulder beyond repair, but she had to do it or die trying. The other option was to just die. Biting down on her lips, bracing herself for the inevitable pain, she executed the maneuver again. With a snap, her hands were free. The pain bent her double and sapped some of the giddiness out of her freedom but she didn't have time to acknowledge either.

Their captor had been careless in tying her wrists to the bike cable. The knot was fashioned to tighten when pulled or yanked but, once the pressure was released, Savvy was finally able to work it loose. Once again, she mourned the missing backpack, the knife and scissors it contained, but there was no time to dwell on it. She turned her attention to Kristen, dealing with the knot at the bike cable and then the tether that bound her hands to her feet. Freed of that, the girl started working her hands under her hips.

She showed Kristen how to put the point of the can opener at the ratchet point of the tie and how to twist it then told her how to snap the ties on her wrists when she could stand.

"As soon as you're free, get dressed."

Hobbling to where he had flung her clothes, she assessed her options. Her jeans were no more than scraps but they could be used to bind her foot. Her shirt was much the same. She found her bra and put it on, hooking the one hook that was still attached and tying the straps around her neck like a halter. Stripping the tattered curtain from the nail above the closet door, she wrapped it around her waist and tied it, sarong style. She wrapped her feet with the remnants of her jeans and slid her boots on over the make-shift socks. It wasn't comfortable but it was protection. Working as fast as she could, using short pieces of shoestring to tie alternating eyelets together, she was cautiously confident that the boots would stay on her feet. He must have removed her coat, hat, and gloves while she was in the back of his van, as she saw no sign of them now, but she would have to worry about that later. Right now, she needed to find a weapon.

She stepped back into the closet and found it wasn't completely empty after all. Wadded in a corner was a dirty pair of bib overalls. They weren't in much better shape that the curtains but they would cover more of her than was covered at the moment. Tossing them onto mattress she'd vacated, she went to work on the clothes rod which, having just been fitted into notches cut into the brace boards on the walls, lifted out easily with a simple twist that broke the brittle paint that glued it in place. Stepping into the middle of the room, she took a practice swing. Fresh pain stabbed through her shoulder but, if it meant their freedom, she would take the pain.

Putting the club behind the stairs she sat down and started working the overalls over her boots. Dust bunnies and dirt clods fell to the mattress and she sucked in a startled breath when one of them scuttled away as she tugged them up. As they slid over her thighs and brush against her panty-less bottom, she was positive there would never be enough soap or hot water to make her feel clean again.

Feeling slightly less exposed, she went back to where Kristen, free of all her shackles, was now dressed and waiting for further instructions.

"Hand me that rope," she told her, motioning toward the tether and picking up the one that had bound her also. It wasn't heavy cord, but there was no give to it. Excellent. She tied a knot in the end of each and then tied both of them together at the unknotted ends. Handing the rope to Kristen, she said, "Take this up the stairs until you find a crack or loose step on the far side of the steps, no more than shoulder high, that you can wedge the knot, on either end, under or into solidly. Pull on it to make sure it can't slip out. Lay the rope across the back of the step so it can't be seen easily, then set at the top of the steps while I finish down here."

Kristen's teeth began chattering like castanets. "Wh..at if he c..c..comes b..ack?" she whispered as though she had already heard him above.

"Turn off the light and come back down the stairs as quickly and quietly as you can."

"Why don't we just leave?"

"One, we don't know where we are, and he does. Two, it's very cold out there and I'm hardly dressed for rough country running. Three, we have a better chance of getting out of this alive if we can incapacitate him, find the keys to the van, and drive out of here."

Hesitantly, the girl nodded and started slowly up the steps, feeling each as she went.

The knot of the rope dangled three steps below the landing. She pressed it against a baluster and laid it along the step above, hoping he would be blinded by the light, as she had been, when he first turned it on, and over-confident that he faced no threat from his captives to pay close attention to his feet.

She took a final look around the room before whispering up the stairs for Kristen to turn off the light and come back down. When Kristen felt her way to where Savvy stood, she put the knot of the rope in her hand. "When he turns on the light, his eyes will take a second to focus. If you pull the rope tight as his foot hits the second step, I don't think he will see it. If it works, he should fall and hopefully break his neck but, if not, I can get a good swing at him and we can tie him up and get away. Leave him here until we can get help."

"I hope you're right." Kristen's teeth had stopped chattering.

Me too, Savvy crossed her fingers. Feeling under the stairs, she retrieved the closet rod and, with a reassuring pat on Kristen's back, took her place closer to the bottom of the stairs but still partially tucked out of sight.

WHERE IN THE HELL WAS he? Savvy wondered for the hundredth time in as many hours, or so it seemed. The inky blackness distorted time. Was it possible he had been captured? Or, horror, had he seen what she was doing down here and was just playing with them? That fear had been chewing on her for a while now. Almost as long as they'd been sitting here in the dark. And the longer they sat in the dark, the softer their whispers became, as though they might miss the sound of footsteps if they spoke.

"I have to pee," Kristen's whisper was barely a breath as they drifted to Savvy's ears.

"Let me get the rope," Savvy whispered back, using the rod as a cane to stand, "and the use the closet."

"The closet?!" the girl hissed in alarm.

"It's as private as you're going to get unless you want to look for an outhouse." Savvy found her hand and took the rope. "I certainly won't be able to see anything."

With only a slight hesitance, Kristen released her hold on the rope and her fingertips made a soft rustle as she followed the wall to the closet.

"I feel icky," Kristen whispered when she returned to take her place.

"Just think how great that first bath is going to feel," Savvy reminded her.

A sigh was the only response. Savvy returned to her position.

"I can't keep my eyes open," Kristen whispered a little later.

Savvy had been fighting off sleep too. They couldn't maintain this vigil much longer. Her foot was swelling inside her boot and the fabric around it was squishy. The constant pain in her foot radiated up her leg to join forces with the throbbing in her shoulder and create a clang of agony in her head. Deep breathing wasn't helping, nor did trying to move her mind beyond her body. The darkness didn't bring her any serenity, only memories of past nightmares that kept dragging her back to the present. She did her best to ignore her damaged shoulder but her heel needed attention if she didn't want to risk blood poisoning.

Would she even be able to swing the club if she had the chance? She thought about the discolored space on the wall by the closet. The first aid kit she'd seen in the nightmare? Once again, she wished for her backpack. How much longer could they do nothing? Damn!

"Let's go," she said.

"Really?!" Kristen's voice managed to hit a chord somewhere between eagerness and fresh terror.

"I'll go up first," Savvy gripped the club tighter. He could be waiting for them behind any door or tree. "You follow me when I turn on the light."

Kristen moved up behind her and touched her back, moving with her to the foot of the stairs. "Maybe we'll need the rope?"

"Get it when you come up the stairs," Savvy said.

At the top of the stairs, she fished for the light switch, eyes squinted against the burst of light. Kristen blinked up at her from the bottom. She hadn't had an opportunity to see the lever or, whatever, that opened the door from this side. It took her a minute to locate it while Kristen busied herself working the rope free. The girl's anxious breath brushed Savvy's neck as she eased the door back and stepped into the kitchen. With a cautioning hand, she halted Kristen while she took stock. Two rooms. This, the main one, and a bump out with a bed that took up most of the space.

Her knit hat and a coat, that was not hers, hung on a peg by the door he'd brought her through. There was another door on the opposite wall but it didn't look like it was rarely, if ever, used. A window beside it, covered with years of grime and cobwebs, was so dark she almost missed it at first. The urge to grab the coat and hat and just take off running was as overwhelming as it was impractical. Every step she took, reminded her of that.

"Check out that bed room," she told Kristen, softly. "Find anything you think we can use." She continued her search as the girl angled off without comment.

There was no sign of her backpack. It might still be in the van but if the van wasn't here, it was just as gone. Using the tiny counter top to take the pressure off her foot, she checked through the one cupboard and the two small drawers for anything that could be useful. Keys preferably. Not hands full of salt, pepper and condiment packets. She threw them back in the drawer. She found a partial tube of antibiotic ointment and a broken hacksaw blade which both went into an overall pocket. She refused to speculate what the blade might have been broken on. A sound drew her attention to Kristen, who had come up behind her.

"Thank God," Kristen said. Savvy heard the grind of the faucet, and then smiled inwardly when she heard the "Ewww," at the splash of water. "Does he drink this?"

Savvy shrugged. He must have bottled water somewhere but they couldn't take a lot of time to look for it, no matter how thirsty they were.

"Did you find anything we can use?"

"I found a pocket knife." Kristen held up her find and put it in her pocket at Savvy's nod.

She found a small ball of twine under the sink and a bottle of bleach. She shuddered at the sight of it. With nothing else in the room except the coat and her hat, she put them on before scrubbing a spot on the window with her elbow. The sky was half lit but the hours in the black basement had screwed with time so she couldn't tell if it was pre-dawn or twilight. Or even what day it was. How long had they been down there? A rough track angled off to the right and down sharply to disappear into the juniper and scrub brush taller than a man. If memory served her correctly, the van, if it was here, would be up the hill and in the trees to the left. Opening the door, which groaned loudly making her wince, she stuck her head out. Seeing nothing, she beckoned Kristen forward onto the ice-crusted ground.

"If anything goes wrong, you take off running. Follow the road but stay out of sight as much as possible. I think they are already searching for you, so, if you see a helicopter, do whatever you can to attract their attention." Savvy headed for the trees, leaning heavily on the closet rod.

"Wait, I thought we were taking the road," Kristen fell into step behind her.

"It will be easier if we can find the van." Which turned out to be easier than she expected. Within a few yards, she could see it. Feeling freedom looming for the first time, her heart lifted. "Let's find the keys," she grinned at Kristen.

We don't need keys," Kristen crowed. "My boyfriend is a mechanic. He taught me how to hot-wire a car."

Not all education came from books, Savvy acknowledged silently, yanking the driver's door open. "Can you drive a stick shift, too?" she asked hopefully.

"Nope," Kristen answered from the other side.

Savvy's heart sank. She'd learned to drive on George Surrley's tractor but that was twenty years ago and her feet hadn't been shooting lightning bolts of pain straight into her skull. She crawled behind the wheel and dropped the visor. No keys. Running her hands under the seat, she directed Kristen to do the same on her side. Still no keys but she located a leather pouch of tools. She slid them into the overalls.

Savvy's nerves were jangling. He'd been gone too long. "If you can hot-wire this thing, you'd better get too it," she said, nerves adding an edge to her words that seeped into Kristen's eyes.

Leaning over the gear shift, the girl started fishing under the dash.

"Looking for these?" The chilling voice froze all thought as though she'd been thrown into an Arctic blizzard. The wind howling like a banshee in her ears. The keys dangled from the finger that wagged at her window. A knife glinted dully in his other hand. Kristen's scream penetrated through the roaring in her head and the ice sheered away.

"RUN!" she screamed at the girl as she slammed her door open, with all the strength her terror could muster, into the face that leered through the window. He'd seen the way she froze and her reaction wasn't what he expected. The door handle hit him square in the chest. He staggered back, trying to suck in the breath that had been driven from his lungs. Kristen whose door hadn't even been fully closed, was out it like a flash and Savvy made a dive toward it, away from the killer and the knife that he still held. "GO! GO!" she yelled at the girl who had paused, reaching back for Savvy's hand.

She'd known, deep in her heart, she couldn't move fast enough to get away from him but, if Kristen was as fast as she said, she stood a good chance of getting away and sending back help. And, if this psycho was more worried about Kristen getting away, maybe he wouldn't have time to kill her outright. But the girl paused too long. Savvy felt the van dip as man grabbed the door and swung into the seat, knife pressed against her ribs.

"One more step and I'll gut her where she sits!" he screamed at the girl. The threat stopped Kristen in her tracks.

Raptor's Kiss
is available In eBook and Print
from Amazon, Barnes&Noble,
and other fine retail stores.
Audible has the audiobook.
Excerpt from *Raptor's Kiss* Copyright © Lois Jaye Evenson 2023 .
All rights reserved.

Don't miss out!

Visit the website below and you can sign up to receive emails whenever Lois Jaye publishes a new book. There's no charge and no obligation.

https://books2read.com/r/B-A-UXYRB-JKVPD

BOOKS 2 READ

Connecting independent readers to independent writers.

About the Author

Lois Jaye is a true Wyoming Native, living and writing in the state where she was born and raised. Although she loves to travel, she's happiest at home behind her omputer. She truly loves to tell stories that highlight the beauty and majesty of her state and, if her stories give her readers goosebumps and laughter in equal measure, she considers it a huge success.